Reader, I
Married Me

First published in Great Britain in 2019 by Trapeze Books,
an imprint of The Orion Publishing Group Ltd
Carmelite House, 50 Victoria Embankment,
London EC4Y 0DZ

An Hachette UK company

1 3 5 7 9 10 8 6 4 2

A CIP catalogue record for this book is
available from the British Library.

ISBN (mass market paperback) 978 1 4091 7760 9
ISBN (eBook) 978 1 4091 7761 6

Typeset by Born Group

Printed and bound in Great Britain by Clays Ltd, Elcograf S.p.A.

MIX
Paper from
responsible sources
FSC® C104740

www.orionbooks.co.uk

Reader, I Married Me

Sophie Tanner

TRAPEZE

For anyone who has ever felt adrift –
you're not drowning but waving x

To love oneself is the beginning of a lifelong romance

Oscar Wilde

Chapter 1

Is it just me who finds sharing a hot tub with colleagues a bit awkward? Though I spend half my life with these people, I've no desire to touch naked flesh with Keith from accounts.

We're staying at log cabins in the New Forest for a team bonding experience and most of my workmates are already outside, submerged in frothy bubbles.

I stand under the unforgiving spotlights in the deluxe bathroom in a green polka-dot bikini, inspecting myself in the full-length mirror. I wasn't expecting to be sporting swimwear in the middle of January.

I've always had quite an athletic frame but my winter of too much content has made me considerably puffier. It's not my fault they start selling Christmas treats in October and then discount them all in the New Year.

I scoop my red hair into a bun, pull on a white towelling robe and eye up the packets of individually wrapped slippers in the cabinet. No: far too frivolous. I don't want to contribute to some massive only-worn-once slipper graveyard.

Right, time to take the plunge. Must be less British. I'm sure in places like Scandinavia co-workers are always strategising in steam rooms, perfectly comfortable with each other's barely concealed genitalia.

I stride through the lounge in bare feet, nodding at the few people sitting on the sofas, looking sheepish.

'Not joining us?' I ask.

'Got a verruca.'

Shit, should've worn the slippers.

On tiptoes, I grab a bottle of Prosecco from the fridge in

the kitchen and poke my head through the glass doors. My breath bites crystals in the cold evening air as I quickly assess the occupants of the two hot tubs on the outdoor wooden terrace.

In the tub to the right is my boss, Giles. He owns Top Banana, the digital marketing agency I work at in Brighton. Conker-brown from his Christmas Caribbean holiday, he's rubbing his copious blonde chest hair and waving his arms around as he talks.

The sweaty account managers around him are edging as far apart as possible and attempting to look professional despite their scanty attire.

The tub to the left hosts the younger contingent of Top Banana. Giles likes to hire savvy digital natives who have no memory of life before mobile phones. The girls are shrieking so loudly the birds in the trees have probably all flown the nest.

I climb the steps and breathe in the earthy scent of the forest. Hmm, I really should join Giles's tub and attempt to engage in some top-level business chat. Senior management need to start recognising me as one of their own. I'm thirty-five years old and still just an account executive on a poxy salary. I have jumped around a bit in my career but, still, surely my years of experience should count for something.

'More bubbles, guys?' I brandish the Prosecco as I approach Giles's tub, dropping my robe and swinging a leg over the side as nonchalantly as possible.

My foot slides on the plastic seat and I inadvertently lunge towards Giles. There's a resounding crack of skulls as our foreheads clash.

'Argh!' Giles clutches his head as I scrabble to disentangle myself from his long slippery limbs. Jess, the HR manager, comes to my rescue; grabbing the bottle and pulling me down next to her by the back of my bikini bottoms while Theresa, the office manager next to her, howls with laughter.

'Shit, sorry, Giles!' I hunch my shoulders in mortification, rubbing my forehead and sinking up to my chin in the hot water.

'Christ, I'm used to ladies throwing themselves at me, but not like that!' Giles's eyes are watering and he now has a reddening bump directly between his brows.

Clearing his throat, Keith, the finance director, leans forward. His glasses are opaque with condensation. 'As I was saying, Giles, Top Banana is maturing and we'll soon need to revisit our business plan.'

Giles slicks his sandy hair off his forehead. 'Yah, absolutely, Keith, time to get our ducks in a row – once we've peeled the onion I'm sure we'll find plenty more windows of opportunity.'

Keith looks at him in confusion. 'I'm not sure I . . .'

'My main focus this year is more business profile pieces on me – in the *Telegraph* and *Guardian* and whatnot,' Giles continues.

'I'm happy to help with that,' I pipe up, keen to make amends for my inadvertent head-butting.

'Excellent – it's what you PR girls are good at, after all.' Giles turns to me, his eyes gleaming aquamarine, matching the hot-tub water.

Giles is obsessed with his reputation as a successful entrepreneur. He's already heir to the Harper's Biscuits fortune – his grandfather invented the Viennese Whirl – but he likes to show his family how well he can do on his own. Even though he's hardly ever in the office and I'm pretty sure it's thanks to Keith that the agency is still afloat.

'With a bit of careful planning we can continue to grow the top line at a decent pace,' Keith persists, catching my eye. I purse my lips and nod thoughtfully. I can't say I've ever actually understood exactly what the top line is. Or the bottom line, for that matter.

As Keith launches into a complicated dissection of the agency's finances, I feel a sharp elbow digging into my ribs.

'Fuck, is it weird that I feel horny?' Jess murmurs next to me. Her blonde bob is mussed up and mascara streaks down her flushed cheeks.

'I wouldn't say our agency's full of talent.' I lower my voice, looking around the tub; there're more than a few beer bellies and moobs on offer. 'Who've you got your eye on?'

'I'd hump anyone right now, Chlo. Typical, the one time I actually feel like having sex and my husband isn't even here.'

'It's true what they say about married sex then?'

'Yep. After ten bloody years of living together and two kids it just feels like another chore. One of the more tedious ones. At least doing the laundry gives me a sense of achievement – and the washing machine is more likely to make me come.'

I wrinkle my nose in sympathy. 'It could just be a dry patch.'

'Yeah, so dry we're in danger of a fucking forest fire. John doesn't even get there's a problem – he leaves the bathroom door open when he's having a crap, for Christ's sake! You wait till you're married with kids – you'll see.' Jess points an ominous finger at me. 'Isn't it time you and your bloke tied the knot anyway?'

'What, after your glowing review?' I laugh. 'Ant's definitely my soul mate but there's no rush.'

Though Ant and I have only officially been a couple for three years, we first met at Goldsmiths uni when we were eighteen. Having both grown up in the sleepy English countryside, we were bedazzled by the bright lights of London and plunged headfirst into the capital city like kids in a sweet shop, trying everything at least once. I was drawn to Ant's impish nature; he was always playing practical jokes on people. He'd raise his dark eyebrows and flash me a cheeky grin and I wouldn't be able to resist. We were partners in crime but I never thought of him like *that*. It was only later that we realised our attraction was physical.

'Aren't you at least going to move in with him?' Jess squints to focus on my face.

'He says it'd feel too crowded.' When Ant moved to Brighton two years ago, he bought a one-bedroom flat with inheritance money and he's quite precious about it.

'Then get a bigger place between you and share a mortgage.'

'It'd make sense,' I admit. 'My flatmate *is* doing my nut in at the moment.'

When I first arrived in Brighton after travelling, I moved in with my mate Dom, who I'd met at a blogger meet-up in LA. He's a fashion vlogger/model and is one of the most charismatic people I know. We had an amazing few years living together, dancing around the lounge in our PJs and throwing outlandishly themed parties, but last summer he bought a flat with his Greek boyfriend. Unfortunately the girl who replaced him, Saffron, is a total fucking nightmare.

'I hate the way she always burns patchouli incense. It makes my clothes stink,' I moan.

'Ugh, I couldn't cope.' Jess shudders. 'You can't keep living like a student, Chlo, you have to settle down sometime.'

'I guess.' I smile as I think of how much Ant hates the phrase 'settle down'. He's always had a bit of a problem with convention; nothing terrifies him more than the idea of buying a nice semi-detached house in the leafy suburbs and staying in the same office job for the rest of his life.

I understand his sense of claustrophobia; the world is such a big place and there's so much to see – which is why I went travelling just before I turned thirty. Then Ant joined me out in Central America and we explored together. Ant is definitely happiest when there's no routine and he can be impulsive, which is why I never pressure him with boring domestic stuff. We're having too much fun; I don't want to ruin it.

'I don't know how you two still do so much partying. I'm way too old for all that now.' Jess pokes the skin around her eyes. 'Look at these crow's feet!'

I flick water at her. 'Jess, come on, we're the same age. You're just mega tired cos you're a mum. And a total MILF at that!' She is; she has an hourglass figure and cherub face with adorable dimples. But I know from experience that there's no reasoning with her when she's on a self-deprecating rant.

'Hardly! Have you seen these spaniel's ears?' Jess wiggles her breasts. 'And I've got an empty pouch of flesh round my middle like a nineties bum bag.'

'I know what you mean, Jess. I've never felt less attractive.' Theresa, sitting next to Jess, leans forward. 'My son brought home a painting of our family from school and he'd given me scarecrow hair and black shadows under my eyes, the little shit!'

I glance at Theresa's mass of stiff straw-coloured hair. To be fair, it does have a touch of scarecrow about it.

'And look, he actually bit me yesterday!' Theresa holds up her arm; there are visible red indents on her wrist. Most people in the hot tub are parents; they stop talking and stare at her bite marks.

'Ouch! Have you tried giving him regular snacks?' Jess suggests. 'Maybe he's getting hangry.'

'Or give him a pillow to punch when he's feeling frustrated,' Keith chips in.

'Or try yelping loudly next time he bites you, then roll on the floor and play dead.' I nod sagely.

'But you don't have children, Chloe, do you?' Theresa looks puzzled.

'No. But my Labrador, Dora, had biting problems when she was a puppy.' I wave my hand. 'It's the same principle.'

A few people exchange doubtful glances and then everyone starts talking animatedly about childcare. I sigh as the usual lifestyle chasm opens up between us. Whenever I try to join in with the frequent family-rearing discussions I'm always met with condescension. As if the parents are soldiers on the frontline of some bloody war and I'm just a deserter who stayed at home under the pretext of growing potatoes.

A cork pops behind me and raucous laughter erupts from the other hot tub, making me regret my decision to join this group. I am interested in children. I enjoy hanging out with my mates' kids and I even have a goddaughter, Maisie, who I love to bits. She calls me 'odd mother' because, well, I like to make her laugh. But there's still so much Ant and I want to do before we commit to raising an actual human being. And Ant can't even keep his cactus plant alive.

'Chloe, we have a code red emergency.' A voice hisses urgently in my ear and I swivel around, happy to be diverted from the heated debate on off-road prams.

'What's up?'

Verity, from the fashion team, crouches behind me in a coral bikini. Her caramel-streaked hair is pulled up in a high ponytail and her flawless face has a dewy glow.

'It's Simone. She's just been dumped and she's locked herself in our bathroom. She might do something stupid. I left my tweezers in there.' Verity bites her bottom lip; her perfect white teeth gleam.

'What do you think she's going to do – pluck herself to death?'

'You never know with her.' Verity widens her china-blue eyes; her wet lashes stick out in spikes.

'OK.' I climb out of the tub and steam rises from my skin.

'Where are you girls going?' Giles hooks an elbow over the back of the hot tub, shooting a sidelong glance at Verity's yoga-toned body as she straightens up.

'No sweat, G, we've got it covered.' Verity puts a hand on her hip and sticks her chest out, smiling at the group in the tub. Most of the men purse their lips as they studiously avert their gaze from her perky nipples, whereas the women gape at her with open fascination.

'Come on, Chlo.' Verity swishes her wet ponytail and struts off across the terrace, apparently immune to the cold.

'Look at Verity's thigh gap!' Jess howls as I hurry after her. 'I can't even walk ten metres without my thighs chafing.'

'Ugh, Chloe, you need to swerve that boring baby chat,' Verity says as we walk through to the kitchen.

'Well, I did hear some great tips on how to manage stretch marks.'

'Ew, I am so not popping sprogs. I wouldn't do that to my body.' Verity presses a hand to her six-pack. 'These days you can just grow them in a Petri dish, can't you? Like, designer babies.'

'Yeah, but you still have to get pregnant.'

'Humph, well I'll just hire a surrogate who needs the cash.' Verity gasps as I slide open the kitchen drawer and take out a butter knife.

'You don't think Simone will get violent?'

'No, it's to pick the lock. Just a little trick I learnt from Ant. Come on.' I slip the butter knife in my robe pocket.

We walk through the cabin lounge and up the wooden stairs to the bedrooms. Verity and Simone are sharing a twin room which has a cream carpet, slatted wooden blinds and dark green bedcovers. Each bed is covered in a tangled mess of clothes – way more than you could possibly need for a forest minibreak. I point at a pair of strappy high heels.

'When are you planning on wearing them?'

'We might bump into someone who's having a massive country mansion party or whatever. Like they do on *Made in Chelsea*.' She kneels by the door of the bathroom and raps on it with her knuckles.

'Simmy, I'm here with Chloe. Are you alive?'

We hear a wet snuffling noise and a thump.

'Babes, he's obvs a total flake. You've got to move on, yeah?' She turns to me. 'They were shagging but then he went totally off-radar.'

'Actually, I saw he was playing our "schexy time" playlist on Spotify yesterday,' Simone protests through the door.

'He is thinking about you then,' Verity croons comfortingly. 'Maybe he just needs a bit of time out and he'll come grovelling back.'

'Yeah, but he won't answer my calls and he's blocked me on WhatsApp.' Simone's voice wobbles. 'No one wants me. I'm fat and ugly. What's the fucking point?'

We hear some more thudding and I put my palms against the bathroom door, speaking clearly.

'Sim, I know how shit you must feel but you *will* get over him, I promise. How long were you together?'

'Three weeks.'

'That's it? So, you didn't even know he existed a month ago! Come on, Sim, you can do better than this knob-head.'

'But I don't want to be on my own,' Simone whimpers. There's a clatter of what sounds like glass smashing and Verity jumps.

'Quick – get us in there.'

I bend over the door handle and insert the butter knife between the door and jamb, applying pressure to the tip of the lock's latch until it gives. Verity and I heave our body weight against the door and stumble into the bathroom.

Simone is slumped on the slate floor tiles by the bath in jogging bottoms and a bikini top. Her short brown hair is damp and sticks to her blotchy cheeks. She's staring disconsolately at the glass of wine she's just smashed in the bath. Red wine stains the porcelain like blood.

'Oops.' She looks up at us with watery brown eyes.

I grab a hand towel and start collecting the larger shards of glass.

'Up you get.' Verity sits Simone on the wicker chair in the corner. 'Don't be such a freakazoid.'

'It was an accident.' Simone sniffs. 'S'all right for you, Vee, all the boys love you. Even now you're living with Gavin.'

'Yeah, I know. But even basic girls find their bae eventually.' Verity perches on the edge of the bath and crosses her long legs. 'You just have to go through the shit ones first. Right, Chloe?'

'Hell yeah. Dave – the guy I met when I graduated – was a total arsehole.' I put the glass in the bin and run the shower-head over the bath.

'Was he the jealous one who told you what clothes to wear?' Simone asks.

'Yes, I wasn't allowed anything too short except in the bedroom otherwise he'd get well moody.' I sit next to Verity on the bath. 'I was a doormat. I let him ban me from seeing friends he considered a "bad influence" and he'd watch porn over my shoulder while we were having sex.'

'Bastard!' Simone and Verity say in unison.

'Yup. Thank God my sister, Emma, helped me build up the courage to leave him. Dave went mental, but we stood our ground. After that, I was single for years and I *loved* it,' I say pointedly to Simone. 'Then I went off travelling on my own and started writing my blog, *Chloe Wanders.*'

'I'd never have the guts to do that,' Simone says.

'You never know till you try.' I smile at her. I still remember the heady mix of euphoria and fear I had when I got on the plane. 'I know it's nice to have a partner to share stuff with, but life can be just as exciting when you're not holding someone else's hand.'

'I'm too chicken,' Sim says morosely, looking into her lap. 'I'd just think everyone was laughing at what a sad boyfriend-less loner I was.'

'Aw, Sim.' I shake my head. 'There's no shame in not having a boyfriend; it's not a measure of how cool or attractive you are. You should only choose to be with someone because they complement your life. Don't settle for anything less.'

'Exactly.' Verity nods. 'Your man should treat you like a princess, else you kick him to the kerb. Like Chloe's Ant. He came halfway across the world to declare his love when you were doing your *Eat, Pray, Love* stuff in Mexico, didn't he?' Verity gestures at me impatiently.

I laugh. 'Well, something like that.'

I thought I'd accidentally swallowed a mezcal worm and was hallucinating when I first spotted Ant's familiar shaved head at the salsa bar. He turned and grinned at me, wiggling his hips in a poor attempt at Latino dance. I ran into his arms and, when he pressed his face into my hair, I knew something had changed between us. It was as if I suddenly understood the words to a tune I'd been humming all my life.

'It's just like a film.' Simone sighs. 'Walking off into the sunset together.'

'There were some epic sunsets on the Caribbean coast,' I admit.

When Ant and I first kissed, I felt my entire body glow. When we had sex, I felt the imprint of him inside me, under my skin. Neither of us had ever experienced such intense feelings before; every morning we woke up together we'd giggle in disbelief and touch each other's faces to check we weren't dreaming.

'But you'll have your own sunset moment one day, Sim,' I promise her. 'You're only twenty-five – don't waste your life crying over men that aren't worth it. Love will come along when you're not desperately seeking it.'

'Yeah, but maybe seek it a little bit. You don't want to wait as long as Chloe and end up some crazy old cat lady.' Verity stands up and inspects herself in the mirror, pouting appreciatively. 'We're still young and beautiful.' She casts a critical glance at Sim. 'Or young, at least. Reel them in while you can, Sim.'

'Verity, it's not all about looks . . .' I protest.

'Said no man ever.' Verity yawns. 'Come on, let's bounce. Have you got your selfie stick, Sim?'

'Yes!' Simone gets up and tugs off her joggers. 'We can put some hawwwt tub shots on Insta; then he'll be sorry he ever ghosted me.'

I frown as we head back downstairs, not convinced Sim's quite got the message. In the kitchen, Verity grabs another two bottles of wine from the fridge. 'Let's get smashed.'

We jog across the terrace to the hot tub on the left. Verity and Sim plunge straight into the foaming water, squealing and splashing water at the sales guys. I straddle the tub carefully, not wanting to repeat my disastrous lunge.

Rudy, one of the geeky tech guys, openly stares at my body, letting out a low wolf whistle. Verity, who is eye-level with my crotch, narrows her eyes at him in irritation. Suddenly she reaches out and tugs my bikini bottoms down an inch.

'Omigod, Chlo, I didn't realise you were a natural redhead,' she observes loudly.

Everyone in the tub cracks up and I accidentally round-kick Rudy in the face in my haste to plunge my errant ginger pubes under the water.

Chapter 2

It turns out hot tubs aren't a great place to binge drink into the wee hours. The next day, most people are suffering from dehydration and nausea.

We spend the morning doing outdoor activities with our forest ranger, foraging for edible wild food and lighting campfires with flint and steel in the forest clearing.

'There are many health benefits to pine-needle tea.' The ranger throws more pine needles into the mess tin of boiling water. 'It can help with high blood pressure.'

I kneel next to him, scribbling in my notebook; I'm writing up a blog post on our trip. My colleagues are leaning against trees and sitting on wooden stumps, observing proceedings with varying degrees of interest.

'Here, try this.' The ranger pours some pine-needle tea through a sieve into a cup and I take a sip. It's fragrant and soothing; a balm to my throbbing temples.

'It's also rich in Vitamin A, which improves the quality of your skin and hair.' The ranger smiles at me.

'Give me some of that.' Verity grabs the cup from me. She's wearing a garish pink velvet Hollister tracksuit. 'I literally haven't slept.'

The ranger hands out more cups of tea as my colleagues stagger over.

'I think that hot tub boiled my internal organs.' Rudy groans, his skinny frame folding as he clutches his stomach, his pale skin almost alabaster.

'That gonna be your excuse now, is it, Rudy?' One of the boys claps his hands to his cheeks and looks towards his crotch in mock-alarm. 'Honey, the hot tub shrunk my penis.'

'Right then, troops.' Giles steps into the middle of the clearing, in a tweed flat cap, shiny new Barbour jacket and inappropriate loafers. 'Before we have our company review back at the cabin, we have the option of den-building. Who'll join me?'

He's in a particularly perky mood and beams around the group, oblivious to our hangovers. He's one of those squash-playing, clean-living types who think that three consecutive pints is debauched.

'I can't, G, I'm totally whacked,' Verity pouts. 'I need to go back and have a nap.'

'Right, no problem.' Giles flicks her a grin and slaps his arms against his sides. 'Anyone else?'

There's silence and the forest ranger frowns at our blatant lack of enthusiasm. 'We'll be building a basic tipi structure and covering it with ferns and moss.'

A few of the men nod assent and step forward and I join them. I mean, if there's a zombie apocalypse then I'll need to know how to build a survival shelter, right?

The ranger leads our small group into the forest and points out a fallen tree that will form the base of our den, then sends us off in search of branches.

'This is the life, eh? Away from all the noise and traffic.' Keith looks up as a bird trills in a tree, his red anorak stretching over his portly stomach. 'I'd quite happily live in a treehouse out here, enjoying the peace.'

'Yeah, it's great getting a bit of headspace,' I agree.

'You want to get yourself a man shed at the bottom of the garden, Keith,' one of the men wheezes, scrabbling at the moss underneath a trunk. 'Perfect excuse to get away from "her indoors".'

'Haha, I'm with you on that, gents.' Giles looks up from fiddling with a compass. He's assumed the role of finding a north-facing entrance to our den but doesn't appear to be too savvy with navigation. 'I've got a little pad in Knightsbridge which is a wife-free zone.'

Keith looks disapproving. 'I didn't mean I want to escape my wife.'

But none of the men are listening; they move away deeper into the forest, grunting loudly as they break up wood.

I dump my bundle of sticks by the fallen tree. 'God, I was considering moving in with my boyfriend but it sounds like familiarity definitely does breed contempt.'

'Oh, don't listen to any of that nonsense.' Keith rubs his lower back. 'You youngsters are too independent these days. There's nothing more rewarding than making a home together.'

I imagine Ant and me decorating a brand-new flat, choosing paint colours and furniture from IKEA. We could get a place by the beach, with a spare room for Ant's music equipment and a garden for Dora.

'I remember when Margaret and I bought our first cottage – we didn't have any furniture so we slept on camp beds and sat on boxes to watch TV.' Keith stares into the middle distance. 'But it was all ours, you know – every brick.'

'That does sound fun.' I smile as we tie our branches into a frame.

Maybe it is time I had a serious chat with Ant about buying a house. We're definitely compatible. When we were travelling, we often shared a hammock or tent. I can always sense when he needs space because he gets monosyllabic and twitchy. I just go and do my own thing for a few hours and he's usually fine by the time I return.

'It would be amazing not to waste money on overpriced rent,' I say. 'I could just about manage half a mortgage.'

Keith winks. 'Salary reviews are coming up in April – might help with how much you can borrow.'

'Ooh, yes.' Feeling inspired, I sidle over to Giles, who is inexplicably knocking the trunk of an oak tree. He has to understand what an asset I am to Top Banana. When I joined two years ago, PR was new to me so I agreed to start at the bottom, but I've picked it up quickly and my clients are always happy. Plus I'm a good writer and my blog, *Chloe Wanders*, has a big online following. It was one of the main reasons Giles hired me.

'Hey, Giles, I'm writing up a blog post on how nature boosts creativity,' I say, noticing that he takes a wary step back as I approach; he still has a red bump on his brow from our last encounter.

'Ah, sounds interesting.'

'I thought we could share it with our clients and maybe consider inviting a few of them out here to work on new marketing briefs.'

'Possibly.' Giles brushes a stray feather from his mustard chinos.

'It'd be a great chance to bond with them outside the office,' I enthuse. 'We could be known as the digital agency that takes online inspiration *off*line.'

Giles ducks as a bug whizzes past his head. 'The problem is, not everyone enjoys the rural life, Chloe. It can be a bit . . . rustic.'

'Oh, but there are so many hidden surprises. I mean, look at those stinging nettles, for example – you can eat them raw, you know!' I gesture towards the undergrowth and Giles purses his lips in disbelief.

'Seriously, you just have to use a certain technique.' I pluck the top few nettle leaves from the plant, pinching the stem with my fingernails. So far, so good.

Giles is watching in alarm and I give him a confident smile as I roll the leaves into a ball with my fingers. This used to be my favourite trick when I was younger; the idea is to break the fine hairs that contain the sting, and then just pop them into your mouth and . . . ouch!

I slap a hand over my mouth as the nettle stings my tongue, frantically chewing it between my teeth to turn it into pulp before it stings me again . . . fuck! My bottom lip is on fire.

'Erm, Chloe, should I get the ranger?' Giles is baring his whitened teeth and I swallow and stick my tongue out to air it.

'No, that's supposed to happen. Mmm, delicious!' I nod at him reassuringly then run to get my bottle of water from my rucksack.

Back at the cabin, we gather on the sofas in the lounge for our annual company review. Most people are really flagging now; I see Rudy holding his eyelids open with his fingers, hiding behind his curtain of blonde hair.

I hold an ice cube wrapped in a tea towel against my stinging lip and lean back against the cushions as Giles takes us through an obscene number of PowerPoint slides, showing a selection of intricate graphs and diagrams. I'm looking forward to getting back to Brighton and snuggling on the sofa with Ant and Dora. He's been looking after her while I'm away.

I catch Verity's eye; she's curled up on an armchair like a cat, with her head on Simone's lap. She lolls her tongue out of the side of her mouth and mimes shooting herself in the temple.

'Now, obviously we score very highly in many areas of business.' Giles pauses on a graph with a row of lime-green columns. 'But I'm afraid the results show a glaring failure in our otherwise spotless record.' He points to the shortest column. 'Can anyone guess what it is?'

Jess, on the sofa in front of me, says, 'Is it gender equality?'

'Don't be ridiculous. We have free female sanitary products in the toilets, don't we?' Giles glares at Jess and her cheeks redden.

A few of the women exchange mutinous looks. As Jess is in charge of HR, she has visibility of everyone's salaries, and her discretion often wanes after a few wines at the pub on Friday evening. Let's just say the gender pay gap is substantially larger than Verity's thigh gap.

'Is it flexible working?' Theresa asks. Giles is very keen on presenteeism. If you want to work from home you basically have to be at death's door. This month he refused to allow Theresa time off to watch her son play the wolf in the school's pantomime, *Little Red Riding Hood*. Thinking about it now, it probably didn't help her son's biting fetish.

'No! We're very tolerant to family pressures.' Giles shakes his head crossly, then claps to bring us back to the point.

'What we're failing at is brand awareness; Top Banana might be fantastic at marketing its clients but it doesn't do a good PR job on itself. I want *everyone* out there talking about our agency. I want Top Banana to be famous!'

He walks to the flip board in the corner.

'If Top Banana was a celebrity, who would it be?' He points at our receptionist, Suki.

'Ooh.' She scans the ceiling, searching for inspiration. 'How about Gordon Ramsay?'

'He's not exactly edgy.' Giles tuts, his pen hovering over the paper on the flip board. 'Anyone else?'

'Ed Sheeran?'

'Robin Williams?'

'Robin Williams is dead, for God's sake. You younger lot, help me out here – who's hip at the moment?' He turns to the cluster of tech lads who are sprawled out on cushions on the floor.

'Abella Danger?' Rudy smirks and the boys around him crack up.

'Oh yes? Is she a YouTuber?' Giles asks, writing her name down.

'She's a porn star, G.' Verity rolls her eyes from Simone's lap.

'Oh, honestly.' A faint blush creeps up Giles's neck. 'I want Top Banana to be a big player - like Kanye West! Come on, guys, you're the creative brains. How do you suggest we get our name out there?'

'You could speak at digital marketing events, Giles?' I call out. 'And give industry insights on your social channels.'

At the moment, Giles's Twitter feed is mainly dedicated to his numerous holidays and fine-dining experiences.

'Thought leadership.' Giles scribbles it down. 'That's an excellent plan, Chloe.'

'And maybe Top Banana could do more in the community?' I add. 'There's loads of charities in Brighton we could partner with.'

'Ooh yeah, can we work with a puppy charity?' Simone squeaks. 'I'm so up for that.'

'Volunteering work is great for publicity, you're absolutely right.' Giles writes it down.

Verity raises herself from Simone's lap. 'If you wanna be more famous then we should win loads of cool awards.'

'Yes, Verity, now you're talking.' Giles points the pen at her. 'We could enter the Most Awesome Place to Work in the UK awards this summer.'

Verity smiles smugly as he puts it on the flip board in capitals.

'I'm looking for a team champion to lead on project "Make Top Banana Famous".' Giles turns to us. 'Who's keen?'

I raise my hand. This project sounds way more interesting than my existing clients – Best Bathrooms and Net Casino. I spend most of my working days trying to make grouting and online gambling sexy.

About ten other people also raise their hands, but then Verity stands up and jiggles about like a cheerleader without the pom-poms. 'Me, me!'

Giles's gaze travels quickly over me and fixes on Verity.

'Yes, Verity, I think you're the woman for the job. We can discuss our award entry over lunch next week.' He winks at her. 'And now, finally, the moment you've all been waiting for. As you know, every year we give out a "stellar staff" prize to the most promising member of the team.' Giles looks around the group, smiling magnanimously as everyone sits up a bit straighter.

'I've closely assessed who's shown initiative over the last year and chosen one person who stands out as a shining example to us all.' He takes an envelope from his back pocket and waves it in the air. 'Our star will receive a spa weekend in Sussex with a plus one. Champagne included, of course.'

An excited murmur goes around the room and I nibble my knuckle in anticipation. Maybe Giles does notice my efforts but is just really good at hiding it. Imagine Ant's reaction this evening when I tell him I'm treating us to a spa weekend away! It's just what we need after a long, cold winter.

'Without further ado, the winner is . . .' Giles withdraws a piece of paper and pauses dramatically, as if he's Simon Cowell on *The X Factor*. '. . . Verity Winterbourne! Would you look at that, this girl is on fire!'

Verity does a little victory jog on the spot. 'Yaaaaaaaaasssssssssss, slayed it!'

I prod the swollen bumps on my lip with my sore tongue as she accepts her prize with a long, emotional speech, trying not to look peeved.

Verity's the laziest workmate I've ever had; she spends most of her time on Snapchat, always avoids client calls, deletes her inbox messages if they're a few days old, and has lengthy meetings outside the office about made-up topics. Like that time I caught her and Simone shopping at a Ralph Lauren sample sale one afternoon, on my way to the post office, and they said they were doing 'market research'.

'And finally, I'd like to thank Chloe.'

I look up in surprise as Verity delivers her last words, clutching Giles's forearm as a single tear trembles on her lower lashes. 'Chloe's ten years older than me and she's shown me just how easy it is to let time slip by without any clear goals. So, thanks, Chloe, for inspiring my ambition.' She nods at me gravely. 'Be the change you want to see, people!'

Chapter 3

I'm relieved to walk through the ticket barriers at Brighton station early that evening. Verity spent the entire train ride home planning all the treatments she's going to have at the spa weekend. As if she doesn't spend enough time on maintaining her appearance.

I know she won't give the 'Make Top Banana Famous' project a second thought; it's just so unfair when I'm gagging for something interesting to work on. Just thinking about the online guides to bathroom furniture I have to write next week makes me want to weep.

I say goodbye to my colleagues and cross the station concourse, past a hen party wearing bunny ears and pink leotards. They screech loudly and my hangover throbs; it's like walking past a chicken farm.

I walk up the steep hill to Ant's flat. Seagulls wheel and cry above me, white ghosts in the night. Yesterday's conversations about settling down are playing on my mind. If I lived with Ant, I don't think work would get to me so much. At least one area of my life would be harmonious.

The bass of Ant's music is making his front door vibrate. He'll be mixing with his headphones on so probably won't hear the buzzer, but, of course, Dora does. I hear her barking frantically, and when the door opens, she shoots through it like a bullet, hurling herself at my legs.

'Hello, darling.' I drop to a crouch and run my hands over her glossy black fur. She's a spinning blur of thwacking tail and wet nose. She whimpers with ecstasy at our reunion, as if I've been missing for centuries rather than days. Dora is a beautiful black Labrador and I absolutely adore her. See what I did there? She even has her own Instagram account: @adorethelabrador.

'And hello, darling.' I rise to greet Ant, who's standing in the doorway in a hoodie and jeans, with his headphones round his neck.

'Hey.' He smiles, rubbing his droopy brown eyes. I pull him into a tight hug, breathing in his peppery smell. Ant drops his head on my shoulder but there's something stiff about him.

I rub his short brown hair; it's soft like velvet. 'What's up?'

'Nothing, just tired.' He yawns, dragging a hand down his face and blinking at me. 'Come in, how was your work thingy?'

'Humph, the usual office bollocktits.'

I follow him down the wooden corridor to the lounge, where he flops onto the L-shaped sofa. His decks are set up in the corner, blasting music from his huge speakers. Vinyl is scattered all over the floorboards.

'Well, at least you got to hang out in a forest.' He yawns again.

'Why're you so knackered?' I sling my rucksack down by the wide-screen TV and sit next to him. Dora jumps up and nudges my arm out of the way so she can lay her head in my lap.

'Tough week at work. There's so much pressure.' He rests his head on the back of the sofa.

'Aw well, it's the weekend now.' I give his knee an encouraging rub but he just wrinkles his nose.

Ant has been working as a recruitment agent at Warren Recruitment for two years now; he fell into it when he moved to Brighton. He's quite persuasive and can charm anyone when he puts his mind to it, but he's never really found a job he loves. His main passion is electronic music. He studied it and he mixes his own tracks but he hasn't found a way to get paid for it yet.

'I might look for a new job. New year and all that.' He looks at me sideways.

'Really?' I'm surprised; Ant usually lets things slide. The floor starts thrumming as a particularly heavy bass line kicks in and I stand up; now feels like a good time to discuss our future. 'Can I turn the music down a bit?'

Ant shrugs and I turn down the volume, taking a deep breath.

'Actually, Ant, I've also been thinking about making a few changes this year.' I turn to face him. 'My work review is coming up soon and I'm going to demand a pay rise. And then, well . . .'

'What?'

'Maybe we could . . . buy a house together?' I blurt out.

Ant's frown deepens but I continue. 'Think how much you'd save if you split a mortgage with me! You could work shorter hours so you can do your music. And there'd be loads more space for your equipment, plus a spare room that our mates could stay in.'

I stop abruptly, realising I've taken on a wheedling tone.

Ant holds up both his hands. 'Chlo, slow down, I don't want to sell yet. This flat is my mum's legacy.'

'I know it is, hun.' When we were in our mid-twenties Ant's mum died of cancer. I'd met her several times; she was a warm, generous woman and they were so close. I went to the funeral and held Ant against me while he wept, my whole body shaking along with his. All his sparkle and cockiness had drained away. He was like a lost little boy, his bottom lip trembling with fear.

'I just wondered if you might want to upgrade – with me.' I sit back down, facing him. 'I'm sick of flat-sharing. And we spend so much time together I thought it'd make sense.'

'I'm not ready, Chlo. I like my space.' Ant's face creases in distress and his leg starts jigging up and down; it's definitely a bad time to talk about this. 'I'm sorry, I would say move in here but there just isn't enough room for all your stuff and mine. And the dog.' He glances at Dora, who is watching our exchange anxiously.

'Don't worry,' I soothe. 'I just thought I'd ask. But it's cool, maybe I'll just look to get a studio flat.'

'Hmm.' Ant runs his hands over his head. 'To be honest, I'm considering renting this place out and doing something really different – like learning to sail.'

My mouth falls open at this unexpected bombshell.

'What?' He widens his eyes to mimic me. 'You know I love the water. I was reading up on commercial yachting, and if I trained up as crew, I could basically sail all over the world and get paid for it.'

'You want to . . . leave Brighton?' Though I'm used to Ant's restless nature, he's never actually this decisive.

'I don't know, sort of. It's more your place than mine.' He bites his lower lip.

I feel a fluttering panic in my stomach. I can't believe he sees it like that. There I was thinking we could buy a house together and he's talking about leaving town.

'But what about me?'

'I could just do short berths – and obviously I'd come back to see you in between, silly!' He squeezes my shoulder.

'But I'd miss you!' My voice wobbles.

'You could always learn to sail with me.'

I tut. 'You know I can't do that.'

'Why not? What happened to the adventurous girl who dreamt of living in the jungle and tracking mountain gorillas?'

'I'm still that girl – I still want adventures. But I've done lots of travelling . . . I just want to, I dunno, focus on developing my skills. And I love living in Brighton. I thought you did too.'

Ant sighs. 'Look, it's just an idea. I'm feeling a bit trapped, trying to figure out what I want.' He leans forward, pressing his forehead against mine, and kisses me. 'Don't be upset.'

I blink as my eyelashes brush against his. 'Well, you're worrying me. If you're feeling crap then talk to me, we can sort it out together.'

Ever since Ant's mum died, he's been prone to periods of melancholy. He hides it well, cracking his usual jokes and acting the fool. But I see it, like black ink spilling across a script.

'I shouldn't have said anything, Chlo, ignore me. I probably need a break, that's all. Maybe some sunshine.'

'Yes, sun.' I seize on the idea with relief. 'I could look at cheap flights.'

'We could recline by a villa pool with a salty cocktail and a selection of continental snacks.' Ant licks his lips enticingly.

'I'll have an extra gherkin, please.' I touch my index finger to the groove at the top of his lip; it fits perfectly.

We kiss and I run my hand under his hoodie over his warm back, suddenly horny. 'Shall we go to bed?'

'Actually, I'm expecting a Skype call from a client in Australia.' Ant stretches. 'It could take a while so there's no point in you hanging around. Shall we just meet tomorrow for lunch?'

'You're working on a Friday night?' I was hoping to stay over.

'I told you it's full on. I have to do international hours, innit.' Ant opens up his laptop on the coffee table. 'Dora hasn't had much of a walk today so you'll probably wanna take her along the beach.'

'Right.' I stand up and Dora gives herself a shake, her collar jingling. I put on my rucksack and clip her lead on, still reeling a bit from the conversation.

'Where shall we go for lunch? The Wonky Rabbit has a new menu.'

'Yeah, whatever.' Ant stares at the screen.

'Whatever, excellent. I love whatever,' I say huffily, clomping down the corridor.

'Hey, don't be like that. The Wonky Rabbit sounds great.' Ant follows me to the door and chucks me under the chin.

'See you then, then.' I give him a peck and walk down the steps, turning to wave as I hit the pavement, but he's already closed the door.

I march through the North Laine area towards the beach, past the vintage boutiques, tattoo parlours, indie coffee shops and pubs, where twinkling fairy lights line the steamed-up windows.

I'm really offended Ant doesn't want to live with me. I can't believe he's been thinking of leaving town without properly discussing it. I thought it was a given that we'd make all our life decisions together – isn't that what a partnership is supposed to be about?

As we cross the road to Brighton Palace Pier, the coloured lights reflect on the sea's glossy black surface, stretching out across the water in glittering columns of red, yellow and blue. Brighton definitely feels like my home right now; but then, Ant is my home too.

Dora gallops down the steps to the left of the pier entrance, and races after her ball as I hurl it across the pebbles towards the white foam glinting in the darkness.

I listen to the gentle whisper of the waves, running over Ant's words. I know his first impulse is to run away from problems but he's also really quick to change his mind. Hopefully his sudden fascination with sailing is just a passing whim.

Dora has abandoned her ball and, nose to the ground, is sniffing a roving path around the lamp-lit promenade. Her back legs start shimmying outward at right angles in typical pre-poo behaviour.

Sure enough, her back humps and she does a poo on the pathway whilst gazing out at the ocean; a loo with a view.

I pull out a poo bag and bend to pick up her turd; there is red stringy stuff poking out the top of it.

Immediately my brain whirs with possible medical emergencies. Has Dora just shat out some of her intestine? Is it a worm? Maybe I should take her to the vet.

I grasp the corner of the object through the bag and, as it uncurls, I see it's a scrap of lacy material.

Binding my lips together in an appalled grimace, I hold the thing closer to the light. Recognition dawns in a sickening retch; it's a woman's G-string covered in dog crap. And it's not mine.

Chapter 4

Ant answers on the fourth ring, his voice gravelly with impatience.

'I'm expecting a Skype call, Chlo.'

'Yes, I know. I'm just wondering why Dora's shat out a lady's G-string?'

There's a few seconds' silence, then Ant laughs uncertainly. 'Maybe she raided your knicker drawer.'

'I don't wear G-strings, Ant, you ought to know that.'

'OK, then she probably picked it up in town, down on West Street.'

'And you didn't notice her eating underwear?'

'Jesus, Chloe, what is this?' Ant snaps.

I rub my forehead and look at Dora, who offers me a conciliatory paw. 'I don't know, it's just really thrown me.'

'Well don't have a go at me about it, especially when I've got this important call any minute.'

'OK, fine.' I hang up.

We climb the steep steps to Marine Parade and walk past the grand Regency buildings, arranged in pristine white tiers like wedding cakes, to Kemptown village.

I feel all shaky and so I go into my local pizzeria, Pizzaface, and order a Vesuvius with extra chilli. Carrying my warm box of pizza, I turn down my street, where rows of three-storey townhouses are lined with black railings and delicate webbed balconies.

As I open my front door, I hear yelling from inside the flat. Dora's hackles rise and she growls and bounds up the stairs. I look around the entryway for a weapon, grabbing a large umbrella from the coat stand and rushing after her.

I'm expecting to see some kind of fight going on in the lounge, so am confused to find eight grown adults lying on their backs on mats, screaming and waving their limbs in the air like dead bugs. Their eyes are screwed up tight and a few of them are kicking their heels hard against the floor.

Saffron, my flatmate, sits cross-legged at the front, serenely observing them. She's wearing a gold tunic and red leggings and her thick black dreadlocks are wrapped in an Indian scarf.

'What's going on?' My voice is drowned out by the cacophony of petulant wailing. I lower the umbrella as the noise crescendos and eventually dies down. Several people roll onto their sides, flushed and giggling.

'Saffron, are you all on acid?' I ask with a forced smile and she waves at me with both hands, her bangles tinkling.

'Oh, hi, Chloe! Haha no, it's tantrum yoga – to release your inner child? Grab a mat, I'll talk you through it.'

'Erm, no thanks, I was hoping to crash in front of the TV actually. How long are you going to be in here?'

Some of the group turn to glare at me, as if *I'm* the disturbance.

'Two hours or so,' Saffron says breezily. 'Then afterwards we'll do some shared reflection.'

'Why didn't you tell me you were planning this?' My skin prickles with anger.

'Chill, Chloe, you're ruining the vibe.'

The yogis in my lounge are now all looking at me resentfully. One woman pouts and puts her thumb in her mouth; she's clearly enjoying channelling her inner toddler.

'Saffron, can I have a word out here, please?' I try to keep my voice even. She sighs, then gets up.

'Just hold on to your feelings of frustration, guys. I'll be back in a tick.' She nods to the group and they resume their whingeing as she follows me down the landing into our kitchen.

Even though I cleaned the flat before I left, the sink is now piled high with dirty pans, and there are bright yellow splodges of turmeric all over the worktops. Saffron adds turmeric to everything: porridge, smoothies, tea. I get that it has beneficial properties but it stains like a bitch if you spill it. And she always does.

There is also a pile of her 'recycling' wedged in the corner by the draining board. But, of course, it's still dirty; baked bean tins crusted with congealed beans, plastic milk bottles that stink of cheese and boxes of cereal that haven't been flattened.

As a self-proclaimed hippy, Saffron really hasn't nailed the eco-friendly living thing. In fact, I'd go so far as to call her a raging *hippycrite*. I had to put my foot down when she tried to keep a wormery in the corridor; it kept overflowing because she never emptied it. She said I was being unreasonable, but no one wants fucking worm juice on their carpet.

I slide my pizza onto a plate as Saffron leans against the doorframe, twiddling her nose ring.

'I don't mean to be a killjoy but this isn't the first time you've had loads of people over without asking me, is it?'

Last September Saffron hosted a full-moon party; our flat was filled with people dressed as goddesses chanting and praying over crystals. It went on all night and I didn't sleep a wink.

Then she bought this massive gong and installed it in the lounge, blocking the entrance to our roof terrace. She now has regular group 'gong baths' and I can feel the vibrations of it from my bedroom.

I mean, I'm not against spirituality; it'd just be nice if she respected the fact that we share this flat.

'I've got to earn my rent somehow,' Saffron says. Her green eyes are slanted like a Siamese cat's.

'What, those guys are paying you for this?'

'Yeah, I did a weekend's course in tantrum yoga so I'm fully trained to teach it.'

'Well then hire a bloody studio – don't use our lounge!' My voice rises with indignation. I don't even know what Saffron does for money; she's always at home wafting about in a kimono and talking for hours on her mobile.

Saffron cocks her head. 'I can tell from your aura that you're agitated. You'd really benefit from joining us. It's only sixteen pounds for the session.'

'No!' I take a bite out of a pizza slice and Saffron eyes it disapprovingly.

'You do realise that poor nutrition doesn't help with negative mood.'

'It's got rocket on it. Look, go ahead with your tantrum fest – just give me some notice in future, OK?'

'Fine. I thought you might stay at Ant's tonight anyway.'

'Yeah, well, apparently not.' I cross the landing into my bedroom and shut the door, leaning against it and breathing deeply. Dora goes to curl up in her bed in the corner tucking her nose under her tail with a heavy sigh. Suddenly the events of the past few hours rush in on me, making me want to scream and cry at the same time. Maybe I will have a temper tantrum after all.

I put the plate of pizza down on my bedside cabinet and collapse on the bed, resting my head against the pillows and looking around the room, with its sloping ceilings and wonky walls. My wardrobe on the far wall is overflowing with clothes and the corner bookshelves are cluttered with ornaments and books I've had since I was a kid. My old school desk sits in the attic window alcove, looking out over the jumble of Brighton rooftops towards the sea.

I listen to the frenzied bawling coming from the lounge and chew my pizza despondently. When I first moved into this flat I found my quirky attic bedroom really cosy, but now it just feels cluttered and stifling. I don't want to spend this evening stuck in here, on my own, with all those randoms in the lounge. I want to be with Ant. But he doesn't seem to want to be with me. My lower lip trembles as I allow this thought to creep in, followed by another, more terrifying: *Does he want to be with someone else? Someone who, perhaps, wears a red G-string*.

I need to talk to someone who knows Ant and me; who can tell me if I'm overreacting. I need to talk to Emma.

Emma's my sister. Well, stepsister if you want to be precise, but the prefix is irrelevant. Basically, my dad married her mum, Janice, when we were both twelve years old, and I was instantly in awe of Emma; she was really pretty with corkscrew blonde curls, went to a private boarding school and had friends with posh nicknames like 'Tabs' and 'Bunty'. She always seemed to be doing impressive things like learning musical instruments, taking dance classes and running cross-country.

At first, whenever I visited Dad, I would stay out of Emma's way just in case she was territorial. But then one afternoon she appeared at my bedroom door in a leotard and tutu, beckoning to me urgently.

'Quick!' she whispered, holding up a small bottle of red liquid. 'Help me put this on – I want two dribbles coming out of my nostrils.'

'What? Why?' I took the bottle and squeezed it so that a viscous bubble ballooned from the nozzle.

'Mum won't let me skip ballet unless I have a really good excuse. I hate it, the teacher always prods me in the bum with her cane.'

Giggling, I applied the fake blood to Emma's nostrils and then she ran out into the corridor, moaning, telling her mum the nosebleed had come out of nowhere.

Janice threw a fit because Emma had stained her ballet outfit and made her lie on her bed with an icepack on the bridge of her nose. I joined her, and we spent the rest of the day obsessing over Britpop.

'Now there's two of us, we can join forces.' She grinned.

Now there's two of us. Being an only child had its bonuses – I had all my parents' focus and attention – but sometimes that was also a burden. Having someone my age to help fight my teenage battles was much better.

After that, we became really close and were both offered a place at Goldsmiths, where I studied theatre and English and Emma studied music.

Emma met Ant first, in a lecture. She invited him out to the pub with us and we did Jägerbombs all night, then went back to his for a house party. He proudly introduced us to his friends as the 'life and soul sisters'.

Emma always says she knew Ant and I would be together from that very first night, but then it's easy to say that with hindsight. I suddenly need her opinion really badly, even though she'll probably be up to her neck in child duties. She's the mother of my spirited five-year-old goddaughter, Maisie, and a brand-new baby boy, Toby.

'Chloe, my God, it's so good to hear another grown-up. I feel like an inmate in an asylum.' Emma answers the phone panting. 'My ears are ringing with the screaming and Toby won't take my milk, even though he's obviously hungry. My boobs are like massive scarlet swollen udders; you would not believe how painful they are. I'm basically a cow. A trapped, insane cow with tinnitus.'

'Shit, is there anything you can take for the pain?'

'Painkillers aren't working, but the midwife came this afternoon and milked me with her bare hands. I just sat there in my dressing gown watching her milk my tits into a cup! A serious low point.'

'Oh, Christ.' I let out a horrified snort at the image. 'That sounds horrendous! And poor little Toby; he must be starving.'

'Yeah, James is giving him formula now.' Emma lets out a huge sigh. 'Think twice before you have kids, seriously.'

'Ha, that's not exactly on the cards.'

'What's up?' Emma picks up on my dejected tone.

I tell her about my conversation with Ant and, when I get to Dora's surprise G-string package, she lets out a stream of expletives that I hope Maisie isn't listening to.

'The sneaky fucking fucker!'

'But don't you think Dora could've eaten the G-string outside somewhere?' I'm dismayed that she's immediately concluding the worst.

'No, I don't, Chlo. I think she ate it right there in Ant's flat. He must've had a girl there. Think about it; the culprit is always someone close to you, never a stranger.'

'Well yeah, but this isn't a murder.' Emma watches a lot of crime dramas.

'Same difference. You need to go around there right now and ask him to his face. You know what he's like – you'll read him like a book. I bet he's totally freaking out since you called him.'

I stand up and reach for my trainers. 'You're right, Em, I need to confront him before he has a chance to make up some story.'

'Yes. Go now! I'm so sorry, hun. I never thought he'd do this. He's always been a bit flaky but he definitely loves you. I can't believe this is happening.'

'Maybe it's not.' I feel adrenalin coursing through me. I'm not prepared to accept that Ant would betray me. 'I'm getting a cab there now. I'll let you know how it goes.'

Chapter 5

'Can you pull up here, please?' I ask the taxi driver in a trembling voice as we get to Ant's road. I can't believe I feel so nervous; this is *Ant*, my best friend.

I get out and stand on the pavement, looking up at Ant's bedroom window. I haven't told him I'm coming because he'd only put me off.

I climb the steps for the second time this evening and press the buzzer hard until my fingertip goes white.

The door swings open and Ant stares at me in confusion.

'I thought you were Deliveroo.'

'I need to talk to you. If you still have your work call, I'll just wait.' I fold my arms.

'I've had the call. But it's getting late and I'm knackered, Chlo.'

'Yeah, I'm tired too. Are you going to let us in or what?'

Ant chews the inside of his cheek as his eyes dart over my shoulder to the road, then he takes a step backwards.

Dora pushes ahead, snuffling the corridor skirting boards. I follow her through to the lounge and stand by the window, drawing the long navy curtains so that no passers-by can look in.

Ant sits on the sofa, pulling the cuffs of his hoodie over his hands. There's an awful silence between us. Words are cluttering up my throat, making me want to vomit.

Ant blows his cheeks out and, with what seems like a huge effort, lifts his eyes to meet my gaze.

'What's up then?' Although he's trying to smile I can see the fear in his expression.

I make myself say it. 'Ant, did you sleep with someone else?'

His Adam's apple bobs and the sound of his dry swallow fills the room. He pinches the skin above his nose and looks at the floor.

'This is about the G-string again.' He gives a scoffing little laugh. 'We've known each other all this time and you've suddenly decided you don't trust me.'

'I want to trust you, of course. This is hideous for me too.' I break my composure and go to sit down next to him on the sofa. 'It's just . . . the way you were being earlier. You seemed so detached. What am I supposed to think?'

Ant's dropped all attempts at light-heartedness. His nostrils flare as he looks at me with serious brown eyes.

'Chloe, I told you. Things aren't great with me right now. I wish I could explain it to you. I'm just questioning everything. It's all right for you, you're content here. I just feel like there's more out there for me.' He waves an arm vaguely and I want to shake him.

'OK, Ant, I get it: you're a free spirit. But you're not questioning *us* though, right?'

There's a ringing in my temples and I clutch his sleeve. '*Ant?*'

He just stares at me.

Suddenly the buzzer goes, making Dora jump up and bark.

'That'll be my takeaway.' Ant gets up and goes to the front door. I wander into his bedroom and look around – at the box on top of his wardrobe overflowing with wigs and funny hats, the wooden Mayan mask that we each got in Mexico, the framed photo of us on Brighton beach. I'm pulling a face at the camera and Ant is laughing up at me, his eyes creased with affection. This doesn't feel real. I was expecting Ant to reassure me when he saw how anxious I was.

I stand over his bed; the grey stripy bedsheets are crumpled. I hear Ant clattering in the kitchen as he serves up his food. Then he appears in the doorway with a bowl and chopsticks.

'Do you want some Chinese?' he asks.

'I'm not hungry.'

He shuffles hesitantly. 'Look, shall we just watch a movie then go to bed? Sleep on it?'

'Sleep on what though, Ant? I'm not the one who's acting so strange,' I snap.

Ant just chews on his chow mein, watching me. I feel a stab of annoyance. How can he eat at a time like this?

'So, did you shag her in this bed?' I ask faux pleasantly, patting the duvet.

Ant groans. 'Argh, Chloe, would you stop with this?'

'Come on, Ant, tell me right now. You can't lie to me. Did you fuck someone else? I'll find out, you know.' I'm yelling now.

Ant looks terrified as I advance on him. The chopsticks he's holding are frozen mid-way to his mouth; a noodle falls back down to the bowl. I won't let him look away from me.

'Did you cheat on me?' My heart is beating so loudly that I can barely hear him when he says it.

'Yes.'

Even though I knew it deep down, I still feel dizzy with shock. I sit abruptly on the bed. My legs don't work any more.

Ant puts his bowl down on the carpet and kneels in front of me, holding on to my knees and talking fast.

'I did have a girl here last night – it wasn't planned. We had a bit to drink and I started opening up about, you know, my mum and stuff. Things I've been bottling up. She was really understanding; she knows a lot about bereavement. We didn't mean to . . . it just happened.'

'You slept with her because she . . . gets bereavement?' I gape at him; my mind is working sluggishly.

'No! We were drunk.'

'And did she make a nice change from boring old *me*?'

Ant grinds his knuckles into his forehead. 'Chloe, don't do this.'

'And my dog, *my fucking dog*, was watching you the entire time and you didn't even realise she'd eaten her G-string – she could have choked.'

'Of course I didn't, it's so weird!' Ant looks over his shoulder at Dora, who's watching us from the corridor, and she sinks her head between her paws in shame.

'You were shagging right here, on these sheets.' I look at the pillows and clutch my arms over my stomach, feeling sick. 'Who is she, Ant?' I whisper.

Ant squeezes his eyes shut. 'No one you know. Just a friend. Chloe, I'm so, so sorry. You know I'd never want to hurt you.' His voice breaks.

I hold out my finger and put it in the groove above his lip. There's a pressure building in my chest that threatens to engulf me. I try to imagine what life would be like without Ant in it; I can't. It would be an impossible life.

'Do you even love me any more?' I ask. It takes all my strength to watch his response. His face crumples and his shoulders heave up and down.

'I don't know.' It comes out in a sob and triggers my own avalanche of despair. I howl and then his arms are wrapped tightly around me and he's biting 'I'm sorry' into my neck.

It is the smell of him, the scent of safety and solidity, that finally chokes me and I feel a deep, dark well open inside me. I desperately cling to his shoulders, because I know I'll drown if I let him go.

Ant and I stay up most of the night. I almost feel sorry for him having to watch me thrash about on his bed – lurching between denial, fury and utter anguish – a complete dribbling mess.

By morning's grey light, I'm utterly exhausted. I lie awake, still fully clothed, staring at Ant's motionless back. I've seen him sleeping so many times; I've seen him naked, crying and sick. I thought this man, who I've loved so hard, was mine for keeps.

I limp to the bathroom to inspect my ravaged face. Sure enough, I look monstrous – two shiny swollen slugs have taken up residence on my lids, hovering over my bloodshot eyes, and I have huge purple bags. My damp red hair hangs limply over my mottled cheeks and my top lip is crusted pink from tear salt.

I go into the kitchen, open the fridge and take out half a cucumber, mashing it directly into each of my eye sockets.

I hear the clickety-clack of Dora's claws on the kitchen tiles and lower the cucumber. She sits and watches me dolefully, her tail sweeping the floor in a half-hearted wag.

I go to crouch in front of her and she puts both paws on my shoulders and licks my ears tenderly, making grunty noises in her throat. Then she tries to lick the cucumber in my hand so I hold it away from her.

I feel untethered, not sure where I want to be. I'm definitely not a functioning member of society. In fact, there's only one person I can bear to see me in this state. I pull my phone from my jeans pocket.

'Mum.' Before she can start speaking, I gulp the words out. 'Ant broke me – broke up with me.'

There's a sharp intake of breath as Mum absorbs the magnitude of the situation. When she replies, her voice is firm.

'Come to me. Get a train right now.'

Feeling stronger now I have a plan, I pull on my bobble hat and coat and wrap a scarf around the lower half of my face. I find a pair of sunglasses in the lounge and put them on, even though it's grey and drizzly outside.

I stand in Ant's bedroom doorway, observing him until he stirs and sits up, squinting in the light from the corridor.

'I can't see your face,' he says with a half-smile. 'It's pretty hard to tell what expression you're pulling right now.'

'Abject disappointment,' I say flatly. 'You've ruined everything.'

He drops his chin to his bare chest and pleats the duvet. 'Chloe, I've told you, I didn't . . .'

I walk away before he sees the renegade tears slide from under my shades. When I slam the front door, I feel the heavy vibration deep in my heart.

Chapter 6

'I never liked 'im anyway.' Mum's West Country accent is thick with loathing as she grinds her cigarette out in the ashtray, narrowing her grey eyes against the smoke. We're sitting on the patio overlooking her back garden, drinking black coffee. She's wearing a navy woollen jumper dress which swamps her skinny frame, and her strawberry-blonde hair is pinned up.

I'm still swaddled in my bobble hat, scarf and sunglasses. I got some funny looks from my fellow passengers on the train here; it didn't help that I kept letting out little squeaks of misery. Even the conductor gave me a wide berth, holding up his hand and telling me not to worry as I fumbled for my ticket.

'You did like Ant, Mum,' I protest. 'He always cleaned your windows and washed your car for you.'

'Pffft!' Mum waves a dismissive hand in the air. 'He was sucking up to me. But I saw through his act all right.'

I resist the urge to defend him. I know she's only saying it to comfort me anyway. She loves Ant as much as I do. I remember a few months after his mother died, he came to visit us in Dorset and Mum pulled him into a ferocious cuddle, telling him he could always turn to her.

'I admit, when he went chasing you 'alfway across the world I thought he might be made of sterner stuff,' Mum continues, shaking her head tragically. 'But I should've known better – he's just like the rest. There's a reason they call men the weaker sex, Chlo. They've got two brains and I can tell you which one's stronger.' She points down towards her crotch and grimaces.

'But I just don't get it!' I wail. 'Our sex life was great.'

'Shh!' Mum puts a finger to her lips and nods towards the neighbour's house. 'Kenneth has his prayer group on Saturdays.'

I lower my voice. 'It never crossed my mind that Ant would look at other women.'

'Oh, he'd 'ave been eyeing up every piece of skirt that walked past,' Mum says darkly. 'The first thing men do when they meet a woman is imagine 'er naked.'

'Yeah, but they don't have to act on it. It's not like Ant wasn't getting any. I thought he fancied me.' I gaze morosely at the rhododendrons. 'Though I have let myself go a bit recently; maybe that's it.'

'It i'nt!' Mum makes me jump as she slams her hand down on the wooden table, all concerns about Kenneth's prayer group forgotten. 'You can't be blaming yourself for this, Chlo, it's not right. I bet you some harlot gave him the eye and flattered his pathetic ego. Men'd risk everything for a quick shag. Look at that chap who cheated on Beyoncé – Jayz, was it?'

'Jay-Z,' I sniff.

'Yeah, Jayz. If he can mess about a woman like Beyoncé then there's no hope for any of us.'

'True.'

The table wobbles as Dora dives out from under it after a blackbird on the lawn. Mum watches her, slowly shaking her head. 'What a way to find out, though. With a dog turd. You couldn't write it.'

'I know. I don't think Ant would have volunteered the information.'

'Oh no, course he wouldn't.'

'I want to know who she is. It's driving me mad. She must've known he had a girlfriend, the bitch.' I clench my jaw.

'I know how you feel, love.' Mum flicks her side fringe out of her eyes and presses her lips together in a grim line. 'When I found out about your father and his secretary I was like a woman possessed.'

Mum married Dad in her early twenties, then left him when I was seven. She made no secret of his affairs. In fact, by the time I went to secondary school, I was very well versed in the bastardry of men. I still loved my dad though; I just knew better than to talk about him in front of Mum.

'She thought she was so flash with her fancy sports car and expensive highlights.' Mum lights up another fag. 'Her Audi wasn't so smart by the time I'd finished with it though, was it?' She blows smoke out of both nostrils, looking like a vengeful dragon. Mum's not averse to a bit of car-keying to make her point.

'No, you certainly told her.' I look at Mum with familiar sympathy. She's not had much luck in either marriage. She met her second husband, Leo, when I was ten. He was an absent-minded classical musician and wore his dark hair in a long ponytail. We lived with him in a ramshackle old cottage in Somerset. He was nice enough to me but unfortunately he also turned out to have a talent for infidelity.

'The problem is, it's not just men you can't trust, it's women too.' Mum drags hard on her cigarette so the tip glows. 'They act all nicey-nicey, pretending they want to be your friend, when all they're after is your man.'

'I thought you said you were giving up smoking?' I think it's wise to change the subject at this point; I can sense Mum's building up to one of her well-oiled rants.

'I never. There's no point anyway, I'll probably pop my clogs soon.'

'Don't say that, Ma. You're only sixty.'

Mum exhales. 'Nicotine's one of my last pleasures in life.'

I sigh, feeling even more depressed. I hate the way Mum's always so negative; I should have thought twice about coming to her to cheer me up. The sound of people singing a hymn drifts over our garden fence and I feel the spit of rain on my cheek.

'I'm going to have a bath and then shall we go into town for dinner?' I suggest.

'Good idea.' Mum's face lights up. 'Shirley from flower group told me that the owners of that new Indian restaurant have a son with Tourette's. Let's see if we can have a gander.'

'He's not a zoo attraction.'

'I've never seen one before though.' She shrugs. 'I wonder if he effs and blinds while we're eating our curry.'

People say heartbreak puts you off your food, but that doesn't seem to be true in my case. Mum and I get a table for two at Bombay Dreams and I munch my way through a large portion of chicken masala, pilau rice and dahl while Mum regales me with the local gossip.

Shillingborne is a quaint market town in Dorset. Mum moved here fifteen years ago when she finally left Leo. She works for the district council, which gives her inside info on the latest town plans and developments.

'Barbara and Mark, who used to live two doors down, have just moved into one of those new houses up on Green Ridge.' She breaks a poppadom in two. 'I didn't tell them that we're building a school right next door – serve them right to have screaming playground kids ruining their retirement.' She smiles wickedly.

'Mum! You could've at least given them a heads-up.'

'Why should I? Toffee-nosed couple they are, never invite me to any of their dos. Shirley told me Barbara was mouthing off about divorcees in the delicatessen. Ha, I'd like to see her reaction if she caught Mark knobbing his secretary.'

'She might not have been referring to you though, Ma.' I sit back in my chair, clasping my hands over my swollen stomach. The restaurant has purple wallpaper and blue lighting, making it feel a bit like a casino lounge. Most of the tables are full, with families and couples tucking into silver dishes kept warm on hotplates.

'Oh, you can bet she was. I'm telling you, Chloe, if you're single you're counted as a second-class citizen.'

'Surely not these days.'

'You wait and see.'

'I can't get my head around the fact that I'm suddenly single. It's like a bad dream.' I take a gulp of red wine. 'I haven't

41

spoken to anyone yet apart from you. It's going to be horrible telling our friends, especially the Goldsmiths lot.'

Ant and I meet our old mates from uni at least twice a year; our break-up will throw a real spanner in the works.

'If they're true friends they'll stick by you. Something like this sorts out the wheat from the chaff.'

'Yeah. Emma will be furious – at least she'll be loyal to me; she's my sister.'

'She's not your sister.' Mum's mouth twists. She doesn't approve of my friendship with Emma, despite showing an unhealthy interest in Emma's mother, Janice.

'Is your father still spending a fortune taking that Janice away on holidays?'

'I think they're going to Dubai soon.'

'He could spend that money on you, you know. Help his daughter out with buying a flat. Especially now you don't have Ant to team up with.'

'I'm not sure he's got *that* much.'

'He's bloody rolling in it. You know I'd help you out if I had any spare cash. I should've taken your dad to the cleaners when I had the chance.'

'Mum, it's fine, I don't need your help.' My voice rises in irritation as I feel another lurch of panic at a future without Ant.

'Shit, there's Barbara!' Mum suddenly hisses, looking over my shoulder and ducking.

I turn in my seat and see an older couple pushing open the restaurant door. The man wears a tweed coat and has a shock of silver hair. The woman is in a white jacket with a coiffed grey bob and her eyes are bulging, making her look like a startled frog. She immediately spots Mum and says something to her husband.

'Mum, I'm pretty sure they've clocked you,' I murmur, as Mum slides further down in her seat, raising her napkin in front of her face.

'For fuck's sake,' Mum says under her breath as the waiter, wearing a purple apron, brings the couple over to sit at the table right next to us. She stands up to greet them. 'Hi, Barbara, Mark. What a nice surprise! I haven't seen you in donkeys.'

'Hello, Joy. We've been busy with the move.' Barbara hangs her jacket on the back of her chair.

'Yes, I hear you had a lovely house-warming,' Mum says sweetly.

'Haha, just a few close friends,' Mark blusters. 'We're loving our new place so far – don't get any hooligans on motorcycles up that way. We do like our afternoon naps.'

'Oh, I know you do, Mark.' Mum winks at me as they sit down.

'And it's Chloe, isn't it?' Barbara is ogling me with open curiosity. 'Still living in Brighton?'

'Hi, yep, I am.' My tone comes out clipped but I'm really not in the mood for small talk.

'Such an odd place, terribly bohemian – I don't think I could cope.' Barbara wrinkles her nose. 'And your husband is the chap with the shaved head, isn't he?'

'Hmm, he's not my husband.'

'Whoops, my mistake. You can't presume these days. Still, I'm sure you'll settle down soon.' Barbara nods, opening the menu in front of her as the waiter hovers nearby with his notepad. 'Will we share a lamb pasanda, Mark, with the mixed starters?'

'You've got it, Babs.' Mark smiles at me. 'She always knows what I'm going to order before I do. What am I having to drink, dear?'

'A bottle of Cobra, and I'll have a . . .'

'Savvy Blanc,' Mark finishes for her. They both titter smugly and the waiter laughs along with them. Mum rips a naan bread into small pieces, breathing heavily through her nose.

'Our daughter's only just had her first, and she's thirty-two.' Barbara turns back to me. 'Though our son started early – he's had three already.'

'Sorry? Three what?' I rub my temple, feeling the beginnings of a headache drill through my skull.

'Psychotic breakdowns,' Mum mutters, as Barbara says, 'Children, silly!'

'We had a full house this Christmas.' Mark chuckles. 'Not that I'm complaining – nice to play games and watch the grandkids open their pressies. I expect you were swamped with family too, were you, Joy?'

I spoon more chutney onto my plate, not catching Mum's eye. Christmas is always tricky for Mum as both her parents are dead and her brother lives in New Zealand. I don't like to leave her on her own but Ant's dad and stepmum invited us to theirs this year and Mum insisted she was fine. Then, when I rang her on Christmas Day, she'd been on the sherry and started crying on the phone about how lonely she was.

'I spent most of it pissed in my armchair, if I'm honest, Mark,' Mum says. 'Bought a turkey breast but burnt it, so ended up having a Pot Noodle.'

Barbara and Mark look at each other and a flicker of confirmation passes between them.

'Ah well, all the more reason for Chloe to hurry up and bring little feet pitter-pattering to your door.' Barbara smiles as the waiter puts down their drinks. 'You career girls need to get your priorities straight.'

I bristle. 'Actually, Barbara, I've just split up with my boyfriend so babies are definitely not on the cards. I'd rather not talk about it if you don't mind.'

Mum nods at me approvingly and nudges me under the table with her foot.

'Oh dear, what a pity.' Barbara looks at Mark for help and he purses his mouth thoughtfully.

'Gosh, well, you know what they say . . .' He cocks his head at me.

No, don't fucking say it, I plead with him in my head.

'. . . plenty more fish in the sea.'

'Shut up, wanker!'

For a second, I'm horrified that I've spoken my thoughts aloud, but then I see Mum and Barbara sit up like meerkats, staring at the young Indian boy who's appeared in front of the beaded curtains.

'Stick it up your bum!' the boy shouts, looking directly at Mark. He flicks his head back and clacks his teeth together. I want to applaud.

A woman appears behind the boy, circling an arm around his shoulders.

'Sorry, sorry.' She raises a hand at the diners, grimacing in embarrassment and leading the boy back behind the curtain.

'How rude,' Barbara tuts, reaching out and putting her hand over Mark's. 'They shouldn't allow him to wander around freely, insulting people like that.'

I put my knife and fork down next to my plate, a white-hot anger surging through me. 'Actually, Barbara, I think you are ruder than that boy. He can't help it. You, on the other hand, should keep your opinions to yourself.'

I throw a twenty-pound note down on the table and stand up; my head is really throbbing now. 'Mum, I'll meet you outside.' I grab my coat from the hook by the door and go to sit on the steps of the monument at the bottom of the high street.

My bottom lip plumps outward as I think how hilarious Ant would have found that situation. He'd have poked fun at Barbara without her realising and I'm sure I'd have been choking back laughter rather than tears.

'That's my girl, you told them!' Mum crows as she joins me. 'You shoulda seen their faces when you left, sucking lemons they were. Serves them right, think they're the bollocks with their stupid happy families.'

She links her arm through mine as I stand up. 'Ignore it, Chlo, you don't want to end up like them anyway.'

I nod miserably as Mum lights up a fag, still chuckling with glee. The problem is, I don't want to end up lonely and bitter like my mother either.

Chapter 7

'Here, have a drink. Hashtag Friyay!' Jess, the HR manager, plonks a chilled bottle of craft beer on my desk as she passes.

There's the usual Friday feeling in the office, when everyone gets hysterical about their upcoming two days of freedom — bingeing on booze, food and box sets before the inevitable crash that is the Monday blues.

Most people have given up pretending to work and a big group has gathered in the break-out area near the kitchen, which has AstroTurf flooring, a foosball table and giant coloured beanbags. Whitney Houston plays on the jukebox in the corner, adding to the party atmosphere.

I'm too engrossed in my new hobby of online stalking to join them. It's been three weeks since Ant and I broke up and I've not spoken to him once. He's ignored my calls and messages and all I can do is picture him having rampant sex with *her*.

I just need someone to pin my anger onto. Right now, it's like all the women in the world have melded into one evil femme fatale. I find myself glaring in paranoia at other girls laughing on the street when they pass me, wondering if they're the woman who stole my happiness.

Well, fine, if Ant isn't going to tell me then I'll find out myself.

I take a slug of beer, smacking my lips at its odd bubblegum flavour, and roll my office chair closer to my computer screen. Ant's Twitter account isn't giving me much intel; he mainly just shares articles on music and politics.

LinkedIn is similarly dry, though he hasn't indicated that he's changing jobs; a good sign that he's not pursuing this crazy sailing idea. He has, however, been watching a few ocean documentaries on our shared Netflix account.

I click onto his Instagram and gasp as I see he's added a new photo . . . of two gin cocktails, complete with a mint garnish. *Two glasses!*

'Is Ant having drinks with shitty G-string girl?'

Alerted by my gasp, Verity and Simone have rolled their chairs up behind me and are peering at Ant's update with suspicion. Verity is in a black jumpsuit with a chunky gold necklace and Simone wears a low-cut red top and short denim skirt.

'He better not be!' I click on the people who have liked the cocktail photo. 'Ugh, who is "Katypops69"?' I groan as I scroll through photos of her doing yoga, working out at the gym and going for runs on the beach. She's got a great figure and long chestnut-brown hair.

'Savage!' Simone grips the arm of my chair. 'Do you think that's her? Look, she must work with him.'

She points to a Warren Recruitment team shot. In the photo, Ant is holding two fingers up behind Katypops69's head in the classic 'bunny ears' prank. I feel my stomach lurch with jealousy.

'Hmm, she's mega beige,' Verity says dismissively. 'What about Facebook?'

'There's not much there.' I click on Ant's wall and Verity quickly scans his updates.

'He's tried the new sushi place, watched the latest *Star Wars* film, done a 5k run. Christ, he's a barrel o' laughs!' she drawls. 'Come on, girls. Time for a rendezbooze at The Lobster.'

'Defo.' Simone grabs her make-up bag from her desk and starts applying lip liner.

I check my Facebook page and frown as I see the sponsored ads on the right-hand side of my feed. One has a cartoon picture of a crying emoji and the text reads 'Why the long face? Do you hate yourself? Find out why in this depression quiz.' Another one, further down, is offering me bipolar treatment.

I clap a hand to my mouth in horror. 'Oh my God, Facebook knows I've been dumped,' I whisper.

''Course it does. It probably analysed all your borderline-suicidal status updates and the articles you kept sharing about why relationships are toxic,' Verity says.

'My mum sent me them – I thought they were interesting.'

'They're crazy.' Verity stands up and pulls on her silver padded jacket. 'Come on, it's time you got back in the saddle. Let's set you up on some dating apps.'

'Hmm, dunno. I've never really done online dating.'

'You'll soon get the hang of it.' Simone links her arm through mine as I stand up. 'I'll be your guru; I've been doing it for years.'

The Lobster is our favourite after-work venue; it's a large cafe-bar next to the pier, with a glass front so you can look out onto the beach. It has an open log fire, battered but comfortable chesterfields, an eclectic range of artwork and a stuffed goat, called Maude, who stands proudly in the corner wearing a tiara.

We order a round of Aperol spritzes and sit on a sofa near Maude. Office workers are filtering through the doors, shedding their winter coats and loosening ties.

'Right, gimme that, let's get you on Tinder.' Verity grabs my phone and starts downloading new apps.

'You'll feel way better once you start seeing other people.' Simone leans across the table. 'I'm so over the guy who ghosted me.'

'Really? You seemed pretty upset.'

'Totes, he's dust. This new bloke I met on Bumble is *obsessed* with me. It's literally the best sex I've had in my entire life. And he made me breakfast the other day. Or at least, he gave me a protein bar from his sports bag. Look . . .' Simone shows me a picture of a beardy bloke on her phone. 'Isn't he salty?'

Verity pauses and looks at the headshot with a quick frown.

'Oh, him. I matched with him ages ago; his chat was tedious.' She feigns a yawn and turns back to my phone.

'What do you mean? You've got Gavin.' Simone looks deflated.

48

'So? I don't meet up with them. I just keep my hand in, because duh.' Verity shrugs, then suddenly her face lights up and she jumps to her feet, waving.

'Look, there's Dom.'

My best friend, Dom, is at the bar, wearing a Burberry trench coat and a maroon scarf looped around his neck. His shiny dark quiff flops over his high forehead as he waves. Most girls instantly fall in love with him, despite the fact that he's gay as a fruit bat. He's so good-looking it's ridiculous; you could just sit and stare at his sculpted face for hours, like you might a beautiful painting.

Dom's also kind of famous. He has a YouTube channel called 'This Old Thing' – a tongue-in-cheek fashion vlog in which he scours charity shops and car boot sales, styling and modelling a bizarre collection of sartorial discoveries with his own unique flair. He just needs to put a tea cosy on his head and his huge fan base swoons.

'Ladies, you all look ravishing as ever.' Dom flops down beside me and plants a kiss on my cheek. 'What an exhausting week!'

'Are you modelling at the moment?' Verity asks interestedly.

'Yes, darling, I'm fronting Gucci's new spring campaign. But there's only so much standing around looking fabulous one man can cope with.' Dom massages his forehead, sliding me a wry look. 'And how's the casualty?'

Dom's been an amazing support these past few weeks. I've spent many nights at his flat on Marine Parade, crying into my wine while he and his boyfriend, Yannis, try to cheer me up. They're both so good at hugging; when I'm sandwiched between their spongy pecs, breathing in their expensive aftershave as they stroke my hair, everything seems a little bit more bearable.

'We're just setting Chlo up on some dating apps. She needs her leg over someone new.' Simone simpers at Dom, blinking her eyelash extensions.

'It's going to take more than a few weeks for me to move on, Sim.' I frown. I can't take advice on my love life from someone who changes her boyfriends as often as her skinny jeans.

AJ, the bar manager, brings over an ice bucket with champagne and four glasses to our table.

'Celebrating, are we?' He's a strapping Caribbean man in his fifties with a ready smile.

'Commiserating,' Dom corrects him, squeezing my knee. AJ makes a little moue of sympathy.

'If you managed to get out of bed today, you're winning.' He winks at me before gliding off to tend the other crowded tables.

Dom pours us all a glass of bubbles as Verity taps at my phone with gold fingernails.

'What're you looking for, Chloe?' she demands. 'Happn's good for hook-ups but OkCupid's better for soul mates.'

I bite my lip and stare at her helplessly. 'Uh . . .' What I want is not to feel like weeping every morning I wake up alone. At least during the week I have to get up for work, but I've started to dread weekends. When I look at the empty pillow next to me, I have no idea how to fill the day ahead. Ant's left a huge gaping chasm in my life.

Sensing my despair, Dom rummages in his man bag and pulls out a crocodile-skin notebook.

'It'll help if we make a checklist. Don't think too hard about the answers; just say whatever comes into your head. Top three qualities you look for in a guy?'

I consider what I like best about Ant. 'Great humour, interesting chat, amazing kisser.'

'What about looks?' Dom scribbles in his pad.

I close my eyes. 'Short dark hair, brown eyes, firm lean body.'

'Occupation?'

'Something creative.'

'Interests?'

'Outdoorsy, sociable, likes festivals and parties, does kung fu and surfing.'

'Chloe, are you describing Ant?'

I open my eyes. 'No,' I say defensively. 'It's just my type, that's all.'

'Hmm. Do you want a man with a high income?'

'Don't mind.'

'Do you want kids?'

'Dunno.'

'What about height?'

'Height? What's that got to do with anything?'

'Oh, it matters – I don't look at guys under five-eight,' Verity says firmly. 'Right, I think we've got enough info. Now we just need a profile pic.' She scrolls through a few headshots of me. 'What about this one of you in a rainbow wig? That way they won't know you're a ginge.'

'Chloe is not hiding her gorgeous Titian locks, they're one of her best features!' Dom leans forward. 'Use that one of her hugging Dora; she wants someone who loves dogs.'

'OK. Description?' Verity looks at me appraisingly.

'Ooh, can I do this?' Simone squeaks, clapping her hands. 'Artistic redhead, sexy smile, up for laughs. What colour are your eyes? Err, they're like browny-greeny-bluey-grey? How tall?'

'They're hazel. I'm five-six,' I say. 'You think my smile is sexy?'

'Sure. Though I'm not a lezzer, yeah. Just to be clear,' Simone says hastily, as Dom looks between us in excitement.

'And how old do you want to be?' Verity purses her mouth. 'I reckon we can get away with thirty-two.'

'Why? What's wrong with thirty-five?' I ask.

'The closer you are to forty the less interest you'll get. Men will always try for ten years younger at least.'

'I'm not lying about my age!'

'Whatevs. Done.' Verity puts my phone on the table and stretches. 'Send us screen grabs of any bizarre messages or dick pics. Always good for a laugh. So, guys, I wasn't going to say anything but guess what?' She holds both hands up as if stopping traffic.

'What?' Simone's eyes are wide.

'Gav's been acting shady and my mum let slip that he had lunch with my dad, which never happens . . . I reckon he's going to pop the question!'

Simone's screech is deafening; several people's heads snap round in our direction.

'That's great, Vee!' We clink glasses and Dom puts an arm around me as Verity launches into other giveaway signs of Gav's incoming proposal.

Maybe I've been a total mug all along. It never bothered me that Ant and I didn't discuss marriage – it's like we skipped all the usual first-stage insecurities in our relationship. I just presumed that we'd grow old together but now I'm questioning whether he was committed to me at all. Maybe he was just using me as a stopgap until something better came along. I swallow in panic. What if Verity's right? What if no guy will look at me once I hit forty and totally pass my sell-by date? Then I really will end up like Mum. I've only got five years left! Shit, shit, shit.

I gulp my drink and Dom looks at me closely.

'Do you want to go and get fucked up? I heard about this warehouse rave over in Portslade.'

I wrinkle my nose, tempted. I feel kind of reckless; like, if someone offered me some acid and a one-way flight to Timbuktu I'd take it.

'Or is it better if you have a Horlicks and a few episodes of *The Walking Dead*?' Dom puts a thoughtful finger to his lips.

I sigh; Dom knows me so well. 'Unfortunately I think the latter would be most wise.' I nod. 'Else I may do something silly.'

I gather my stuff, then, swaying slightly, make my way home up St James's Street past the crowded pubs, where roars of laughter spill out onto the pavements, and sex shops with mannequins wearing bondage in the windows.

I go into Sainsbury's and browse the groceries, throwing a random selection of vegetables into my basket. The man next to me glances at me sideways. Is it my imagination or is he looking at me pityingly?

Suddenly cooking a meal for one seems pathetic. I thrust my chin out and wedge a massive family pack of Frosties under my arm. That'll show him. How does he know I don't have loads of people waiting for me back home?

I throw some pouches of baby food in my basket, giving the man a weary but brave smile.

'Can't always cook from scratch, hey? Sometimes you just need a day off,' I say, grabbing a bumper pack of disposable nappies for good measure. The man nods, avoiding my gaze.

Moving down the aisle, I automatically take a jar of green pesto from the shelf, then freeze. I don't really like green pesto; it's too tart. I much prefer red. It's Ant that likes it green.

I slowly put the green pesto back and replace it with a jar of red. 'Fuck you, Ant,' I mutter out loud. My head is swimming a bit; the strip lights are really bright.

A woman has joined the man next to me and is nuzzling his neck. 'Shall we get some of those Gü puddings, babe? They're on offer – two for one.'

'Ooh, *two for one*. How clever.' I mimic her under my breath and they both look at me sharply. I think I might be a bit drunker than I realised.

I quickly round the corner, colliding with a garish pink cardboard display of teddy bears, roses and chocolates. A heart-shaped sign says: 'Treat your loved one to a romantic night this Valentine's Day!' I'd totally forgotten it was next week.

'Oh, for Christ's sake.' I plonk my basket on the floor with a clatter. My forehead's getting really hot. I lift my fringe and waft a packet of spice mix underneath it like a fan.

The couple are looking at me in concern. 'Allergies,' I tell them. 'I'm allergic to romance.' I snort with laughter and feel my bottom lip wobble dangerously.

My bill comes to a lot more than usual and I wrestle with several large bags of shopping home, stopping to pick Dora up from her dogsitter on the way home.

'So sweet, she's been snuggling on the sofa between us, watching movies.' The sitter laughs, gesturing to her boyfriend, who waves at me from under a blanket. I grimace back at him through a crippling wave of desolation.

I follow her gaze as she eyes the nappies under my arm.

'Early incontinence,' I tell her, relishing her look of alarm.

I'm almost glad to hear that Saffron is home; I don't think I can deal with an empty flat right now. She's in the kitchen humming along tunelessly to some creepy panpipe music as she burns the stir-fry in her wok.

I dump my bags on the kitchen counter and grab a tea towel from the back of the door, flapping it in the air to get rid of the smoke. 'Careful, the alarm will go off in a minute,' I say, as the smoke alarm emits a piercing shriek. Dora immediately starts barking.

'Ohhh, stupid thing.' Saffron's dreads fly everywhere as she reaches for a broomstick and bashes it into the alarm on the ceiling.

'Wait, no need to break it.' I stand on the footstool and take the battery out.

Saffron leans across the sink to open the window. She's in a short purple velvet dress; not her usual style.

'That dress doesn't look like it's made of hemp,' I say, putting a pouch of baby food in the microwave to heat up. I may as well eat it now I've bought it. 'What's the occasion?'

Saffron glances down at herself. 'I'm just trying on stuff ready for Valentine's Day next week.'

I sigh. 'Not you too. Surely you think it's useless commercial bullshit?'

'Yes, obviously – but it's also an opportunity to express love; nothing wrong with that.' Saffron slides her blackened stir-fry into a bowl and shakes turmeric on top.

'I didn't know you were in love,' I say, spooning blended carrot into my mouth.

'There's a lot you don't know about me.' Saffron taps her finger against her silver nose ring. Her green eyes slide over me. 'Are you eating baby food?'

'Yeah, so?' I suck the spoon defiantly.

Saffron shakes her head. 'Honestly, Chloe, it's been weeks since your break-up – you really need to stop moping about. Self-pity is so unattractive. Haven't you read the tea towel?

'Huh?'

She unfolds the discarded tea towel and holds it open. It shows a picture of the Buddha, with a quote written underneath: 'Peace comes from within, do not seek it without – Buddha.' She reads the words in the same deep spiritual tone she reserves for yoga class.

'It's hard to be peaceful when your boyfriend's just cheated on you.'

Saffron sighs. 'Buddhist theory says you shouldn't get too attached to things; people aren't your possessions.'

'You can't help getting attached to your own bloody partner!'

'Yeah, but he made his choice and it isn't you. If you love somebody, set them free.'

'Isn't that a song lyric from Sting?'

Saffron tips her head back in exasperation. 'Yes, but it all means the same thing.'

'Right.' I grab the box of Frosties. 'Thanks for that, Saff, great help.'

I go into my bedroom and switch on my iMac, turning up *The Walking Dead* to its highest volume so that the dry rasp of the Undead quickly fills my room.

Dora jumps up next to me as I flop on my bed and cram my mouth full of sugar-coated flakes. Saffron and everyone else is completely right: I do need to let go of Ant and move on.

But there's only one way I'm going to get a sense of closure. No more faffing about on social media – I need hard evidence. I need to find out who shitty G-string girl is, once and for all.

Chapter 8

I'm 99 per cent sure 'Katypops69' is shitty G-string girl; I've gone through all of Ant's social media posts in the last year and she's liked his stuff over eighty times. I mean, how obvious can you get?

The plan is simple. Today is Valentine's Day and I bet Ant and Katypops have booked some cosy romantic meal together. So, I'm going to turn up at Warren Recruitment's offices, catch them leaving for their date, and confront them directly. I've got a really good speech that I've rehearsed in the mirror, which is so scathing I'm sure it'll leave them cowering in repentance.

In my revenge fantasy, I'll then perform some complicated *Kill Bill* move which temporarily paralyses them both. I'm hoping I'll instinctively tap into my inner martial-art skills, like those women who display extreme strength and lift cars off their trapped children.

Warren Recruitment is based in Hove so I've arranged to leave work early for an appointment at my doctor's, which is also, conveniently, in Hove.

'How can I help you today, Ms Usher?'

My GP, Dr Fletcher, finishes typing something, then steeples her hands under her chin. Her dark hair is scraped back in a bun and she has a regal nose. Despite her focused gaze, I sense that there are a million things whirring around in her head. It must be incredibly tiring being a GP – with so many people needing you to help them.

'I haven't been sleeping well, I have loads of headaches and I've been crying a lot,' I say in a small voice. 'The other day, in the supermarket, I couldn't breathe.'

It's all true, anyway. I probably do need help. Facebook clearly thought I did.

'Have any recent events triggered this anxiety, do you think?'

'Yeah, my boyfriend dumped me. It's taking a while for it to sink in.'

'How long ago was this?'

'Nearly a month. Surely I should be over the worst by now? Is there something you can give me for it? Like sedatives, or, you know, whatever those crazy Hollywood housewives have?' I bite my lip hopefully.

The delicate lines around Dr Fletcher's bright brown eyes deepen as she contemplates me. She's obviously realised I'm a complete fraud. I dig my fingernails into my palms and hang my head. I can't believe I'm wasting NHS time; I'm a terrible person.

'People underestimate the health impacts of heartbreak,' she says gently. 'The associated stress hormones can physically affect everything: your skin, your muscles, your stomach . . . your heart.'

I look up. Her compassionate tone makes me want to hurl myself onto her lap.

'But Chloe, I'm afraid there's not a magic pill I can give you. When relationships end, in a way your sense of self ends. Don't expect to miraculously bounce back. It will take time.'

'Yeah, I know, I just don't know what to do with this *awful* feeling inside.' My voice quivers.

'It helps if you surround yourself with loved ones. And maybe try some new hobbies or volunteering – get a different perspective. I can recommend some fantastic local charities.'

I nod. Everything she says makes sense. 'And would you recommend unleashing furious vengeance on those who've wronged me?'

Dr Fletcher smiles, as if I'm joking. 'If you're still feeling depressed in a few months, come back. I can refer you to a counsellor, we can consider antidepressants or we can look at holistic practices like meditation – there are plenty of options.'

'Have I got a proper mental disorder then?' I put a hand to my chest, suddenly scared.

'Your mental wellbeing can change from day to day. The important thing is to pay attention to it and improve your chances of coping. Coming here today was an excellent choice.'

I promise Dr Fletcher that I'll return if I need to and quickly leave the surgery. The sky is darkening to a deep navy as I walk down Church Road, past the Regency townhouses and artisan shops. The Valentine's window displays are cascading with shiny paper hearts and lips; a raw red blur in my peripheral vision. I pull my hood up over my head.

I'm wearing a voluminous old parka that nearly reaches my ankles. I found it at the back of my wardrobe; an ill-advised purchase during my Britpop days. It's the best disguise I could think of at short notice.

Warren Recruitment is in a big ugly building set back from the road. I glance furtively over my shoulder as I enter through the back car park and climb the grassy bank, ducking behind a row of bins.

From here, I can see directly into the open-plan office, starkly lit with artificial strip lighting. Rows of grey Formica desks line the faded blue carpet and people sit hunched on their swivel chairs, their faces blanched by the glow of their screens.

I breathe in sharply as I see Ant by the whiteboard at the end of the room, writing figures with a board marker pen. A small group of people stand around him, smiling.

He bows with a flourish and his colleagues clap; one girl reaches out and punches him lightly on the shoulder – it's Katypops69.

Like a starved person, I devour the details of her, making swift and uncompromising comparisons to myself. She is muscular but graceful, with a long neck, round, generous boobs and thick brown hair running down her back in a plait. Her features are delicate, like a china doll. She wears minimal make-up and her cheeks glow pink under the strip lights.

As she turns and walks past the desks across the room, Ant follows. Her long corduroy skirt restricts her steps so that they're quick and precise. She carries herself with an air of primness, like an actress in a period drama. Is that what tempted Ant – a sense of conquest? Or maybe the fact that she's completely different to me.

I shuffle sideways, following their progress to the kitchen. It's like I'm watching a scene in a horror film; I want to cover my eyes but the draw of it is too strong. I stuff a knuckle in my mouth, barely registering the fat rain drops that have started splattering my hood.

Katypops69 is talking as she bends over to retrieve a Tupperware from the fridge. Ant stands behind her, both hands in his back pockets. Is he looking at her arse?

I try to read his expression, to remember how desire spelled itself on his face. She straightens and turns, cocking her head to one side, inches away from him. I'm sure I see his gaze travel from her eyes to her lips. I ache for him to look at me like that again.

I look around at the people gormlessly tapping on their keyboards – surely everyone else in the office is picking up on this outrageous flirting? It shouldn't be allowed. Any minute now they're going to start removing their clothes. I feel like calling the HR manager to intervene.

I bet they're discussing their Valentine's date. Now he and I have split up, they can celebrate going out in public together. They can sit in a crowded restaurant and gaze at each other across a candlelit table, touching hands. They'll tell each other endearing personal stories that add that extra frisson to coupling with someone new and interesting.

I dig my hands deep in my parka's pockets, holding my breath. My hand finds a plastic lump with a chain – a keyring? I grip it tightly.

As Ant leans towards the girl, I take a step forward, onto the bottom bar of a bin, and the lid flips open, letting out a rotten belch. My head jerks back and I lose my footing, my arms still stuck in my pockets. I slide feet-first down the damp bank, pushing the bin in front of me.

I free my arms too late, and as I land heavily on my coccyx, a sharp pain shoots up my spine. The bin lands on top of me, spilling mouldy orange peel and empty crisp packets.

Somewhere, an ear-piercing siren sounds, loud and insistent. I lie on my back in the falling rain, limbs splayed, eyes rolling in panic as I try to locate the noise. It seems to be coming from me.

A row of faces appears at Ant's office window. They're looking down at me, peering into the shadows.

'No, oh God, please no.' I grapple with the bin, shoving it further down the slope, and roll onto my side, spilling garbage everywhere. Raindrops creep across my hairline and splash onto the grass. The siren only seems to be getting more deafening. I raise my right hand and realise a small ring and chain is hooked around my index finger.

Ant's palms are flat against the glass and he's frowning in recognition. Behind him, Katypops69 rests her chin on his shoulder, casually intimate.

On all fours, I pat the wet grass around me and find the black plastic fob that has fallen from my pocket. I have inadvertently detonated a rape alarm.

I have a vague memory of some self-defence workshop I went to review for my blog. I must have pocketed the free personal alarm and completely forgotten about it.

Cringing in mortification, I fumble with the chain and insert the pin back into the hole just as a security guard rounds the corner of the building. The siren chokes dead.

'Can I help you, miss?' The guard strides towards me, turning his collar up against the rain.

I crawl up the slope, trailing litter, hoping my big coat will obscure me and that the unwelcome onlookers will think I'm just some old tramp who was looking for dinner.

'I'm talking to you!' the guard says aggressively. 'This is private property.'

'I know, all right, let go!' I squeal as he grabs my arm and hauls me to my feet. 'Can we just . . . do this over here?' I try to move to the other side of the bank but he yanks my hood down and tightens his grasp.

'You let off an alarm?'

'Yes, it's a rape alarm.' I hold it up miserably. My hair is plastered to my face.

'Have you been attacked?'

'No, only by a bin. I'm fine.'

'Are you drunk?'

I shake my head, raising my eyes to the lit window. Ant is staring at me, his face a pale oval of shock. His colleagues are all talking at once, poking him; one of them is bent over, laughing. Katypops has clasped both hands over her mouth.

'Right, well it's time to leave,' the guard says firmly, giving me a shove towards the exit.

'Yes, I'm going, OK, there's no need to . . .' I let my voice die along with the last shreds of my self-respect as I am frog-marched from the premises. This is me moving on, Ant, just watch me.

Chapter 9

'I shouldn't laugh.' Emma laughs anyway, and her corkscrew blonde curls tremble. She's wearing a turquoise wrap dress with kimono sleeves that matches her blue eyes. 'Sorry, it's just the image of you wrestling with a bin.'

'Yeah, it wasn't my finest hour. I stank of litter for days.' I dip a digestive into my tea and it instantly disintegrates.

Just over a week later, it's Saturday afternoon and my sister, Emma, is sitting on the Indian pouffe on my lounge floor. Her baby, Toby, is sleeping in his carrycot next to her and my five-year-old goddaughter, Maisie, is playing on my roof terrace.

'Have you spoken to Ant since?'

'He sent me a text.' I show her.

> *Hi Chloe, I'm not sure if you meant to be outside my office but I really think we should put some distance between us right now. Ant*

'In other words, "stay the fuck away".' Emma presses her lips together. 'I'm sorry, hun, but you know Ant, he always shies away from confrontation. Remember he refused to come with us to tell your horrible ex, Dave, you were leaving him?'

'Yep, total let-down. You sure made up for it though.' I smile, remembering Emma facing up to Dave, even though he was several feet taller than her, her fists clenched at her sides, her blue eyes blazing.

'I was terrified inside.' She pulls a face.

'So was I, I thought he was going to hit you. That's when I finally realised he was a complete nutter. Christ, I do pick 'em, don't I?' I say, looking over at sleeping Toby. A tiny fist is curled at his flushed cheek.

Emma giggles. 'Remember Monologue Jonny?'

'Oh, don't!' I groan. I dated a guy called Jonny in my late twenties for about a year. He was an international tour guide but, unfortunately, his lengthy anecdotes weren't as engaging as the destinations he'd visited. 'How do you get it so right and I get it so wrong, Em?'

'It's not your fault Ant's been a total wanker,' Emma says through biscuit crumbs. 'I'm not speaking to him.'

'Thanks – it means a lot. I reckon some of the Goldsmiths crew will still see him though.'

'Yeah, I think Linda is in touch.' Emma wrinkles her nose apologetically.

'I don't care. She can do what she wants,' I huff. Linda is my least favourite of our uni friends; she's always been bossy and a bit of a snob. Emma gets on with her much better than I do.

'Mummy, can we get a fat man?' Maisie shouts through the French doors from my roof terrace, which overlooks a row of back gardens.

'Maisie, don't insult Chloe's neighbours,' Emma reprimands.

'Actually, I think she's talking about the brass Buddha statue out there,' I say. 'Saffron got it for Christmas; she's obsessed with Buddhism.'

Maisie comes over to where I'm nestled on the big blue sofa and grins, baring a neat row of perfect little teeth. She's wearing a red corduroy pinafore dress and has her mother's blonde curls, which frame her angelic face endearingly.

'Can I wake Dora up?' She points to Dora, who is curled up in her bed in the corner, nose to tail, twitching and making wheezy grunts as she races across her favourite dreamscapes.

'No, Maisie, Mummy's talking. Go and finish your *Frozen* jigsaw puzzle.' Emma points to the toys she has laid out in the corner of the room.

Successfully diverted, Maisie goes to lie in front of her puzzle, sticking her tongue out in concentration as she lines up the jigsaw pieces.

Emma leans her elbows on the coffee table. 'Chlo, I'm sure there's someone out there much better suited to you than Ant. People get married a lot later these days. Have you tried online dating – isn't that what everyone does now?'

'Kind of. I've been chatting on a few apps but I'm not really feeling it.'

'Why?'

'It's just not very . . . romantic. I mean, can you imagine the wedding speech: "The moment I first laid eyes on her Tinder profile I knew she was 'the one'." It doesn't make you feel very special, knowing a guy's swiped right on your face along with a hundred other girls that week.'

'But you have to meet them to see if you have chemistry, right?'

'Chemistry's a complex and magical thing – how can you predict who you'll fall for based on a photo, or their height, or the fact that you both like cheese? In fact, in all the greatest love stories I've read, the romantic couple are always the most unlikely match!' I slam my hand down on the table as it occurs to me. 'On paper they would *never* choose each other.'

'Like who?' Emma narrows her eyes sceptically.

'Like Romeo and Juliet; they were from feuding families.' I try to recall classic romantic literature from my degree. 'And Jane Eyre falls for Mr Rochester, even though he's her snooty employer. And Elizabeth Bennet actually hates Mr Darcy when she first meets him; she thinks he's an arrogant prick.'

'Oh yeah! And in *Pretty Woman*, Vivian's a prozzy, and in *Titanic*, Rose and Jack are from different classes.' Emma is warming to the theme. 'And in *Beauty and the Beast* . . . well, he's an animal – it's practically bestiality.'

'Exactly!' I grin. 'It's the basic formula of romance – totally unexpected and accidental. You think any of that lot would've matched on Tinder?'

Emma shakes her head, looking a bit dazed.

'The whole idea of true love is that it happens when you least expect it,' I continue dreamily.

'Chloe.' Emma's voice is so heavy with sarcasm, it's dropped an octave. I look at her in surprise.

'What?'

'Hello? We're not in Disneyland. Those are just stories. In real life, by the time you actually marry and have kids, all the romance has gone. Believe me, a ripped perineum is quite the passion killer.'

'A what?'

'The bit between my clit and anus, split open by that little angel.' Emma points a finger at Maisie, who is holding a jigsaw piece so close to her face she's gone cross-eyed.

Emma laughs at my horrified expression. 'And we're just too tired to have sex anyway. I can tell you, hand on heart, I would much rather watch *Prime Suspect* and have a massive glass of Malbec.'

'But you and James are so good together, he's, like, the perfect husband—'

'Haven't shagged in eight months,' Emma interrupts, her face impassive.

'Really? Well, sure, you've just had Toby.'

'Even before I was pregnant it was a totally rare occurrence. I just don't feel sexy. All I ever wear is maternity or nursery clothes.'

'Em, come on, you always look amazing.'

'Hmmph, being in Brighton makes me feel like such a frump, it's so bloody colourful. We just walked past a transvestite in red high heels and an Amy Winehouse beehive wig and no one batted an eyelid. You wouldn't get that in Surrey.'

Emma lives in a lovely house with her husband, James, and her two children. She used to work in music production and live in a flat in Soho, but when she got pregnant with Maisie, they decided to move south of London where there was more space.

'When James said he was coming to Brighton today, I jumped at the chance to get out,' she continues. 'Honestly, Chlo, the most exciting thing that happens in our town is the farmers' market on Fridays and I've worked my way through every preserve on offer.'

I look from Emma's pained expression to Toby's scrunched-up face. The dome of his head is as delicate as an eggshell.

'I know it's hard, Ems, but it won't be like this forever; they'll grow up and you'll have your freedom back.'

'What, in eighteen years? I won't even know where to start – I'll be like an alien landing on a new planet. I know this sounds awful . . . but sometimes I feel like dumping everything and running away. I carry my entire household around with me like some dung beetle: the pram, the nappies, the bottles, the clothes, the wipes, the toys – not to mention the children.'

I lower my voice to a whisper. 'Maybe you *could* run away? You know, change your name to Dympna, get a new passport and move to Poland? I'll come with you. We'll have to shave our heads though, because your crazy curls and my red hair stand out a bit.'

Emma snorts through her nose. 'We could pretend to be Hare Krishnas.'

I close my eyes and start chanting, 'Hare-hare-hare Krishna,' and Emma lets out a volley of hysterical giggles.

'Seriously though, Em.' I stop chanting. 'If you're saying true love doesn't exist and fulfilled marriage is a myth then what's the bloody point of any of it?'

'Dunno.' Emma shrugs unhelpfully and we stare at each other. 'But you may as well get back out there – Ant's not hanging around pining for you, is he?'

The sound of the doorbell makes Dora spring up from her bed with a startled *woof*.

'That must be Dom, he's early.' I uncurl from the sofa and catch Emma rolling her eyes. 'What?'

'Nothing, I just didn't realise he was joining us.'

'Well, we're going shopping in a bit.' I go to buzz Dom in. Unfortunately there's not much love lost between my two closest friends; they always seem to disapprove of each other's lifestyle choices.

'Brrr! It's colder than a witch's tit!' Dom clutches his mustard cashmere scarf against his chest and his quiff bounces as he prances up the stairs towards me.

I give him a hug and Dora circles around his legs, panting with excitement. 'Emma's just popped in for tea.'

'Oh, a yummy mummy on a pouffe!' he exclaims as we enter the lounge. 'Interesting combo.'

He takes his overcoat off and throws it on the armchair. He's wearing a green pussy-bow blouse, skinny leather trousers and Cuban heels.

'How're you, Dom?' Emma says, her expression blank with dislike. 'I saw on Instagram that you were in the Caribbean. Do well for holidays, don't you?'

'Yes, I was looking at tropical island couture.' Dom flops on the sofa next to me.

'Must be nice earning money just sitting on a beach in a thong.' Emma doesn't bother to conceal her envy.

Dom casts me a wounded look and I laugh. 'Em, there's a bit more to fashion vlogging than that,' I tell her.

Dom crosses his legs and appraises Emma with a snide eyebrow. 'Well, you could always start a mummy blog about living the suburban dream. I suppose you're completely out of touch from the London music scene now?'

As if sensing his mother's chagrin, Toby wakes up with a gurgling cry. His tiny hands starfish open and his eyes goggle at us as if seeing for the first time.

'Ah, it's feeding time. You don't mind, do you, Dom?' Emma says sweetly, fiddling with a tie at the front of her top so that an engorged breast bobs into view.

'No, of course, you go right ahead.' Dom examines the ceiling as Toby sucks her nipple robotically, his eyes closed in ecstasy.

'He's latching on better now?' I ask.

'Yes, thank God, but not before I got nipple thrush. The candida fungus spread to his mouth and he got white spots all over his gums,' Emma says conversationally.

'Gosh.' Dom grimaces. 'Poor lad's got an STD and he's not even a year old.'

'It's not sexually transmitted – obviously.' Emma tuts. 'It's a yeast thing.'

'Urgh, "yeast" has got to be one of my least favourite words.' I flap a hand in the air, trying to lighten the atmosphere.

Dom laughs. 'So, are we going shopping to cheer you up?' He throws a pointed look at Emma. 'Chloe's had such a rough time, I'm just glad I've been around to pick up the pieces.'

'Sure,' I say. 'Where do you want to go?'

'I was thinking maybe Beyond Retro in the North Laine? I'm looking for antique cufflinks, floppy handkerchiefs and maybe a walking cane. I'm doing a vlog on dandyism.' Dom's blue-grey eyes are wide with enthusiasm.

Emma makes a scoffing noise and shakes her head at Toby as she moves him from one boob to the other.

'OK, I might look for something to wear on a date,' I say, plucking at my old sweatshirt. 'I haven't bought any new stuff for ages.'

'What, you're going on a date?' Dom holds a hand up. 'I thought you hadn't had any luck.'

'Em persuaded me to try.'

'We've had a *sisterly* heart-to-heart.' Emma smiles at Dom triumphantly.

'I'll give it a go,' I say, getting my phone out. 'But I really don't know which messages to respond to.'

'You need to delete the inane "Hellos" and "How you doin's" instantly. *So* unimaginative.' Dom leans against my shoulder as I scroll through my inbox. 'You might just about get away with that in a bar, Joey-from-*Friends* style, but it simply doesn't translate online.'

'And get rid of any that have poor grammar; who don't know the difference between "you're" and "your".' Emma shudders. 'And the ones who spell "definitely" wrong.'

I grin. 'I have actually had a few "definatelys".'

'You want a guy with observation skills.' Dom grabs my phone from me. 'Yes, this Liam from OkCupid is asking about Dora. He's a teacher from Hove and likes music festivals and good food. Cute, huh?' He holds up a photo of a guy with straight jet-black hair and a tan, standing on a paddleboard and laughing.

'Oh yes, he looks nice,' Emma says approvingly.

'Ask him for a drink right away,' Dom instructs. 'No point beating around the bush when you want your bush beaten.'

'Dom!' I whack his thigh. 'I'm not sure I'm ready to sleep with anyone yet.'

There's a loud bang in the corridor, followed by a scraping sound. Saffron appears bum-first in the doorway, dragging a cardboard box. She's wearing an orange angora kaftan and her dreads flap over her back.

'Having a de-clutter are you, Saff?' I say, surveying the overflowing contents of the box, which includes Indian throws, bongo drums, a selection of crystals, yoga mats and a ukulele.

'Yes, it helps cleanse the mind.' Saffron straightens up. 'And I'm down-sizing because I'm going away for a bit.'

'Ah, right.' I smile. It'll be nice to have the flat to myself, without a lounge that doubles as a holistic studio.

'And I'm going to Airbnb my room.'

'What?' I say sharply. 'I don't want random strangers having a set of house keys and traipsing in and out.'

'But I need to cover the rent and bills somehow, don't I?' Saffron's carefully modulated voice snaps like a sulky teenager.

'If you can't afford a holiday, then don't go away!' I stare at her, incredulous.

'Actually, Saffron, I think you'll find when you check with the landlord that it's illegal to sub-let,' Dom interjects. 'You'll have to find another way to subsidise your trip.'

'What*ever*. I'll just cancel all my plans then, shall I? God, I knew you'd be unreasonable, Chloe!' Saffron turns on her heel. Moments later we hear her bedroom door slam.

'Whatever, whatever, what*ever*!' Suddenly Maisie, who has been watching our exchange curiously, stands up and starts stomping her feet hard on the carpet, grabbing fistfuls of her blonde curls. Her face is a perfect imitation of Saffron's scowl.

Dom, Emma and I erupt into helpless laughter and I revel in the rare moment of harmony between my two closest friends.

Chapter 10

I can't believe it works; you can just order a male online. I'm sitting at a table in The Lobster the following Saturday, waiting for Liam from OkCupid to come and join me for dinner.

There's a relaxed atmosphere, with groups of friends sharing platters and couples flirting with each other over candlelight. Later this evening a highly recommended hip-hop band will play on the stage at the back.

I look out at the beach through the glass front; the lights of Brighton Pier flash across the pebbles. There's no sign of Liam yet. I've been through his photos loads of times. I definitely fancy his face. He has a square jaw, a high forehead and expressive dark eyes.

But what if I'm not attracted to him in real life? What if he has a crap personality and really irritating mannerisms which completely turn me off?

Apparently you know if you fancy someone in the first ninety seconds of meeting them. And I'm not great at hiding my feelings, so if I'm not into him then he'll instantly clock it and we'll have to sit there and make fake small talk for hours.

I feel a hot flush rising from my chest and push my chair back from the table, breathing hard. A few nearby diners glance at me curiously. This is the most awkward scenario in the world. Why do people do this to themselves? I could just leave now.

'Everything OK, Chloe? Would you like to order food?'

I look up to see the bar manager, AJ, smiling down at me over a menu. His bald head gleams a rich mahogany in the soft lighting. 'Our special of the day is miso-glazed sea bass.'

'Hey, AJ. I'm fine with just a drink for now, thanks. I'm . . . waiting for someone.' I fiddle with my wine glass self-consciously.

'Well, you look lovely.' AJ gives me a wink and turns to the table next to me.

'Thanks.' I smooth my dress down over my thighs. Dom helped me choose this green skater dress with sequin detailing. It's quite flattering, though my exposed arms feel a bit flabby. I pinch the spare flesh critically. Here I am wondering if I'll fancy Liam, but what if he takes one look at these borderline bingo wings and turns on his heel?

I fidget on my wooden chair; my mouth's gone dry and my tongue feels way bigger than usual. I never realised there are so many different ways to sit; I lean forward with my elbows on the table, but that feels too eager. So I slump backwards and gaze into the middle distance like a brooding intellectual, then realise I'm staring too hard at a diner eating linguine as he meets my eye and frowns.

I'm just experimenting with straddling the chair backwards when I hear a deep voice behind me.

'Chloe, is it? Need a hand with that chair?'

I quickly stand up. 'Liam? Hah, I was justh . . . testhing it.' I wiggle my swollen-feeling tongue in panic and turn the chair round so it faces the table again.

'Sure, well it's great to meet you. I recognised your lovely red hair.' Liam grins and I just stare at him. There are cute dimples in his cheeks and he's wearing a khaki bomber jacket, white T-shirt and black jeans. His choppy dark hair falls over his forehead. Fit – he's definitely fit.

What do we do now – shake hands? I give him a weird little wave just as he leans forward to kiss my cheek and end up rubbing his chest . . . which is warm and firm. He smells of citrus and wood smoke.

'I got us a bottle of red.' I gesture to the table. 'But it's fine if you'd rather a beer, I'll just drink it. I mean, uh, maybe not the whole bottle . . .'

'I love wine, thanks.' Liam takes off his jacket and sits down, looking around admiringly. 'This is a great place; I've never been here before. I'm more a Hove boy.'

'Yep, it is. That's Maude.' I point to the stuffed goat on her gold pedestal to our left. She stares glassily ahead. 'If you're a fan of taxidermy.'

Liam turns to look at her. 'Not exactly.'

I laugh too loudly and search for another conversation topic as I pour him some wine.

'So . . . erm, do you like cheese?' I blurt out.

'Actually I'm trying veganism at the moment.'

'Ah, well done. I tried it for a bit – I definitely felt healthier.'

'Why did you stop?' Liam's dark eyes travel over my face.

'Well, mainly because I really like cheese.'

'Yeah? What's your favourite?'

'Hmm, good question.' My mind is a total blank. 'I guess . . . Cheddar?'

Oh God, this is so lame. Why am I being such a dick? I take a gulp of wine and look longingly at the exit.

'How're you finding online dating so far?' Thankfully Liam takes control of the conversation. He leans back in his chair and tilts his head. He's so confident.

'I'm quite new to it really, just trying it out.' I shrug, attempting to mirror his casual body language. Obviously I'm not going to tell him that it's my first online date ever and I'm currently nursing a broken heart. 'What about you?'

'Ah, I dabble, you know.' He gives me a cheeky grin. 'I must say seeing your dog was a real bonus. She looks gorgeous.'

'Thanks, she is.' I nod. 'You can't get more loyal than a Labrador.'

'More loyal than men, huh?' Liam teases.

'Yeah.' I feel a lurch in my chest but attempt a brazen smile. 'But then, I don't keep my men on a lead. Not always, anyway.'

Liam chuckles. 'You're very pretty.'

'Thanks.' I stare at the table, willing myself not to go red. I hate not having control over the colour of my face; people who never blush don't realise how lucky they are.

'And what are you looking for, Chloe?'

'Oh.' Not this again. 'Well, personally I like surprises.'

'Riiiiiight.' Liam cups his chin in his hand. 'I've never had that answer before.'

'What do other women say then?'

'I once went on a date with a lady who had a checklist.'

'No!' I pull an incredulous face. I really must dispose of the ultimate list Dom drew up for me.

'Yep, she sat there with a notepad. She wanted to get pregnant and asked me about my family's medical history, if I owned a house and what sort of pension I had. She was totally unapologetic about it – just said she'd had enough of time-wasters.'

'Woah.' I blow out my cheeks. 'That is thorough!'

'Yeah, but then I kind of get it. There's way more pressure on women to have kids, right? Even the word "child*less*" implies they're missing something.'

I'm impressed by Liam's understanding. I smile; I can already feel my tongue returning to its natural state. 'You don't feel pressure to have kids then?'

'Nope. I'm a primary school teacher so I'm already surrounded by them. Anyway, I've never been one to follow the herd, as you could probably tell from my profile.' Liam winks.

'Oh yes, doesn't it say you're from Hawaii or something?' I note his olive skin. 'It must have been amazing to grow up there.'

'What? No, I'm tanned because I was in New Zealand recently. I actually grew up in Peterborough; my childhood wasn't glamorous at all. But I soon made up for it when I got to Brighton. That's what I love about this city – it's so open-minded.'

'Ah, not sure where I got Hawaii from then. And yes, cheers to unconventional Brighton!' I raise my glass and we chink.

By the time we've had dinner and finished our second bottle of wine, The Lobster is crowded. People gather in the space in front of the stage, where the band is tuning up. Liam and I have to shout over the din and he pulls his chair right up next to mine. I'm enjoying his company; he seems really intelligent and interesting.

His arms are strong and muscular and I keep staring at his clean pink fingernails. He's totally different to Ant; taller and chunkier and kind of . . . more polished. But I am attracted to him. The wine swirls in my head and I feel a giddy rush of elation.

I take back everything I said about online dating. This is great. We definitely have chemistry. In fact, Liam asks me more questions than Ant ever did. He seems really interested in who I am.

'Hello, Brighton!' The female lead singer turns to the crowd and speaks into the mic. 'We're The Wallflowers.'

There's applause as the four-piece band start playing. They're wearing *Game of Thrones*-style clothing and play an interesting hybrid of folk and hip-hop. Somehow, with a double bass, banjo, guitar and excellent vocals, they manage to do the best cover of 'Gold Digger' I've ever heard.

'Nice!' Liam stands up. 'Shall we?' He holds out his hand and I take it. We thread through the crowd towards the stage to dance. His body moves perfectly in time to the music; he's got good rhythm. I keep sliding sideways glances at him and laughing as I catch his eye because he's doing exactly the same.

We're both out of breath by the time the band play their last song.

'Shall we go outside?' Liam's face is flushed.

We walk out onto the beach promenade and I stand with my hands in my coat pockets, looking out to sea. Liam moves closer to face me and the pier's coloured lights turn his skin blue, then red, then green.

I swallow and lift my face to his. His eyes are shiny black, as if his pupils have expanded so much they've drowned his irises. He puts a hand behind my neck then kisses me, pulling me close against his torso.

I close my eyes and run my hands up over his back, over this new shape of a man. His kiss is harder than Ant's but there's something exciting about his assurance. His fingers lightly tug on my hair.

'So, can I come and meet your dog?' he murmurs.

I hesitate. 'Is that a euphemism?'

'If you want it to be.' He kisses my neck just under my ear and an involuntary shiver runs down my spine.

Sleeping with someone who isn't Ant will be the final nail in the coffin. But then our relationship is dead anyway.

I look over Liam's shoulder at the dark water swelling around the pillars holding up the pier. Sometimes I feel like my bedroom is haunted by memories of Ant.

'I mean, we could go back to my flat, but I think Lucy is feeling a bit rough,' Liam is saying. 'You'll have to come over some other time though. I'll cook for us all.'

'That'd be nice.' He obviously likes me if he already thinks I'll get on with his flatmate. 'Come on then, let's go to mine,' I say decisively, lacing my fingers through his.

Dora's black nose snuffles feverishly along the small gap under the front door as I unlock it. Then she hurls herself at us, jumping up at Liam as if she's known him all her life.

He crouches down, rubbing her behind the ears, then, when she tips her head back, scratches her underneath her chin. Her eyes close in bliss, her tongue swinging with wild abandon.

'Wow, you know her sweet spots!' I smile as Liam buries his face into her neck.

'I grew up with dogs.'

I open my bedroom door and drop my bag on the floor. 'I think there's some wine in the kitchen,' I begin as Liam joins me, but he shakes his head and shuts the door behind him.

'Not thirsty,' he says, pulling off his T-shirt. His chest is much more defined than Ant's.

76

I stand motionless as he steps closer, allowing him to unzip my dress and slide it down over my hips. All my nerve endings are zinging.

We land on my bed in a flurry of limbs and Liam rips open a condom packet with his teeth. I lie back against the pillow and watch him roll it on and he suddenly pauses.

'You do want this?' His expression of concern is touching and I put my hands around his neck and pull him towards me.

'Oh yes, I do.'

We twist our way through a variety of positions and when I flip onto my front I feel the first ripples of an orgasm pulse through me. I bite the pillow and clench my hand over Liam's fist. He kisses the back of my neck, his breath hot in my ear, slowing down his movements so he goes deeper. I moan and squeeze my eyes shut and imagine for a moment that it is Ant behind me.

I remember the amazing sex Ant and I had on New Year's Eve when we got back from a friend's house party. We were still a bit high; we gave each other a massage with my jojoba oil and played drum 'n' bass and shagged until dawn's light turned my room pink, our skin all slippery and buzzing. And then we lay, entangled, looking into each other's eyes. And he told me how much he loved me. Liar.

'Chloe, are you OK?' Liam whispers; he's stopped thrusting. 'Your face is wet. Are you crying?'

'Mmmmmmmnnnnnn. Nope, all fine.' I swipe my cheek with my palm and nod quickly.

'Are you sure?' Liam sinks onto his elbow, trying to get a closer look at me, but I avert my cheek.

'Absolutely.' I reach around for his buttock, giving it a reassuring squeeze and guiding him back into me. 'Don't stop. I always cry when I come. It's just my thing.'

Chapter 11

Brighton is rammed full of visitors over Easter weekend. Crowds stand on the pavement in front of the pier, gawping at the dancing lights.

'Excuuuuuuse me!' I call as Dora lowers her head and pushes between their knees, making them squeal in surprise.

I'm on my way to Sunday lunch at The Lobster with the Goldsmiths crew. Linda, who lives in Hove, has organised it. I'm hoping seeing mine and Ant's mutual friends won't be a setback. Meeting Liam has really boosted my self-esteem. This past month, we've had several dates that always end up back at mine. He's great in bed. And I've developed a technique that prevents me from crying during sex, which Google tells me is called a 'crymax'. I just have to make sure I'm facing Liam and looking him right in the eyes, then I repeat his name over and over. That way no rogue thought of Ant creeps in. It really works.

'Look, it's Chloe!' Emma's pushing Toby's pram along the promenade towards us.

'Odd mother!' Maisie, in flowery dungarees, lets go of Emma's hand and takes a running leap at me, her blonde curls bouncing.

We slide open The Lobster's glass doors and are immediately assailed by the loud chatter of diners and an enticing combination of aromas. AJ waves at me from behind the bar.

Emma wheels the pram over to a long table at the back, by the window. 'This is us.'

I lower Maisie to the ground and she crawls under the table with Dora, sticking her tongue out and copying her panting.

'How many of us are there, again?' I ask.

'Four couples and us two, plus all the kids. James can't make it; he's bloody working again.'

'And you're absolutely positive that Ant isn't coming?' I check, helping Emma set up the highchairs.

'A hundred per cent. I told Linda it'd be really awkward if he's here. She was cool with it.' Emma lifts Toby into a chair and adjusts the foot board.

'Hmm, I don't think I've ever seen Linda *cool* about anything,' I say and Emma straightens up laughing, but then quickly stops as she looks over my shoulder.

'Oh, hi, Linda. We, er . . . how are you?'

I turn to see Linda standing behind me in navy trousers, a cream blouse and a peach-coloured pashmina. Her coral lips are fixed in a brittle smile as she chooses to ignore our slight.

'Chloe, awful news about you and Ant. It's obviously taken its toll; you look ghastly.' She kisses the air next to my cheeks but I move my face in the wrong direction and end up briefly sucking her earlobe, which tastes of Jo Malone's Pomegranate Noir. 'It won't be the same without him here.'

I open my mouth to protest but she's enveloping Emma in a big hug.

'Emma, you're a total knockout as usual. And is this Toby? Aren't you a gorgeous chap!' As Linda bends over Toby's highchair, her ash-highlighted hair falls onto his face and he blinks at her perplexedly, knitting his pale eyebrows together.

'Look, it's the life and soul sisters!' Linda's husband, Tom, appears with their young daughter, Saskia, and son, Roscoe. Maisie emerges from underneath the table, blinking up at the other children shyly.

I kiss Tom's cheek, marvelling at how different he looks these days. He always used to have the half-starved, rakish look of a model but now he's filled out so much, his denim shirt strains over his belly, and when he takes off his panama hat, his monk-like bald patch is larger than ever.

'Look, there's the rest of the gang.' I point through the window as our uni friends appear at the top of the steps by the pier, holding onto excited children and pushing a selection of buggies. They spot us and wave.

There's Scottish Morag and Duncan, who used to be in a band together when we were at Goldsmiths – they were about to be signed by Island Records but then their singer went loopy and tried to chop his own finger off. They've now moved back to Edinburgh and have a young daughter and a baby boy.

Then there's Heather and Ray, who were rebellious goths throughout university but now live in Putney with their son and both work for English Heritage.

Finally there's Jeremy and Polly, who've been together since they were fifteen and kind of exist as a single entity, so their combined couple nickname is 'Jolly'. They're very chilled out and run an alpaca farm in Kent. They have two kids, called Raven and Blaze.

'Right, operation Goldsmiths Easter lunch.' Emma moves a coat stand aside to make more space. 'Let's hope we don't scare everyone away.'

After much manoeuvring, we're finally all settled, with drinks on the table. Morag and Duncan sit on my left, opposite Emma, with their baby in a highchair next to Toby's. Heather and Ray sit on my right opposite Jolly, and Linda and Tom pull up chairs across from me.

Linda is still in rhapsodies over the news that Heather is pregnant again.

'I was wondering if you might have some special news for us,' she crows as Heather strokes her six-month bump. 'Don't think I didn't spot you drinking cranberry last time I saw you. It was either that or cystitis.' She bursts into peals of laughter, her face shiny with foundation.

'Yep, we're multiplying faster than ever,' Heather says proudly, tucking her glossy dark hair behind her ears. 'Here's to making it to adulthood. Cheers, everybody!' She holds up her bottle of J2O and we all clink.

'I can't believe it's fifteen bloody years since we graduated,' Morag says, looking around the table, her sweet freckled face crinkled with a smile. 'How times have changed. Remember when we were all living in dodgy flats and getting off our tits every weekend?'

'Oops, I'm pretty much still doing that.' I grimace.

'Oh, dear Chloe, ever the rebel.' Linda tuts. 'Surely it's time to grow up.'

'What does it even mean to be a grown-up?' I challenge her.

'Good point, Chloe.' Polly, next to Tom, comes to my defence, a dreamy look in her pale eyes as she twirls her wispy blonde hair around one finger. 'Growing up is a state of mind. In fact, we're always growing.'

'Oh, nonsense,' Linda says, gulping her white wine. 'It's very simple.' She holds up a large hand and ticks off on her fingers. 'Marriage, reputable employment, mortgage, children. All these things make you a responsible adult.'

'Well, we've fallen at the first hurdle then,' Polly says, nudging Jeremy and grinning. 'We're not even married.' Jeremy strokes his goatee and looks unconcerned.

'I'd rather spend the money on more land.'

'Typical Jolly.' Linda exchanges critical looks with Tom. They got married in the Cotswolds in their mid-twenties; it was the most expensive wedding I've ever been to.

'Are you still planning a loft conversion, Linda?' Emma asks, deftly changing the subject.

Linda heaves a big sigh. 'Actually, no. Tom and I have decided to move back to Fulham, haven't we, darling?' She pats his knee. 'It has many more PLUs.'

'What're PLUs?' Emma frowns.

'You know, "people like us".'

I let out a snort of laughter. 'Are you serious? You only want to be surrounded by people who are *exactly* like you?'

Linda sniffs as AJ approaches with his notepad, wearing a red and white striped apron that matches the deckchairs outside. 'Well, Brighton's changed – it has some very unsavoury types these days. I'd rather socialise with people I have things in common with.'

AJ's eyes bulge comically as he overhears her comment.

'I'll have the roast beef,' Linda orders. 'But first, can you tell me the provenance of the meat?'

'Pardon?' AJ purses his full lips.

'The *provenance*,' Linda emphasises. 'We're ethical carnivores. I heard Waitrose play classical music to their cows in the abattoir before slaughter – to stop them releasing stress hormones, you know.' She looks round the group and Jolly gape at her in horror.

'I see. I will check with the chef, ma'am.' AJ inclines his head then looks at me, his pen poised.

'Hm.' I frown at the menu. The slaughter chat has put me off a bit. 'I'll have the mushroom wellington, please.'

Thankfully, Linda and Tom start regaling Emma with a detailed account of their skiing holiday, leaving me free to catch up on the others' news. Jolly tell me about their new alpaca clothing range and I promise to help them with their website and PR, and Heather discusses the different colour options for her new nursery.

'And are you guys still playing music?' I ask Morag and Duncan. 'You were so good.'

'God, no,' Morag laughs, her brown curls bobbing. 'Those days are long gone; I haven't picked up a guitar in years.'

'When you have children you don't have time for hobbies, Chloe,' Linda interrupts, having finished bullying Emma into agreeing to get Maisie on the slopes. 'It's all about their needs. Isn't it, Sasky?' Her daughter, Saskia, is sitting between her and Tom. 'Mummy can't be selfish now she has to look after her darlings.' She puts on a crooning baby voice that makes me want to punch her.

Our group exclaims appreciatively as AJ and another waiter bring steaming plates to our table. AJ puts Linda's roast in front of her and clasps his hands behind his back.

'I can confirm that it is traditionally reared, grass-fed Sussex beef, ma'am,' he says. 'And the last thing they hear before slaughter is most probably deathcore.'

'What?'

'Deathcore, ma'am. It's a type of heavy-metal music, usually involving a lot of mindless screaming and growling. Apparently the farmer has a real passion for it.' AJ's expression is perfectly deadpan and Jolly and I bite back giggles as Linda nods pompously.

'Right then, see, it's worth knowing about the food you serve.'

'Absolutely, couldn't agree more.' AJ retreats, tugging an invisible forelock and shooting me a mischievous glance.

I can't manage the last of my mushroom wellington, so subtly slip it past my lap into Dora's waiting mouth. Encouraged, she slinks out from under the table and stares up at the highchairs with interest, watching Duncan feed his baby.

The baby locks eyes with her and gabbles in delight, hurling bits of chicken and butternut squash at the floor and screeching as Dora devours each scrap.

Linda observes the scene over her wine glass, already boss-eyed with booze. She's always been a lightweight. 'So then, Chloe, isn't it time we mentioned the elephant in the room? Your dog has strange defecation habits, I hear.'

Her overbearingly loud voice carries across the room and I clench my fists as Tom lets out a bellow of laughter.

'Uh oh, G-string-gate! It's a cracker of a way to get busted.' He slaps his thigh and shakes his head. 'No offence, Chloe.'

I curl my lip at him. 'Yeah, real funny story, huh, Tom?'

'My book group nearly died when I told them,' Linda hoots, grasping onto Tom's arm. They both judder with suppressed laughter.

'Guys, don't be mean.' Emma nudges Linda.

'Chloe, I'm so sorry, it must have been awful.' Morag's Scottish lilt is soft. 'How are you?'

I look down at my plate; everyone is staring at me.

'I'm getting there,' I mumble.

'Well, I'm hoping you can be mature about it,' Linda says. 'It was terribly awkward for me having to leave Ant out today.'

I glare at her, speechless with indignation.

'I think he'll understand, Linda,' Emma says. 'He knows he's messed up.'

'He doesn't mind,' Duncan suddenly chips in, spooning more food into the baby's mouth.

'You've spoken to him recently then?' I pounce on the news.

'Ah, yes. He called me last weekend.' Duncan shoots me a guilty look over his shoulder.

'Ha, he won't even talk to me. What did he say?' I notice my friends glancing at each other as I lean forward urgently.

Duncan flushes and fiddles with the baby's bib. 'Hmm, he mentioned that he's moving to Portsmouth to do a sailing course.'

'He's going through with that then? I can't believe it!' My stomach lurches when I think of Ant leaving town for good. 'And did he mention his new fancy woman?'

I know I sound hostile but I can't help it; it's the first opportunity I've had to find out what Ant's been up to.

'Well, he didn't say too much but, yes, I think she's still on the scene . . .' Duncan trails off, looking pained.

'He's still seeing her?' I whisper. My chest feels tight and I put down my fork. I've been tormenting myself with visions of Ant and Katypops69 for the past two months, but deep down I didn't really believe he'd do this to me.

'Yes, I've invited them to our leaving party this summer – I can't be expected to ignore him forever.' Linda sniffs self-righteously.

My mouth falls open. 'What about me?'

'You're here today, aren't you?'

'You can't not invite Chloe, that's not fair,' Emma says.

'Of course it is – none of us wants any drama.' Linda turns to Emma. 'Don't worry, you and James are on the guestlist.'

I look at Emma in dismay. Her nostrils flare and she frowns miserably. 'We won't come, Linda. I'd rather not see Ant at the moment, let alone his girlfriend.'

'Oh honestly, how petty.' Linda rolls her eyes crossly. 'I always said it was a bad idea to get into a relationship with a friend in the first place. It completely ruins the group dynamic.'

'No, you did not. When did you say that?' I clench my jaw, feeling bile swirling in my stomach.

'Look, let's not talk about Ant, it's still very raw. I'm sure Chloe will find someone else soon. Brighton's full of hot guys,' Emma says soothingly, pouring us all more wine.

'Ha, you'd be hard pushed to find a man who's not a poofter in this city.' Tom winks at me. 'I have to keep my back to the wall every time I go out.'

'What's poofter?' Maisie pipes up from her chair next to Emma, tilting her head quizzically.

'It just means that Tom's an awful bigot, Maisie, my love,' I say. 'He really shouldn't open his mouth around children. And actually, for your information, Tom, I already have a new boyfriend; he's called Liam.'

'Ooh, it's serious then?' Emma's eyes widen.

'Yes, we're official,' I lie. I mean, we've been seeing each other for a month; surely it's only a matter of time before we have 'the chat'. 'We just clicked instantly; we have so much in common. We go for loads of country walks and pub dinners and stuff.'

We've been for one country walk. But now the weather's getting warmer I'm sure we'll be doing more.

'What does he do?' Linda narrows her eyes.

'He's a primary school teacher,' I say proudly. 'But he's also got a degree in ancient history and can speak four languages. His parents are academics.'

'Hmm. Teachers don't earn much.' Linda refuses to look impressed.

'Yeah, well, he owns a massive flat in Palmeira Square, actually,' I say. I'm not sure if he owns it, but whatever. 'And his family have a country estate in Peterborough and a townhouse in London.' I'm blatantly just making stuff up now but at least everyone's stopped looking at me with pity.

'He's way more focused and active than Ant,' I continue. 'He has Duke of Edinburgh qualifications and runs marathons. And he's going to volunteer on an education project in Sri Lanka this summer. I'll probably go with him.'

'Wow, he sounds amazing. I'm so happy for you, Chloe, well done!' Morag grabs my forearm and I feel a bit bad about exaggerating, but Liam and I *are* getting on really well. He hasn't actually asked me around to his flat yet, but I'm sure he will. The main thing is, he can't keep his hands off me. I bet we have more sex than Ant and shitty G-string girl.

Satisfied with my seemingly healthy love life, everyone starts up other conversations around the table. Emma leans forward with Toby on her lap, her blue eyes sparkling.

'I can't believe you didn't tell me all that about Liam. I can't wait to meet him. Didn't I say it was worth online dating?'

'Yeah, maybe it can be romantic after all.' I grin, beckoning for her to pass me Toby. He gives me a big gummy smile and immediately clutches my hair, rubbing it against his cheek.

'Aren't you the most delicious thing in the world?' I coo at him. His dark grey eyes widen and his head jerks backwards as if he's having a mind-blowing revelation, then he lurches forward and snuffles contentedly into my neck.

'It's such a shame, isn't it?' Linda slurs. 'She's so good with them.'

I look up to see her nudging Emma and realise I'm the third person she is speaking of.

'What should I be ashamed of now, Linda?' I grit my teeth.

'It's all very well having a new boyfriend but it'll probably be too late to have kids by the time you get your act together.'

'Maybe I don't want kids,' I counter. 'I might want to focus on different things – like creative projects, or my career.'

'Oh yes, are you still an account executive at that Google-wannabe agency?' Linda titters bitchily.

'Actually, I'm being promoted to account manager,' I say. Apparently I've become quite adept at stretching the truth.

'Ah, Chloe, that's fab news – finally!' Emma cries and my smile falters.

Linda folds her arms. 'The point is, no job can ever be as rewarding as rearing a family. There's nothing on earth like having your own little "mini me" running around.'

'True.' Heather rubs her pregnant belly in circular motions. Her constant bump-caressing is really starting to annoy me now.

'Yeah, well, I'm perfectly happy as I am, thanks,' I say stubbornly.

'Children aren't the be all and end all, guys. They can be a right pain in the arse,' Emma joins in.

'But you can't *possibly* know what love is until you have children.' Linda's face is slack with sentimentality as she breathes sour white wine fumes over me.

'I know what love is.' I hear my voice wobble unconvincingly and bend my head to the soft blonde down covering Toby's scalp, trying not to succumb to a quake of panic. I'm holding a sleepy baby, for fuck's sake, I'm completely defenceless.

Linda shakes her head. 'Believe me, no amount of bloody Labradors will ever match up to it.' She gestures dismissively at Dora, who is lying by the highchair, watching me with soulful brown eyes.

I look at my beautiful dog, who makes me laugh every single day. Something inside me snaps. 'She's not a "bloody Labrador". Don't mock my life, Linda; it's just as important as yours. Not everyone's a fucking *PLU*, you know, that's what makes the world so interesting.'

Linda clutches her pashmina, and her mouth opens and closes like a goldfish.

'Hey, hey, calm down, Chloe.' Emma takes Toby from me as he starts to cry. 'Come on, this is supposed to be a nice catch-up. Linda, Chloe's a bit sensitive right now.'

'Don't patronise me.' I glower at Emma. 'I just don't like ignorant bullies.' I push my chair back. 'I'm going to the loo.'

As I leave the table, I hear Linda tell everyone in barely hushed tones that she thinks I'm having a breakdown.

In the toilet cubicle I text Dom with shaking hands:

Am at The Lobster about to stab smug, homophobic, entitled dickheads, Linda and Tom, with a fork – please save me!

I wash my hands in the sink and look in the mirror; my face is red and my eyes look a bit wild. I powder my nose and smooth my fringe down. I can't have everyone telling Ant that I've lost the plot.

As I leave the ladies', Duncan is coming out of the gents', running a hand over his bushy black hair. He sees me and smiles lopsidedly. 'Wine's gone straight to my head.'

'Hey, Duncan.' I cross the corridor to join him, barricading his way with my arm. 'When you spoke to Ant, did he mention that he works with his new girlfriend at all?'

'Hmm, I really can't remember where he met her.' Duncan steps towards the exit but I move in front of him.

'Is her name Katy? Please, Duncan, this is important. Try to remember,' I beg.

'Katy, erm, I'm not sure that was it.' His face scrunches up in concentration and he closes his eyes. 'I think it might have been something like . . .' His eyes pop open and I stare at him, inches from his face.

'What?'

Duncan blinks. 'Can't remember.' He hiccups.

'Chloe, what are you doing?!' I turn to see Linda standing by the exit.

'Huh? Nothing.' I realise I'm clutching the front of Duncan's shirt and quickly let go. 'We were just having a little chat.'

'Chloe cares about Ant a lot.' Duncan gives my shoulder a hearty pat, nearly knocking me over. 'S'understandable.'

'Gosh, well there's no need to attack him.' Linda glares at me, giving me a wide berth on her way to the ladies'.

I turn and stick my middle finger up at her retreating back and Duncan dissolves into giggles. 'She's got a massive arse, hasn't she, Linda? You could rest your mug of tea on that.'

★

I keep Duncan and Morag engaged in conversation while we order dessert, ignoring the increasingly disapproving looks Linda is throwing me across the table.

Then, with a flash of relief, I see Dom at the window. He's wearing a bright orange blazer with fur trimming, white satin trousers and pointy winkle-picker shoes.

He winks at me, then strides through the doors towards our table, panting.

'Dom, what are you doing here?' Emma says, flicking a suspicious glance at me.

'Sorry to barge in on your lunch but I'm afraid I need Chloe; there's been an emergency,' Dom announces dramatically.

Linda's gossip radar twitches. 'What's going on?'

'You must be Linda? An honour to meet you.' Dom extends his right hand across the table and grasps hers firmly.

'What kind of problem?' Linda tries to remove her hand but Dom keeps on shaking it.

'Well, it's all rather delicate. I'm afraid my boyfriend, Yannis, has managed to get something . . . stuck.' Dom finally lets go of Linda's hand and raises his right index finger suggestively.

I nearly choke on my water and Morag lets out a bellow of laughter.

'What on earth do you mean?' Linda looks appalled.

'I don't want to spell it out but . . . we got rather carried away in the bedroom.' Dom widens his eyes.

Jolly shriek in unison, slapping each other with mirth.

'Please! There are children present.' Tom puts his hands over Saskia's ears and frowns at Dom. 'This isn't some seedy nightclub, you know.'

'Oh, what?' Dom grasps his lapels and looks around as if in shock. 'Isn't it? Where am I?' He starts flailing and squinting as if blinded by the light.

I crack up. 'Oh dear, I'd better go and help. Sorry, guys.' I stuff the last of my Bakewell tart in my mouth and stand up.

'Is that a dwarf? A bald dwarf?' Dom is grasping the high-chair and goggling at Morag's baby in alarm. 'Arrrrggghhh, no, don't look at me, vile offspring!' He holds up two fingers in the shape of a cross, as if to ward off evil spirits.

The baby shrieks happily and bangs its spoon on the table. Most people around the table are laughing now, except Emma, Linda and Tom.

'This is ludicrous, you're winding the children up!' Linda is all puffed up like a goose.

'OK, OK, we're going. Come on, you.' I blow kisses around the table and take Dom's arm as he staggers towards me, his arm still shielding his eyes.

'Let's go get some pliers and Vaseline. Bloody poofters!' I roll my eyes pointedly at Linda and Tom as we leave and they sit frozen in their seats, wearing matching expressions of scandalised distaste.

Chapter 12

Great, now Emma keeps asking me about my new job role and boyfriend and I have to fob her off with sketchy half-truths. No wonder they call it a web of lies; our conversations have got very sticky since the Goldsmiths lunch last week. I can't admit to her how humiliated I am by the news that Ant's moved on so quickly. I'm sick of feeling like a loser.

Still, hopefully today I can prove myself; I have my appraisal with Giles and I'm not leaving his office until I get a pay rise.

I press the 'latte' button on Top Banana's coffee machine and it starts gurgling as I read through my notes. I jotted down all my work accomplishments this past year and it makes quite a long list.

'Morning.' Simone slopes into the kitchen in joggers and a sloppy T. She's barely wearing any make-up and her hair is in a messy ponytail.

'Hey, want a coffee?'

'Black, please.' She sits on the bench, gazing out of the window to the high street below.

'You OK? How's it going with beardy bloke?'

'Oh, *him*. He gave me the stupid "ex"cuse – says he's still in love with his girlfriend.' Simone sighs and her breath steams up the glass pane.

'Shit, sorry, mate.'

'I'm so over men, they're bad for me.' Simone draws a penis in the condensation on the window. 'I'm going on a man diet.'

I put her cup on the table. 'What does that involve?'

'I've deleted all my dating apps and booty calls. I'm not even going to *think* about men. Maybe if I stop looking for love, it will find me.'

'Good for you, Sim. Men take up a lot of headspace.' I smile ruefully.

'Have you done any more stalking? Now you know Ant's defo seeing that bitch?'

'No, I can't risk getting caught again.'

'Well, at least you've got Liam. He's keen, isn't he?'

'I *think* so.' Liam still hasn't asked me over and sometimes he takes ages to reply to my texts, but when he does come to see me he's really attentive and complimentary. 'I think he's biding his time because he knows I'm still recovering from my break-up.'

Simone draws a broken heart in the condensation. 'Hey, d'you want to come over to mine to watch girl-power movies like *Bridget Jones* and *How to Be Single* and eat a shit ton of ice cream?'

'Sure. That sounds like fun.' I grin at her.

'Christ, I can't bear the tension any more.' Verity strides across the kitchen tiles to the retro orange fridge, taking out a smoothie bottle. She's wearing a navy and cream suit and her hair is pleated in a stylish chignon.

'What's up?' Simone looks Verity up and down. 'You look smart.'

'Gav and I are going on the spa retreat I won this weekend and I have a feeling he might propose. I can't cope with the pressure. He better ask me on the first night so I can relax.' Verity tips her head back and gulps the smoothie.

'Aw, poor you,' Simone says doubtfully. 'I don't s'pose you've had any thoughts on bridesmaids yet, have you?' She draws a ring under the penis on the window.

'Nope, still deciding.' Verity licks her lips, then looks at me. 'Chloe, don't you have your review with Giles now?'

'Yes.' I clutch my notebook against my chest. 'How did yours go?'

Verity throws a quick look over her shoulder. 'Don't tell anyone, but I've been promoted to account manager and had a £5k pay rise.'

'Result!' Simone claps her hands together. 'No wonder you look so slick. Maybe you'll get one too, Chlo.'

'Great news, Vee! Let's hope so.' I hold up crossed fingers and walk determinedly across the AstroTurf towards Giles's office. I'm wearing an expensive suede skirt and new white silk shirt which is, unfortunately, a bit see-through. Hopefully Giles won't notice though – he'll be far too impressed by my business-like manner.

I wait outside Giles's office door because his red light is on. He had traffic lights installed outside so that he can indicate to staff when he's available or engaged.

I do the maths in my head; if I get a £5k pay rise I'll just about be eligible for a mortgage on a studio apartment. I can already picture it in my head: a sunny bijou flat with a mezzanine floor. I'd use clever storage and minimalist Scandinavian design. Even if the space is small, it'll mean I'm totally independent; as Virginia Woolf said, all one needs is 'a room of one's own'.

Hugging myself with anticipation, I bend to look into the giant aquarium that makes up Giles's glass wall. The tropical fish have delicate translucent tails and stunning neon colours. Maybe I'll get a fish tank for my new home. An orange and white stripy fish that reminds me of Nemo floats past.

'Hey, Nemo!' I wave my little finger at him. Then, through the plant fronds, I suddenly make out Giles. He is throwing Velcro darts at his dartboard.

I straighten up and wait patiently; perhaps playing darts helps to focus his mind before important meetings.

After another five minutes, the light changes from red to green and Giles opens his door, sighing as if I've rudely interrupted him. He's wearing a baby-blue cashmere jumper and tan trousers and is running his fingers through his golden hair distractedly.

'Come in, Chloe. This'll have to be quick; I've got to be in London soon.' He sits at his desk and gestures at the chair opposite. I take a seat, feeling my confidence wane. He doesn't look like a man about to deliver good news.

Giles's office is nearly the same size as our open-plan floor. His window overlooks the curved white domes of the Royal Pavilion and is flanked by an arcade machine and a beer fridge. A self-massage chair sits in the corner and a drone perches on top of his shelving unit like some alien insect.

'Right, well, I've listed the improvements you said I should make in last year's review,' I say briskly, opening my notebook. 'And I'm pleased to say I've addressed every one of them.'

I look up to see that Giles is staring at my chest. I follow his gaze; you can quite clearly see my black bra. Dammit.

I feel my face go hot and hunch my shoulders, raising my voice to compensate.

'As well as all my extra-curricular projects, every account I work on has seen increased ROI and I've gathered some direct client appraisal. I think you'll agree it's all very positive.'

I hand him a printout of client quotes; I was touched at how happy they were to help. 'I was hoping we could discuss my suitability as an account manager and a salary increase that reflects my work.'

I've been practising ways of asking for more money and this phrase sounded the most professional.

Giles ignores my request and scans the quotes, his face impassive. 'Hmm.' He puts the paper on his desk, then taps on his iMac keyboard. 'Actually, Chloe, I have some in-house feedback for you here too. As you know, every year we ask some of your colleagues to comment on your work as part of an anonymous process.' He frowns at his screen, then looks at me. 'I'm afraid your score was underwhelming.'

'What?' I'm taken aback. 'But I work really well as part of a team.'

'Well, it says here that you can often be careless and do a botch job.'

'That's not true! Who said that?'

'It's an anonymous process, you can't ask that.'

'But it's not fair to slate me without any evidence. How am I supposed to defend myself?'

'Someone else has said that recently you've been "over-emotional" and "a bit nuts",' Giles continues.

I rub my forehead in consternation. I have spent a fair amount of time crying in the ladies'. I can't help the way sudden memories of Ant ambush me when I least expect them. 'I've had a bit of trouble in my personal life recently but I'm doing my best to get past it.'

'Ah, yes.' Giles's blue eyes widen lasciviously as he recalls the office gossip. 'Didn't you catch your boyfriend doing something dirty with your dog?'

'No! It wasn't like that.' I shift forward in my chair. This is not going how I'd hoped. 'Look, I admit I've had a temporary lapse but you can't deny what I've achieved over the past year.'

'Chloe, in this instance, I've decided not to promote you.' Giles is now bouncing a ball made entirely of rubber bands on the carpet. 'However, I've given you a salary increase in keeping with inflation, which is a two per cent rise.' *Bounce. Bounce.*

My sunny bijou flat disappears in a sickening rush. 'What?! So I'm stuck as account executive for yet another year? Surely I've got enough experience to become a manager by now. How can Verity be more qualified than me? She's ten years younger!'

'Ah, but have you seen her Instagram stories? They're very clever.' *Bounce. Bounce.*

'Pfff,' I scoff; most of Verity's stories involve semi-nudity. 'What about my blog, *Chloe Wanders*? I sent you the post I wrote after our forest trip. It did really well; a few of our clients shared it.'

'Your writing is good,' Giles concedes. *Bounce. Bounce.*

'Verity might be able to film her own cleavage but her grammar is crap. She told me she doesn't read books because "all the words hurt her eyes".'

'Look, Chloe, it's an ever-evolving world.' Giles sighs. 'I think you can learn a lot from Verity. In fact, I've made her your line manager.'

'What? You can't have *her* managing *me*!' I splutter with outrage.

'Chloe, you're a solid member of the team but if you want to impress me you need to stand out. I want to be dazzled by your creativity.' Giles cups his elastic ball in his hands.

'I'm trying, Giles, but you always put me on really dry accounts.' My voice rises in resentment. 'There's only so much I can do with bathrooms and gambling.'

'Well, then you have to think outside the box.'

'Can't you at least give me an opportunity to prove myself? You could put me on the "make Top Banana famous" project.'

'Not this time.' Giles stands up and throws the ball across the room into his big-boy toy chest, then rifles on the shelf behind him, pulling out a glossy book with the words 'Rising Above Average' in big green lettering on the front. 'Here, if you like reading you can borrow this – I'm sure you'll find it very inspiring.'

I stand up and take it begrudgingly. My motivation to be brilliant decreases exponentially with the length of time I'm stuck on the same rung of the career ladder. Especially now I have to go another year with a salary that doesn't qualify me for the property ladder.

My life is like a really shit game of snakes and ladders right now.

'Right, I'll get back to work then.'

'Good to chat, Chloe.' Giles types on his keypad and chuckles at his screen. 'Remember, your only limit is yourself!

'Ah, Chloe, can I have a quick word?' Verity is sitting in the break-out area on a neon-green beanbag with a MacBook Air on her lap. She beckons me over.

I go to sit on a pink beanbag next to her, unable to summon a smile.

'So, Giles told you the news about me being your line manager, huh – isn't it exciting?!' She holds out her fist and nods at me until I raise mine for a fist bump. 'I reckon I can really help you improve; none of us like a botch job.'

She pivots her laptop so that I can see her screen. 'Look, I've made a spreadsheet of all your weaknesses. It'll take a while to work through them but don't worry, we're in this together. What's that noise?' She looks up.

I stop grinding my teeth and shake my head. 'Dunno, coffee machine?'

By the time I leave work that afternoon, all my nerve endings are screaming. Verity insisted on shadowing every little thing I did, giving me a running commentary on what I was doing wrong. She even made me reorganise my email filing system and her method is completely counter-intuitive.

I stomp home along the beach with Dora; dark clouds rumble across a white-tipped sea. I automatically take out my phone and feel a stab of dejection when I remember that I can't talk to Ant as I usually would. Instead I text Liam.

> *Hey babe, whatcha up to this eve? Had a rank day at work, would be good to hang out x*

Since when have I become so average? I fling Dora's ball across the pebbles ferociously, nearly wrenching my shoulder from its socket. My university tutors always said I was full of such promise and I managed to get a first-class English degree.

I always thought that by the time I was in my thirties I'd have a brilliant career which helped change the world for the better. Yet somehow none of my office jobs have been as stimulating as I imagined. I feel like I'm only using half my brain. Or half of the 10 per cent of our brains that we supposedly use; which means just 5 per cent. God.

Even *Chloe Wanders* has ground to a bit of a halt. I try to remember the last time I felt really inspired and stayed up late writing a blog post.

My phone pings in my pocket. It's Liam.

> *Hey hey sexy lady. Would love to but am doing a pub quiz tonight with Lucy. Let's hook up soon though, can't wait to take your clothes off xx*

I try not to feel hurt that he didn't invite me along to the quiz. It's early days; I shouldn't be too needy. Anyway, at least he still wants to undress me.

As I put my key in the lock, my front door opens. Ant is standing right in front of me in a Superdry hoodie and jeans. After all these weeks, his sudden proximity starts a whole chemical reaction off in my body; I feel like I'm falling from a great height.

'Chloe, shit.' He takes a step back. Dora jumps up at him, pawing his thighs and whimpering.

'What are you doing here?' I snap, cross at the effect he's having on me.

'Uh, I was just . . . collecting some stuff.' His face twitches with panic. 'Saffron let me in.'

'You weren't going to wait to see me?'

'Well, yeah, I mean, if you want.' His voice cracks a little and he reaches out for the doorframe, his hand almost touching mine.

As I stare at him, a strange numbness seeps through me. 'Fine, come on then.' I gesture for him to follow me up the stairs.

Saffron hovers in the corridor wrapped in a tiny towel. A tattoo of a rose curls around her right ankle and up her calf. She is casually sweeping her finger along the banister – as if she ever notices dust.

'Feel free to let all my ex-boyfriends into our flat, Saffron,' I say sarcastically, as I lead Ant into my bedroom and shut the door.

Ant sits on my bed and grabs Dora in a bear hug as she jumps up to join him. I look at the tawny curve of his neck as he rolls her over onto her back, her paws pedalling happily. My throat constricts and I turn away.

'So, what stuff did you want then?' I go to my wardrobe and pull out one of the bottom drawers.

'Huh?'

'You came to get your things – what do you want back? Your socks? Your old T-shirts? Your stupid comic books?' I start throwing his stuff into a plastic bag. 'Everywhere I look there's little reminders of you, Ant, please take them all away!'

'There's no need to shout, Chloe,' Ant says in a hurt little boy voice.

'Uh, yes there *is*! I've had a shit day and you've made it worse. I can't believe it's taken you this long to show your face. I never knew you were *this* much of a coward.'

'What do you mean?'

'I *mean* we've been best friends since we were eighteen but you've just cut me out of your life and left me to suffer.' My chest heaves.

'I thought it'd be good to give you time to process it. There's not much I can say to make you feel better.' Ant looks at his hands, lying limply in his lap.

'There's plenty you could say!' I rage. 'Or at least you could just be there to listen to me. These past few months have been . . . torture. I've never felt more alone in my life.'

I gulp; if I allow tears to flow they will scald the skin on my cheeks. 'Have you considered how gut-wrenching it is for me to think of you with *her*?' I continue. 'All our friends have heard about her and I don't even know who she is. It's like she's just stolen you from under my nose.'

'It's not her fault.' Ant closes his eyes; his bushy eyebrows are furrowed. I know every fibre of his being wants to run away and hide from this. 'It's mine.'

'Don't you dare!' I hiss, taking a step towards him. 'Don't you sit on my bed and bloody stick up for her. Is she your girlfriend now?'

Ant shakes his head, then nods.

'Christ, how can you live with yourself? You've just discarded me like I'm an old toy and she's a shiny new one.'

'It just happened,' he says tonelessly.

'Well, you're a massive shit and I hate you, I hate you both. I wish you'd never followed me out to Mexico and told me you loved me. You're the biggest waste of my life.' I want to collapse on the floor. I can hardly be bothered to hold myself together any more.

A muscle in Ant's jaw jumps. 'Fine, well you'll be pleased to hear that I'm leaving in two weeks. I've finished at Warren

Recruitment and I'm renting my flat out and moving to Portsmouth to do a sailing course.'

'Good. Fly, fly away, free spirit. The sooner you're gone the better.' My hands are trembling as I reach up to my bookshelf and take down my wooden Mayan mask that matches the one Ant has, and stuff it in the bag. 'And how will lover-girl deal with that?'

'She'll probably join me,' Ant whispers.

I just stand and stare at him with my mouth open; there are no words left. I chuck the bag on the bed next to him and he takes out the mask.

'I can't take this – we're supposed to have one each.'

'I don't want it.'

Ant looks down at the mask in silence.

'Don't think I know what I'm doing, Chlo,' he says at last. He leans forward and kneads his knuckles into his eyes. 'I'm fucked.' And then he's crying into his hands, great creaking sobs; he sounds like an old rocking chair.

Dora wriggles next to him, nudging her nose underneath his hands and licking his wet cheeks, which makes him cry even more.

I give him a tissue, resisting the urge to sit down next to him and try to solve his problems. They aren't mine any more.

Ant takes a juddering breath and blows his nose loudly. 'My mum would be really disappointed in me right now, wouldn't she?' he croaks pathetically.

All the anger drains out of me. 'Oh, Ant. She would . . . but she'd still love you.'

When Ant's dried his tears, we go out into the corridor and he turns at the top of the stairs.

'I'll be back some weekends – maybe we could meet for a coffee?' His cheeks are damp and blotchy. 'I'd like to stay in touch.'

'Maybe,' I say. I've spent weeks longing for Ant to contact me, thinking that if we met up he might be able to make sense of what has happened. But now I'm not sure I even want to look at him again.

'Chloe, are these your new boyfriend's pants? I found them in the bathroom.' Saffron opens her bedroom door. Liam's green boxers are swinging from her finger.

Ant pales; he looks as though he's been socked in the gut. 'Are you fucking kidding me?' he snarls.

'Nice one, Saffron.' I snatch the boxers from her. 'Great timing.'

Ant's lip curls as he looks at me. 'You have a go at me when you've already got a new boyfriend? You've got some cheek.'

I meet his eye coldly. 'Don't start, Ant. You've not got a leg to stand on. Liam has really helped me – I'm not explaining myself to you.'

'Anyway, why would you care?' Saffron taunts, narrowing her slanted green eyes.

We both look at him; for once I appreciate Saffron's condescending nature. Ant's eyes flick between Saffron and me warily.

'Well, do you care?' I persist. 'Have you ever actually given a shit about me, Ant?'

Ant looks at the boxers in my hand and opens his mouth as if to say something, then shakes his head.

'Fuck this.' He turns and jogs down the stairs, then the front door slams. Not quite the closure I'd hoped for.

Chapter 13

Finally. Liam's invited me over to his flat this evening. He's cooking dinner for me and his flatmate, Lucy. I weave my way through the Saturday crowds on the seafront towards Palmeira Square. The sun glints off the golden poles of the carousel as the wooden horses move up and down to the merry-go-round music. I'm hoping tonight will mark the next step in our relationship.

I think I've turned a corner since Ant came over to get his stuff; it's actually a huge relief to know he's leaving town this Monday. I imagine him sitting in his empty flat with everything in boxes – the way it was when he moved in two years ago. We were so knackered from hefting everything about that we just set up his flat screen on the lounge floor, got into sleeping bags and ordered pizzas. I was so excited to have him in the same city as me.

But that chapter is closed now and I'm finally getting myself back: the person who exists without Ant to define her. I turn The Stone Roses up on my iPhone and look out over the sparkling blue sea, catching a waft of sun cream and the tang of seafood from the oyster hut. It's been a hot May day and most people are in flip flops and sunglasses. The lowering sun casts a sepia light over the pebbles and seagulls waddle lazily in front of me.

I'm filled with a welcome positivity, I'm going to say 'yes' to everything this summer – do new things, meet new people and maybe even look for a new job, somewhere that actually values my input. And I'm going to do more writing for *Chloe Wanders* – I'm sure Liam will be up for exploring with me; he's pretty adventurous.

Liam also seems more sociable than Ant; it'll be good to meet his circle of friends. I think he'll get on really well with most of mine. I imagine taking him with me to one of Linda's precious dinner parties and grin to myself. He'd make short work of her snobbery. He's very eloquent and quite political; I'd love to see him react to her 'you don't know what love is until you have children' bollocks.

I walk past the rows of coloured beach huts and across Hove Lawns, where people are lounging about on picnic rugs. Liam lives in a stately terraced house on Palmeira Square, where opulent heritage buildings form an elegant curve facing the sea.

'Helllllllloooo, Chloe.' Liam answers the door with a tea towel over his shoulder and a smudge of flour on his cheek. 'Welcome to my humble abode.'

'I was beginning to think you lived in a bus stop.' I kiss him then follow him down the corridor into a large lounge with cream carpet, a dark grey corner sofa and curved windows looking out over the crescent. A dark-wood dining table stretches the length of the far wall.

'Wow, what a beautiful place.' I go to admire the view. The bright sky is studded with clouds like fish scales.

'Sometimes I have to pinch myself; it's almost too good to be true,' a female voice says behind me, and I turn to see a petite girl with a blonde bob in a zebra-print dress.

'Hey, I'm Lucy.' She holds out her hand; it's the size of a child's. 'Liam's told me all about you.'

'Good.' I grin at him as he ducks through the open arch into the kitchen. 'Nice to meet you, Lucy. How long have you lived together?'

'Three years, still going strong.' Liam raises a fist in acknowledgment.

'Do you want help, babe?' Lucy joins him, lifting the lid of a bubbling pan.

'No. Too many cooks. Get your mitts off!' Liam swipes at her with the tea towel.

'D'you want red or white wine, Chloe?' Lucy asks, as I sit on the sofa.

'I'll have red, please.' I notice that the bookshelves are stacked, probably because they're both teachers. And the mantelpiece is crowded with framed photos of Liam and Lucy together in various locations. They're obviously close; I'd better make an effort to get to know her.

Lucy puts our wine glasses on the coffee table, then sits down next to me, tucking her feet up underneath her.

'So, I presume you're a grammar Nazi, like Liam?' I ask.

'What? Ha, no, my spelling's shit. I dunno how I got through uni.' She shakes her blonde hair carelessly.

'Isn't spelling quite important in your job though?

'Nah, as long as I have clear pronunciation I'm fine.'

'Right.' I frown. 'It must be pretty exhausting working with kids.'

'Oh, I don't much. You know what they say – never work with kids or animals!'

'Ah, so it's mainly adults then?'

'Yeah.' Lucy gives me a strange look. 'Mainly adults.'

'Right then, ladies, dinner is served! Sit yourselves down and prepare to be impressed.' Liam plonks a huge pie on the dining table along with bowls of vegetables. 'It's Quorn mince but you won't know the difference, I promise.'

Lucy and I 'ooh and ah' appreciatively as we carry our glasses to the table. She pulls up a chair right next to Liam's, though there's plenty of space around the table, and I slide in opposite them.

'Wow, if I'd known you were this good, I would've got you to work in my kitchen!' I say to Liam. 'Which reminds me; I'm cooking Mexican at mine soon. Up for it? Be good for you to meet some of my mates too; we might even do a bit of salsa dancing.'

Liam spoons pie onto our plates with a vague smile. 'Maybe, baby.'

'Omigod, Liam, do you remember when we tried those salsa classes in Portslade? You were the only guy who could actually move – all those other awkward men, typical Brits!' Lucy laughs.

'We were the best in the class.' Liam gives Lucy the lazy grin I find so attractive. Is it my imagination or are his eyes lingering on her lips?

Halfway through the meal my skin is prickling with discomfort. I can't shake the feeling that Lucy and Liam are being really flirtatious; they keep touching each other. At one point Lucy even stroked Liam's cheek.

And Liam keeps catching my eye and nodding as if to get my approval on how wonderful and entertaining Lucy is. If I'm honest, I'd rather she just piss off to her bedroom and leave Liam and me alone.

'Hey, Liam.' I interrupt him as he tries to push more vegetables on Lucy's plate. 'I was thinking of taking some time off work and going to Wales or somewhere. Want to come?'

'Eat your greens, Lucy!' Liam is prodding Lucy's closed mouth with asparagus. 'Hmm, Wales? I can't take holiday during term time.' He glances sideways at me.

'Gerrrroooff!' Lucy spits out the asparagus, giggling. 'I love Wales. Liam and I spent a week camping in Pembrokeshire last summer – it was epic!'

I force a smile as they reminisce. I ought to be pleased that Liam has close female friends. Cursing Ant for making me so suspicious, I redouble my efforts to bond with Lucy.

'So, Lucy, what subjects do you teach?'

'Huh?' Lucy blinks at me. 'I don't teach.'

'Oh! I thought Liam said you were a teacher, like him.'

'God no, I can't imagine anything worse!' Lucy gags. 'I'm an actress. I have an agent in London.'

'Oh, wow! Sorry, I don't know where that came from.' I pour us all more wine, feeling stupid. 'Have you got any jobs coming up then?'

'Yes, actually! I've just landed a part in *Holby City*. We're filming in Yorkshire so I'll have to leave this one on his own.' Lucy pouts Liam an apology and he laughs.

'Hey, I can look after myself. I've just demonstrated my cooking skills.'

'Yeah, but I'm more worried about you pining.'

'Well, I can always invite the secondary round.' Liam winks at me.

Lucy's face crumples and she looks down at her plate.

'What's the matter, had enough pie?' Liam nudges her shoulder and she shakes her head and mumbles inaudibly.

'Hey.' Liam gently takes her chin and turns her face to him. 'You're my number one, remember.' He leans forward and kisses her. On the lips.

I blink at them. Did I just hallucinate? No, I didn't. Liam kisses Lucy again, cupping the back of her head like he does with me.

'What the actual fuck – what are you doing?' I demand, and they pull apart and look at me.

'Kissing,' Liam says.

'Uh, have I just slipped into an alternative universe here? Since when is it normal to snog your flatmate in front of your date?'

'Lucy is my primary.' Liam says it as if reminding me of a really simple fact I'd forgotten.

'And what the hell is a primary?'

'She's my primary lover.'

'Not a primary school teacher then?' I clarify.

Lucy snickers, a swathe of blonde hair falling over her face. 'That's why you thought I was a teacher?! No, I'm his girlfriend.'

'But how can you be lovers when I'm going out with him?' I ask her. I feel as if my brain is working extra slowly.

Lucy puts her small hand on Liam's arm. 'Honey, I think Chloe might have the wrong end of the stick.'

'I thought you realised, Chloe.' Liam looks sloe-eyed. 'Lucy and I are poly. It says it on my OkCupid profile – I haven't tried to hide it.'

'Poly? What do you mean?'

'Polyamorous. Lucy and I are in a relationship, we're partners. But we can also have relationships with other people –
our secondaries.' Liam adopts a patronising tone, as if speaking
to his pupils.

'Polyamorous.' I screw up my face in disbelief. 'What? I
thought poly meant Polynesian – like those islands, you know
. . . Hawaii?!' I wave my hands around in frustration.

Lucy bursts into peals of high-pitched laughter. 'She thought
you were Polynesian!' She whacks Liam's thigh. 'Oh God,
I'm going to die!'

'It's my exotic good looks.' Liam chuckles, swigging his wine.

'Err, this isn't just some big joke!' My mouth has fallen open
as I watch them. 'You seriously thought I was your secondary?
Your sloppy secondary?'

'Hahaaaa, sloppy secondary! That's good!' Lucy bends over
the table, cracking up.

'Oi! You can't just fuck with someone's feelings and then
take the piss.' I throw up my hands in indignation.

Liam pulls a face. 'Come on, Chlo. It's not my fault you
didn't read my profile properly.'

'I didn't realise four little letters carried so much meaning!'
I explode. 'Everyone knows you skim-read those things – and
you wrote a bloody essay. Anyway, you could have brought
it up when I met you. Or any of the times we've seen each
other since!'

'I have mentioned Lucy, quite a lot actually.' Liam squeezes
Lucy's hand.

'I should bloody hope so.' She narrows her eyes at him
playfully.

'How stupid of me to assume you were talking about your
flatmate!' I say. 'How old-fashioned of me not to pick up on
your bloody weird terminology. I mean, "primary" – couldn't
you just say "girlfriend", for fuck's sake? If you'd explained it
properly I certainly would not have slept with you!'

Liam looks cagey and I gasp in realisation. 'But of course
– you wanted a shag! Which is why you were so deliberately

vague.' My voice wobbles as the unfairness hits me. 'What did you expect tonight? A threesome?'

Liam and Lucy exchange sideways glances.

'My God, you did.'

'Well, I'm owed a threesome,' Liam says, sounding petulant. 'We haven't had two girls for a while.'

I cannot believe I've been so duped. I stare at Lucy, who has the grace to look slightly ashamed; she avoids my eye and picks at a splinter in the table. I feel as if I've walked into a complicated Woody Allen film.

'Don't you mind your boyfriend fucking other girls?' I ask bluntly.

Lucy winces, then raises her chin. 'Actually, jealousy is just a signpost for other insecurities and should be explored. You can't expect to satisfy all of your partner's sexual needs – it's unrealistic.'

Her words hit a raw nerve and I shake my head. 'That's fucking bleak, isn't it? I may as well give up now.'

Liam chuckles. 'It's not bleak – it's a more mature approach to commitment. We have a lot of married friends who are polyamorous; it keeps their relationships healthy.'

'Healthy, right.' I let out a bark of laughter.

Liam tilts his head. 'You've got to admit, it's quite a compromise to be with just one partner your entire life. You end up comparing them to other people, wondering what you're missing.'

'Well you shouldn't be so bothered about what you're *missing* if you already have someone by your side.' I'm suddenly trembling with anger. 'Haven't you ever heard the expression "don't have what you want, want what you have"?'

Lucy sighs. 'Look, Chloe, we have clear parameters and we're open with each other, so neither of us gets hurt.'

'Congratulations on being so emotionally stable!' I stand up and clap. 'You may be honest with each other but you certainly weren't with me. You crack on with your poly-bollocks; I'm off.'

I grab my coat and head back down the corridor. Liam follows me, pulling Lucy with him.

'Look, this has all been a big misunderstanding. When you've had a chance to digest it, give me a call. You can't deny we have great chemistry,' he pleads.

I turn at the front door and look at him scathingly. 'Liam, you're an arrogant prick. I'm not fawning over you along with the rest of your bloody harem.'

Liam puts a hand on my shoulder, his eyes glittering with a strange intensity. 'Aw, come on, Chlo, don't be like that.'

'Leave it, babe, she's not into it.' Lucy wraps both her arms around Liam's waist and glares at me. 'Next time pick someone who's not such a prude.'

I yank the front door open and run down the steps on wobbly legs. When I look back, Liam is staring after me and Lucy has her head buried in his chest.

'Arrrghhhh!' I let out a strangled cry of frustration as I cross Kings Road onto the beach. The sea is molten silver under a moonlit sky.

Well, that was a fucking disaster. Whoever heard of a love story that ends with three people walking off into the sunset hand in hand? Surely the whole point of finding 'the one' is supposed to be just that: one person you love over all others, one person to make you happy, one person who completes you.

I can't believe I was so desperate to get over Ant that I failed to see Liam was using me; his desire flattered my shredded ego. I feel like a total mug.

Tears roll down my cheeks and I swipe them away. If this had happened to Simone, I'm sure I'd be shaking my head at her naivety. I cringe as I remember smugly telling her not to waste her life crying over men that aren't worth it. Look at me now; I'm no better than her. It's time I took my own advice.

I reach Brighton Bandstand and climb the steps, walking down the black and white chequered tiles until I stand directly under the ornate dome. I gaze up at the buttery moon, which is nearly a full circle.

I'm so over all these negative emotions – shock, sadness, fear, loneliness, anger, bitterness, denial. I feel like a hungry vampire has sucked the life out of me and I miss optimistic, happy Chloe. I want her back.

'I'm done,' I say aloud, grasping onto the railings. It's time for me to start healing. And, right now, there's only one man I need to see. He might not want to speak to me but I'm not going to take no for an answer.

Chapter 14

I shift the litre bottle of gin under my armpit and hold down the buzzer. It's nearly 11 p.m. If he doesn't want to see me then I'll just say my piece and leave – at least I'd have got it off my chest.

Footsteps sound in the hall and the outdoor light comes on. The door swings inwards and Dom stands there wearing flamingo-pink shorts, a silver shirt, a cropped Fair Isle tank top and cowboy boots. His hair is even wilder than usual; it rises inches above his forehead like a cresting wave.

'Chloe, what a nice surprise!' He gives a delighted laugh. 'Yannis is away so I've been stuffing my face with sweets and singing on my karaoke machine. Come on up, we can do duets!'

'Wait, first I want to say something. Before we get carried away talking about other stuff.' I hold up a hand and Dom looks at me curiously.

'OK, sure. What's up?' He eyes the gin under my arm. 'Are you drunk?'

'Not yet. I just wanted to say thank you, Dom. These past few months I've felt so hopeless and crap and you've been my lifeline – my Brighton rock. I know it's tedious listening to someone else's pity party – I've bored myself enough – but you've never once complained. All you've done is try to cheer me up.' My voice breaks a little and Dom dips his head and gives me a bashful smile.

'I know we don't do "serious" too often,' I continue. 'But I want you to know how much your friendship means to me. I love you, Dom.'

'Oh!' Dom gulps and clasps his fists to his mouth. 'Chloe, are you trying to make me cry? You'll ruin my eyeliner!'

'No, no more tears,' I say firmly, pulling him into a hug.

'I love you too. Of course,' Dom says, resting his chin on my shoulder.

'Cool. Right then.' I hold the gin aloft and grin at him. 'Let's go get smashed.'

Yannis and Dom's flat is stunning; it makes mine look like a rabbit hutch. It has a massive open-plan living space with high ceilings, white wooden floorboards, floor-to-ceiling sash windows and a little wrought-iron balcony that overlooks the sea. The feature wall is lined with designer wallpaper covered in tropical fruit.

A sapphire-blue velvet sofa and chaise longue faces the large TV in the corner, which is hooked up to Dom's laptop and currently shows the lyrics to 'Dancing Queen'. A wireless microphone lies on the gold coffee table along with several bowls brimming with Candy Kittens sweets.

I throw myself into the scarlet love seat by the windows and curl up like a foetus in a plush womb. Dom mixes us some gin cocktails in the kitchen area, which is all black marble and stainless steel.

'I can't believe the cheek of Liam! What a self-serving greedy bastard,' he rants. 'And he sounded like such a nice guy.' He puts our glasses on the table, then flops onto the chaise longue opposite me. 'God, I wish I'd seen your face.'

'I know, I actually thought I was going mad when he first kissed her!' I take a deep swig of my drink. 'I'm so dim; Liam was taking me home for a threesome – like some cat bringing home a mouse – and I had no bloody idea. Duh!'

'They played you, darling, but you're not stupid. You're just honest and open. Unfortunately not everyone is.' Dom sighs and fiddles with the orange slice in his glass. His handsome face darkens with worry.

'Shit, is there trouble in gay paradise?' I sit up, alert.

'I don't know, maybe I'm overreacting. Yannis and I had a big row before he left for London. His sister's getting married in Greece this November, and even though she invited me, he says he'd rather not take me as his plus one.' Dom takes a jelly pineapple from the bowl and nibbles on it, his dark quiff drooping. 'Apparently he doesn't want to make his extended family uncomfortable and "rub it in their faces".'

'But you guys have the best relationship I've ever seen!' I exclaim.

'I know we do, I have no doubts about us. I thought he felt the same.'

'He does! He adores you, Dom.'

'Hmm, well now he's made me feel like his dirty little secret.'

'No! You're not dirty and you're not a secret.' I quickly crouch by his laptop and tap on the keyboard, then walk over to the door, turning dramatically, with my head bowed.

'What are you . . .' Dom tails off and starts grinning as I stride towards him in my best wide-legged Patrick Swayze gait.

'Nobody puts Dommy in the corner,' I say in a low growl, offering him my hand. 'C'mon.'

Dom pushes his hair off his face, grabs my hand and leaps to his feet as the lyrics to *Dirty Dancing*'s finale, 'I've Had the Time of My Life', appear on the TV screen.

I hand him a mic and grab one myself and we both start singing; pelvic-thrusting our way across the floorboards and screwing up our faces as we belt out the words: 'I owe it aaaaall to youuuuu-ooo.'

Two hours later and I'm feeling totally euphoric with singing power ballads back-to-back.

'They should prescribe karaoke as therapy,' I enthuse from the kitchen, topping up our glasses with ice and generous measures of gin. 'It makes you feel brilliant and not give a shit about the wankers.'

'Great idea!' Dom leans across the marble counter and clacks his glass heavily against mine. 'Karaoke therapy against bastards – fuck Ant, fuck Liam and fuck Yannis!'

'Yeah! We don't need them – we're fabulous without them.' I weave my way to the sofa and perch on the arm. The room seems a little blurry but in a good way.

'Right, time to get serious.' Dom grabs a hoodie from the back of the sofa and puts it on, then bends over his laptop. 'This is it, Chloe.'

Familiar piano chords fill the room and I jump up as the urgent guitar riff of Eminem's 'Lose Yourself' kicks in. Gin sloshes over the rim of my glass as I raise my hands.

Dom pulls the hood up over his head and adopts a casual rapper stance, fixing me with an intense stare. He points at me, asking if I had one shot to seize everything I ever wanted in one moment, would I capture it, or just let it slip?

I clench my fists in excitement; I love it when Dom sings Eminem – he knows every single lyric and expertly adopts his deep Detroit accent.

Dom jumps up onto the love seat and spits out the words fluidly to an invisible audience. I also leap onto the couch cheering him on, occasionally yelling out the odd phrase like 'mom's spaghetti' and 'oh, there goes Rabbit' until we get to the chorus, and then we're both singing in unison and waving our arms to our imaginary crowd.

'You *own* it, you better never let it go-go!'

I laugh triumphantly, feeling goose bumps run across my arms as the song plays out, tense and unrelenting. It's just as I'm bouncing in the air, singing at the top of my lungs, fuelled by gin, that it comes to me: I'm enough, just as I am.

The song ends and Dom collapses on the love seat, panting. 'That tune is quite the tongue twister.'

'Dom, I've just realised something,' I say dazedly, stepping off the sofa and tottering over to the sash windows on tiptoes. 'I *enjoy* being me – I *love* me.' I throw my arms wide.

'Yes, Chloe! I fucking love you too. And I love me. And I love . . . *gin*!' Dom shouts, tipping his head back.

I open the window and look out over the darkly shimmering ocean. A gust of night air buffs my cheeks.

'And I love Eminem. And I love my cowboy boots. And I love eating refined sugar while Yannis is away,' Dom continues defiantly, throwing a handful of jelly sweets at his mouth and missing.

'But I want to celebrate this feeling properly,' I say with fervour. 'Why is everyone so obsessed with *romantic* love? All the songs and films and books go on about it. What about loving *yourself*? Shouldn't that be just as important?'

'Totally. People should definitely love themselves more.' Dom blinks rapidly, trying to focus on me as I pace up and down, gesticulating drunkenly.

'Yeah, they should celebrate themselves! Well, you know what, Dom, I'm going to do it.'

'Do what?'

'I'm gonna own it and make a proper commitment to my*self*. I'll do what everyone else does when they find love – have a special ceremony!'

'What, d'you mean like . . .' Dom's eyes widen and an incredulous smile plays on his lips.

'Like a *wedding*. Yes. I'm going to marry myself.' I nod emphatically, about thirty times.

There is a pause and then Dom lets out a gurgling shriek, flapping his hands in front of his face. 'Omigod, Chloe, are you serious?'

'Yes, Dom, I am.' I put a hand to my chest. '*I* am perfect for *me*.'

'This is bloody brilliant. Oh shit. OK, hold it there. Let's do this the right way.' Dom falls to his knees by the coffee table, rummaging around in the bowl of sweets.

'Aha, here we go.' He holds up a red jelly ring with a yellow jewel on top. I take it and give it a quick lick.

'Raspberry, nice.'

Dom laughs, then claps his hands. 'Right, now go for it – propose.'

'OK.' I take a deep breath, then sink to one knee on the floorboards, bowing my head. 'Chloe Usher, I love you,' I announce, with deep passion. 'Will you marry me?'

I feel my pulse speed up as I slip the jelly ring on the fourth finger of my left hand. There is silence and I hear Dom give an emotional sniff. I clasp both hands to my chest, then rise to standing.

'Yes, Chloe, I will,' I say proudly.

'She will, she will,' Dom echoes, punching the air. 'This calls for bubbles, my darling!'

Swaying slightly, he goes over to the kitchen and pulls a bottle of vintage champagne from the wine rack along with two flutes. 'Obviously you'll need a proper wedding ring; that jelly won't last long.'

'True.' I hold my hand out in front of me. 'It'll need to be a bit different – a ring to mark my contentment as a single person.'

'A ringle!' Dom declares, popping the cork across the room.

'Yes – a ringle! Perfect!'

'You can get one especially made. Now, to the blushing bride.' Dom hands me a flute and we toast. 'This will be the wedding of the year! We have to make it public right now, so you don't back out. Shall we put it on Facebook?' He pulls his laptop towards him.

'Even better, I'll announce it on my blog,' I say.

'Yes! Your followers are going to love this.'

I squint at the laptop as I type my login. The screen's swimming a bit but I haven't felt this excited about writing for ages.

I type frantically, reading the words aloud to Dom, who chips in with the odd phrase. I'm so wired I actually feel like I have more clarity of thought than usual.

Dom takes a photo of me laughing and holding up my jelly ring and we upload it to the article.

After an hour of tinkering, we're onto our second bottle of fizz and the coffee table seems to be wobbling as I lean on it. My eyelids feel very heavy.

'OK, I think thass the best I can do. Ready?'

'Abslolootly,' Dom slurs, a big streak of eyeliner running down his cheek. 'Do it.'

I suck in my breath, then click 'publish'.

I'm Engaged . . . With Myself!

05.05.18

Helllooo reader!

You may've noticed my blog's been tumbleweed recently. That's cuz I've been going through a shitty time – and I've been doing less wandering and more WONDERING. And so, this blog post is not about a destination, but it is about a journey ☺☺

I won't over-share but basically I was cheated on and dumped by the man I thought I'd be with 4eva. Ughhh.

Surely that's not sposed to happen once you've finally found 'the one'? You're sposed to prance off into the sunset (rain clouds), scrape together enough cash for a flat, go to IKEA, get IVF treatment and ignore each other's signs of ageing, right?

WRONG! Turns out even a match made in heaven can turn out to be HELL – the one person you thought would always have your back can stab you right between the shoulder blades. NEWSFLASH: no one's relationship is 100 per cent safe!

So, what d'yu do when you're the unlucky reject? You quickly try to squash another guy into your boyfriend-shaped hole before anyone can shout 'single'!

Because there's something seriously wrong with single people, right? All of them have a hideous personality disease that isn't visible to the naked eye. Oh yes, they might **look** OK, they might even be vaguely attractive, but behind closed doors they line up their voodoo dolls in pairs and stick pins into them whilst furiously cry-wanking (cranking).

OK, that was sarcasm and I'm a bit (a lot) drunk. The fact is, tonight I've realised that it's time I stopped being so afraid of being ALONE and remembered how much I enjoy my own company. I don't need an 'other half' to 'complete me', I am already whole, thank youuu very much!

I'm sooo over finding 'the one' – I've decided I am 'THE ONE'. And I need to love myself. That's not an empty promise, I've gotta give myself the same respect I give everybody else. Let's face it, if you don't like yourself you end up being a bit of a wanker.

And so, dear readers, to honour my self-love in the traditional way, I'm going to put a ringle (single ring – see what I did there?) on it and have a WEDDING! Yes, you read that right: I'm going to marry myself!

My self-wedding will be in Brighton this summer and it's going to be MEGA! I'll keep you posted and hope to have an open invitation to my reception. After all, who doesn't love a big party?! YAY!

Yours forever wondering,
Chloe x

Chapter 15

The sound of the key in the lock jerks me awake.

'Gaaah!' I gargle drily, clawing the air and sending sofa cushions flying. It takes me a moment to realise I'm in Dom's lounge.

'Aha, hello, Chloe!' Yannis comes through the front door wheeling his tweed case behind him. He's dressed impeccably in a tailored chocolate-brown suit and tie. His black hair curls at his forehead and his trimmed circle beard neatly frames his chiselled jawline.

'Oww.' I sit up and the dull pain in my temples fires into life.

'What exactly were you taking last night?'

'Um.' I blink at him blearily, resting my chin on the back of the sofa. 'Nothing. Gin. Champagne. Whisky.' My voice crackles with dehydration.

'Uh-huh.' Yannis fills a glass of water at the kitchen sink and brings it over to me.

'Thanks, saviour.' I sit up cross-legged and gulp thirstily. Sunlight is flooding into the room under the blinds. 'What time is it?'

'It's 2 p.m. So, do you remember what you posted online at approximately 3 a.m. this morning?' He perches on the sofa arm, his hazel eyes crinkling behind his tortoiseshell glasses.

'I . . .' My memories whirr sluggishly as last night comes back to me: Liam's Quorn pie, him and Lucy kissing, the night sky from the Bandstand, making cocktails at Dom's, singing Eminem.

'Just the small matter of marrying yourself?'

Ah, fuck. I lift my hand; the red jelly ring is still on my finger.

'How do you . . . Oh God, I posted a blog about it, didn't I?' I groan. I should never ever publish things I've written whilst wasted. I made that rule years ago when I ill-advisedly posted a schmaltzy poem about the African sunset; it was so cringe-worthy. Luckily my followers thought it was a parody and I didn't correct them. 'Did you see it on Facebook then?'

'Did I see it? Chloe, you've pretty much broken the internet. Your blog has been shared all over Twitter and Facebook; your face is popping up in all of my feeds. Talk about a bombshell – people are going nuts over it.' Yannis shakes his head and chuckles.

'Shitting hell, really?' I gnaw at my cuticle. 'What are people saying about it? Do they think I'm insane?' I grab my phone from the coffee table but the battery's died.

'I mean, there are some very mixed reactions . . .' Yannis trails off diplomatically.

A jubilant roar echoes down the corridor and we turn as Dom skids through his bedroom door brandishing his phone, wearing only purple tartan boxer shorts and a green silk eye mask pushed up on his forehead.

'Chloeeeee! Your post has had three thousand shares already – result!' He starts doing a tribal dance of victory around the lounge, shaking his butt and holding both arms aloft.

'Told you, it's spreading like wildfire.' Yannis hands me his phone and I click through to my Twitter feed; there are loads of messages already.

@ChloeWanders This is the most offensive example of narcissism I've ever heard.
@ChloeWanders I'm usually a fan of your blog posts but this is RIDICULOUS, I think you should stick to travel writing #disappointed
@ChloeWanders Are u OK hun????

'Yeah but it's not exactly positive engagement, is it? Oh no, what have I done?!' I slump back on the cushions. 'Now no one will take my blog seriously!'

'So it isn't all a big prank then?' Yannis tilts his head.

'No, baby, it's no joke.' Dom slings an arm around Yannis's shoulders and gives him a kiss on the lips. 'It's a very brave act. We should all take a leaf out of Chloe's book and embrace who we are – no hiding.' He hovers inches away from Yannis's face and a frisson of frustration pulses between them.

'But I *could* quickly delete it and say it's a joke.' I go to put the kettle on and the floor lurches in front of me as if I'm on a ship.

'No way. You're seeing this through, my darling.' Dom follows me into the kitchen, rubbing a hand over his taut naked belly, and opens the fridge. He takes out a bowl of fruit salad and plonks it on the breakfast bar.

I feel like I'm sweating gin from every pore, so bend over to lean my face against the soothing cold marble of the counter. I'm getting the fear, big time.

'You can't force her to marry herself if she doesn't want to, Dommy.' Yannis perches on a stool, clicking his tongue.

'She does want to, though! You should have seen her last night; she was magnificent. Surely you don't regret what you said, Chloe?'

I roll my cheek on the marble. 'Well . . . no, I meant what I said. But I don't want to piss people off.'

'Ah well, you can't cast a pebble without causing ripples,' Dom says merrily, biting into a slice of watermelon that's almost as wide as his grin.

When I borrow Dom's charger and my phone lights up, there are loads of notifications cluttering the screen. I've got missed calls and social media messages from mates I haven't spoken to in ages; Emma and Mum have both tried calling me and I read Ant's text aloud:

> *Chloe, if this blog post is your idea of revenge, I think it's totally childish. I can't believe you're airing our dirty laundry so publicly – just as well I'm leaving town now. Thanks for nothing. Ant*

'Hah, he's the one who made your laundry dirty!' Dom exclaims. 'With a G-string covered in dog shit, to be precise.'

'That is a very good point,' I say, immediately replying:

> *It wasn't my dirty G-string though, was it, Ant? I hoped that you'd be happy for me but you're just thinking about yourself as usual. Bon voyage.*

'That's my girl, sod what Ant thinks.' Dom hands me some strong painkillers.

'Now, Chloe, if we can't find an official person to marry you, I'll quite happily get ordained so I can do it,' he says as he kisses me goodbye. 'I think I'd make a great minister. I've always fancied wearing a cassock and white collar.'

It's starting to spit with rain as I walk home along the beach and cold air whips around my bare legs.

I stop in at The Lobster to get a takeaway cappuccino. 'Can you make it a double espresso shot please, AJ?' I ask.

AJ, wearing his deckchair apron, nods and dashes around behind the bar, surprisingly light on his feet for such a large hulk of a man. He puts the coffee down in front of me and stares at the cup, then throws up his hands and comes around the bar.

'Chloe, I think it's utterly marvellous you're marrying yourself.' His eyes are shining. 'I always think your blog posts are interesting but today's post on self-love was an absolute revelation. I've been single for years now and I can tell you, I'm a damn sight happier than I was in my second marriage!'

'That's so good to hear, AJ, thanks!'

'We're supposed to be a sophisticated culture – I mean, look at how many different types of coffee we have, for goodness' sake.' AJ gestures to the coffee menu behind him. 'But we only ever focus on *one* kind of love – romance. It's all anyone ever talks about. I think self-love should get just as much airtime.'

'Exactly! I'm so glad you get it.' I sip my cappuccino. 'And you don't get lonely, on your own?'

AJ's forehead wrinkles as he contemplates this. 'No. If I need human contact I'll seek it. I'm hardly a social hermit.' He gives me a cheeky grin that suggests this is quite an understatement.

I smile back, intrigued. 'Well, thanks for the support, AJ, it's just what I needed.'

Feeling more positive, I head across the pebbles. It's raining harder and I pull my coat collar up around my ears. My hangover's making everything seem intense today; it's just a silly little blog post to make people think. It's not like I've properly committed to anything.

My phone vibrates in my pocket. Emma is calling me again.

'Hey, Em, sorry, my phone ran out of juice earlier.'

'Why the hell didn't you tell me about this crazy wedding?!'

'I only decided last night, at Dom's.'

'*Of course* Dom was involved. Christ, Chloe, can't you just be quietly single and miserable like everyone else?'

'Haha.'

'I'm serious, why do you always have to make such a big song and dance of everything? It's so unnecessary.'

'What?' I'm taken aback by her cranky tone. 'Why shouldn't I have a song and dance? You had a big flashy wedding!'

'Yes but – duh – I had a husband! Look, Chloe, I know your life is all cool and alternative but you can't totally lose touch with reality, it's embarrassing!'

'Sorry I embarrass you, Em,' I say hotly. 'God, you're starting to sound like Linda.'

'So? She's not that bad.'

'Are you joking? She was a total bitch at that lunch and you didn't exactly leap to my defence.'

'Do you blame me? Linda told me how you pinned Duncan up against the wall and grilled him about Ant. There's no need to lash out at us just because our lives are sorted.'

'What? Duncan didn't mind! Do you realise how difficult it was for me hearing about Ant's new girlfriend? Imagine how you'd feel if James cheated on you!'

'I'd deal with it like an adult. Not get my gay best friend to come save me. Honestly, Dom is so juvenile, he's such a bad influence on you.'

'Don't you dare say that! He's been right by my side this whole time, which is more than I can say for you!' I'm yelling now, and small globules of spit fly from my mouth. A group of people walking past turn their heads to look at me.

'What, so now *I'm* neglecting *you*? I'm the one who's stuck inside all day bringing up children.'

'I bloody know that, Emma, and I understand how hard it is to be a mother, OK?'

'You don't have the first clue, Chloe. And now you're making a mockery of the whole thing.'

'I'm not mocking you, Emma! Why are you taking this so personally? For Christ's sake, the entire universe is centred around marriage and family.'

'Yes, cos that's what normal people do.'

'Wow, so now I'm not *normal*. I'll understand if you want to disown me.'

'Don't be so dramatic.'

'I think you'll find you're the one overreacting. I'm going.'

I hang up. My whole body is trembling and the rain is hammering down, soaking my shoulders.

Emma and I have never spoken to each other like that before. It's like we've just lifted the lid of a can of ugly worms. Is this what she's always thought about me?

I consider calling her back and smoothing things over but a stubborn part of me refuses. There's clearly something bigger going on between us, but right now I don't have the mental capacity to deal with it.

Bonnnnnnnnng. Bonnnnnnnnnggggggggg. When I get home, I'm greeted by a deep oscillating noise that makes my teeth rattle. Dora's ears flatten against her head and she growls.

Great, Saffron's got her gong out.

I head straight for the sofa in the lounge regardless, and stretch out on the cushions.

Saffron is sitting cross-legged by the roof terrace doors in her red silk kimono. Her dark beaded dreads hang down her back, almost touching the floor. The gong is in front of her; a massive bronze disc suspended on a wooden frame with wheels. Her eyes are closed and she's muttering some chant as she strikes it with a fluffy mallet.

I turn the TV on, flicking through Netflix and selecting *Love Island*, which I turn up full volume.

Saffron opens her eyes mid-strike.

'Excuse me?'

'Yes?' I prop my head up with my hand to look at her.

'I'm practising.'

'What's to practise? Don't you just hit it over and over again?'

'No, actually it takes a great deal of skill to prime it and produce the right notes.' Saffron sniffs.

'Right, well can you do it in your room?'

'No – I was here first!' Saffron strikes the gong and a harsh sound punctuates her objection. Dora whines and slopes off down the corridor with her tail between her legs.

'That's not fair; you spent every evening practising in here last week. Do you really expect me to stay in my little bedroom while you make all this din in here?'

'God, most people would love living with a meditation teacher!' Saffron yells, jumping to her feet.

'I've got nothing against meditation – there's just a time and a place.'

'That's crap. You're the least spiritual person I've ever met. I can't believe you have the audacity to pretend you're so enlightened!'

'What do you mean?' I frown in surprise as she paces agitatedly up and down.

'You copied me. I should tell everyone you're a fraud!'

'Saffron, what are you talking about?'

'Your blog post about self-love!' She rounds on me, her

eyes flaming. 'My favourite yoga guru shared it this morning. That was totally *my* idea!'

'Huh?' I blink at her a few times. This conversation has taken a strange turn.

Saffron makes a squealing noise, then storms out of the room. Dora reappears in the doorway, cocking her head.

'Don't ask me, pup,' I say.

'This!' Saffron comes back, holding out her Buddha tea towel and reading the words: '"Peace comes from within, do not seek it without." *I* showed you this; *I* introduced you to the ways of Buddhism. And now you're pretending you've had this big epiphany about self-compassion.'

I stare at her, astounded. This has to be the most unexpected reaction I've had so far.

'Saff, I can promise you, the tea towel had nothing to do with my decision,' I say carefully.

'Yeah *right*. Well, it's backfired now anyway, hasn't it.' Saffron rolls her gong back against the wall. 'Everyone thinks you're unhinged.'

'Not everyone, actually.' I pick up my phone and tap on Facebook. I have hundreds more notifications; my mates are definitely finding the news hilarious but they're a lot nicer about it than some of the strangers on Twitter.

'There's no way you'll pull this wedding off with any dignity. You're an insult to spirituality; look at the trash you watch on TV!' Saffron gestures at the screen, where various couples are writhing about under duvets, grunting and squeaking in a poor attempt at subduing their orgasms.

'Erm, actually *Love Island* is very anthropologically interesting.' I insist as she stamps out of the room again. I roll my eyes and scroll through the Facebook comments. One of my ex-colleagues has put a row of cry-laughing emojis, saying: *I hate to rain on your parade, mate, but marrying yourself can't possibly be recognised by the law or church.*

'He's right, you know,' I say aloud to Dora. 'There's no way it's going to be legal.'

With something like relief, I turn my attention back to *Love Island*, where a heated debate about fake boobs is raging. Tomorrow I'll go to the register office – if self-marriage isn't possible then I'll just cancel the whole thing and blame it on the rigid conventions of society.

Chapter 16

The register office is in Brighton Town Hall, just around the corner from Top Banana. I call first thing on Monday and make a lunchtime appointment, telling the receptionist I'm a journalist with a few questions on marriage.

I lay awake late last night, fretting about the reactions my blog post has caused. I was worried my colleagues would take the piss this morning but luckily most of my floor's empty; the fashion team are in the boardroom with a new client called Pelican – a high-end clothing label that does prints and textures inspired by wild creatures. Giles has gone all out trying to impress them; our office has been decorated like a jungle, with vines and camouflage netting draping the walls, and there's a wildlife-themed soundtrack blasting out over the speakers, including Toto's 'Africa' and Basement Jaxx's 'Back to the Wild'. There's even paper animal masks on everyone's desks; I got a gorilla mask which I'm currently wearing pushed back on top of my head.

At midday, I turn off my computer, remove my mask, and slip out of the office. Brighton Town Hall is a grand cream building with giant fluted columns. I announce myself at the main desk and the receptionist directs me to the waiting area where several couples are sitting. They look breathless and excited and keep squeezing each other's hands. Every now and then they glance over at me, sitting on my own; they're probably wondering why I'm there without a partner. I just offer them a mysterious smile and flick through the out-of-date wedding magazines.

Eventually I hear the *swish swish* of cheap fabric on plump thighs and look up to see a large bald man with a pallid complexion regarding me.

'Miss Usher? Kevin Bliss, Superintendent Registrar.' He offers me a damp palm to shake. 'Please come with me.'

I jump up and follow him to his office, which smells distinctly of burgers.

'Which publication is this interview for?' he says, gesturing to the chair opposite his desk.

'It's called *Chloe Wanders*, a lifestyle and travel blog.' I sit down.

'Ah, a blog.' He seems underwhelmed. 'Well, I have a lot of appointments today so can only answer a few questions. What do you want to know?'

'So, basically, I'm researching the idea of, uh, self-marriage.' I take out my notepad and biro. 'Is it possible to marry yourself?'

There is silence while he waits for the punchline.

'Like, could such a ceremony be legally recognised?' I press. 'Have you heard of anyone doing it before?'

'No, I certainly have not!' Kevin finds his voice. 'I heard about that artist marrying a rock and I think there were stories about someone marrying their dog – but it's all absolute nonsense of course. Why on earth would someone want to marry themselves?'

'As a gesture of self-acceptance, you know, a celebration of being happy with yourself.' I shift in my chair as he frowns at me; he reminds me a bit of my headmaster at secondary school.

'And what is wrong with having a big birthday party?' He leans back, folding his arms across his protruding belly.

I stare at my notepad, thinking hard. 'Well . . . because birthdays aren't really rituals, are they? Everyone has them every year. But a wedding is a one-off milestone which marks a step up in life. Marriage is supposed to be, like, a stamp of approval – so that you can go ahead and live "happily ever after".'

'Yes, and finding a partner to share your life with is a basic human need; married couples are the foundation of society.'

I scribble in my notepad. 'I don't see why that has to be the only option. Sure, everyone needs meaningful relationships in their life, but there are loads of ways to connect with other people. I just don't see why everything should be geared towards getting coupled up. I think sometimes you need to stand in your own power and I can't think of a better way to make this point than by having a self-wedding.'

'Hang on, so you are actually planning on marrying yourself are you?' Kevin massages his temples and looks at me with mild despair.

I wrinkle my nose sheepishly. 'Uh, yeah. That's the plan. I mean, there aren't any other rituals out there to celebrate self-love, are there? I thought I'd just borrow from the format of the wedding for now and redress the balance a bit. As a single person I should be just as entitled to have a significant rite of passage.'

Kevin lowers his head for a moment, breathing heavily.

'Miss Usher, I do not appreciate time-wasters. The answer to your question is a resounding *no*. It is not possible to marry yourself.' He opens a folder on his desk and runs a stubby finger down the page. 'Marriage is, and I quote, "the union of *two* people to the *exclusion* of everybody else".' He looks up, a pious fire in his gimlet eyes. 'Do you understand?'

'See, this is what I mean; "the *exclusion* of everyone else" – it's a bit harsh. No wonder single people can feel so isolated.' I glare back at Kevin, and in these few mute seconds, the doubt that's been gnawing at me for the past day falls away. I blink in fascination. I've never felt more certain about anything in my life. I swear I hear a sort of choral humming, and it's not just the fax machine in the corner.

'Mr Bliss, thank you for your time.' I snap my notebook shut decisively. 'You've been a great help. I am going to have a cultural ceremony to celebrate my unity, to the *inclusion* of everybody else. Whether it's legally recognised or not.' I stand up.

Kevin also hefts himself to his feet, his jowls quivering with affront. 'Miss Usher, this is utterly ludicrous. You will not be taken seriously, I assure you.'

'Then consider me one of life's clowns.' I bow at him with a flourish and back out of the room.

As I return to my desk, I see Verity and Simone; they're both wearing animal-print dresses and masks and carrying a tray of tea through from the kitchen. I wave at them but they look straight ahead as if they haven't seen me. They're probably keen to get back to the boardroom to schmooze Pelican.

I feel a spike of longing; I haven't worked on an exciting account for months now. I hoped that at least now Verity's my line manager she'd give me opportunities to stretch myself, but she just gave me a car parking client who has a tiny budget and is notorious for being difficult.

As I open the document I'm working on for Best Bathrooms, Jess comes jogging across the room, a monkey mask pushing her blonde hair back from her forehead.

'Chloe, is it all a hoax or what?' She pulls up a chair next to me, her wide eyes searching my face. 'Marrying yourself? I nearly died when I read it on Facebook last night!'

'Yup, I'm going to do it.' I smile at her firmly.

'Fair play to you.' She cracks up. 'I'd do it myself if I had the chance. I fucking *crave* my own company. I'd give anything to have the whole double bed to myself for just one night without John snoring away next to me like an old warthog.'

I giggle as she does an impression of her husband, gargling at the back of her throat, and the few people at their desks look over, frowning.

'And then he'll throw a big hairy limb over me as if I'm just a pillow.' Jess shudders. 'I mean, it's practically abusive; who can possibly fall asleep under those circumstances?'

'Yeah, I do sleep better on my own,' I admit.

'And don't get me started on meal times – John is the noisiest eater I have ever heard,' Jess continues. 'He doesn't just chew his food, he *sucks* it at the same time!' She does another loud demonstration, causing Theresa to tut pointedly. Jess ignores her.

'I've started eating dinner early, with the kids. I can't bear to be in the same room as John when he's chowing down.'

'D'you know, I think there's actually a word for that.' I open a Google browser. 'Yes, look, there you go: "misophonia" – it's a phobia of specific sounds.'

'Hmm.' Jess looks unconvinced. 'A phobia of husbands, more like.'

'Hubbaphobia?' I suggest and Jess screeches with laughter, slapping my knee.

'Yes, Chloe, that's exactly it. Hubbaphobia!'

It's difficult to concentrate on the scintillating copy I'm writing about waterproof adhesives because Dom keeps pinging Pinterest boards of wedding inspiration ideas to my phone. I'm just looking at a bizarre mermaid wedding dress when Mum calls me for the fourth time today.

'Hey, Ma, I'm at work,' I answer.

'Yeah, I know, but I logged on to the Facebook this morning and there's all this hullabaloo about you being engaged.'

'It's not "the Facebook", Mum, it's just Facebook.'

Mum only got a Facebook account last year; Shirley helped her set one up. She treats it with great suspicion; friend requests terrify her and she's always worrying that people are spying on her.

'Did you write that thing about marrying yourself? Or was it someone having a laugh? You should report them, you know – they shouldn't be allowed to use your photo.'

'It's fine, it's my blog, Mum. I was going to call you tonight and explain . . .'

'Hahahahaha!' Mum cackles. 'You've got the right idea, Chlo, who needs men? Fuck the lot of them!'

'Shhh! It's not like that, Mum,' I say, cupping my hand around my phone.

'I don't blame you, girl. I'd do just as well marrying my bird table than another man.'

'Yeah, but this is about me loving my*self*. I reckon I'll have the ceremony some time in August.'

'What, in real life? Not on the Facebook?'

'Yes, in real life – it'll be a real wedding.'

Mum draws in a sharp breath. 'This is my fault, isn't it? With my failed marriages. I've set a bad example to you.'

'No, Mum – it's not a negative thing.'

'Are you inviting your father and that Janice? Because I'm not sure I could bear to see them all over each other, Chlo, not with me on my own all these years.'

I snort. 'Believe me, Dad and Janice aren't likely to rub your nose in it with PDAs; they've had separate bedrooms for as long as I can remember.'

'But how sad will it look if the mother of the bride hasn't got a partner?'

'Mum,' I sigh in exasperation. 'The *bride* isn't going to have a partner – that's the whole point!'

I look up as I hear a clinking in the kitchen. Jess is lining champagne flutes up on the table. It's probably something to do with the new client. 'I've got to go. I'll ring you later.'

I stand up as Simone rushes through with a bunch of gold helium balloons and starts tying them up around the office.

'Hey, Sim, what's going on?' I call to her and she frowns.

'As if you don't know.' She tugs her zebra mask down around her neck.

'You want a hand?' I walk over and take a balloon from her, tying it to the top of the jukebox. 'Hey, it was cool hanging out at yours, d'you want to come to mine next time? I've bought the new *It* – scary clown fest!'

Last week was the first time I've been to Sim's flat. We were supposed to be watching girl-power movies but then realised we both had a passion for horror and ended up scaring ourselves stupid with slasher films.

'I don't think it's a good idea under the circumstances,' Simone says coolly, moving away from me.

'What circumstances?' I stare after her as the rest of the fashion team file back onto our floor.

'Did you have a good meeting with Pelican?' I ask Verity as she puts a folder on her desk. She scowls, looking thunderous.

'What's wrong?'

I'm interrupted by Giles, wearing a leopard-print suit and a lion mask on top of his head, standing on the kitchen bench and clapping his hands.

'Attention, troops! As per the email I sent, we're finishing a little early today. We've just had a very successful meeting with Pelican, I think they were really swayed by our wildlife theme today. And also not one but *two* of our members of staff have a very special announcement!'

He holds a bottle of champagne in my direction. 'On behalf of the company I'd like to offer both Chloe and Verity congratulations on their engagements!'

'You guys!' I laugh appreciatively as Giles pops the champagne cork across the room, and suddenly 'Chapel of Love' is blaring out on the jukebox and my colleagues are pulling party poppers and cheering.

I turn to Verity, holding out my arms for a hug. 'Yaaaaay! So Gav finally got round to asking? You must be so happy!'

But Verity backs away from me, shaking her head. 'Don't pretend you didn't see it,' she spits.

'See what?' I drop my arms.

'The adorable selfie of Gav and Vee on the beach at sunset.' Simone stands by Verity's side like a protective bodyguard. 'Gav wrote "She Said Yes" in the sand.'

'Ah, how sweet – he's such a romantic!'

'He built me a sandcastle and put my ring on the top. And he brought a picnic basket of champagne and strawberries.' Verity's voice trembles.

'Well, that's awesome, isn't it?!' I don't get why she has a face like a slapped arse.

'It was!' she shrieks. 'I put it on Insta on Saturday night and it got the most likes I've *ever* had. But then *you* suddenly decide to announce your pathetic engagement and steal my limelight.' Verity glowers. 'It's such a sad attempt at attention-seeking!'

'Oh, honestly, I didn't even see your announcement. I'm not marrying myself to spite you, Verity!' I object.

'Yeah *right*. Ever since I had the promotion you just can't deal with my superiority.' Verity's red lips are stretched thin with fury. 'After all I've done for you, helping you with your love life and your career.'

'Oh yeah, your advice has been invaluable.' I laugh sarcastically.

'Massive congrats, girls!' Jess says, carrying over a rainbow cake with mini sparklers on top. She puts it down on my desk. 'Can I see your rings?'

Verity raises her left hand to reveal a huge sapphire glinting on her finger. 'It's very rare,' she says in hushed tones, tilting her hand so that it catches the overhead light. 'Gav had it imported from Sri Lanka.'

'Bloody hell!' Jess breathes out in admiration and they all stare at it transfixed.

'Where's your ring, Chloe?' Simone snarls. 'I bet you don't have one.'

I hold up my left hand with similar reverence. I'm wearing another jelly ring; this one is green. Dom gave me a whole bag of them.

'It's made from the finest gelatine.' I gaze at it lovingly. 'And I'll be getting a ringle made for the wedding.'

'What the fuck?' Verity recoils in disgust. 'Total piss-take.'

'Ah, the blushing brides.' Giles joins us, looking at me with unusual interest. 'Chloe, I'm impressed by the splash you've made on social media. What a fascinating idea you've come up with, marrying yourself. Have you been reading that book I gave you – *Rising Above Average?*'

'Mm, yeah,' I lie, stuffing a slice of rainbow cake in my mouth. The book is sitting untouched in the drawer of my desk.

'Maybe you're not the wallflower I thought you were.' Giles's mouth twitches as he jokingly bumps his shoulder against mine. His aftershave smells of cloves.

'Wallflower!' I protest, spitting coloured crumbs.

'I thought *I* was supposed to be your rising star.' Verity stamps her foot, looking furious.

'Verity, you know I think highly of you,' Giles says smoothly. 'It just seems Chloe has a knack for pushing people's buttons, which is the whole point of PR. In fact, it might be worth her helping you with Top Banana's entry to the Most Awesome Place to Work awards. What do you think?' He smiles at me.

'Yes, that'd be great,' I say.

'But I've already filled in the bit about company culture,' Verity says sulkily. 'Like, I talked about our sushi nights, foosball table and life-drawing classes and stuff.'

'Jolly good.' Giles blithely ignores her outrage. 'Chloe can have a look at the application too – "many hands" and all that. I know weddings take a lot of organising but please make sure they don't take priority over this project. I'm relying on you, girls.'

He gives us a double thumbs-up then walks briskly to his office, shutting the door and flicking on his red light.

Jess moves away to refill glasses and Keith dad-dances over to us as 'Crocodile Rock' starts playing, carrying a bowl of crisps and with a plastic snake around his neck.

'So, your fella finally decided to make an honest woman of you, eh, Chloe?' He winks.

Verity rolls her eyes. 'Keep up, Keith. Chloe's boyfriend dumped her. And now she's marrying her*self* because no one else will have her. It's the most important time of my life and she's ruining it.'

Keith blinks rapidly as he digests the information. 'Gosh, you modern women. It's a whole new world. Have you set a wedding date then?'

'I'm thinking about an August wedding,' I reply.

'Bloody typical,' Verity fumes. 'You would have to have your wedding first!'

'What? I don't even know when yours is!'

'December: I'm having a winter wonderland. If you copy me in anything else I'll report you to the police.'

I snort. 'What exactly will you report me for?'

'Sabotage and harassment.' Verity holds a warning finger up close to my face.

'And stalking. You've already got a history of it,' Simone chimes in.

'Would any of you girls like a crisp? They're posh ones.' Keith holds his bowl out, looking uncomfortable. Simone reaches for a handful and Verity slaps her wrist.

'Simone, I told you – no saturated fats before the wedding. I'm not having plump bridesmaids!'

She gives Keith a withering look and barges past him towards the kitchen with a sheepish Simone in tow.

I stare after them, biting my lip. Great, so Verity's taken my self-proposal as some sort of nuptial challenge. The last thing I need is Verity as an enemy; she's a pretty difficult friend as it is.

'Marrying your*self*.' Keith brushes crisp crumbs from the front of his jumper, looking baffled. 'Can't say I understand you independent women, but then I'm a bit old-fashioned, me. I was chuffed to bits when I walked my daughter up the aisle; lovely chap, her Paul. Nice to know she's got someone looking after her.'

'Yeah, I'm sure it is.' I have a sudden memory of Ant surprising me when I could barely move with flu last winter – he turned up at my flat with a basket of all my favourite foods, then wrapped me in blankets on the sofa and cooked me dinner. 'You stay there, my little sausage,' he said. 'Let me take care of you.' I remember how loved I felt then, despite my burning chest and streaming eyes.

'I'm sure your father would want the same for you,' Keith is saying.

'Hmm. I'm telling him this Saturday.' I scoop some saturated fats from his bowl. Dad's on holiday at the moment and he never checks social media, so I'm planning on breaking the news in person. He and Janice are quite conservative so they'll probably need a bit of time to digest it. 'I'm sure he'll be pleased; all he wants is for me to be happy, after all.'

Chapter 17

Dad lives with Janice in London Fields. It's nearly midday when I get off at the train station and walk through the park to their house for Saturday lunch. The sun is shining high in a cloudless blue sky and groups of hipsters lie on the grass, drinking beers and ham-fistedly trying to light barbecues. I duck as a frisbee whizzes past my head.

I walk past the lido and onto leafy Richmond Road. Dora would love it here but Janice won't allow dogs in the house; she says she doesn't want their claws scratching the expensive wooden flooring. She isn't much better with children; whenever I visited as a teenager she used to look at me as if she wanted to tidy me away with the old newspapers. I don't know how Emma copes with such a frosty mother. The last time I was here, on Boxing Day, Janice got cross with Maisie for getting sticky fingerprints on the door jamb and made her sit quietly on the sofa, telling her 'children should be seen and not heard'. I could tell it really upset Emma; she disappeared to the bathroom for ages.

I haven't spoken to Emma since our row on the phone last Sunday, so was pleased to hear she's coming to lunch today. I'm hoping it'll be a good opportunity to make amends; we're usually a united front when it comes to our parents.

As I approach their semi-detached Georgian house, I see Janice in the front garden snipping at a pot of fresh herbs. She's wearing a plum pencil skirt, blouse and beige heels, and her white-blonde hair is so neatly coiffed it doesn't move as she turns.

'Hi, Chloe!' She waves her secateurs in the air. 'Dressed for the occasion, I see!' She titters at her own joke and I look down at myself. I'm wearing my army-print jacket, a T-shirt, rolled-up jeans and flip flops – clearly too casual for Janice.

'How was Dubai?' I cross the driveway to give her a quick hug, and her pearl necklace clacks against my collarbone.

'I was impressed with our hotel, very comfortable. Good for shopping too, you ought to go.'

'Hmm, I've never really fancied it – I've read that Dubai is built by slaves and driven by hyper-consumerism.'

'Haha, typical Chloe!' Janice holds me at arm's length and inspects me. 'Now, you've lost a bit of weight, I think?'

'Yeah, a bit, I've been doing more running and hula hoop classes.'

'Hula hoop? Honestly!' Janice shakes her head. 'Your fringe has grown far too long; you'll get a squint.'

I follow her through the open front door and her heels clip the walnut flooring in emphatic staccato, drowning out every other word as she gives me grooming advice. I'm tempted to point out that high heels probably do more damage than dogs, but manage to bite my tongue.

As we pass down the corridor, I glance into Janice's overly floral boudoir, then Dad's minimalist bedroom with its olive-green walls and leather chesterfield.

We walk across the pristine lounge, which always feels like a show home, and, with a tug of affection, I see Dad sprawled out on the swing seat in the adjoining conservatory. He's wearing navy corduroys and a speckled jumper, reading the *Financial Times*.

'Hi, Pops!' I sing. He lowers the paper and slides his reading glasses down his nose, looking mildly surprised for a minute as he re-engages with the real world.

Then he puts his glass of wine down, unfolds his rangy form and stands up to give me a big dad-hug. I breathe in his spicy aroma of Imperial Leather soap and French cigars. When I was younger, I used to steal one of his jumpers to take back home to Mum's, sleeping with it under my pillow because it still smelled of him.

'How was your holiday?' I ask.

'Tedious.' His voice rumbles in my ear. 'I was mainly working.'

Dad works for a top auditing and tax services firm and Janice is a property manager, but if Janice has her way, they'll probably soon retire and spend their golden years seeing the world from the deck of a luxury cruise ship.

'Janice, bring Chloe a glass,' he calls, gesturing me to the armchair. 'Now tell me, what's going on in Chloe's world? I hope you've severed all contact with that moron Anthony?'

I sink back into the foamy cushions and take off my jacket. 'Pretty much.' I haven't seen Dad since Ant and I broke up. When we've spoken on the phone I've kept the details to a bare minimum. It feels weird talking to Dad about how betrayed I feel because I know he did exactly the same, if not worse, to Mum.

'You deserve better, Chloe. He was a lily-livered layabout – what you need is a real man, not some . . . recruitment agent.' Dad nods as Janice brings in another wine glass and bowls of snacks.

'Thanks, Janice.' I pour myself some wine from the bottle, which is already half empty. 'What does it take to be a "real man" then, Pops?'

'Well, Ant wasn't exactly an alpha male.' Dad sighs and crosses his socked feet. 'He was a bit scatty and sensitive, if you ask me. What you need is a powerful man, someone who has clear direction. You know, like Emma's James – he's very competitive, from what I gather.'

'Yeah, alright, we all know how amazing James is.' I wrinkle my nose. It's always bugged me how much Dad idolises James just because he earns a huge salary at a London advertising agency. Personally I find him quite aloof; his work rules his life and he's always staying late at meetings or taking business calls on his mobile.

'I don't really care about status, Dad. It'd just be nice to go out with someone who was honest and respectful. Not cheating on me would be a good start.'

'Hmph. Indeed.' Dad's face twitches as he tops up his glass. 'And how's work? Emma mentioned something about a promotion.'

'Ah, yes, well actually they're putting it on hold for the moment.' Dad frowns in disappointment. 'But my boss has just given me the important job of raising Top Banana's profile. I'm going to strengthen our community links in Brighton – it's really interesting.'

'They need to give you a pay rise soon; at your age you ought to be earning considerably more.'

'Yes, Dad, I realise that,' I say through gritted teeth.

'Ooh look, there she is!' Janice trots through the conservatory and out the back door as Emma's Volvo pulls up in the driveway.

'When are you going to learn to drive, Chloe?' Dad leans forward to watch Janice greet Emma. 'I don't know how you've managed without a car all this time.'

'I haven't ever really needed one. I walk most places, or get the train.'

We both stand up as Emma comes in.

'You haven't brought the kids?' I ask. I was looking forward to playing with Maisie.

'No, James is looking after them at home.' Emma stands stiffly as I kiss her on the cheek.

'It's good for him to bond with them, anyway,' Janice says, patting Emma's shoulder. 'While you enjoy some adult company.'

'Hmm, we'll see how he gets on; he hardly ever has to look after them both.'

'Ha, I never knew one end of a nappy from the other,' Dad says cheerfully as he kisses Emma. 'Would you like a small wine?'

'Go on then. I guess we're celebrating, after all.' Emma raises a sardonic eyebrow at me.

'Are we?' Janice's head tilts like a bird's as she looks between us, immediately picking up on our tension.

I glare at Emma; I want to wait until Dad's had a few more drinks before I tell them my nuptial news.

'Actually, Emma, my job promotion is on hold. So it's a bit premature to celebrate yet,' I say.

'That's odd, you seemed so certain.' Emma's blue eyes are cold; she's clearly not ready to smooth things over. I feel indignation rising. I haven't done anything wrong, so if she expects me to grovel she's got another thing coming.

'Lunch is ready, come on through!' Janice trills. I jump up and follow her into the lounge, pleased our stilted conversation has been interrupted. Emma has barely looked at me since she arrived and has deliberately kept Dad and Janice talking about their holiday so we don't have to communicate.

'Ta-daaaa!' Janice throws her arms wide as we enter the dining room. Emma and I scan the room in puzzlement.

'What?' Emma says.

'The carpet!' Janice tuts. 'It's brand new! Cost an arm and a leg.'

'Ahh.' Emma prods the cream carpet with the toe of her ballet slipper. 'Very nice, Mum.'

'Yes, very . . . soft,' I agree, looking down.

'Come on then, I'm bloody starving.' Dad moves towards his chair at the head of the table, eyeing the huge dish of lasagne in the centre.

'Hang on!' Janice suddenly cries. 'Napkins.'

We all hover behind our chairs as she rummages in the chest of drawers, pulls out some purple napkins and pushes them into decorative silver rings, giving a satisfied 'there' as she puts them down and we all sit.

I reach to unroll my napkin but Janice yelps, 'Wait!' and my hand goes back to my lap.

'Music!' She bends over the stereo. 'Now let me see, what shall we play . . . ah, I know: Ed Sheeran. He's a bit of a dish, no?'

Emma and I laugh politely without comment. Janice settles back down with a wiggle and beams as Ed starts crooning.

'That's better.' She slides her napkin from its ring and unfolds it onto her skirt. We all follow suit and Dad uncorks a bottle of red wine.

'So, Emma, have you enrolled Maisie at Marsden's yet?' Janice asks as she spoons lasagne onto our plates. Marsden's is a highly esteemed prep boarding school in Surrey; Janice has been going on about it since Maisie was born.

'No, Mum, I told you, I'm not sending Maisie there. I don't want her to board.' Emma scowls.

'She wouldn't have to board for a few years yet; it'd just be good to get her familiar with the place.'

'I don't want her to board at all.'

'Why ever not? Didn't do you any harm, did it?' Janice's tone is light but there's a steeliness to her smile that makes me shudder.

'It did do me harm,' Emma says quietly, helping herself to salad, and I feel a pang of sympathy for her.

Unfortunately, when she was in her teens, Emma was bullied by some girls who were jealous of her popularity. She confided in me that just before bedtime they used to soak her sheets and steal the light bulbs in her room so that she had to change the covers by torchlight. Janice refused to let her move schools, insisting it was just 'girlish pranks', but Emma and I campaigned so hard to go to the same sixth form that eventually she gave in.

'And how's James getting on with the Porsche account?' Dad changes the subject. 'I told my pals at golf that he's behind the recent advert. They couldn't believe the costs involved.'

'He's working really hard on it. They're very demanding,' Emma says.

'And Ant, is he doing well at work?' Janice's beady grey eyes fix on me. 'Or is he still distracted by that DJ business?'

'Ant and I broke up in January, Janice.' I spear a cherry tomato.

Janice's bland expression wavers at my sharp tone and she pats her hair. 'Oh yes, your father did tell me.'

'Good riddance,' Dad mutters.

'And is there a new man on the scene? Any dark, handsome stranger sweeping you off your feet?' Janice wiggles her head.

'I'm not sure I'd care how handsome he was if a stranger knocked me off my feet.' I smirk at Dad but he's gazing out of the window ruminatively, swirling his wine in his glass.

'But surely one of your friends can set you up with a nice eligible bachelor? I hope you're not being too fussy. Emma, you must know some suitable men?' Janice purses her lips.

'I'm not sure Chloe is bothered about finding a partner, Mum.' Emma looks at me sideways.

'What do you mean? Of course she wants a partner.' Janice looks perplexed.

'Thanks, Emma.' I take a deep breath. 'I actually have something to tell you both. Dad, will you listen for a moment please?' Dad's head swivels round.

'Well, the fact is . . . I'm going to marry myself, in a cultural ceremony in August. I'd love it if you both came.'

There's a silence and Dad's brow plunges, then he lets out a strangled bellow. 'Good God, you're just like your bloody mother.' He says it like he's got a bad taste in his mouth.

Janice gives a slightly hysterical giggle, then looks down at her plate miserably.

I stare at Dad. 'What exactly do you mean by that?'

'A man-hater.' He pours himself more wine. His lips are stretched thin.

'I don't hate men! You just said yourself that I deserve better and I agree. My wedding is to celebrate my self-worth.'

'Oh, this whole self-respect business is absolute tosh!' Dad explodes. 'Joy kept on about that when she left me and now look at her – a frigid old divorcee.'

'Don't call her that!' I yell.

Janice's hands flutter on the tablecloth. 'Obviously this is some sort of joke, Roger – as if Chloe would humiliate herself in public like that.'

'It's not a joke, Mum; Chloe wrote a ranty blog post and now it's all over the internet,' Emma says.

'It wasn't ranty!' I say.

'Erm, slagging off couples and saying everyone's relationship is doomed? I would call that a rant.'

'I didn't say that! And actually, I've had emails from journalists asking me for interviews,' I snap. '*They* think I'm making an interesting cultural comment.'

'You are not speaking to the papers! If my colleagues find out about this, I'll be a laughing stock,' Dad growls.

'Yes I am! And I came here today to ask for your blessing, Dad – I was going to ask you to give me away.'

'Give you away to what?' Dad barks. 'Thin air!'

Emma laughs and I turn on her. 'Since when did you became so small-minded, Emma? I'm presuming you aren't interested in being my maid of honour?'

'Ha – no way! I don't want any part in your stupid wedding. And don't call me small-minded!' Emma lashes back, her face screwed up in anger. 'You think you're so "out there", don't you? In your stupid Brighton bubble. Well, one day you'll turn round and all your drifter mates will have moved on and you'll be completely on your own. At least I'll have my family to look after me.'

Her words are like ice in my blood.

'I didn't realise we were in such competition,' I whisper, putting down my knife and fork.

'Look, this is nonsense – you cannot marry yourself, Chloe, I just won't hear of it.' Dad slams his fist on the table and Janice jumps.

I push my chair away from the table. 'Don't lecture me on marriage, Dad; you fucked yours up.'

'How dare you! I was young and men make mistakes.' Dad shoots Janice a panicked look, his Adam's apple bobbing up and down.

'Oh please, you're an insult to manhood.' I look around the table, my stomach churning with distress. 'Some family you are. I'm going to marry myself with or without your support.'

'Well, I'm sure you'll be very happy,' Dad says in a scathing voice.

'Yeah, just like you and Janice. You're obviously living in total marital bliss.' I stand up. 'Still in separate bedrooms, I gather?'

Dad's eyes bulge. 'Don't you bring our relationship into it.' He gesticulates at Janice, accidentally striking the neck of the wine bottle, and as if in slow motion, it goes careering off the table, spurting red wine in a high arc.

'Noooooo!' Janice leaps up as if electrocuted, her hands snatching at the air. 'My carpet!'

It's too late: the wine has splashed against the wall and an ugly red stain is seeping into the cream carpet. Emma groans and catches my eye and for a moment I think she'll relent, but then she shakes her head and says, 'Look what you've done now.'

'It wasn't me!' I shout, backing away down the corridor. Janice is on her knees, mopping at the stain with a napkin, practically weeping. Dad is cursing and spinning in useless semi-circles. As he throws another napkin at Janice, he gives me a look of such contempt that I turn on my heel and run.

Chapter 18

'Single Bride Gives Up Desperate 20-Year Search For A Husband And Resorts To Marrying Herself.'

Shit, maybe Dad was right, maybe I shouldn't have spoken to the papers. I stare in horror at the *Mirror*'s write-up of my interview on my office computer; they haven't exactly quoted me verbatim. And the article is accompanied by an image of Ant and me that was taken a few years ago at Glastonbury festival. I look like I need to be sectioned; I'm screaming at the camera, covered in mud, wearing a rubber chicken hat, swimming costume and wellies. Ant is gurning in a stained panda suit. The photo has a dramatic jagged tear down the middle between us.

'What's up?' Jess comes to perch on my desk. 'Ah yeah, I saw that.'

'I've not been desperately searching for a husband!'

'Don't worry, babe, it's just tabloid clickbait. They've included a link to your blog post so people can see the real story.'

'Yeah, but no one ever really reads beyond the headlines, do they? Oh God, Dad will not like this at all.'

'At least it's got people talking. No, don't read the comments!' Jess grabs my forearm as I scroll down.

What an attention-seeking schizophrenic freak, she needs to be locked up.

They used to burn people at the stake for this bullshit — she's a witch — kill her!

She's obviously a self-obsessed nightmare, no wonder she's single.

I swallow hard and feel the blood rush to my face, noticing a few of my colleagues on the beanbags looking over at me.

Theresa is talking behind her hand to the receptionist, Suki, and they're both shaking their heads, their eyes wide with gossip.

'Why are these people so angry? I'm not hurting anyone,' I whisper, licking dry lips.

'Of course you're not.' Jess sighs. 'They're nasty trolls. Don't pay any attention to them.'

'But it's not just them . . . It's my family too. I don't understand why people are reacting so strongly! I thought it'd be a fun celebration that encouraged everyone to think a bit more about self-love, you know?'

'Yeah, I totally get it.' Jess chews her fingernail. 'People obviously think it's selfish to put your own needs first, which is bullshit – you shouldn't be a sodding doormat all your life!'

'I know. Even when I try really hard to please people it doesn't work – all I ever wanted was to make Ant happy and look where that got me . . . and I try to impress people like Dad and Giles all the time but they always expect more!' I tip my head back in frustration.

'Oh Chlo, you're looking at the archetypal self-sacrificing chump right here!' Jess jabs a finger at her own chest. 'My entire life is spent either pacifying petty office squabbles or in domestic drudgery. Only yesterday I had to resolve a point-less dispute between Verity and another account manager, stay late at work to courier Giles's passport to the airport because he hadn't packed properly for his holiday, and then, when I got home, the cat had been sick all over the kitchen. Do you know how my dear husband and children had dealt with it?'

'Oh God, how?' I can't help giggling at Jess's disgusted expression.

'They had placed a sheet of kitchen towel over each pile of vomit so it wouldn't offend their delicate senses and then ordered a takeaway for dinner. As soon as I walked in, they started complaining about how the smell was putting them off their pizza!'

'No!' I slap a hand over my mouth. 'Your husband didn't clean it up?'

'What, John? Chloe, sometimes I think my husband believes in magic. There are so many things that just miraculously happen in our household: hoovering, laundry, ironing, cleaning, tidying, cooking, washing up, paying bills, paying insurance, school runs, childcare, supervising homework.'

I stare at her as she counts off her chores on her fingers, feeling exhausted just listening to her.

'Jesus Christ, I'm never going to complain about my flat-mate again,' I say.

My phone vibrates loudly on my desk and I curse when I see it's a text from Ant:

> *Chloe, this has gone far enough. We need to talk. I'm back in Brighton this weekend, can you meet me then? Ant*

'Haha,' Jess says as I hold it out for her to read. 'Bet this has really put the shits up him.'

'Um, sorry to break up this little social, but Chloe, we have a team meeting in the ball-pit room *now*.' Verity appears next to my desk in stripy hot pants and a boob tube, with a hand on her hip. 'In Giles's absence, I am in charge.'

The ball-pit room on the first floor is, well, basically a room full of coloured plastic balls. The tech lads are predictably pelting each other. One of the balls hits Verity in the chest as we enter and she shrieks.

'Enough, everybody! Can we be a bit more professional please?'

The boys nudge each other and whisper as I wade past them and sink down in the corner between Simone and Rudy.

Verity perches on a white stool and switches on the wall-mounted cinema screen. 'As you know, Pelican have just signed a six-month contract and we need to wow them with our brilliant creative ideas. I'm putting together their beach collection campaign.'

She clicks onto a webpage showing hot models in animal-print swimwear. 'I'm looking for interesting angles. Anyone?'

Rudy raises his hand. 'But Vee, we work on tech – why're you asking us?'

Verity tuts. 'I can't be expected to come up with all the ideas myself! Come on, anyone can be creative. We're in a bloody ball pool, aren't we?' She points at Theresa. 'Theresa, what sort of things do you look for in a new swimming cossie?'

Theresa pats her dry bushy hair and looks disconcerted. 'Gawd, I don't know, a strong gusset?'

Verity makes a moue of revulsion and turns to Rudy. 'What about you, boys? What would make you buy a pair of swimming trunks?'

'Rudy needs a helluva lot of padding,' one of the boys calls out, and Rudy quickly turns scarlet as he chucks a ball at him.

'Fuck off.'

'How about making a feature of the wild animals?' I say. 'You've got all these prints – snake, tiger, leopard, zebra, giraffe . . . you could get people to do a beach personality quiz, called something like "unleash *your* beast".'

'Yeah, I like that – unleash the beast!' Rudy says. 'People love sharing quiz results on social media.'

Verity tosses her hair back. 'I don't think so. Way too obvious.'

'What about doing something on how empowering it is for women to wear thongs?' Simone says.

'Yes!' Verity clicks her fingers.

'What's empowering about them?' I ask.

'Erm, hello? Women shouldn't be ashamed of their buttocks,' Verity says, writing down *be proud of your bum*. 'We could get women to post photos of their bums on Insta – even the fat ones.'

'Yes! Hashtag Belfies!' Simone punches the air. 'This is inspired.'

'See, you're not the only one who can be a feminist, Chloe,' Verity sneers.

'Oh please, wearing thongs is hardly a strike against the patriarchy.' I roll my eyes and zone out as Verity and Simone flesh out the #PelicanBelfie campaign.

I scroll through the recent messages from Dom on my phone, asking me if I've decided on a wedding venue yet, feeling a flutter of panic when I think of all the organising I need to do.

'Hello . . . earth to Chloe.' Verity is waving at me. 'I don't expect you've done anything on the Most Awesome Place to Work awards? Probably too busy showing off to the press.'

'Actually, I've spent a lot of time on the corporate social responsibility section,' I correct her. 'At the moment Top Banana doesn't do anything for Brighton's community, so I've contacted a bunch of charities and several have come back saying they'd love to have our staff volunteer.'

'Well, you'll have to get clearance from Giles before anyone does that,' Verity sniffs.

'I already have, before he went away. He's granting everyone half a day a month, starting this Friday. I'll send around an email with the details. There're options to volunteer for a homeless shelter, a food bank or befriending local elderly people.'

Everyone makes interested noises and starts asking me questions, and Verity claps her hands together crossly. 'We don't have time for this now; I want to talk about the kitchen.'

A loud groan travels the room. The kitchen is an ongoing battlefield at Top Banana, with people leaving passive-aggressive Post-it notes on their milk, sandwiches, Tupperware, mugs, sweeteners, etc. There's always some kind of office email chain going round about a misplaced boiled egg or the cross-contamination of Marmite with peanut butter, usually with accompanying images attached.

Verity, who I suspect is one of the more enthusiastic Post-it authors, launches into a tirade about the largely ignored cleaning rota and, overwhelmed with apathy, I allow myself to slide slowly backwards until I'm submerged up to my neck in plastic balls.

As we all walk back through to the second floor, Jess signals to me. 'Your desk phone has been going mental.'

She points to it just as it rings again and I grab the receiver. 'Chloe Usher speaking.'

'Chloe, hi! I hope you don't mind me calling, the receptionist gave me your number. I'm Bianca Mendes, producer and director at Cube Productions. I read about your proposed self-marriage online – congratulations!' Bianca has a husky voice, brimming with enthusiasm.

'Uh, thanks.' I sit down, taken aback.

I see Verity and Simone wheel their chairs closer to me, alerted by my tone.

'I couldn't believe it when I read your article – it's *so* relevant to what I'm working on right now,' Bianca gushes. 'We're producing a TV documentary series with a working title of *New Love*, exploring all the exciting new approaches to love in the twenty-first century – and we'd like to feature your wedding!'

'Wow, OK, you mean film it?' I ask, and Verity lets out a little squeak of rage.

'Yes! We think it'd be really inspiring to capture your journey on camera, including all the preparations as well as the beautiful ceremony itself.'

'Hmm, I don't know if I want cameras everywhere.' I definitely don't think it'd be wise to record the reactions of people like Emma and Dad.

'I promise you won't notice them at all. The main thing is that you get to tell your story in your own words. I think your blog made some excellent points about society's expectations.'

'Yeah, but it's kind of backfired already.'

Bianca lets out a throaty laugh. 'Do you mean the *Mirror* article?'

'Yes – and all the comments.'

'Chloe, don't let that bother you. Trolls are an inevitable part of interactive media.' Bianca's voice deepens with encouragement. 'In some ways the number of trolls you attract indicates success – it means you have a wider sphere of influence.'

'Is that a good thing?' I ask.

'Of course it is, when you have something important to say! I see you as an uplifting ambassador for self-love. Don't worry, Chloe, this documentary will give you an opportunity to spread your message far and wide.'

I hesitate. 'What other stuff will you be talking about in the series?'

'We're shadowing a whole bunch of interesting folk – same-sex parents, open partnerships, cooperative communities, et cetera. They all reflect a dramatic shift from the traditional two-point-four family; as does your act of sologamy – marrying yourself!'

'That does sound interesting,' I admit. I've only been on TV once before, when my primary school was filmed at a nature reserve for the local news. Mum recorded it on video. Whenever she plays it, I cringe to watch myself sporting a short wonky fringe and dungarees, talking earnestly to the camera about frogspawn.

'Can I think about it? It's taken me by surprise a bit.'

'Of course! I'll email you over the details. We'll pay you a fee, of course. Just drop me a line when you've mulled it over. Though we've already started our filming schedule, so if you do want to take part let us know sooner rather than later.' Bianca pauses then says, 'And I just wanted to say, I've recently had my share of heartbreak, and reading about your determination to heal yourself really struck a chord with me. You're kind of like Bridget Jones, but with balls!'

'Ah thanks, that's sweet.' I feel chuffed, despite suddenly having an alarming image of Bridget Jones's big pants bulging at the crotch.

Once we've hung up, Verity and Simone round on me.

'Who was that?' Verity demands.

'Just a TV producer.' I shrug, deliberately vague.

'They do not want to film *your* wedding?'

'Well yeah, actually, they do.

'Wow, cool!' Simone's mouth falls open in awe and Verity glares at her.

'Simone, have you even started inviting people to my pre-wedding events yet?'

'Yes! I've got a list of RSVPs right here, see.' Simone says, turning back to her computer and opening a spreadsheet.

As well as Verity's wedding in December, she is also insisting on an engagement party, a bridal shower *and* a lavish hen do in New York.

Verity barely glances at the list. 'Also, huge crisis, I've just found out that Gavin's sister has got a snake tattoo on her forearm. I do *not* want her ruining my wedding photos by looking like a total pikey. I need you to sort it.'

'What do you want me to do?' Simone looks up, chewing the inside of her cheek anxiously.

'Duh – get it removed, of course!' Verity frowns as I snort with laughter. 'Right, I'm going to lunch. I don't want any calls, I need to de-stress.'

'OK.' Simone nods and starts opening her carton of pasta salad.

'What the hell is that?' Verity grabs it. 'There's seven hundred calories in this, Simone, look at all that mayonnaise! We're getting your bridesmaid dress in a size ten, remember – you've got six months to lose two dress sizes!'

'Please! I haven't eaten today, I've been so busy. I'll just have broth for dinner, OK?' Simone desperately tries to snatch the salad back, her voice thick with unswallowed saliva.

'No. There's plenty of fresh fruit in the kitchen.' Verity marches off with the salad, dumping it in the bin on her way out. Before Simone can follow her, her mobile rings and as she answers it I hear a loud volley of protest.

'Yes, hi, Henrietta. Yes, I'm afraid Verity does expect you to attend the bridal shower *and* the hen do,' she says nervously. 'Well, yes, bridal showers did start in America but loads of people in the UK have them now; it's more a gift-giving party to honour the bride-to-be.'

I raise a sceptical eyebrow at her and she turns her back on me. 'Sorry to hear about your unemployment but, still, Verity will be devastated if you're not there.'

Chapter 19

The office is more energetic than ever this Friday morning, as most people have opted for the half-day volunteering. I've arranged for minibuses to come and pick up staff and drop them at the various projects around Brighton. Verity has ostentatiously declined, stating that she has far too much essential work to do. She keeps going on about 'the Pelican brief', making it sound way more significant than a social media campaign of bum selfies.

I wait with my colleagues in the foyer, next to the Lego reception desk. Since the *Mirror* article on Monday, everyone is acting strangely around me. Theresa has started speaking to me very slowly, with both hands held out in front of her, as if I'm a volatile maniac who might suddenly attack her with a stapler.

'Right, here's our lift, guys.' I beckon to the ten people who've signed up to the elderly befriending charity and we climb into the bright yellow Brighton Befrienders bus.

A woman in the front passenger seat turns around. She has light brown hair in a ponytail, bright hazel eyes and the warmest smile I've ever seen.

'Thank you so much for giving your time today,' she says as we pull away down the high street. 'I'm Kate Dooley, founder of Brighton Befrienders. Our elderly members are all over sixty-five and living alone. You'll be visiting them in pairs today and we've got cakes you can take with you.' She nods at a crate on the floor and Simone stares at it hungrily.

'What if they need the toilet or get sick or something?' Rudy asks. I whack his arm but Kate just laughs.

'Good question. Most of our members are physically well and capable, though they may have poor mobility. You shouldn't have any trouble in the time that you're there, but here's my card anyway – we can be with you in a jiffy.' She hands around her cards.

'What shall we talk to them about?' Simone pipes up. 'The war and stuff?'

Kate laughs again. 'To be honest, love, you could talk to them about paint drying and they'd still be delighted to see you.'

'Right, this is Muriel's place,' Kate calls out as we pull up outside a cream bungalow. 'She's ninety-one years old and has a cleaner and gardener come once a week, but otherwise she looks after herself.'

Rudy lets out a low whistle. 'I don't think I've ever met anyone that old.'

Kate smiles, consulting her clipboard. 'I have Chloe and Simone down for this visit. Take Muriel some mini Battenbergs; she's a big fan of marzipan.'

Simone grabs a handful of cakes and flashes me a petulant look as the minibus leaves us in the driveway.

'Verity's not here, so you can drop the attitude,' I say. 'We're supposed to be cheering this lady up.'

Simone wrinkles her nose and looks down at the Battenbergs in her hands. 'Fine, as long as you don't tell Vee how many calories I eat.'

'You must be my girls!' We turn to see a tiny woman in the bungalow doorway, holding her walking stick aloft. She's about five foot, in a purple skirt, blouse and navy cardigan. She has thinning reddish-brown hair and a beaming moon-shaped face that reminds me of a dried apricot. 'Come on in, I've got a pot of tea ready.' Her voice is high and wavering.

'Hi, Muriel!' I bend to kiss her cheek. 'I'm Chloe and this is Simone.'

'Ooh, it's not often you see a redhead, lovely.' Muriel holds a lock of my loose hair in front of her faded amber eyes. 'And you . . .' She turns her gaze to Simone, drinking in every detail. 'You've got the face of a young Marilyn Monroe, with those pretty round cheeks.'

'Thanks!' Simone looks chuffed.

Muriel shuffles her way slowly down the brown-carpeted corridor, leaning heavily on her stick. I walk next to her, offering my arm, and she takes it gratefully.

'It's my right hip,' she says. 'I had an operation eight years ago and it's never been the same since.'

We go into the lounge, a bright room with rose-pink wallpaper, cream leather armchairs and a large bay window that overlooks the cul-de-sac. At the far end of the room a long wooden cabinet holds lots of framed photos and some postcards. An antique grandfather clock stands next to it, ticking softly.

I lower Muriel into an armchair by the window and she props a few cushions behind her back.

'Help yourselves.' She points at the low table in the middle of the room, which has a tray of tea and biscuits laid out. 'I've got shortbread and ginger nuts there if you'd like them.'

I sit on the armchair next to Muriel and Simone sits down cross-legged on the floor, next to the table.

'I'm supposed to be on a diet,' she says, adding the Battenbergs to the tray. 'But it's not making much difference.' She prods the small roll of fat that bulges over her denim skirt.

'I don't understand these faddy diets.' Muriel shakes her head as Simone passes her a cake. 'We never had them in my day. And people were generally a lot thinner.'

'But then you were on rations, weren't you?' Simone asks, her voice thick with crumbs. 'So you couldn't really binge eat?'

'Well, only in the forties,' Muriel muses. 'But I suppose our portions were smaller.'

'And supermarkets didn't come in until the sixties, either,' I add, putting two cups of tea on the trolley between Muriel and me. 'Which means you didn't have all the hidden sugars and snacks and ready meals.'

'Oh no, none of that. Everything came from our local grocers and butchers, or our gardens.' Muriel fishes about in her cardigan pocket and pulls out a plastic straw. Simone and I watch in fascination as she starts drinking her tea through the straw. 'Sometimes I miss my mouth with the cup,' she explains.

'Did people drink as much booze?' I ask.

'Not really; alcohol was more of a treat.'

'And how did you burn off calories? Did you have gyms and fitness classes?' Simone dips shortbread in her tea. 'I've tried HIIT class but my lungs nearly burst.'

'We didn't have gyms.' Muriel taps her cheek with a gnarled finger in thought. 'But we walked a lot and housework kept us active. And of course, we danced!' She raises both her hands, which are covered in age spots, and beats the air. 'Foxtrot, Charleston, tap, waltz, swing, jitterbug. I used to love visiting the London dance halls; the men would queue up to dance with me. There was one fella called Alfie, boy could he dance, we used to sweep the floor with everyone else!'

Muriel's face shines as she relives the moment and Simone and I gaze at her in awe.

'We don't have anything like that now,' Simone says wistfully. 'We don't have dance partners, we just get wasted and mosh about together.'

'Ah, but I expect the men are still queuing up for you, ladies.' Muriel looks between us, her tawny eyes twinkling.

'Hmm, I'm actually on a man diet at the moment,' Simone sighs.

'Gosh, you like your diets, don't you?' Muriel shakes her head. 'I don't think depriving yourself of something works very well; it usually makes you crave it more.'

'Yeah, you're right there.' Simone looks pained as she reaches for a ginger nut.

'And you, Chloe? Do you have a special someone?' Muriel peels the marzipan layer from her cake.

'I've recently broken up with my long-term boyfriend, Anthony . . .' I tail off and Muriel nods, briefly squinting her eyes shut in empathy. 'I'm actually meeting him this weekend.'

'Are you?!' Simone exclaims. 'Ooh, is he going to have a go at you?'

'Probably.' I shake my head at Simone to show I don't want to tell Muriel about my self-wedding. It might confuse her and, anyway, I'm more interested in what she has to say.

'What about you, Muriel?' I change the subject.

'Ooh yes, did you marry Alfie?' Simone asks.

Muriel giggles. 'No, I married Brian in the end.'

'Oh!' Simone sounds disappointed. 'Alfie sounds great – why did you let him go?'

Muriel shrugs peaceably. 'You don't regret anything at my age, pet; it's all worth it, even the heartbreak and the mistakes. It's what life's about.'

We fall silent and I try to imagine a time when Ant will be just a distant memory.

'That's Brian and me in America the year before he passed.' Muriel points to a framed photo in the centre of the cabinet. 'He died twenty years ago – heart attack.'

Simone and I go to look at it; Muriel and Brian are standing in front of a waterfall grinning at the camera. Muriel is taller and straighter, and auburn curls tumble over her shoulder.

'That's when I still had hair.' Muriel pats her bald patch self-consciously.

'You've been on your own for twenty years?' Simone's mouth is hanging open as she looks around the room. 'What do you *do*?'

I frown at Sim but Muriel is chuckling. 'Oh, I amuse myself: gardening, reading, watching TV. I did used to play bridge and go to bingo.' Her face clouds over. 'It's more trouble to get out now, mind. This damn hip.'

'Do you have family nearby?' I ask, sitting back down.

'No, my daughter passed away when she was sixty and my son lives in Spain. He visits when he can but, you know, he's got commitments.' Muriel gestures vaguely.

'What about friends? You must have loads.' Simone is pacing the room, examining the ornaments on the shelves.

'Dear, when you get to my age I'm afraid your friends start dropping like flies.' Muriel slurps her tea through the straw.

'But your neighbours . . . ?' Simone pauses by the window, peering across the cul-de-sac.

'They're busy, got their own lives.' Muriel follows Sim's gaze resignedly.

'What about the internet?' I feel a growing incredulity that this sweet woman is so hidden away.

'I'm too thick to use computers!' Muriel chortles. 'I can just about manage to work the TV.'

I start to protest but then close my mouth. Sometimes I forget just how radical technology must seem for people from Muriel's era. She did, after all, grow up in a world of telegrams and post boxes; she can't be expected to adopt computers as seamlessly as my generation. And anyway, I don't even know if going online is the answer to her isolation.

'So how often do you have people like us come and visit you then?' Simone says, looking just as shocked as me.

'Kate Dooley is an angel.' Muriel smiles widely at us. 'She sends me volunteers at least once a fortnight – always such lovely people like yourselves. I was going through a bit of a bad patch when she called me five years ago. It was like a lifeline.'

There's silence; only the sound of the ticking grandfather clock fills the room.

'Well, I'm certainly visiting you again,' I say and Simone nods, her brown eyes wide and serious.

'So am I,' she agrees. 'Just try and stop me.'

The next hour passes so quickly; Muriel shows us round her garden, gives us her secret recipe for Bakewell tart, and is just offering her theory on the murder of John Lennon when the doorbell rings.

'Did you have a good time?' Kate hugs Muriel tightly in the corridor.

'It's been the highlight of my week.' Muriel grips our hands as we reluctantly say goodbye.

She stands in the doorway as we drive away and Simone and I wave madly from the back window. I feel a lump in my throat as I watch her tiny figure recede, imagining the hours and hours she'll have to fill until the next visit. My other colleagues seem similarly emotional.

'We met a D-Day survivor called Frank. Amazing he was, got out all his medals.' Rudy shows us pictures on his phone. 'And he gave us a sherry.'

'How many elderly members did you say you had, Kate?' I call out.

'Ten thousand in Brighton and Hove, love. We're trying to expand into surrounding areas too.' Kate smiles at me in the rear-view mirror.

I rest my head against the bus window and stare out at the rows of houses as we pass, unable to comprehend that there are thousands more people like Muriel in this city, living alone and forgotten behind closed doors.

Chapter 20

The next day, our befriending visit is still on my mind. I wander around my flat in a daze, wondering where I'll be living in fifty years' time. That is, if I'm still alive.

Saffron isn't in so I sit on the roof terrace in peace, drinking tea and looking out over the back gardens; in one a man is hosing his flower beds, in another two children practise cartwheels.

'Come and get your swimming costumes on,' their mother calls through the back door. As they run into the house, one of them sees me watching and waves.

I feel a swoop of alarm to think that I'll end up like Muriel one day; unable to leave the house unassisted. I look down at my crossed legs and feel ashamed at how often I curse the shape of my calves. I totally take my mobility for granted. In fact, I take a hell of a lot for granted.

I tilt my head back and feel the morning sunshine on my face. Visiting Muriel's given me a new perspective on my life, which is just as well because I'm meeting Ant for a drink at The Lobster.

I spot Ant immediately, hunched at the corner table, in a T-shirt and boardies. His hair has grown a bit longer and curls at his temples.

'Hey.' I walk over and Dora starts wiggling furiously, licking his bare knees.

'Do you have to take that bloody dog with you everywhere?' He moves his legs to the side and pushes her away.

'Yes,' I say evenly, pulling up a chair opposite him. 'She's my spirit animal.'

Ant huffs and rests his elbows on the table. His skin looks sallow and there are dark smudges under his eyes.

'How's the sailing course going – found your sea legs yet?'

'It's really tough actually, we have to get up so early, even at weekends.'

I suppress a smile; Ant's always loved his lie-ins. 'Have you got some time off now then? Where are you staying?'

'Only two nights. I'm crashing at a mate's.' Ant doesn't meet my eye and I assume he's staying with his new girlfriend. I bite my tongue; I'm not going to quiz him.

'Well, at least you're following your dreams, huh?' I remind him. 'I don't expect you feel so trapped any more.'

Ant glowers at the sugar bowl. 'You have no idea.'

'What can I get you, Chloe, my sweet?' AJ appears at our table in a Hawaiian shirt and yellow shorts. 'We have a new summer menu of fresh juices, inspired by my Caribbean roots.'

'Ooh lovely, why don't you surprise me, AJ.' I wink at him and he bows with a flourish.

'Why're you so perky?' Ant mutters when AJ's retreated behind the bar.

'Why're you so moody?' I retort. 'It's a lovely day; the sun is shining, the sea is . . . splashing. What's not to like?'

'Jesus, I never thought you were this vindictive. Are you trying to ruin my life?'

'Ant, you can do what you want with your life; I don't care any more.' I drop my breezy tone. 'I'm just trying to get on with mine, OK?'

'Uh, what, by marrying your*self*? Why on earth would you do that!'

'Because it's time to love myself.'

Ant rolls his eyes. 'Don't tell me this isn't a deliberate attempt to make me look like the bad guy.'

'You seriously think I'd do this for revenge?' I stare at him. 'My face is plastered all over the tabloids, for fuck's sake!'

'Well, yeah, I know,' I admit. In the past week, the *Sun* and the *Mail Online* have picked up the story, using headlines similar to the *Mirror*'s. 'But they lifted that photo from Facebook – I didn't give it to them.'

'It's an awful photo!' Ant yells. 'I'm gurning my tits off.'

'Here we are!' AJ sings, putting a massive glass of golden juice in front of me, decorated with a slice of pineapple. 'It's called "Lust for Life"!'

I take a sip of the drink and smack my lips at the tangy taste of passion fruit and kiwi. 'Yum!'

'And would you care for some Lust for Life, sir? It looks like you need it.' AJ turns to Ant with such exaggerated consideration that I have to take another gulp of the drink to stop myself laughing.

'No, I'm fine with this.' Ant gestures curtly at the coffee he's nursing.

'Look, Ant,' I say softly when AJ's left. 'You might be the one who's gone sailing but I've been totally lost at sea.' I search his familiar face but there's not a flicker of compassion. I continue the nautical metaphor as I try to get through to him. 'Come on, throw me a bloody life jacket.'

Ant slams his hands down on the table, his face twisting with malice. 'Trust you to blame the entire thing on me. Oh, poor little Chloe left to survive all on her own.' He affects a falsetto that makes me recoil. 'Have you ever considered that *you* might have played a part in our break-up? You always wanted me to be this funny and interesting person, there to make you laugh. Everywhere I turned you'd be there, waiting for entertainment.'

'Whaaaaaat?' My mouth falls open in disbelief.

'Don't deny it!' He points at me. 'You don't know how much pressure it was, having to perform.'

'Oh. My. God.'

'And with sex, too – you were always offering yourself on a plate. The whole point of relationships is that you're supposed to hold a bit back, keep a bit of mystery.' Ant plumps his bottom lip out defiantly.

'So you went and shagged someone else because I wasn't

mysterious enough?' My voice is shrill. I push my juice away, suddenly not thirsty.

'You know what I mean.' There's an intense yearning in his gaze. 'You used to be so fearless, like that night our bus broke down on the border of Guatemala and those dodgy locals crowded round us. You just strung our hammock up between two trees and said they could stare all they liked.'

I swallow, remembering how Ant climbed into the hammock and I stayed wide awake, keeping an eye on our unwanted audience and watching the stars fade to dawn as he drifted off next to me, his limbs heavy on mine.

'The Chloe I knew disappeared.' Ant is whispering now as Dora stirs between our legs. She nudges her snout up into Ant's crotch and cold air wafts between my legs as she wags her tail. Ant looks down at her black nose. 'You became too needy, Chloe,' he says. 'Just like your dog.'

That does it. I push my chair away from the table and stand up.

'Fuck *you*, Ant!'

Ant looks around the cafe in alarm and waves his hands to shush me as Dora dances about, galvanised by the sudden change in energy.

'No, I will not *shush*! How dare you throw that cliché at me – it's not my fault you got bored! Here, if you want something more exotic, have this!' I grab my glass and throw my drink over him; juice splashes his face and the pineapple flops wetly in his lap.

There's cheering behind me and I turn to see AJ and another waiter clapping loudly.

'Bravo, Chloe!' AJ calls. 'I was very close to doing that myself!'

Ant clambers to his feet, swiping at his face with a napkin.

'You're pathetic, all of you,' he spits, and AJ hops backwards, clapping his hands to his cheeks in mock fear. 'Just don't talk about me to anyone else.' Ant raises a warning finger in my face. 'It's time you got over me.' He storms out without a backward glance and I let out a bellow of ridicule.

'Oh believe me, I'm over you!' I yell at his retreating back. AJ comes up and puts an arm around me, handing me a new, bright red juice.

'This one's called "You Go, Girl!"' he says. 'And it's got a shot of Jamaican rum in it.'

By the time I get home, the orange sun is dropping in the sky, squeezing the clouds into syrupy layers of red and pink. I sit back on the terrace with a G&T.

It's turned out to be an unexpectedly delightful afternoon and I'm a bit pissed. After Ant left The Lobster, I sat on a deckchair outside drinking more You Go, Girl!s with AJ. He told me I'd dodged a bullet with Ant and that he's clearly an arrogant diva. He was so understanding that I ended up telling him all about my row with Emma and Dad.

'Chloe, the world would be a boring place if everyone listened to their parents.' AJ flashed his bright white smile. 'Your family doesn't always know what's best for you.'

Then he played Madonna's 'Papa Don't Preach' over the loudspeakers and told me about the massive fight he had with his dad when he left home. It made my argument seem very tame in comparison.

Dom came to join us, keen to sample our newly invented cocktails. Fired up by Ant's disapproval, I called the Bandstand and found it is available for my wedding in mid-August, so I paid the deposit on my credit card. And, just as we were leaping about with excitement, AJ kindly offered The Lobster as the wedding reception venue.

'It would be my honour,' he insisted.

So, now I have the venues sorted out, it's all starting to feel more real. I suck my slice of lemon as I watch my neighbours cooking sausages on their outdoor grill, silvery smoke drifting towards me on the warm air.

In the spirit of self-acceptance, I run over my conversation with Ant. Even though I'm glad I chucked a drink over him and a lot of what he said to me was out of order, there might be a *tiny* grain of truth in his words. Maybe I did expect too much from him and allowed myself to become a watered-down version of the person I used to be. Ant and I have always been separate people and I should be responsible for my own happiness.

The realisation makes me sit up. The more I think about what it means to take control of your life, the more important this wedding seems. I open up my laptop, feeling inspired to start writing my wedding vows.

A bunch of social media notifications distract me. Since the tabloid articles this week, I've had several persistent trolls on Twitter. One guy, called @HotRod, has been tweeting me almost every day:

> @HotRod @ChloeWanders YOU ARE A DESPERATE MENTAL OLD FRUMP!

I've ignored him all week but now I can't help responding:

> @ChloeWanders @HotRod All right, no need to shout.

He replies immediately:

> @HotRod @ChloeWanders I'VE NEVER SEEN SUCH A SAD ATTEMPT AT ATTENTION-SEEKING IN ALL MY LIFE

I reply:

> @ChloeWanders @HotRod Well, at least now I have your attention, that's all I ever wanted.

I giggle, picturing him sitting in front of his screen. I wonder what he looks like and why he's so angry.

I click through to my *Chloe Wanders* inbox and open an email from Bianca at Cube Productions, asking me if I've had a chance to think about them filming my wedding. I scroll through my other emails as I deliberate; Dom and AJ told me I should definitely do it.

'The way I see it,' Dom said, 'you're trying to raise the profile of self-love, and talking about it on TV is a great start.'

An unopened email suddenly makes me gasp. The address is Katypops69@hotmail.com – the girl from Ant's office. Maybe she's finally getting in touch to confess their affair! I click through and start reading.

Dear Chloe,
I hope you don't mind me mailing you out of the blue. I just had to get in touch because your blog post about committing to love yourself meant SO MUCH to me.

Firstly, I'm sorry about the way Ant treated you. I actually work at Warren Recruitment and was there that day you turned up at our offices. I felt soooo awful for you when you were under that bin, I nearly ran outside to pull that horrible security guard off you! I used to think Ant was all right but he never mentioned that he cheated on you – what a knob!

Anyway, when I read your post about how you don't want to be afraid of being alone I . . . well, actually I burst into tears. You really made me think. Because – I never tell anyone this – I basically feel empty and numb ALL the time and I don't know why.

I'm twenty-five, with a great job and boyfriend and flatmates, and Brighton is an awesome place to live. By rights, I should be really happy. My mates from uni always say they're 'well jel' of my life – I guess because I often post 'smug Brighton' photos!

But the fact is, I'm just going through the motions. There's a huge shadow behind me, chasing me. I'm constantly pretending it's not there – as if I'm an actress playing a character's role. As long as there're people around me I can keep it up.

But when I'm on my own, the shadow catches up with me and suffocates me and I'm so scared, like I'm a kid drowning in the dark, but I can't call for help.

I don't know why this happens – it's got worse recently and I do anything to avoid it. Sometimes I drink booze to obliterate it, sometimes I . . . do other stuff.

It was when you said you needed to start loving yourself that I suddenly stopped and thought, why am I ignoring the drowning kid? She needs me. I'm not sure if I'm brave enough to help her yet but thanks for making me even consider it, Chloe.

I'm really sorry for pouring this shit out on you when you already have your own to deal with. I just wanted to say I think you're great, keep writing.

Love Katy xx

I blink several times, my skin tingling with sympathy. I was not expecting that. HotRod's jibes pale in significance when I think of what courage it must've taken Katy to confide in me. I feel honoured that she found my words a comfort.

I quickly click back to Bianca's email and write:

Hi Bianca, yes, I've thought about it and I would welcome the opportunity to be part of your documentary. I will happily take on the role of 'ambassador for self-love' ☺ Give me a call and we can discuss possible filming dates. Cheers, Chloe x

I reopen Katy's email and read her words again carefully. I sit back and look at the bruised evening sky, remembering what Dr Fletcher said to me about mental wellbeing. Then I hit 'reply' and start to type.

Chapter 21

'So, the bad news is that I can't take an online course to become a wedding officiant. Apparently that only happens in American sitcoms.' Dom sucks his smoothie through a stripy straw.

A week later, we're having al fresco Sunday brunch at a cafe in the Lanes. The sun is beating down on the walkway and there's the sugary scent of hot fudge in the air. Shoppers weave their way past us, dressed in beachwear.

'And the good news?' I lower my shades to look at him.

'Is that I'll just bloody do it anyway,' Dom says breezily, stretching his arms behind his head. He looks very nautical in a long-sleeved Breton shirt with a red neckerchief.

'We're really milking our artistic licence, aren't we?' I grin.

'And why not? Life imitates art.'

He looks so pleased with himself, I burst out laughing. '*You* are a piece of art, Dom.'

Dom bows his head in acquiescence, then picks up his phone. 'Look, there are loads of brilliant costumes I tried on at the fancy dress shop. Here's me as the Pope, and as a vicar, and I thought I'd try Jesus just for a giggle.'

I scroll through the photos and crack up at Dom's pious poses. 'Oh wow, that pope's hat really suits you! So, we're going for a religious minister vibe, are we?'

'Yeah, unless you want it totally secular?'

'Hmm, not sure what the church would make of self-marriage. Though actually,' I slap a hand on the table as it occurs to me. 'Isn't one of the ten commandments "thou shalt love thy neighbour as thyself"? Meaning they must value self-love.'

'Jolly good point,' Dom says. 'I'll pick one of these then, it'll give the ceremony an air of pomp. And I might do a religion-inspired collection for my vlog; there's so many cool accessories! And what about your wedding dress? When can we go shopping?'

'Hmm, I've only got a small budget and the priority was hiring the Bandstand, so the dress can wait. I might get a second-hand one – I'll only wear it once anyway.'

'Sure. Beyond Retro usually have a good selection of vintage wedding gowns,' Dom says. 'And you want men *and* women to your hen do, right? I'm loath to call it a "hag" do though – ugh!'

'Yep, definitely. What about "sten" do?'

'Hmm, not much better.'

'I was hoping Emma would help plan the whatever-it's-called but I haven't heard from her since that awful lunch at Dad's.'

It's felt so strange arranging the wedding without consulting Emma. We haven't spoken in nearly a month, which is the longest time we've ever gone without communication. It's a constant gnawing anxiety inside me but I still can't bring myself to offer the olive branch. *She* attacked *me*; it's her call.

'Darling, Emma would probably insist that you stick to a traditional hen do and plan some ghastly twee affair with stuffy afternoon tea and pottery classes.' Dom pulls a revolted face. 'Seriously, leave it to me. I've already got some brilliant ideas. Now, shall we go and look for ringles?'

'Let's do it.'

We stroll down the maze of alleyways, where fetish lingerie shops rub shoulders with contemporary art galleries and independent record stores. I pause outside a bespoke jewellers. 'Ooh, I quite like those.' I point to the unusual silver rings streaked through with wood.

'They're wood?' Dom recoils.

'Yeah, so? I like trees.' I push the shop door open and a little bell rings. The jeweller is behind the counter, peering through a magnifying glass. He has thick grey hair and eyebrows, reminding me a little bit of Father Christmas.

'I'm particularly fond of this reclaimed wood collection,' he enthuses when I ask to try some on. 'Wood is symbolic of confidence and wisdom, you know.'

I end up ordering a silver band with cherry wood running around the centre.

'Good choice: cherry is the tree of the heart,' the jeweller approves as he measures my finger.

'Would you be able to engrave it with the words "I complete me"?' I ask and he nods, quickly scribbling in his notepad. 'Ah yes, that's a common one.'

'Er, no, sorry.' I lean over the counter. 'Not "you complete me", "I complete me".'

'Ah.' He frowns, twiddling the end of his moustache. 'Right you are.'

We've only taken a few more steps when Dom pauses in front of an artisan chocolate shop called Choccywoccydoodah.

'Have you ever seen anything like it!' He's gazing at a massive marshmallow pyramid cake with dripping white chocolate oozing down its sides. 'Come on, any wedding cake worth its weight needs to be slathered in lashings of chocolate!'

We go into the shop and marvel over the lavish hand-made cakes, confectionery and chocolate sculptures in the most amazing shapes. After many, many samples, we finally decide on a three-tiered cake with truffle filling, enrobed in a white Belgian chocolate coating.

'We can add any bespoke touches if you want to make it more personal,' the shop assistant offers.

'Could you do yellow chocolate sunflowers to add to the base?' I ask.

'Certainly.'

'And maybe a bride on the top?'

'Ooh yes, an edible bride, I'll do her in white chocolate. And shall I put the groom in white chocolate too?'

'Hmm, no. Don't worry about a groom for now.' I give her a knowing wink and she looks puzzled.

'Okaaaay. No groom. Gotcha.'

172

'Eek, I think I might be confusing everyone,' I wince as we leave the shop.

'Don't worry, they'll take it in their stride,' Dom laughs. 'This is Brighton.'

As we wander past the boutique clothes shops, Dom turns to me. 'So, what're you wearing when you meet Cube Productions tomorrow?'

'Erm.' I look down at my white shorts and silver vest top. 'Probably just something summery like this.'

Dom frowns. 'I think you need to give your media profile a bit more thought. The first thing people will notice is your appearance, believe me.'

'Really?' I chew my lip. I've been trying not to get too nervous about being filmed. Bianca was delighted that I've agreed to be part of their documentary. They're coming to my office first to have a chat with some of my colleagues and then we'll go to my flat and they'll get some interior shots of my home life.

'And you've prepared your flat so it gives the right impression?' Dom presses his hands together in front of his lips, watching me in concern as I shake my head cluelessly. 'A television crew will be nosing around your home in twenty-four hours, Chlo – come on, there's no time to waste!'

Dom's fervour is catching. As soon as we arrive at my flat, I begin panic-tidying.

'We'd better move Saffron's junk for a start. I haven't seen her for a week – God knows where she is.'

'It's probably just as well. You don't want her ruining the atmosphere with her faux hippy bullshit.' Dom is laden with bags of props, which he dumps at the top of the stairs, then starts removing the psychedelic cotton wall hanging.

'Saffron got that from Goa,' I say.

'It's hideous.' He bundles it under his arm and sweeps her collection of crystals off the corner shelf, replacing them with a potted orchid.

In the kitchen, he hides all the supermarket value products

in the cupboard under the sink. 'You want to ooze sophistication and good taste.'

He pulls a box of Waitrose Duchy Organic biscuits out of his bag along with a tin of loose Earl Grey tea and puts them by the kettle, then lines up a selection of potted plants on the kitchen windowsill. 'Basil, coriander, aloe vera.'

I kneel in front of my DVD collection in the lounge as Dom puts a soft grey throw over the red wine stain on the sofa.

'Hmm. My taste in films gives off quite a confusing message. *The Little Mermaid* and *Legally Blonde* on top of *Wolf Creek* and *Scum*.'

'It shows you have a light and dark side.' Dom lays out glossy hardbacks on the coffee table and I read out the titles doubtfully.

'*Vogue: A History, Erotica Through the Ages, A Thousand Years of Japanese Manga*. Dom, what on earth are these?'

'They're to show you're a liberal intellectual, Chloe, with an avid interest in culture.'

Dom replaces the damp faded towels in the bathroom with some fluffy white bath sheets and hides my razor blades and old bars of soap in the cabinet. Just as we're leaving, I gasp and dive for the bin, retrieving an empty box of Canesten.

'I don't want them thinking I'm riddled with thrush!'

My bedroom proves the most difficult to style, with its odd shape, sloping ceilings and overflowing storage. Dom drapes some silk over my corner bookshelves to hide all the books I've kept from childhood, plus my collection of Care Bears.

He frowns at my old school desk. 'Chloe, why have you even got a desk with an ink well? Quills went out of fashion a while ago.'

'It's nostalgic,' I say firmly.

Eventually he gives up and turns his attention to my wardrobe. 'Right, let's select a few outfit options – you've got to look the part.'

By the time we're finished it's 8 p.m. and we open a well-deserved bottle of wine and collapse in front of the TV. 'I haven't even thought about what I'm going to say yet!' I turn to Dom in panic. 'What if they ask me loads of really awkward questions?'

'You don't have to answer anything you don't feel comfortable with,' he assures me. 'You work in PR so you know the deal; just stick to your story and you'll be fine.'

I nod, kicking my legs up to rest in his lap.

'Hey, have you heard any more from HotRod?' Dom rolls his head towards me expectantly. Our Twitter conversations have become quite entertaining; I almost look forward to the next insult.

I read out the latest:

@HotRod @ChloeWanders IT'S A SHAME YOU'VE RESORTED TO MARRYING YOURSELF, YOU PROBABLY WEREN'T EVEN THAT UGLY – A FEW YEARS AND KILOS AGO
@ChloeWanders @HotRod Flattery will get you everywhere ;)

Dom laughs loudly. 'Wow, this is quality flirting.'

'Ah, yes,' I breathe. 'Girl who marries herself falls for Twitter troll – it's a post-modern romance.'

Chapter 22

After lunch on Monday, Giles calls a quick meeting in the beanbag area. 'We need to pull out all the stops when Chloe's film crew arrive this afternoon, people.' He's topped up his tan on his recent holiday and is wearing a navy polo shirt, shorts and a well-cut blazer. His sandy hair is swept back from his brow, looking considerably lighter than usual.

'Had your highlights done especially, Giles?' Rudy calls out cheekily, and Giles pretends not to hear him.

'Prospective new clients might watch this documentary, so I want you focused, professional and charming, please. Remember, we're at the cutting edge of digital media.'

Verity, standing next to me, rolls her eyes. She's acting as if the whole thing is a big bore but that hasn't stopped her wearing a knockout gold mini dress, with her blonde hair flowing in glossy ringlets down her back.

Back at my desk, I check my *Chloe Wanders* email account. I've been contacted by a whole range of people from all over the world – PhD students, journalists, divorcees, Christians, single men looking for love, angry misogynists, curious supporters. One woman in Australia says she's going to arrange a self-wedding as a coming-of-age ceremony for her teenage daughter.

I'm pleased to see I've had a reply from Katy; we've exchanged a few emails this past week and I've been thinking about her a lot.

Hey Chloe,
I can't explain how much it helps just to have you take me seriously. I tried talking to some people close to me, like you

said, but I think they're scared or something because all I get is 'why don't you do more yoga?' (boyfriend) or 'we all have days when we feel a bit blue' (Mum). I know they mean well but it makes me feel even more alone. I wanted to yell at my mum, 'At least blue is a colour!' The way I feel most of the time, there is no colour in the world at all.

I get the theory that doing positive things will make me feel happier, but some days just mustering the energy to get up and wash myself seems like the most pointless waste of time. The other day I went bowling with my friends and I felt so detached, watching them all have fun. I had to keep pulling faces that made me look like I was enjoying myself. It's not even like I was sad . . . I just didn't feel anything. That's the problem: I can't just 'get over it' because 'it' is 'nothing' – a big empty hole of nothing.

Sometimes I wish I didn't have people who care about me – then maybe I wouldn't feel duty-bound to exist.

Anyway, sorry, I'm just having (another) one of those days. Ignore me.

Love Katy xxx

I breathe in deeply. She does not sound good. I click onto her Instagram account; this past week she's posted photos of a seagull stealing her boyfriend's chips, herself doing a handstand in a bikini, showing off taut abs, and her group of friends bowling. It's bizarre to think that this seemingly happy-go-lucky young girl can have so much darkness in her head. I don't know what advice to give her. I start typing slowly, deleting sentences as I try to find the right words to persuade her to see a professional.

An hour later, the receptionist calls my desk phone to tell me the Cube team are coming up. My pulse starts racing and Jess stands up, flapping her hands. 'They're here, everyone, they're here!'

There's a flurry of activity and my colleagues start acting as if they're auditioning for a soap opera, moving in jerky wooden movements and talking like they're reading from a script. Theresa picks up a phone that isn't even ringing and starts laughing hysterically.

I smooth down the yellow gingham dress Dom and I agreed on last night and check my hair and make-up in my compact mirror, then go through the double doors.

'Chloe Usher!' Bianca's husky voice makes her sound as if she's been partying all night. She holds out slender arms as she steps from the lift. She's wearing a short lime-green playsuit and her shoulder-length ombré hair is a rich chestnut fading to blonde. I'm immediately intimidated by her uber-trendy vibes.

She kisses my cheeks, then jerks her head at the two guys emerging behind her. 'This is Seth and Tariq, my camera bitches.'

They both have their hands full of equipment so just nod and smile, looking me up and down with interest. Seth has a mop of messy brown hair and is tall and slim in jeans and a Superman T-shirt; Tariq is a handsome, petite Indian guy in a black vest and shorts.

'We've cleared a meeting room for you,' I say.

'Fab thanks, we'll set up a tripod in there, so we can do sit-down interviews then we'll use hand-held cameras when we look around. Wow, cool office!' Bianca whistles as I push the doors open and she clocks the AstroTurf flooring, foosball table and hi-tech kitchen.

'We like to offer our staff an artistically stimulating environment,' Giles booms, striding towards us. 'I'm Giles, the Managing Director.'

'Great.' Bianca shakes his hand. 'We'd just like a quick chat with a few of you and some action shots of you guys working, so please' – she raises her voice to my obviously ear-wigging colleagues – 'just carry on as normal.'

Someone lets off a loud fart sound and Giles whips around to glare at the huddle of boys around Rudy's desk. 'Let's start with the grand tour, shall we? You will not believe your eyes when you see our ball-pit room!'

★

178

Bianca's bright smile is a bit forced by the time we return to the second floor. 'What a fascinating agency. It reminds me of Google's offices.'

'We can certainly play with the big boys.' Giles preens.

'Right, Chloe, we'd like to capture a slice of your working life, so do you mind sitting at your desk and just . . . getting on with whatever you're doing?' Bianca asks me, as Seth positions his camera next to my work pod.

'Uh, OK.' I turn towards my computer but bump into Keith, who is standing frozen by my desk, staring at the camera fixedly. 'Excuse me, Keith,' I say.

He makes a strangled sound and hands me an expenses form, then shuffles sideways towards the kitchen like a crab.

I feel his pain; suddenly my face feels all hot and I don't know what to do with my hands. I sit down and look at my computer, hyper-conscious of the black eye of the camera to my left. In my screen's reflection I see that my fringe has managed to get a weird kink so it sticks out at an angle from my forehead. I quickly try to pat it down.

'Chloe, just relax.' Bianca and Giles are watching me, a few feet away. 'These are just background shots – we won't even put a mic on you. Maybe do some emails, chat to your colleagues . . .'

Verity, who's been ostentatiously thumbing through papers on her desk, immediately spins around in her chair.

'Now might be a good time to talk about the Pelican brief, then. Simone, are you listening?' She clicks her fingers and Simone reluctantly turns to face us.

'I've managed to secure some amazing influencers for our Belfie campaign,' Verity says, showing us some printouts of various YouTube and Instagram profiles.

'How did you select them?' I ask.

'They've got loads of followers – duh!' Verity looks affronted. 'KerazyKat has over a million subscribers and her last vlog, where she baked a unicorn cake, got four million views!'

'OK, and what's the angle again?'

'The angle is "wear our bloody bikinis and take a photo of your arse",' Verity says through gritted teeth.

'Sounds great.' Giles can't bear being on the sidelines any more; he comes over to sit on the edge of Verity's desk. 'How about an update on the Most Awesome Place to Work award entry, girls?'

'I've got the CSR bit covered,' I tell him. 'I've filled in loads of info about the three different charities I've signed Top Banana up to this year. Simone and I are also helping Brighton Befrienders with their marketing so there's lots to talk about.'

'Are you?' Verity snaps at Simone. 'Surely you don't have time for that – you're supposed to be planning my wedding?'

'There's always time for charity,' Giles says, smiling at the camera with his best Bob Geldof expression.

'Are you getting married too then, Verity?' Bianca calls out, her eyes flicking between us with interest.

'Yes, I'm marrying an actual man,' Verity sneers. 'We're having a winter wonderland wedding.'

'Ooh, lovely.' Bianca scribbles on her clipboard. 'It might make a nice contrast to Chloe's experience. Would you mind doing a quick interview with us?'

'Absolutely.' Verity smirks. 'I'd love to give you my thoughts.'

I keep anxiously checking my computer clock, Verity's spent over twenty minutes talking to Cube; God knows what she's telling them. Eventually they emerge from the meeting room and Bianca looks delighted as she bounces over to my desk. 'We've got some great stuff from your colleagues and everyone's signed release forms. Shall we whizz over to your flat in our van and we can chat to you properly there? Tariq's off so it'll just be me and Seth, nice and informal.'

'Sure.' I turn off my computer.

'Do you have any cats at home by the way, Chloe?' she asks idly, as she taps on her phone.

'No. But I have a dog, she's at her sitters right now – I didn't know if you'd want her around.'

'Oh, perfect! Yes, let's pick her up on the way – we don't want to leave her out.'

I'm so thankful Dom helped me prep my flat; as I lead Bianca and Seth up the stairs I'm suddenly aware of how dirty the magnolia walls are, and the beige carpet looks really drab.

'Here we are then, it's just a rental so . . .' I trail off and stand awkwardly on the landing.

'Lovely.' Bianca's head swivels. 'Is that the lounge? Seth, do you want to set up in there?' She motions to Seth, then walks past me towards Saffron's bedroom. 'How many people live here?'

'Just two. My flatmate isn't here at the moment.'

Bianca throws Saffron's bedroom door open and I'm about to explain why it looks like a junkyard but there's no need because everything has gone. Her room is completely empty, aside from her old futon on the floor. Even the curtains have been taken down.

'Oh!' I exclaim. She must have cleared everything out while I was at work today. With a sinking feeling I realise this doesn't bode well for her paying her rent this month.

'Anything wrong?' Bianca is looking at me.

'Hmm, it's fine. Let me show you the rest of the flat.'

As we go through to the lounge, Seth is filming the coffee table books. '*Erotica Through the Ages*?'

'Yeah, it's pretty interesting.'

'Is it now?' Seth is opening the book and scanning one of the pages. 'Crikey, are those dildos?'

I curse Dom under my breath and turn away abruptly to hide my blush. 'This is the roof terrace.'

Bianca joins me, ignoring the view and looking down at the empty gin bottle that I forgot to clear away.

'I'm a gin girl too.' She winks at me.

Dora comes through the doors, threading her body between my legs.

'Ah look, she's like your shadow,' Bianca says as I crouch down to pet her. 'Seth babe, get this. Aww, so cute!'

Starved of my attention all day, Dora gets a bit carried away and, with her paws on my shoulders, starts licking my ears and making little grunty noises. I laugh and screw my face up, feeling self-conscious.

'Haha, all right, Dora, calm down. Gah!' I push her away as her tongue swipes across my nostrils, frowning up at Seth's camera. 'So did you want to interview me then? Shall I sit on the sofa?'

'For sure – would you mind putting on the clothes I grabbed you from wardrobe?' Bianca asks.

'Oh, is this no good then?' I pluck at my gingham dress in disappointment.

'It's lovely, but I'm afraid some patterns come out blurry on screen. Don't worry, I picked out some cool stuff.' She hands me a big cotton bag. 'You go change, we'll wait in here.'

I'm not convinced about Bianca's choice. I stand in front of my bedroom mirror in an all-in-one pink trouser suit with shoulder pads. I look like something from *Dallas*. Still, she's the expert.

When I walk back through to the lounge, Seth is on his knees filming my DVD collection. He looks up and lets out a wolf-whistle, and Bianca claps her hands. 'See, there you go! Bright colours really work on TV. Take a seat.'

I sit on the sofa and Bianca pulls up the pouffe opposite me. 'Actually it'd be good to get your hair off your face. Can I just . . .?' She pulls a clip from her pocket and reaches forward to fix my fringe up. 'Perfect.'

She checks the camera is rolling, then gives me a big grin. 'So then, Chlo, we're all dying to know: why did you decide to marry yourself?!'

I grimace and stroke Dora's ears. 'God, where do I start?'

Bianca tucks her legs up underneath her, her attractive face sympathetic. 'Tell you what, just pretend I'm your mate and start at the beginning. It doesn't matter if you ramble on, we can cut out any of that. Rant away!'

'Hmm, yeah, but I don't think it pays to be bitter. My decision to marry myself is less about anger and more about acceptance.'

'True, but I love what you were saying on your blog, about how there's so much stigma around being single. I get it all the time!'

'Are you single then?' I ask interestedly.

'I am now. Some men don't know a good thing when they've got it!' She pouts at Seth in mock-resentment and he frowns into the viewer, looking embarrassed.

Bianca winks at me as if to suggest she'll tell me their history later and I smile back, intrigued.

'Come on then, what's so good about being single, Chlo?' she asks.

'Well.' I tip my head against the cushions in thought. 'For a start, I don't have to deal with someone else's bad moods.' Bianca nods vigorously and I settle back into the couch, feeling more relaxed. 'And I can do whatever I want, whenever I want.'

I'm quite happy with the way the filming has gone; aside from a cringey moment in my bedroom when the silk draping fell down and revealed my collection of Care Bears, I think I come across as quite a reasonable person.

'You work well on camera, Chlo, you're a natural,' Bianca says as she passes me a contributor contract to sign.

'Thanks.' I scan the page, feeling excited. I've always wanted to see how filming works behind the scenes. I've helped out on a few promotional client videos at Top Banana but they're nothing compared to this.

'We're so honoured to come to your wedding. I'll look into getting a filming licence for the Bandstand tomorrow.'

'Oh yeah, I hadn't even thought about that. It must be such a fascinating job,' I say. 'What other documentaries have you done?'

'Hmm.' Bianca rubs her nose. 'We did a great one about clubbing in Ibiza.'

'And that one about gap year students,' Seth reminds her, packing up his boom mic.

'I'd love to see some,' I say.

'Sure, I'll send you some links some time,' Bianca says vaguely. 'Oh, can I just grab the trouser suit back?'

'Of course, one sec!' I jog into my bedroom to change, taking one last look at myself before I remove the suit. Maybe shoulder pads do work after all.

When I return to the lounge, Bianca and Seth have disappeared.

'Hey, guys?' I call, walking down the landing. I see them in the kitchen; Seth's bent over, filming something on the worktop.

'Whatcha doing?' I ask and Bianca turns, a strange look on her face. 'Is Saffron your flatmate, Chloe?'

'Uh, yeah. Why?'

'She left you a note.' Bianca stands aside and I see for the first time that there's a letter propped up against the kettle. I recognise Saffron's loopy handwriting and pick up the piece of paper with trepidation. Shit, I bet she's doing a runner. I knew something was going on.

Sighing, I scan the first paragraph, then feel my face stiffen in shock. Time slows right down and each word leaps out at me, jolting my vision.

Hey Chloe,
It's not easy for me to tell you this and I've actually been through a mental time myself recently, OK? Basically, I need to clear my head and so I've moved out and put all my stuff in storage. I've cancelled my rent and told our landlord that I'm over-stressed and you'll arrange a replacement tenant for me – it's not like you gave me a choice.

I find you very difficult to live with because you're really uptight about everything and I need to surround myself with people who are positive and caring.

Anyway, there's another thing I'm not proud of but at the same time it's not really my fault – Ant and I have fallen in love. We didn't expect it!! The fact is, we've got loads in common – he's a free spirit like me and we nurture each other.

That time you were away in the forest, I went to his flat to teach him meditation and somehow we ended up connecting physically, and since then, it's like we're each other's destiny.

It's against my values to hide it any more. Ant didn't want to tell you yet but seeing as how you're sooo enlightened you're marrying yourself I figured you can deal with this!!

I'm staying with Ant in Portsmouth while he does his sailing course. We're both really happy and we'd rather you didn't contact us — I really don't need the hassle at the moment. It's not all about you, you know.

I hope you find a new flatmate who is more suited to you. We all need harmony in our lives.

Namaste,
Saffron

I hold the letter in front of me, staring at it. Then I walk over to the wall next to the fridge and start banging my fore-head against it, slowly and deliberately.

'Erm, Chloe. Is everything OK?' Bianca asks behind me. Her voice seems tinny and faraway.

'Saffron was shitty G-string girl all along?' I whisper, still banging my forehead on the wall. The thud echoes comfort-ingly in my ears.

'Pardon?' Bianca says.

'What a mug. What a total mug.' I let out a wild yelp and turn. I'm staring directly into the cold eye of Seth's camera. He lowers it and frowns at me.

'Chloe, you don't look well. I think she needs to sit down,' he says to Bianca, who tuts and turns to me.

'Is Ant your ex-boyfriend, Chloe?'

I feel my skin tightening as recollections start spooling through my head like clues in a thriller. Why didn't I bloody realise?

I take a step towards Bianca and Seth, feeling as if I'm walking in quicksand.

'How about you tell us what just happened?' Bianca nudges Seth and he points the camera at me again. 'It might help to get it off your chest.'

'I . . . he . . . she . . .' My breath is coming in little bursts and I'm not sure what sort of noise will come out of me next. 'No . . . I can't. Can you go, please? I can't do this right now.' I bend over, resting my hands on my thighs, and Seth shakes his head at Bianca.

'Yeah, fine, we'll leave you to it. Catch you later, Chloe.' He tugs Bianca with him back out of the room.

I reread the note, waiting for the slam of the front door, then let it slide to the floor through numb fingers. I walk slowly to Saffron's bedroom door and open it. Blood-red skylight streaks the empty room, making it look like a murder scene.

Fresh versions of the truth wash over me until I'm shivering with anger.

'You motherfuckers.' I say it quietly at first, and then I'm shouting it at the top of my lungs. I stamp and hurl myself across the room, lashing out at thin air and bellowing with rage.

Finally, when my voice is raw and I am spent, I flop down onto the futon and lie staring at the ceiling until the room turns black.

Chapter 23

I'm finding it quite hard to love myself right now. In fact, self-compassion seems to have quite quickly crossed the ugly line into self-pity. These past two weeks, paranoia and resentment have crept in on me like sly bullies. It's Saturday morning and I sit hunched in bed, obsessing over all the sordid details I missed. That night I came back from the forest, Saffron had probably just returned from Ant's. How could she look me in the eye when she'd just shagged my boyfriend? How could *he*? And that time I found Ant here at my flat after work – he hadn't come to collect his stuff at all, he'd come to see Saffron. I shudder when I remember Saffron wrapped in her towel; they'd probably just had sex. Being cheated on is bad enough, but when you're lied to, when you realise that there are loads of holes in your version of reality, it's enough to make you go a little bit insane.

I can't believe my dog was a witness. How sick is that? I look down at Dora, who is lying on the carpet, gazing up at me.

'Why didn't you tell me it was Saffron?' I ask her. 'You could have alerted me somehow – like drug-sniffer dogs do.'

Dora yawns sedately, then stretches and lets out a small fart.

'Come on, let's get you breakfast,' I sigh, and swing my legs over the bed.

In the kitchen, I pour her biscuits into a bowl and she pushes it around the lino with her nose in her haste to get every last scrap.

I turn the kettle on and lean against the worktop. Saffron's Buddha tea towel is still hanging on the back of the door; I grab it and ram it into the bin. This flat has too many memories.

It's so unfair, just as I was starting to feel I have control of my life back, Ant's managed to pull the rug from under me yet again. Several times I've started to call him – but his behaviour is so inexcusable that there's no point in trying to make him see how much he's hurt me; if he had respect for me he'd never have done it in the first place. The Ant I thought I loved doesn't even exist and I've lost one of my best friends forever.

Which makes me feel even worse about my standoff with Emma. I can't lose two best friends in one year; I've got to make amends.

I dial Emma's number.

'Hello.' Her voice is heavy.

'I figured I better call you; it's been weeks since we last spoke. You obviously aren't bothered about our friendship.' I take out the milk and slam the fridge door.

'Chloe, I've got a family to look after.'

'I know you have a family. I'm supposed to be part of it.'

'Look, it's not my fault I don't agree with your wedding. I'm allowed an opinion. If you hadn't noticed, half the nation's reacting the same way as me.'

'Right.' I breathe in deeply through my nostrils. 'Couldn't you just be happy for me?'

'Chloe, I don't have time to be happy for *me*, let alone you. Do you realise what a luxury this hippy-dippy "me-time", "self-love" crap is? I can't even have a shit without being interrupted. And I haven't drunk a hot cup of tea in months. Do you know how many half-empty stone-cold mugs are lying round my house?' Emma's voice vibrates with agitation and I raise my tea to my mouth and watch the steam rise guiltily.

'I'm sorry,' I say with effort. I don't really know what I'm apologising for, but I want my sister back. 'I wish I could help.'

'You *can* help – by not being so . . .'

'So what?'

'Different,' Emma says, then snorts. I sense a thawing.

'We might be different but that doesn't mean we can't support each other,' I say tentatively. 'I can come over and clear up those mugs.'

'Hmm. Maisie's been asking about you. I haven't told her about your wedding. I just think it would . . . confuse her.'

I wince; suddenly I feel an urgent pang to see Maisie. 'Em, children are considerably more open-minded than adults. I'm sure she'd be fine but, whatever, we don't have to talk about it any more. I told you, I'm having the wedding anyway, without your blessing, but it doesn't mean we have to be at loggerheads.'

'I have missed talking to you,' Emma admits.

'Er, hello? I know! It's been awful. And you'll never believe what I found out about Ant.'

Emma swallows.

'I found out who shitty G-string girl is,' I continue.

There's a pause and I frown. 'Hello?'

'I know,' Emma sighs.

'What?'

'I know it's Saffron – Linda told me.'

'When?'

'A few weeks ago.'

'You knew and you didn't tell me?'

'What?' Emma's tone rises defensively. 'It doesn't make a difference now. I'm not condoning it.'

'You didn't tell me,' I repeat disbelievingly. 'Everyone's known about it for weeks and I'm the last bloody person to find out.'

I hear Toby start to cry and Emma makes a cross blowing noise. 'We weren't talking, Chloe. And anyway, with this whole wedding thing I thought you'd moved on.'

'Fuck you, Emma.' I hang up and put my elbows on the kitchen worktop, kneading my fists into my eye sockets.

Hurt and rage sear through me; I just want these horrible feelings to go away. Why am I being let down by all the people who're supposed to support me?

I hear the sweep of Dora's tail; she's watching me with her ears flat against her head. Her brown eyes are so steady and trusting that I let out a dry sob.

'You're literally the only thing I can rely on,' I tell her, sinking to the floor. She backs into me and I rest my chin on her rump.

My phone vibrates in my gown pocket and I dig it out, hoping it's Emma calling me back, but it's a new email from Katy.

Dear Chloe,

I am so so sorry to hear about Ant and your flatmate, you must be feeling like complete shit!! I want to give you a massive hug right now! Do you know what I think? I think Ant's massively insecure. He always likes lots of attention and he's scared of not being liked. Which means he's scared of being boring. I reckon he looked outside your relationship because he wanted to reinvent himself – be someone more interesting. Which, when you think about it, is so fucking sad and such a COP OUT because, if he was a bit more mature, he wouldn't need to completely fuck someone else over to feel better about himself! You are worth a MILLION of him and, I know it probably doesn't mean anything to you right now, but this has proved that you are sooooo much better off without him!

Stay strong and mail whenever you need.

Love Katy xxxx

P.S. Thanks for recommending Dr Fletcher. I went to see her at the Hove surgery and she was so nice I basically had a massive fucking breakdown and snotted all over her shoulder. She's made me see that there may be a way out of this. I owe you one.

I sigh in relief, pleased that Katy's contacted Dr Fletcher. I reread her words on Ant and find myself nodding frantically at her take on it.

The door buzzer makes me jump; I'm still in my PJs and I'm not expecting visitors. I answer hesitantly and am filled with a soaring comfort when I hear a familiar West Country accent.

'Chlo? It's your mum.'

She climbs my stairs looking tanned and toned in white shorts and a vest top, with her hair cut shorter than usual in a long bob. She looks me up and down and shakes her head. 'Bloody hell, love, look at the state of you. It's worse than I thought.'

'What are you doing here?' I ask stupidly as she gives me a tight hug.

'Thought I'd come to cheer you up; may as well stay here while you're looking for a new flatmate. I'll exorcise that bitch's room before I sleep there though.' Mum glances towards Saffron's door. 'Has she been back?'

'No, she's obviously steering clear. The landlord's pressuring me to pay her rent and she's totally ignored my emails about it.'

Mum follows me through to the lounge as I plonk despondently down on the sofa. She puts down her weekend bag and looks around the room. 'Well, you can sell that gong for a start.' She nods at Saffron's gong, still standing by the French doors.

'I couldn't! She got it especially imported from Burma.'

'Give a shit, she fucked your boyfriend.' Mum goes over to the gong and starts rolling it across the room. 'I'll put it in my car now, I'm sure we can flog it down the Lanes.'

'Mum!' I give a horrified giggle.

'Look, Chloe.' Mum straightens up with her hands on her hips. 'We Ushers aren't pushovers. We don't lie back and let people like Saffron walk all over us. We fight back.'

I stare at her wordlessly for a moment, then take a deep breath and stand up.

'You're right. I know a good second-hand music shop. Give me ten minutes.'

Mum and I barter with the shop owner and end up getting £700 in cash for the gong. I let out a whoop of nervous laughter as we get back in the car. 'I can't believe we just did that.'

'Why should you have to foot her bill? That should cover it for now.' Mum looks out of her window at the blindingly blue sky. 'Lovely day – shall we take Dora up Devil's Dyke?'

We park at the top of the South Downs and take a walking trail that has stunning views of the rolling chalk valley towards the sea. We watch the hang gliders launching themselves from the top of the hill over the patchwork green fields.

When I tell Mum that Emma already knew about Ant and Saffron and kept it quiet, she is fuming.

'Bloody typical, that is,' she rages, hurling a stick down the slope so Dora goes plummeting after it. 'You mustn't let her lord it over you, Chloe. Ever since you were teenagers Emma's wanted the upper hand.'

'Really?'

'Of course! Don't you remember when she auditioned to be Ariel behind your back?'

'Oh yeah.' When Emma and I were in sixth form, our college put on a production of Shakespeare's *The Tempest*. Emma and I were both doing drama A-level and were keen to be in it. We weren't confident enough to go for the main roles, so we decided to audition as Trinculo and Stephano – two drunken members of the shipwrecked party.

But then, on the afternoon of the auditions, Emma was up before me and I sat watching in amazement as she started spouting lines for the coveted role of Ariel, Prospero's spirit helper.

She'd obviously learnt them off by heart in secret; she was very fluent and really looked the part as she pranced around the stage with her golden locks flying behind her. Our teachers were so impressed they gave her the part right there and then.

'Luckily that turned out all right,' I smirk.

'You made a wonderful Prospero,' Mum says loyally.

When it was my turn to audition, I was so fired up on adrenalin from Emma's about-turn that I read out my favourite soliloquy from the play, by the protagonist. No other girl had tried for Prospero, as it's a male role, but our teachers thought it added an extra dimension to the character and offered me the part.

Thinking about it now, I chuckle at how put out Emma was when I got to boss her around on stage as my servant.

'That girl's got too much of her mother in her to be a good friend to you,' Mum continues, swerving a fresh cowpat.

'But they're not that similar,' I insist. 'Janice winds Emma up all the time.'

'No matter how hard you try, you'll always end up like your mother,' Mum warns.

'Not necessarily,' I argue. 'Sometimes you can learn from other people's mistakes.'

Mum glances at me wryly. 'Is that what this crazy wedding's about? My messy divorces have put you off marriage altogether?'

'Well, you're definitely living proof that diamonds aren't forever, Ma.' I grin.

'I can't help blaming myself – I gave you too much free rein when you were younger.' Mum gazes out over the shimmering valley. 'You were always roaming the countryside, your imagination running wild.'

'What? I had an amazing childhood!'

'And then I let you go off travelling, wandering about like some stray vagabond.'

'That was the best time of my life!'

'Then, of course, some bastard man goes and fucks you up. No wonder you've gone a bit screwy.'

'I've not gone mad.'

'But you've still got a chance at happiness, Chloe.' Mum's face sags with sadness.

'Mum, don't you see, I'm doing this because I am happy – being me.' I slow to a halt on the footpath. 'You've got to *be* the happiness.'

Mum also pauses, sparking up a cigarette.

'Marrying myself is not about me giving up on men or romance at all. I've got *loads* of love to give. The point is that, right now, I'm directing it at myself.'

Mum blows out a stream of smoke. 'So you've not been targeted by some cult then?'

'No!'

'That's what Shirley reckons. She said I should approach you carefully cos you've probably been brainwashed.'

'I'm not in a cult, Mum.'

'And you're not giving up . . . you know.' Mum wiggles her head meaningfully and I frown.

'What?'

'*Sex*.' She whispers the word. 'I'm too old for all that but you've still got years.'

I laugh. 'No way – I'm not giving up *sex*.' I mimic her hushed tones. 'All I'm giving up is putting up with bullshit.'

'Oh well, then. I can live with that.' Mum links her arm through mine and we continue walking as Dora appears over the crest of the hill, her paw aloft, wondering where we've got to.

'Surely you're not too old for "all that", are you?' I take the opportunity to ask – we rarely talk about Mum's sex life, or lack of.

'Course I am. The only penis I've seen in ten years is in Life Drawing classes, Chlo.' She nods grimly toward her own crotch. 'All that's left down there is cobwebs.'

Chapter 24

I haven't had such fun with Mum in years; in her determination to cheer me up, she's dropped her usual gloomy outlook and is acting the fool just to make me laugh. After a long walk on the Downs, we go for a Thai dinner and then to see some improvised comedy. Mum even starts heckling the actors, telling them to stick to their day jobs.

On the way home, we're accosted by a stag party on St James's Street. The men wear police outfits on their top halves, with their legs clad in suspenders and high heels. Mum gets quite carried away and starts whipping one of them with his own truncheon.

It's another sunny day on Sunday and Mum lays out croissants on the roof terrace.

'It's good to get out of Shillingborne for a bit,' she muses, stretching out on the rug. 'Sometimes I feel like the odd one out down there, with people like Barbara and Mark looking down their noses at me.'

'They can fuck off,' I growl.

Mum chuckles. 'They wouldn't last a minute in Brighton.'

'Yeah, *they'd* be the odd ones out here. We don't like judgmental wankers.' I stuff a chunk of pastry in my mouth. 'Do you want to come to my befriending date with Muriel later? You know, the elderly lady I told you about.'

Simone and I have met Muriel a few times this month; Jess has been joining us too. Every time we see her I marvel at her upbeat attitude.

'Why not?' Mum says, leaning back on her elbows. Her features are so much softer when she's not angry.

We walk along the beach to The Lobster, where I've arranged to meet Muriel and Jess. I fill Mum in on the work I'm doing for Brighton Befrienders to get more volunteers and donations.

'We're doing a photo shoot soon with some of the elderly members and their befrienders having a laugh together,' I say. 'And I'm helping them with social media and web copy.'

'That's wonderful, Chlo. Maybe I should see if there's befriending in Shillingborne. I can't tell you how much I miss my own parents.'

As we approach The Lobster, the outside wooden terrace is teeming with groups of people enjoying the sun. I spy Jess and Muriel already settled at a table, under a parasol. Muriel's wearing a blue cotton dress and white sun hat. When she sees me, she pulls her hat off and waves it in the air, her peachy round face breaking into a wide grin.

'Heyo!' Jess, in a tank top and denim skirt, jumps up and pulls two chairs up to the table.

'Ooh, is this your Labrador? What an absolute darling.' Muriel holds her gnarled fingers out to Dora, who raises her head she can be tickled under the chin. 'You like that, don't you? Look at your fur, so soft,' she croons. 'I used to have Labs when I lived in Kent; I'd walk them through the meadows every day. I tried to adopt a rescue dog recently but they wouldn't allow it – said I'm too old!'

'Aw, well I'll bring her with me every time I visit,' I promise.

AJ comes out to take our order, grabbing Mum's hand and kissing it when he hears she's my mother.

'May I offer congratulations on producing Chloe.'

Mum giggles girlishly. 'I'm not sure I can take all the credit.'

'Maybe it's her father's genes then?' AJ suggests.

'Hell no, he hasn't got a decent gene in his body!' Mum looks chuffed when AJ gives his deep guffaw.

'Well I'm sure you're very proud of her, especially with her recent proposal.' AJ beams at me and Mum nods hesitantly.

'I've already bought a new hat for the wedding!' Muriel's eyes dance. I was bowled over by how unfazed she was when I told her about marrying myself. She just blinked a few times and said, 'Times will change.'

'And Muriel, how're you liking my homemade lemonade?' AJ crouches next to Muriel.

She smacks her lips together, grasping his wrist. 'It takes me right back to childhood, very refreshing! And thank you for playing this swing music, I love it!'

'You ain't heard nothing yet.' AJ winks and points to where a five-piece band are setting up in the cordoned-off area outside The Lobster.

'Has John got the kids?' I ask Jess.

'Yeah, he's taking them swimming.' She rolls her eyes. 'He kicked up a right stink, wanted to watch the football. But I told him I had an important date.' She smiles at Muriel.

'Typical man; they'd rather hide behind a newspaper than pull their weight with childcare,' Mum tuts, dragging her chair into the sun. 'When Chloe was young, her father would just as soon talk to the television as play with his daughter.'

'Really?' Jess looks between Mum and me eagerly and I frown. Even though Dad and I have fallen out, I don't like to hear Mum's Dad-bashing. 'Was he quite hands-off then?'

'Oh, he was hopeless,' Mum says with relish. 'Life was so much easier after we'd split up. It was like looking after two children. He'd throw a strop if parenting duties messed with his precious "leisure time"; said he needed to unwind outside of work. Course, at the time I didn't realise "work" involved giving his secretary a seeing-to. No wonder he was always so knackered!'

She smiles grimly as Jess and Muriel gasp in sympathy, and AJ raises his eyebrows while serving our coffees.

'Was it difficult being a single mother?' Muriel asks, stroking Dora's head, which is resting on her knee.

'It wasn't much fun doing it on my own. But it was better than living with an imbecile.'

Muriel looks at me, her hooded eyes astute. 'I don't expect you understood very much of it, did you, dear?'

'No,' I say quietly. It's hard to explain the feeling of being stretched between two opposing parents – watching them hate each other but loving them both.

'Did you get on with your husband, Muriel?' Mum asks.

'My Brian was a gift.' Muriel moves her head from side to side like a tortoise. 'We had our differences but we had them together.'

'Ah, how sweet.' Jess looks wistful. 'It sounds like you fell for the right man.'

'Oh, the falling bit is easy to do.' Muriel waves a dismissive hand. 'It's the staying part that's harder.'

Mum nods fervently, fishing in her bag for a cigarette.

'What are you doing that for?' Muriel turns to her, her mouth pinched in disapproval.

'What?' Mum pauses, the lighter inches from her fag.

'Smoking. It shortens your life.' Muriel holds up a finger.

I can tell Mum's about to give her usual 'I'll probably cark it soon anyway' line but then she bites her lip, looking at the lively older woman in front of her. I'm shocked to see her meekly tuck the cigarette back in its box.

There's a strumming of guitar strings as the band does a sound check and then the female singer introduces them. 'Hello, we're the Merry Widows, here to give you some Brighton rock 'n' roll.'

The seated guests cheer and several groups of people sitting on the beach by the pier look over interestedly.

'Our first song is dedicated to Muriel – are you out there?' the singer calls, shading her eyes and scanning the tables. Muriel waves her hat in the air.

'What we're doing for you now, Muriel, is a little "Twist and Shout"!'

'My favourite! Jess, did you and AJ tell them?' Muriel beams and Jess nods, laughing.

As the band start blasting out the jaunty classic, Muriel hoists herself to her feet with her walking stick. Jess and I join her, swinging her hands back and forth to the music.

Kids from the next table get up and also start dancing, whirling around in front of Muriel.

Encouraged, Muriel lets go of our hands and bravely steps forward, bending her knees and dropping into a low swivel, sliding her feet along to the beat. Her auburn curls gleam brassy in the sunshine as she bops, grinning at the band. We hover behind her, holding out our arms, just in case her dodgy hip gives out. The singer belts out the lyrics and we all sing along: 'Ah ah ah ah . . . shake it up baaaaby nowwww!'

AJ is standing in the entrance laughing over at us, and several people are pointing at Muriel dancing and taking photos. I grab my phone and start filming.

When the tune finishes, we all clap and shriek with admiration and AJ lets out a loud wolf-whistle. Muriel takes a small bow then pats down her dress insouciantly as she takes her seat. 'They didn't call me Queen of the Hammersmith Palais for nothing.'

The band plays an hour's set and people come up from the beach to join in the dancing. Our table proves very popular as children and adults come up to talk to Muriel. One young girl seems really in awe of her and keeps staring at her with big blue eyes. When Muriel tells her she's ninety-one, the girl asks, 'But how are you still alive?'

Eventually Jess, who's giving Muriel a lift home, reluctantly says it's time to leave.

'It's been an absolute pleasure.' Mum hugs Muriel tightly.

I order us some sundowners and olives and we throw the ball across the pebbles for Dora, watching the starlings draw fluid punctuation marks over the pier.

'What a wonderful woman.' Mum shakes her head. 'Puts me to shame, she does.'

I look across at her fondly. 'Thanks for coming to see me, Mum, you've really helped.'

She holds my gaze, her eyes reflecting the sea.

'I am proud of you, you know,' she says gruffly. 'Always have been.'

'Aww.'

'And I'd like to buy your wedding dress.'

'Oh no, Mum, there's no need for that. I was just going to get a second-hand one, something simple.'

'No, I've got a bit saved; if you're going to marry yourself you're to do it properly. There must be some quality bridal shops around here.'

'Wow, thanks, Mum!' I'd written off the idea of frothy designer gowns, but now I feel a little fizz of excitement.

'I know you were always more of a tomboy, mucking about with slow-worms and climbing trees,' Mum continues. 'But there's nowt wrong with feeling like a princess for a day.'

We have dinner back at the flat and Mum goes to bed early. I sit up on the sofa feeling so grateful that she came to rescue me. Hanging out with Muriel and Jess today has really lifted my mood too.

I open my laptop and upload the video I took of Muriel dancing to 'Twist and Shout', watching it over and over again and chuckling at her wild abandon. Her face is glowing and her movements are uninhibited by her elderly body. It's as if she's suddenly been transported back to the 1960s and she's a young woman again.

I click through to my blog and start writing a new post.

One Foot in the Rave

30.06.18

Dear Reader,

Here's a video of Muriel, aged ninety-one, dancing
impulsively to her favourite tune – isn't it
brilliant? It seems like such a novelty, which
makes me wonder why we don't see more elderly

people dancing. I guess in our culture, live music and dancing is often seen as the domain of youth, which is crazy because surely our relationship to music should only get richer with the passing of time. Why should elderly people stand in the wings while the young ones have all the fun?

Well, the answer is probably that they don't get out as much – it's a bit harder when you have to rely on a zimmer and most of your mates have popped their clogs! It doesn't mean that people like Muriel don't want to socialise though; look at her, she loves a rave-up and don't anyone try and tell me it's bad for her health.

Did you know that over half of all people aged over seventy-five live alone? And that a lot of those people have mobility issues and so don't speak to a living soul for days, even weeks at a time?

Thank God for charities like Brighton Befrienders, who assess and train volunteers, matching them with like-minded people over sixty-five and arranging regular dates.

It was through this befriending charity that I met Muriel – and from the first time I laid eyes on her, something special happened. It's not just me – there's a bunch of testimonials from members who say this charity has, quite literally, changed their lives.

So, next time you see an elderly neighbour, spare a smile, a quick chat or a cup of tea. Or, you know, you can always invite them dancing. I'm definitely taking Muriel out again – a date with her is better than any I've had on bloody Tinder ;)

Yours forever wandering,
Chloe x

Chapter 25

Dom arranges my wedding dress fitting for the following Saturday. Mum and I meet him in a cafe in the North Laine and he tells us he's made an appointment at Bridal Desires – a boutique bridal shop that frequently features in *Vogue*.

'Only the best for our Chloe!' he says, hugging me. He's dressed for the occasion in a bright blue chequered suit and gold cravat. 'You're doing so well. I'm still reeling from the shock – surely Saffron is far too crusty for Ant!'

'Too right; all that matted hair makes her look like the back end of a yak,' Mum agrees, stirring her coffee.

'I slept with a Rasta once,' Dom ruminates. 'His dreadlocks kept bashing me round the face – it was most unpleasant. And they stank of hamous.'

Mum cackles and I look around at the other diners. 'Shh, guys, we're in Brighton. You can't slag off hippies.'

'Hey, Chloe!' The cafe door's bell jingles as Bianca and Seth from Cube Productions come in. Bianca looks glam in tight white pedal pushers and a halterneck top, with her two-toned hair pulled into a fat bun. Seth's in denim shorts and a T-shirt with the words 'Cool Story Bro' emblazoned on the front. He's wheeling a big black case behind him.

Bianca sounded relieved when I called her about the dress fitting; I think she thought I'd had some kind of irreversible breakdown the evening I found Saffron's note. She tried to get me to tell her more but I said it was still too raw for me to discuss.

'Chloe, I loved your blog about that old lady dancing – soooooo cute! Everyone's going mad for it, hey?' Bianca's gold hoop earrings swing against my cheeks as she kisses me.

'Thanks, yeah, Muriel's a bit of an internet star at the moment!' I grin. My blog post has been shared loads this past week, and Brighton's local newspaper, *The Argus,* have reposted the video of Muriel dancing. Kate Dooley's over the moon because Brighton Befrienders has been inundated with volunteer requests and donations.

'And you must be Dominic?' Bianca greets Dom. 'I checked out your vlog – I'm loving your work!' She looks him up and down with interest. 'Especially the recent post about religious style – who'd've thought a dog collar could look so hot.'

'Well, I'll need to look the part on Chloe's big day, especially now we're getting her a knockout dress.' Dom winks at Mum.

'Thanks for inviting us today.' Seth smiles at me. 'I don't suppose you have a date for your hen do yet? Just trying to pin down our filming schedule.'

'Aha, well actually' – Dom clutches my wrist – 'I've just had the go-ahead this morning . . .' He grins.

'What is it?'

'I've booked us a float at Brighton Pride's parade in just a month's time! I figured as it's the biggest and best international celebration of love, why not bring a self-love wagon to the party?'

'No way, Dom! How did you manage that?'

'Pulled a few strings.' He winks. 'I've let all your mates know. And, as hens are rather unremarkable birds, I suggested that we all dress up as birds of paradise instead.'

'Oh my God, this is the best idea *ever*, thanks so much.' As I hug him, Bianca and Seth exchange delighted looks.

'We can get some awesome footage of the carnival.' Bianca's jade eyes are shining. 'I've got a great feeling about this, Chloe. I reckon you're going to be the highlight of our TV series.'

'Actually, I wanted to ask you . . .' I hesitate, and Dom and Mum nod at me encouragingly.

'I've been asked to be a guest on ITV's *Breakfast with Britain*,' I say. 'They mailed me a few days ago – would it clash with your documentary?

'Not at all, that's fantastic news, Chloe!' Bianca punches the air. 'I know the production team so I'm pretty sure they'll let me capture the behind-the-scenes action.'

'Great opportunity to get the nation onboard,' Seth agrees. 'They've got millions of viewers.'

'Eeek, I know. I'm not sure I have the guts; I haven't replied yet,' I grimace.

'Of course you must do it – in for a penny, in for a pound,' Dom says, linking his arms through mine and Mum's. 'Right then, ladies, let's go and bag ourselves a gown.'

We leave the cafe and go down a little back street to a town-house painted bright blue, with a gold sign saying Bridal Desires and wooden shutters over the windows.

'It may look discreet but it's definitely the best place in town,' Dom says as we approach. 'They stock a curated edit of designer dresses, mostly handmade in France.'

'The owner of this place is OK with us filming, right?' Seth checks.

'Yep, but are you sure I shouldn't tell her about, you know' – I lower my voice – 'the whole not-having-a-groom thing?'

'Completely sure,' Bianca says. 'It'll make for a more interesting dynamic.'

'Shouldn't make a difference to her anyway.' Seth flicks his fringe out of his eyes. 'She'll still flog you a dress, right?'

The front door flies open and a woman stands on the step with her arms aloft. 'You must be Chloe Usher? I'm Jeanne!'

Jeanne has a French accent and her stiff black bob looks like a Lego helmet. She's wearing a silvery polo neck and pale grey culottes.

'Pleased to meet you.' I shake her hand. 'We're filming everything from now on if you don't mind?' I glance back as Seth gives me the thumbs-up and mounts his camera onto his shoulder.

'Not at all. You're all very welcome at Bridal Desires.' Jeanne waves at the lens. 'And you must be the mother of the bride?' She squeezes my mum into a big hug and reaches out to grasp Dom's hand as she's doing so. 'Please, come with me, meet my babies.'

We follow her down a corridor lined with luxury damask wallpaper. 'Usher is such an appropriate surname for a wedding!' Jeanne says. 'Will you be keeping it?'

'Yes, definitely.' I smile at her.

We let out a collective gasp as we enter the large fitting room; wedding gowns of all hues and textures line the walls – ivory, champagne and rose blush trains billow from the hangers, embellished with intricate beading. Above them, flower arrangements are creatively draped over glass shelves, along with a selection of wedding shoes, twinkling in the soft light from the chandeliers. A huge gilded mirror lines one wall and there's a changing booth with heavy silk curtains in the far corner.

Seth and Bianca carry their equipment across the thick cream carpet to the padded window seat and set the camera up on a tripod.

'Chloe, we won't put a mic on you as you'll be changing, but this should pick up most of the sound.' Seth angles a large boom microphone over our heads.

Mum, Dom and I stand in the middle of the room gaping at everything, and Jeanne trails her fingertips along the rows of hanging dresses. 'Choosing the right wedding dress is like falling in love,' she ruminates. 'You 'ave to follow your gut, your instinct, and, I promise you, you will find "the one". It might be the first you try on, it might be the tenth . . . just keep an open heart.'

'Right.' I touch one of the hand-stitched corsets tentatively.

'As you only have six weeks before the wedding, you'll want a dress that needs little alteration,' Jeanne continues. 'And the shade of your dress will inform the colour of your bouquet, your make-up and even your cake.'

'Really?' I rub my forehead, feeling a bit overwhelmed. 'But I've already decided on sunflowers for my bouquet; they're my favourite.'

'D'accord, then don't choose a gown with blue or purple undertones,' Jeanne says, as if it's obvious.

'I thought all wedding dresses were white?' I frown.

Jeanne laughs uproariously. 'I'll leave you to play while I bring you some refreshments.'

'How're you feeling, Chloe?' Bianca calls from the window seat.

'Erm, well there's a lot to choose from.'

'Don't worry, we'll soon narrow it down.' Dom snaps to attention. 'It's just about deciding what sort of silhouette you want – you've got the ball gown, the A-line, the trumpet, the mermaid, the sheath, the tea-length.'

He starts taking dresses off the rail and hanging them in the changing booth. 'You've got great shoulders, Chlo, we can try strapless gowns with a full skirt. Or you could even pull off a backless number.'

Jeanne reappears with a tray of champagne flutes and places it down on the low table by the window seat. 'Santé!'

She nods at the dresses Dom has selected. 'I see you 'ave a best man with good taste. Come on, Chloe.' She holds out her hand, then looks at mine. 'Where is your engagement ring?'

'I . . . um . . . it's being resized.' I flick a guilty glance towards Bianca and follow Jeanne into the changing booth.

'OK, prepare yourselves.' Jeanne pulls the silk curtains around us. 'The results will be breathtaking.'

Eight dress fittings later and my breath has most definitely been taken; the dress I'm wearing has a corset so tight it's squeezing all the air from my lungs, the layers of stiff material are scratching my skin and the heavy skirt is making my legs sweat. I feel like I'm boiling in a bag.

'Oh Chloe, you're glowing,' Mum gulps. She's already had three glasses of champagne and her expression is soppy.

'Melting, more like,' I say, glancing at my red face in the mirror.

'I think this one is especially flattering; it gives you a tiny waist.' Dom tilts his head.

'But I can't breathe,' I grumble.

Dom sighs. 'What have I told you about fashion and comfort? They *are* mutually exclusive!'

'Now tell me, 'ave you had a little ripple yet, Chloe?' Jeanne asks. 'Maybe the urge to scream out loud or cry?'

'The lace fishtail one was OK.' I shrug.

Jeanne shakes her head. 'Non, "OK" is not enough. Tell me, what kind of person are you going to marry? How did you meet?'

Mum and Dom exchange glances and Bianca sits up straight, gesturing for me to face the camera.

I look up at the decorative ceiling and wrinkle my nose. 'Hmm, I've known her for ages; all my life actually.'

'Aha – a lesbian – I knew it!' Jeanne gasps, then motions for me to continue.

I giggle. 'Well, one night I realised that I'd taken her completely for granted . . . and I told her I loved her.'

Jeanne has closed her eyes and is nodding as I talk, circling a hand by her ear as if she's physically catching my words. 'Beautiful. What do you love most about her?'

I smile. 'I trust that she'll always have my best interests at heart. I love her sense of humour and the way she always tries to find a bright side. I'm proud of how she always tries to be a better person.'

Seth raises his head from his viewing screen and for a moment I catch his eye. An odd tension flickers across his face.

Jeanne moves over to the far rail, muttering quietly. Her palm massages the air above the dresses and then suddenly her index finger gravitates towards a hanger. She unhooks it and swings around, swirling a gleaming ivory satin gown in front of her.

'Try this,' she says, with quiet confidence.

I stand in my pants and bra in the changing booth as Jeanne slips the dress over my head, and at once the fabric is like a cool balm to my feverish skin.

'And this.' She puts a double-layered tulle veil attached to a rhinestone tiara on my head and pulls the iridescent material down over my face. 'Parfait.'

I step out from behind the curtain and everyone in the room goes still. I turn to face the mirror and swallow hard. The dress clings to me like a melting peach-gold cloud at sunset. The sweetheart neckline nestles just below my collarbone and the soft bodice hugs my torso like a second skin.

Impulsively I spin on my toes and the full skirt billows out from my waist, floating weightlessly around me, the crystal beading detail making it sparkle like ocean waves. Laughter bubbles from me and I step towards the mirror and lift the veil up over my head to reveal my wide smile. 'This is me,' I say to my reflection.

'Can you dance in it?' Dom asks, and I do some experimental moves. 'Yeah, it's totally flexible.'

'And do you want to take it off?' Jeanne asks.

'No, actually, I don't. I want to keep it on all day long.' I grin.

'Then it's the one, Chloe, you've found *the one*!'

'Look at her – my girl is all grown up!' Mum hugs Jeanne.

'And try these shoes with it. Aren't they divine?' Dom puts a pair of diamante heels in front of me and I step into them.

'I'm not great in heels. I think pumps might be better. Or even sparkly trainers.' I lift up my skirt and totter around the room in wobbly circles.

'Trainers?' Dom looks horrified. 'Absolutely not. You just need to get your stride on, like this.' He raises himself high onto his tiptoes, then holds his arms slightly away from his body, with his palms outstretched.

Tilting his chin upward, he starts strutting across the carpet like a catwalk model. As he reaches the corner he shoots a sultry look over his shoulder towards the camera and then turns dramatically, flicking his quiff.

I start copying Dom, surprised at how effective the technique is. I'm so busy concentrating on my steps that I don't hear the door open.

'Are you fucking kidding me?'

I spin around to see Verity standing in the doorway wearing a sparkling tiara and a pink wedding gown with the biggest puffball skirt I have ever seen. Behind her, Simone and a dyed-blonde woman, with similar features to Verity, are jostling to get a look at me.

Verity and I glare at each other and Jeanne hastily puts her glass down. 'Miss Winterbourne, I'll be with you très bientôt. Did you try on the whole selection?'

Verity is looking at me like a cat before it pounces on a mouse.

'Where did you get that dress?' she asks with eerie calm.

'I . . . from the rail.' I smooth my hands over the bodice protectively.

'I want it. Mum, can I have it?'

'Yes of course, darling,' the woman behind her murmurs.

'No, we're having it,' Mum growls. 'Who's this?'

'I work with her,' I say, holding Verity's gaze. 'I thought you ordered a dress back in May?'

'It was too small,' Simone pipes up over Verity's shoulder.

'It was too tacky,' Verity corrects her. 'I want that one.' She points at me.

'Well, I'm sure there are plenty more like this, right, Jeanne?'

'Actually, that's a one-off I'm afraid,' Jeanne says nervously. 'It's the last in a couture collection by the great designer Sofia Dubois.'

'Then call her immediately and tell her to make me one,' Verity snaps.

'I'm afraid she died last November,' Jeanne whispers.

'Whaaaaaaaaat?' Verity's screech makes the chandelier rattle overhead and I do a throat-cutting motion at Seth to tell him to stop filming, but Bianca overrides it. She's bouncing on her seat excitedly as she watches the drama unfold.

'You said you would help me find "the one" and I'm telling you *this* is it.' Verity glares at Jeanne whilst jabbing her finger at me. 'If you don't let me have it I will ruin your name; no bride will go near you with a barge pole.'

'Excuse me, young lady, you have no right to gate-crash our fitting and make such demands.' Mum puts her hands on her hips. 'I'm buying this dress for my daughter and that's all there is to it.'

'And if you try to smear Jeanne's name I'll put a stop to it. I have slightly more influence in the fashion world than you do, darling,' Dom adds.

Verity lowers her head and stares at me, breathing heavily like a raging bull. Then, before I can register what is happening, she charges at me, grabbing onto my waist and burying her head in my stomach.

'Arrrrgh!' Already off-balance on my high heels, I go flying backwards. My flailing arms get tangled in the changing booth curtains and there's a loud *riiiiiip* as our combined body weight tears them away from their railing.

I land painfully on my coccyx, with Verity and the curtains on top of me. She straddles me, tugging at my bodice, but I can't free my hands to fight her. I'm swaddled in layers of heavy material and my full skirt is tangled around my legs. I kick them hard and my shoe flies through the air, hitting her on the back of the head.

'Owwwww, bitch!' she squeals, grabbing my tiara and bashing my chest with it. 'Give me the dress!'

'No! Why should I?' I'm wriggling underneath the grip of her thighs; my skin is burning up.

'You haven't even got a man to remove it on your wedding night – it's a fucking waste!'

'I will not accept 'omophobia on my premises.' Jeanne's accent thickens with outrage as she, Dom and Mum surround Verity, tugging at her upper arms in an attempt to pull her off me. 'Lesbians have just as much right to get married!'

Verity pauses, inches from my face, her blazing blue eyes widening. 'Lesbians?' She turns to Jeanne.

'Oui, so what if Chloe's partner ees a woman? Their passion runs just as deep.'

Verity sits back on my pelvis and lets out a bark of laughter. 'Oh God, you don't know, do you?'

'Know what?' Jeanne looks rattled as Mum, Dom and I avoid her gaze. I frown at Bianca, who is silently cracking up on the window seat.

Verity shakes her head; a victorious smile plays on her lips. 'She hasn't got a partner, you fool – it's a total sham. She's marrying herself.'

I take advantage of Verity's distraction and thrust my hips upward hard. She slides sideways and Dom grabs her under the arms, pulling her off me. Mum pins down her shoulders and her long legs thrash underneath the puffball skirt.

Still swathed in silk, I quickly jack-knife my body away from her across the carpet and, panting, end up staring at the pair of red Converse trainers in front of me. My gaze travels slowly upward until I'm looking into a familiar glossy black lens.

'Er, are you gonna give me a hand or what?' I ask crossly as Seth's head jerks up.

'What? Oh, yeah, sorry!' Seth shoves his camera on the cabinet and grabs my elbow, unwrapping the curtain from my body as he does so.

I breathe out loudly and flap my arms as they're freed, standing up straight to view the scene before me.

Simone and Verity's mother are dithering in the doorway, looking aghast but not making any effort to help Verity, who is writhing around on the floor like a demented snake. Mum is kneeling on one arm and Dom is pinning down the other. They're wearing identical expressions of resolute determination. Poor Jeanne is surveying the damage, flinching at the destroyed changing booth. Her eyes finally rest on me.

'Is it true?' She cocks her head. 'You will marry your*self*?'

'Yeah,' I mutter. 'As a gesture of self-love.' I drop my head, suddenly ashamed. Jeanne has been so generous and patient today; I don't want her thinking I'm taking the piss.

'What's your opinion on that, Jeanne?' Bianca says, nudging a motionless Seth towards his camera.

Jeanne looks from Verity to me. She reminds me a bit of Joan of Arc, with her helmet hair and heaving silver-clad bosom. 'My entire trade is built on amour,' she says slowly, in guttural tones. 'I 'ave learned that when you find love, in whatever form, you embrace it fully. Love only breeds love.'

'Hear, hear!' Dom whoops from the floor.

'And furthermore' – Jeanne rounds on Verity – 'I do not tolerate intimidateurs. Now take that dress *off* and get out of my shop!'

Chapter 26

The *Breakfast with Britain* studios are on London's South Bank, overlooking the River Thames. As we drive through the gates, I recognise the familiar vista of St Paul's Cathedral and the Millennium Bridge, which you can see from the studio windows during the show.

Bianca persuaded me to agree to be a guest after the wedding dress fitting. We were all on a bit of a high after Jeanne's dramatic ejection of Verity from her shop. Thankfully the Sofia Dubois dress was intact, despite Verity's grappling. We left with it wrapped carefully in a garment bag and I invited Jeanne to my wedding.

I've never seen Verity lose control like that. Simone and her mum had to manhandle her into a taxi and this past week at work she's completely ignored me, which is preferable to her usual barrage of snide remarks. She's silently seething that Giles granted me time off work to appear on this show.

I can't believe I'm actually doing this; I'm going to be on live television! The presenters, Henry and Jane Pinkman, are such big household names. I hope they're gentle with me; Henry has a reputation for being a bull in a china shop when it comes to nuanced emotional debate and Jane often makes headlines by coming out with some completely un-PC clanger that offends half the nation.

As the driver opens the door for me, I'm paralysed by a tremor of nerves. He gives me a kind wink as he sees my petrified face.

'Don't worry, love, you'll be fine.'

I'm relieved to see Bianca and Seth are already waiting at reception. Bianca, in a chocolate-brown wrap dress, grins. 'Ready for your fifteen minutes of fame, babe?'

'No,' I say. 'Argh, why did I agree to this?'

'Because you've got something to say.' Seth hands me a takeaway cup of tea. He's typically casual in a checked cotton shirt, slouchy jeans and desert boots. 'And it's an interesting experience, right?'

'Yeah, I've certainly never done anything like this before.'

'Henry and Jane will probably rib you a bit, so give as good as you get – go for feisty,' Bianca advises. 'They love a bit of drama on this show.'

'I'll try.' I nod. This week I've watched loads of YouTube videos of Henry and Jane's interviews and jotted down some pithy answers to questions they might ask, but my mind is now drawing a total blank and I can hardly sit there and refer to my notebook.

'Chloe?' I turn to see a girl with pale blonde hair, in a khaki dress, walking swiftly towards us. She's wearing a headset and she pushes the mouthpiece down as she greets me. 'I'm Denise, we spoke yesterday.'

'Yes, hi!'

'Great to meet you. And you guys must be from Cube.' She shakes our hands. 'I'll take you through to the green room; you'll be on our weekly slot called *Strange but True*.'

'Right.' I gulp. 'Are my clothes OK?' I spent ages choosing an outfit last night, with the help of Dom, of course; we decided on a royal-blue velvet pinafore dress and lemon shirt. And I'm wearing my new gold loafers too; Dom said I needed a subtle statement piece.

Denise gives me a cursory glance. 'Yep, fine.'

We follow her through some swing doors and a large warehouse.

'Who else do you have on the show today?' I ask, as we walk down a blue-carpeted corridor lined with framed photos of Henry and Jane Pinkman.

Denise consults her clipboard. 'In this segment we've got a guy who drinks snake venom to stay young; Emma Royd, the lady who only speaks in puns; and a BNP supporter who dressed up as a Muslim.'

Bianca laughs. 'That does sound like an interesting bunch.'

'Strange but true!' Denise sings. 'Here we are.'

She opens the door to the green room, where a woman covered in swastika tattoos sits on a sofa, next to a lean, pale guy with startling yellow eyes and long black hair in a ponytail.

In front of them is a coffee table with bowls of fruit and croissants, and a large television monitor is mounted on the wall, showing Henry and Jane in the studio.

'Take a seat and help yourself to refreshments. I'll come and get you when the make-up team are ready.'

'Will you give me an idea of the questions Henry and Jane will be asking?' I sit at a table in the corner. 'It'd be good to be prepared.'

'Hmm, yes, there should be time for you to meet them beforehand.' Denise presses a hand to her ear, frowning intently. 'Sorry, got to go. Emma Royd has just upset some of our female viewers with a PMT joke.'

'How're you feeling, Chloe? Excited by this opportunity to hit back at your critics?' Bianca asks, angling the overhead mic while Seth films.

'Actually, my entire body seems to have turned to jelly,' I reply, showing her my trembling hands.

'What're you in for then?' The swastika woman on the sofa turns to look me up and down. Her dark hair is short on the sides and long on the top, with a military sheen.

'I'm marrying myself.'

'You what?' Her square jaw juts out.

'It's a symbolic act of self-compassion,' I say, practising one of my rehearsed answers.

She screws her face up in incomprehension, then whistles through her teeth. 'Mental,' she mutters.

'And what are you speaking about?' I ask.

'I went to me local pub dressed up in a hijab, got loads of abuse.'

Seth looks up from his viewer in amusement, pinching the bridge of his nose.

'Why did you do that?' the man next to her asks. He's got amazingly flawless skin.

'I lost out on a bet.' The woman shrugs and bites into a pain au chocolat. 'Made me realise though, not very nice being shouted at.'

'Such empathy!' The man catches my eye and his supple lips twitch. The large bag next to him starts rippling.

'Um, I think there's something in your bag,' I say, watching it transfixed.

'Ah yes, this is Tangy.' We all gasp as he lifts out a four-foot snake. It's orange, with bands of black and yellow running down its long body.

'Get the fuck away from me!' The swastika woman jumps up, knocking over the fruit bowl.

'It's fine, he's a Honduran milk snake; he doesn't bite,' the man says calmly as the snake coils around his neck. 'He mainly kills his prey by constriction. Want to hold?'

He offers me the snake and, fascinated, I tentatively hold out my hands. The snake loops around my arm and over my shoulder, its sinewy body cool and dry. I hold my breath as the snake guy nods reassuringly. 'He likes you.'

The door flies open and a very large woman waddles into the room, her raucous chuckles making all her chins wobble.

'You've got to understand, Emma, we have millions of viewers and many of them are very conservative; you can't poke fun at a serious subject,' Denise, behind her, is explaining.

'All I said is, "Making jokes about PMT isn't funny. Period",' Emma says.

'Yes, but you're obviously implying the opposite.' Denise sighs and Emma winks at me.

'But I was just about to move on to how when you get a bladder infection, urine trouble.'

Disturbed by the activity, the snake is winding its way tighter around my arm and I look at its owner for help.

'All right, Monty Python, no need to throw a hissy fit,' Emma says as the snake guy gently removes Tangy from me. Then her eyes widen as she clocks the tattooed woman cowering in the corner. 'Look, we got a Nazi in our midst. I would make a joke about German sausage right now, but they're the wurst.'

I get the giggles at the look on the swastika woman's face and see Seth and Bianca are also having trouble maintaining their composure.

'Right, I've had enough of this.' Denise runs a hand through her hair, looking harassed. 'Chloe, follow me, please.'

In the hair and make-up studio, several people are sitting in swivel chairs in front of illuminated mirrors, wearing black gowns and having their make-up applied with sponges by glamorous technicians. The counters are cluttered with designer products: liquids, powders, sprays, pencils.

'Hello, Chloe, how would you like to wear your hair today?' A pretty girl smiles at me. 'Redheads are my favourite.'

'Hmm, I usually just dry it and let it do its thing.'

'How about some curls then?' She waves some tongs in front of me enticingly as another girl leans down to peer into my face. 'Gosh, your eyes are a real mix of colours, huh. How about some cool purple tones?'

'You're the experts.'

As the girls swivel me this way and that, covering my face with various substances and twirling my hair, I quiz them about the celebrities they've worked with. They regale me with stories about their outlandish demands and insider secrets.

I'm still reeling from the news that a certain A-lister film star is actually bald as a coot when they spin me around to face the mirror with a triumphant 'ta-daaaaa!'

I stare at my reflection in astonishment. I barely recognise myself; I'm slathered in a pale creamy foundation, my eyes look twice their usual size and my cheeks have a rosy glow. I finger my hair, which falls over my shoulders in shiny ringlets.

'Woah,' I say. I look like a doll.

Denise appears behind me, puffing in frustration. 'Chloe, I'm going to have to rush you – the producer wants you on right away.'

'What? Don't I get to meet Henry and Jane first?' I grip the chair arms in panic.

''Fraid not. We've had to cut short a phone-in on sexuality so we'll just sort you out with a lapel mic, then we'll go through.'

I stand as a man approaches me with a little grey box and wire with a small mic at the end.

'Just clip the box to the back of your dress and thread the wire up under your top. The mic clips onto your collar like this.' He demonstrates but my hands have started shaking so much that the make-up girl does it for me.

'Can I use the toilet?' I jog after Denise down the corridor. Seth and Bianca are waiting ahead by a set of double swing doors.

'Hmm, they're back there; not sure you have time.' Denise mutters into her mouthpiece.

'You look amaze!' Bianca gushes as I join them, but Seth frowns.

'They got rid of your freckles.'

'Yeah.' I move my face experimentally. 'It feels like I'm wearing a mask. Which is probably a good thing – something to hide behind.' I look through the glass and see the *Breakfast with Britain* set, with its grey sofas, lime cushions, black and white floor tiles and large window overlooking the Thames.

The studio floor is buzzing with activity; people move lighting rigs, fiddle with cameras, bend over monitors and, oh God, there's Henry and Jane walking through from the kitchen area.

'Right we've got a news bulletin coming up and then you're on, Chloe,' Denise says. 'Keep your voices down when we go through. Bianca and Seth, you can stand in the production gallery.'

'Shit, I don't know if I can do this.' I start turning in alarmed circles, feeling like a bluebottle trapped inside a glass jar.

'You'll be great,' encourages Bianca. 'Like I said, be as outlandish as you can; it'll make better TV.'

I nod as Denise pushes open the doors and the next minute I'm walking across the set.

'We have five minutes before we're live so make yourself comfortable,' Denise says.

I feel as if I'm in a surreal dream as I approach Henry and Jane, who're sitting side by side on the sofa. Jane is banging a fist in her lap as she berates Henry.

'Everyone knows you don't ask a bisexual person if it's "just a phase".'

Henry runs a hand through his salt-and-pepper hair. He looks larger in real life; his grey suit is straining at the seams. 'Oh for goodness' sake, woman, talk about pot calling the kettle black; you just told the gay man he "didn't sound gay" – that's no better.'

'Guys, this is Chloe Usher,' Denise interrupts, and they both look up, wearing identical stubborn frowns. 'We've got four minutes until we're rolling.'

'Ah yes, sorry, just had a spot of trouble with the phone-in; sexuality is a minefield these days!' Henry stands up, smoothing down his green shirt. 'Pleased to meet you. Remind me what we're talking about now?'

'I'm marrying myself,' I smile, shaking his hand.

'Ooh yes, all very interesting. Welcome, Chloe.' Jane eyes me beadily like a bird spotting a worm. 'Do come and join us.'

I sit on the sofa facing them and cross my legs tightly to stop my bladder bursting, then uncross them as I realise my dress is riding too high. A camera to my left swoops past me, making me jump, and I stare, startled, at the lens. The overhead lights are dazzling.

'If you can just look at Henry and Jane please, Chloe,' Denise calls from the studio floor. I see Seth behind her and he gives me the thumbs-up. 'Right, rolling in sixty seconds.'

I rub my sweating palms on my dress and fix my eyes on Jane's face; her skin is so pink and powdered it reminds me of Turkish Delight and her orangey lipstick bleeds into the fine lines around her mouth.

'Am I doing the intro?' Jane peers at the autocue. 'Ah yes. God knows how we're going to gloss over your gaffe, Henry – the press is probably all over it already.'

'Will you stop going on about it? We'd be here all day if I pulled you up on every mistake,' Henry counters.

Jane speaks out of the corner of her mouth. 'Sometimes I think my biggest mistake was marrying you.' She smiles brightly as a camera moves closer and a loud jangled soundtrack starts playing. 'Hello and welcome back to *Strange but True* – where we talk to the slightly-less-than-normal people of Britain!'

'Many people spend their entire lives searching for "the one",' Henry continues. 'But Chloe Usher, from Brighton, realised that "the one" was right under her nose the whole time. She's recently caused a stir by announcing that she's going to marry *herself*!' He pulls a comical face and turns to me.

'So, Chloe, have you always been bonkers?' he asks conversationally.

'Haha, probably a bit!' I lick my dry lips.

'You certainly seem to be a few sandwiches short of a picnic!' Jane says, and I start as I hear my own laugh booming out loudly over the speakers.

'Huh . . .?' On the large-screen monitor in front of us they're playing a video of me doing the robot dance, dressed as a giant aubergine. 'Ah, that was a friend's party,' I say, recognising the footage my mate took of us pissing about. 'It was a fruit and veg theme.'

I clap a hand over my mouth as another video starts playing, recognising the long-haired grey cat on the windowsill instantly. 'Oh no.'

So, I tried talking to a cat once; hasn't everyone? I feel my face burning as I watch myself eyeballing the cat and letting out a series of drawn-out meowwwwws. At one point the cat replies, baring its pointed teeth and hissing.

Henry and Jane judder with laughter and I try to keep a smile fixed on my face. Why didn't I realise it would be like this?

'But seriously, Chloe, even though you do seem a bit odd' – Jane wipes her eyes – 'surely you're not completely unlovable?'

'Well no, I'm not unlovable; that's the point,' I reply.

'Then why marry yourself?'

'Because loving yourself is as important as having other people love you.'

'You must've had terribly bad luck with men if they've driven you to this!' Jane jives her shoulders up and down gleefully. 'We've tracked down a few of your exes to find out what the problem is.'

'*What?!*' I turn in my seat as two men emerge from behind the screen at the back of the studio. I breathe out in relief when I see that neither of them is Ant but then recoil as I recognise Dave, the controlling boyfriend I had when I graduated from Goldsmiths, and Monologue Jonny, the guy I dated before I went travelling.

'Jesus Christ.' I lace my hands over my head in mortification as they both join me on the sofa.

'Bit of a blast from the past, hey, Chloe?' Henry says happily. 'Welcome, Dave and Jonny. Can you tell us briefly what it was like going out with Chloe here?'

'She was away with the fairies,' Dave grunts immediately. I glance sideways at him; age has not treated him well. He's shaved his head and put on about two stone. Broken veins cluster around his bulbous nose and his neck seems shorter. 'Gallivanting about, chatting to any Tom, Dick or Harry.'

'Oh, please! You'd have kept me locked up if you had your way,' I retort. 'I was only trying to escape your temper.'

'I don't have a temper!' Dave bangs a meaty fist into his palm.

'Oops, hope we're not going to need to call the security guards,' Jane titters, flicking a glance towards the studio floor. 'What about you, Jonny? Why didn't you and Chloe work out?'

Jonny purses his lips and scoops his lank hair behind his ears. He's looking geekier than ever in thick-rimmed glasses and a diamond-print cardigan. 'Well, the truth is, Chloe never really listened to me. I remember once I was telling her friends about the time I chased off a real bear from my campsite in Canada and Chloe actually told me to shut up. Very rude – it was one of the most thrilling times of my life; I can tell you now if you like . . .?'

'No, that's OK, Jonny,' Henry cuts in hastily. 'We get the picture. What do you boys think of Chloe's decision to marry herself?'

'I always knew she was a lezzer,' Dave glowers. 'At least it saves some poor bloke having to end up with her.'

'Oi, I'd rather be alone forever than be with you!' I snap back at him.

'I'm not surprised – she's clearly still very self-involved,' Jonny observes primly, pleating his cardigan in his lap.

'Says the man who loves the sound of his own voice so much he's lost all social awareness,' I scoff, looking around wildly for an escape route. I don't think I can take much more of this, live television or not.

I think Henry and Jane sense that I might bolt because they quickly wrap up their questions and send my exes off back behind the screen.

I sit on the edge of the sofa, massaging my forehead with my knuckles.

'Well, I think we all picked up on the tension there, Chloe.' Jane cocks her head sympathetically. 'Not a happy track record, hey? And from what I gather, your most recent ex-boyfriend cheated on you?'

'Hmm, yes,' I grimace, glancing around in panic.

'Don't worry, he didn't want to join us today,' Henry assures me. 'Typical man, ruled by his you-know-what.' He chuckles indulgently and I feel a spike of irritation.

'I don't think men are any more highly sexed than women.'

'Uh oh, watch out, we got ourselves a bra-burner here.' Henry nudges Jane.

'Hmm, would you say your wedding is a "feminist" statement, Chloe?' Jane makes air quotes with her fingers.

'Well, years ago, a woman had to marry to survive and then she became the property of her husband.' I wrinkle my nose. 'So, I guess marrying myself could be seen as a protest against the patriarchy.'

'Oh, honestly.' Henry tuts. 'What does "patriarchy" even mean?'

'It's a system of society where men hold the majority of power,' I explain.

'Yes, but . . .' Henry blusters. 'It's all a load of nonsense really.'

'I think what Henry's trying to say is that women are much more liberated these days.' Jane attempts diplomacy.

'We are,' I agree. 'But single women are way more stigmatised than men. I mean, there're plenty of "eligible bachelors" out there but how many "eligible spinsters"?'

'Hmm, "spinster" is rather an ugly word.' Jane's blue eyes suddenly flash. 'It's not really surprising, is it? There's a lot of pressure on women: we have to look beautiful, be willing in the bedroom, act like a good wife, bring up the family, age well—'

'Yes, yes, Jane, we know all that,' Henry interrupts, rolling his eyes.

'Don't dismiss me, Henry!' Jane shrieks and he holds up placating hands.

'I'm not dismissing you, I'm just saying that surely marrying yourself shouldn't exclude men, otherwise that would be sexist! Chloe, do you think a man could marry himself?'

'Of course men could do it too; I'm all for equality, and self-love is genderless.' I smile at him. 'And, if anything, society makes it harder for men to express their emotions, so it'd be great to see them openly love themselves. How about it, Henry?'

'Ah, no, I don't think so.' Henry shakes his head as Jane hoots with laughter.

'OK, so maybe we do all need to love ourselves, Chloe,' Jane concedes. 'And I see why you broke up with the exes we've just met. But don't you ever want another man?'

'I'm not saying I don't want men in my life. I just think truly loving myself gives me a strong foundation for all other relationships. And hopefully I'm less likely to pick blokes that aren't good for me.' I give her a meaningful look.

'So would you divorce yourself if you wanted to marry another person?' asks Henry.

'Nope, divorce isn't an option.' I shake my head. 'It'd mean I couldn't live with myself, which is pretty dark.' For a moment I think of Katy; I wonder if she's watching.

'Hmm, I think I'm coming around to your way of thinking here, Chloe,' Henry says, glancing at the autocue. 'If you marry yourself, you get to watch whatever you want on TV plus you don't have a partner nagging you all the time. Ow!' He flinches as Jane gives him a slightly-harder-than-mock punch.

'And at least you won't be disappointed in the bedroom.' He wiggles his eyebrows at me suggestively and I look at him open-mouthed. I remember Bianca telling me to give as good as I get so I quickly match his smirk.

'True words, Henry – I've never had any trouble pleasuring myself,' I say, taking a demure sip of water.

Henry's eyes goggle and Jane makes a little choking noise. I'm aware of some movement on the studio floor and a camera zooms closer to my face.

'Ahem, oh dear. That was your fault, Henry, lowering the tone as usual.' Jane takes over as Henry still looks a bit paralysed. 'Thank you very much for sharing your story, Chloe, we wish you all the best in your marriage . . . to yourself. Now we're going to the weather and we'll be back with you in just a jiffy.'

The camera pans out and Henry lets out a long noisy breath.

'Sorry, I didn't mean to . . .' I trail off as Denise comes over, giving me a slow clap.

'Wow, Chloe, we weren't expecting that.' She grins. 'Thanks, you were fab.'

'OK, please can I go to the toilet now?' I beg.

I shake hands with a rather twitchy Henry and Jane and hurry across the studio floor. Several people point at me, laughing, and Seth and Bianca appear by my side. Seth's cracking up so hard he can barely keep his camera trained on my face.

'Chloe, that was an absolute classic. The look on Henry's face! I can't believe you casually dropped the masturbation bomb on daytime TV.' Bianca laughs huskily. 'How do you feel?'

'He started it!' I say, biting my lip. 'Argh, do you think it was a bit much?'

'Oh, no.' Bianca smiles triumphantly, revealing bright white teeth. 'Not too much at all.'

Chapter 27

So, it turns out that female masturbation is *still* a taboo subject – who knew? By the time I got back to Brighton after appearing on *Breakfast with Britain*, the entire nation was apparently choking on its cereal thanks to my throwaway comment on pleasuring myself. Viewers were 'left aghast' and took to Twitter to rant about my perversity. HotRod, of course, had a field day.

> @HotRod @ChloeWanders THEY SAY THE CAMERA PUTS
> ON POUNDS, IN YOUR CASE I'D SAY STONES

Most of the tabloids covered my interview with Henry and Jane Pinkman, quoting the angry abusive tweets from viewers with relish and publishing unflattering stills of Henry, Jane and me. Henry's reaction is the funniest; his eyes bulge and his mouth twists into a sort of titillated grimace. And there're some awful ones of my overly made-up face; my bright red mouth is frozen in a downward gurn, my hair sticks out in unnaturally stiff curls and I have about three chins.

Still, on the upside, my interview has opened up a lot of debate about female sexuality as well as self-love, and the broadsheets have decided to get in on the conversation.

The following week I sit at my desk eating a sandwich and reading through all the coverage.

The *Guardian* has focused on my comment about a woman's sex drive being as high as a man's, including stats on the number of orgasms a woman can experience in an hour (50–100) compared to a man (3–4 a night). The *Telegraph* reports on the 'rising trend' of sologamy and has tracked down a few other people from around the world who have already married themselves; I smile at the Canadian woman who says, 'self-marriage is an opportunity to celebrate our personal independence, self-reliance and freedom from the chains of convention'. When I open my *Chloe Wanders* emails, my inbox is rammed. I do a fist pump when I see the lifestyle editor of *Stylist* has contacted me, congratulating me on my handling of 'that buffoon, Henry Pinkman', and offering to do a feature on my wedding. I reply immediately, telling her I'd love to chat. Then I eagerly click on an email from Katy:

> Dear Chloe,
> OMG it was awesome to see you on TV! It felt so strange watching you when I've never met you in person, even though we send all these emails. It must have been such a shock to see your ex-bfs appear but you handled it sooo well! That Dave looked like a nasty piece of work. For a moment I thought Ant would come on but I'm sure he's keeping his head well down – haha, serves him right!
> You sounded really confident and I think you're so brave making such a public declaration of self-love. I could never do that, mainly because I don't really see what's worth fighting for and I don't have a strong opinion of who I am. Sorry, that sounded really neggo – when actually things are a bit better. Like, I've recently started crying! And my counsellor says this is great because it means I'm finally feeling SOMETHING.
> Anyway, you're my hero.
> Love Katy xxxx

I sit back. Reading Katy's innermost thoughts is incredible; to think that every day she has to face an uphill struggle against such terrifying apathy. I had no idea depression could be like that.

'Chloe-Usher-is-a-cunt-dot-com.' Verity's crowing voice makes me jolt and I turn in my chair.

'Oh, why thank you, Verity, you're talking to me now?'

'Have you seen this website?' Verity is laughing at her screen. 'They have seriously gone to town on you.' She reads aloud.

'Announcing you're marrying yourself then admitting you're a wanker on live TV? This smacks of desperation – this daft cunt needs locking up . . . no man on earth will obviously have this pathetic sad cunt.'

I flinch at the vicious language. 'Verity, will you please stop calling me a cunt?'

'What?' She applies lip gloss innocently. 'They're not my words. The website's got pages on loads of people!'

'Sounds like you've found the perfect bedtime reading material.' I grimace in disgust.

'It's your fault for being such a show-off in the first place.' Verity kisses her teeth, then turns to Simone next to her.

'Sim, did you manage to get hold of the unicorn breeder?'

'Not yet. They're not really unicorns, Verity – you know that, right?' Simone looks up from tapping at her keyboard. 'They're white horses with fake horns.'

'Yes, I know! But I want to arrive on one at my bridal shower,' Verity whines. 'And I want to be covered in that amazing iridescent body glitter. God, you're not exactly on the ball, are you?'

'I am,' Simone says tiredly, tucking her hair behind her ear and avoiding my gaze. 'I'll make it happen.'

'Gather round, everybody, I have some exciting news!' Giles emerges from his office, bouncing on his tiptoes.

'I've just this minute heard that Top Banana's been short-listed for the Most Awesome Place to Work in the UK awards! We're up against two other companies but the judge told me we have a very good chance of winning – meaning we'll get a shooting-star trophy, a mention in the nationals and an all-expenses-paid corporate day out somewhere swanky!'

Giles smiles widely as everyone cheers. 'The judge also told me which area we scored most highly in and I'd like to thank one particular person for that.'

Verity smirks proudly. 'Thanks, Giles—' she begins, but he interrupts her.

'Chloe's thorough approach to CSR really resonated with the board. They're fascinated by our charity work, especially now you've raised so much awareness for Brighton Befrienders with your excellent blog post about that old biddy dancing. Let's have a round of applause, please!'

Simone gives a triumphant wolf-whistle and Verity's head snaps around. 'Simone!'

'What?' Simone says insolently, lifting her dimpled chin. 'This award will get Brighton Befrienders even more exposure as our partner charity. It's brilliant!'

'And if we do win, Chloe, I'd like you to help me with the acceptance speech,' Giles says.

'Er, really? I'm not sure I—'

'Go on, you know far more about all this CSR stuff than me, and you're already quite the public speaker, right?' He winks.

'OK.' To be fair, it's probably best Giles doesn't attempt to explain our CSR efforts; sincerity is not his forte.

'Shall we invite Kate, the charity's founder, along too?' Simone suggests.

'Excellent plan.' Giles nods. 'And maybe one of the oldies. The judges would love that.'

'Great, let's ask Muriel.' I grin at Simone. 'She's the ultimate socialite.'

The Most Awesome Place to Work in the UK award dinner is held at a posh London hotel near Tottenham Court Road on Thursday evening. Giles invites Keith, Verity, Simone and me to join him, and we meet Kate Dooley and Muriel at Brighton train station. Everyone's wearing smart clothes and there's already a celebratory vibe; Giles buys a few bottles of Prosecco for the hour's journey. He's wearing a tuxedo and his hair is slicked back with gel.

Muriel, in a lilac dress and matching hat, immediately starts flirting with him, grabbing onto his arm and batting her pale eyelashes. 'If I were fifty years younger!'

We get a taxi to the hotel, where Bianca, Seth and Tariq are waiting for us. I thought featuring Brighton Befrienders might add a nice community angle to Cube's documentary on love. When I told Bianca we'd probably all get smashed on free champagne she seemed particularly keen to come along.

'Don't you all scrub up well!' Bianca beams at us, looking professional in a tailored navy trouser suit. 'And I'm honoured to meet you, Muriel.' She shakes her hand. 'I want you to show me some of your moves later!'

We're ushered through to the hotel's ballroom; a grand space with original oak floors, a vaulted ceiling and vintage chandeliers. At the far end is a raised stage, and the hall is lined with round tables covered in pristine white tablecloths and set for a three-course dinner. Other guests are starting to arrive, bending over the tables to read place cards. Waiters circulate with silver trays of champagne flutes and canapes.

Top Banana's table is at the front, near the stage. 'Let's hope we'll be climbing those steps to accept our award!' Keith holds up crossed fingers. His suit jacket is too small for him and barely covers his wrists.

'Got your speech prepared, Chloe?' Giles puts an arm around me and I wriggle uncomfortably. I'm wearing a backless green dress and can feel his damp palm on my bare shoulder blades.

'Yeah, I've made notes. The judge said it'd be a nice touch if Kate and Muriel joined us on stage too.'

'Eek, there are already loads of people here – I think I'd freeze up!' Kate's shiny hair is swept up in a chignon and she wears a long black fishtail dress.

'Oh tosh, just picture everybody naked.' Muriel nudges Kate, her eyes sparkling.

'Shall I come up and talk about our creative environment, G?' Verity asks. She's in a tight red dress with a plunging cleavage.

'No, I've got it covered, thanks.' Giles barely looks at Verity and she vents her rage by slapping Simone's hand away from the breadbasket on the table.

'Look, your dress is already bursting at the seams.' She prods Simone's white halterneck dress. 'What even is this style anyway?'

'It's fifties glam, like what Marilyn Monroe used to wear,' Simone says, patting her wavy hair and smiling at Muriel, who gives her a thumbs-up.

'Right, guys, we've set up an interview room just next to the cloakroom so we can chat to you away from the action.' Bianca gestures towards a swing door by our table. 'Giles, Chloe, do you want to come through and we'll do a test run?'

Verity glares after us as we follow Bianca down the corridor to a conference room with tables and chairs stacked against one wall. Tariq is angling a spotlight towards a single red and gold chair in the middle of the room, which looks a bit like a throne.

Seth crouches behind a tripod facing the chair, looking tidier than usual in a black shirt and charcoal trousers.

'Hey.' He turns when we come in. 'Clip these lapel mics on and we'll record a quick intro.'

'Excellent.' Bianca claps her hands together as Giles and I oblige. 'You can tell us about your entry, then I'll let you get back to your champers!'

When we re-join the table, the ballroom is packed and there're three men in suits standing on the stage.

One steps forward and speaks into the mic, his hair standing up in spikes. 'Good evening, everybody, and welcome to our tenth annual Most Awesome Place to Work award dinner. There are many great places to work in the UK but there's only one *most awesome* place!'

Everyone claps as he holds up a shooting-star trophy. 'We've shortlisted three companies and after dinner we'll find out who has won.'

There's more applause and Giles nudges me and grins expectantly. The host goes on to give sponsor details and I look around for another glass of bubbles, recognising the CEO of a rival agency, White Elephant, holding court at the table next to us, the staff around him laughing as he gesticulates wildly.

Giles shoots him a filthy look. 'Tom Banoff is such a poser,' he says to me out of the side of his mouth. 'He wouldn't know what company culture was if it bit him in the arse.'

The Cube team do interviews with Kate and Muriel, then come to join us for dinner. Verity pounces on Seth as soon as he sits down, pulling her chair up next to his.

'I was wondering if you're available for hire?' she asks as he jerks backwards, clearly wary of her after her meltdown at the wedding dress fitting. 'I want to have a videographer focus solely on me for the whole of my wedding. You know, with close-ups of my face and stuff. Like Keira Knightley in *Love Actually*.'

'Ooh yeah, that'd be really emotional,' Sim enthuses, gazing at the avocado and prawn boat a waitress puts down in front of her.

'No mayonnaise, Sim,' Verity warns, then turns back to Seth. 'When I look back on my wedding, I don't want to watch my relatives and mates getting drunk and trying to shag each other, you know? It's *my* big day; I should be the main star of the film.'

'I can't help, I'm afraid. I only do serious documentaries,' Seth says, shuffling his chair away from Verity towards me.

'It's such a fascinating job,' I say, pouring everyone more wine. 'It must be so hard having to film hard-hitting stuff without being able to help. Like when that baby elephant died in the drought on Attenborough's *Africa* series and the camera crew couldn't intervene.'

'Oh my God, I was in pieces when I watched that,' Simone agrees.

Seth shrugs nonchalantly. 'Yeah, well, cameramen are specially trained to be impartial observers – you know, we're recording it for the greater good.'

'Could I make a toast to you wonderful people for inviting me today?' Muriel's high voice rises above our chat as she lifts up her glass. She's sitting opposite me, on extra cushions, but she still looks tiny. 'The food is delicious and I'm having ever such a good time!' Her joy is so infectious, we all smile at each other and cheers her as she says, 'To company!'

Everyone in the room seems quite drunk by the time dessert arrives. Keith has taken off his jacket and has one arm hooked over the back of his chair as he talks to Kate. I couldn't say for certain, but I think he might be attempting to flirt.

I have somehow managed to collect three different glasses of alcohol: champagne, red wine and rum.

'Argh, can you take one?' I push a glass towards Seth and he laughs and holds up a hand.

'No way, I can't drink on the job, Bianca would skin me.' He nods in her direction just as she looks up. She closes one eye at him in mock-suspicion.

'Did you two used to go out?' I ask, blunt with booze.

'Err . . .' Seth bashes at the burnt sugar on his crème brûlée with a spoon. 'Yeah, ages ago.'

'Why did you break up?'

'Hmm. We didn't bring out the best in each other,' he says quietly.

'But you still manage to work together?'

'Oh, yeah – she's got talent, we're both ambitious.' Seth looks up, his brown eyes amused. 'You're full of questions tonight.'

'Soz, bit tiddly.' I cross my eyes. 'Dunno what I'll do if I have to speak later!'

'You'll be fine. You survived *Breakfast with Britain*.'

'It was cringe!'

'You've had amazing coverage from it though.'

'Yeah, my favourite being Chloe-Usher-is-a-cunt-dot-com,' I say drily.

Seth snorts. 'Ignore the trolls.'

'I'm trying to, I just don't understand how complete strangers can be so hateful.'

'They don't need much of an excuse,' Seth says. 'Everyone in the public eye is fair game, no holds barred: kids with Down's syndrome, old people with Alzheimer's . . . once I filmed an acid-attack victim – her whole face was covered in scars – and they slagged off the necklace she was wearing.'

'Jesus!' I stare at him in disgust. 'Who would do that?'

Seth shrugs. 'People with serious issues. Don't take it personally. Easier said than done, I know.'

'Shh!' Giles leans forward, flapping his hands as the man with spiky hair takes to the stage again. He's followed by two men and two women, who sit down on a row of chairs.

'Ladies and gentlemen, I hope you enjoyed your dinner and are suitably lubricated. That's what these awards nights are about, after all.' He winks and there's raucous laughter across the room. I giggle as a girl on the table next to us goes to sit down and misses her chair completely.

'A big thanks to our judges for offering their expertise. They're going to talk us through their thoughts on best-practice business, then we'll announce our winner!'

Our table is in a state of nervous excitement as the judges take it in turns to speak.

'If bloody Tom Banoff wins, I'm walking out of here,' Giles says. There are beads of sweat standing out on his forehead.

Kate and Muriel clutch each other, squealing with the tension and Simone has her fists clenched at her mouth like a child.

'Giles, shall I come and stand next to you on stage if we win?' Verity leans forward, tugging the neckline of her dress down. 'Even if I don't speak, I'll add a touch of glamour.'

Giles is frowning at the woman on stage as she discusses employee productivity. 'Hmm, no, that won't be necessary, Verity, we don't want it to get too crowded up there.'

Verity glowers at me as if it's my fault and I avert my gaze, watching as the host returns to the mic. 'I won't keep you hanging any longer. Without further ado . . .' He beckons to a woman behind him who hands him a gold envelope and pulls out a piece of card. 'This year, the most awesome place to work is . . .'

Everyone around our table holds their breath and bares their teeth at each other, and the silence seems to last forever before he says, '. . . Top Banana!'

Chapter 28

'Ten years ago, rather than choosing to fritter my time and money away on fancy holidays like the other playboys, I decided to set up my own company.'

I've never seen Giles so unbearably self-important. I stand with Kate and Muriel at the bottom of the stage steps, clutching my notebook and shifting from foot to foot as his acceptance speech drags on for over fifteen minutes. He keeps waving the trophy around and throwing smug looks towards his rival, Tom Banoff, who is slumped in his seat looking like he wants to thump someone.

The host quickly interrupts Giles as he pauses for breath and glances at the judges, who're looking slightly frosty. 'Thanks, Giles. I think one of the overriding factors in the judges' decision was the impressive community links you're building. Can you tell us about that?'

Giles nods obligingly. 'Absolutely! Top Banana is the most successful digital agency in the country, sure.' He pauses for a beat and looks intently around the room. 'But we have a conscience.'

I give Kate an apologetic grin; she's looking up at Giles with an unreadable expression as he starts pacing the stage.

'At Top Banana we realise that we're living in great privilege; there are some people who don't have a roof over their heads, or a warm meal, or a person to kiss them goodnight. Hell, there are some poor people who don't even know it's Christmas time *at all*.'

The host beckons to me in panic as the crowd starts up a cynical rumbling. 'Chloe, would you like a word? And maybe your charity representatives.'

I jog up the steps with Kate helping Muriel behind me, grinning around nervously at the sea of drunken faces. There's a murmur of recognition and someone shouts, 'What a pleasure!' causing a ripple of laughter. Great, my lewd reputation precedes me.

I blink at my notebook. The underlined letters 'CSR' blur in front of me; why oh why didn't I stick to soft drinks?

I watch Kate and Muriel reach the top step and smile as Muriel waves her walking stick in the air. Her unadulterated gaiety reminds me of what matters.

'CSR,' I say into the mic. 'Quite a dry acronym. Or Corporate Social Responsibility. That doesn't sound much more appealing, does it?'

There're some chuckles and shouts of agreement.

'Personally, I think Superman describes it better,' I continue. '"With great power comes great responsibility."'

I try to ignore Giles doing a Superman pose across the stage.

'Businesses are powerful entities but they don't exist in isolation. Everything they do impacts the society around them, right?'

I notice with relief that some people sit up straighter, looking interested.

'Companies like Top Banana don't just have to be about making money,' I continue as Giles mimes rifling through wads of cash in his hands. 'They can also have compassion. Which is why we decided to support the charities in Brighton who are working tirelessly to improve the quality of life for many people in our city.'

I hold out my arm and Kate and Muriel step towards me. 'I have to say, these two have become my very own superheroes of late. Please put your hands together for Kate and Muriel!'

Kate gives a rousing speech about the work Brighton Befrienders does and how businesses can get involved, then Muriel takes the mic and gives a first-hand account of her loneliness before Kate contacted her. By the time she's finished, most people are sniffing and dabbing at their faces with napkins.

The host beams widely as he joins us, and the judges give her a standing ovation.

'And I'm sure most of us here have seen *that* video of you, Muriel; you're not averse to a good dance, right?' the host says, nodding towards the back of the stage. The next minute 'Twist and Shout' is blaring out over the speakers and Muriel's eyes widen as they meet mine. Then Kate and I link arms with her and twirl around the stage, laughing as everyone in the ballroom jumps to their feet, swivelling their hips and singing along to the music.

'How're you feeling, Chloe?' Bianca asks from behind the camera. I lean back in the red and gold chair.

'Pretty pissed, if I'm honest.' We've been drinking solidly since winning and the hotel conference room is spinning a bit.

'It's definitely time for celebration. Can you believe your wedding is in less than a month?! Have you got anything to say to your future bride?' Bianca grins.

'I can't wait to marry you.' I close one eye and point at the camera. 'You're the bessht . . . best thing that ever happened to me. Oops!' A hiccup makes my body jerk. I giggle and let my head loll to the side. 'I need to sleep now,' I say to the carved wooden chair arm.

'Yep, great,' Bianca says. 'We've spoken to the rest of your team so that's a wrap! You guys better get the last train home, huh?'

'Mmm yeah, errr, where's my . . .' I look around vaguely for my possessions.

'Your bag is here and you put your coat in the cloakroom.' Seth catches me just before I barrel into the camera tripod, looping my handbag over my shoulder. 'Cloakroom's just down the corridor.' He opens the door and steers me in the right direction.

'Thanks.' I hiccup again, ricocheting off the walls and squinting at the bright swirly carpet. I peer through the glass door of the cloakroom. The attendant has left and there are just a few coats hanging on the free-standing rail.

'Hello, coat.' I wave through the glass then push the door open. 'Miss me?' I throw my arms around my mac and tug downward but it remains on the hanger as I fall to my knees, spilling the contents of my bag over the floor.

'Ohhh sloppy bag!' I crawl on all fours under the rail, chasing rolling tampons and lipsticks. There's a noise behind me and I turn to see Giles staring at my bum. His shirt's unbuttoned to reveal thick blonde chest hair and his eyes are heavy and bloodshot.

'Ah, there she is, my secret weapon.' He leans back against the door, a satisfied smile on his face. 'You know, I think we make a great team, Chloe. Everyone's been singing your praises tonight.'

'Thanks.' I sit back on my haunches.

'I think I underestimated you.' Giles tilts his head.

'Yeah, you did.' I hiccup, looking up cheekily. 'Not too late to make me account manager though, is it?'

'Not too late.' Giles chuckles, moving closer to stand over me. I tip my head back to look up at him and he holds a hand out. I grab his wrist to haul myself up and suddenly he's got both arms around my waist and is pulling me towards him. His breath stinks of whisky.

'Urrrrgh, Giles, what're you doing? Gerroff!' I twist in his grasp, turning my face to the side as he kisses my neck.

'Come on, Chloe,' he whispers urgently. 'You might know how to pleasure yourself, but I can do better!'

'No, Giles! Get your hands off me!' I push against his shoulders and lean back as far as I can but he grabs the back of my head and presses his mouth against mine. Our teeth bash together and his tongue slips in my mouth, slimy and muscular as a slug.

'Mmmnnnnnnnffff!' I feel his stubble scraping my chin as he pushes his tongue deeper, digging his fingers into my bare back. Anger spirals through me as I struggle to breathe and I jerk my knee upward sharply, aiming for his crotch.

'Ooooof!' Giles gasps and lets go of me, clapping his hands to his groin and bending over double.

I grab my bag and coat and stagger away from him, wiping my mouth in disgust. Giles pants, glaring at me with watering eyes. His fringe is plastered against his sweaty forehead. For a moment we just stare at each other and then I back away through the door and run for the ballroom.

The next morning my shrill alarm clock pierces my stupor and I groan and swipe at it, hitting my glass of water, which clunks to the floor, soaking my face and the pillow in the process.

'Fuck.' I sit up. I'm still in my green dress from the awards and my eyelashes are glued together with mascara. A throbbing headache gnaws behind my eyes. I blink in panic as I see the time is 9 a.m.; I should be in the office right now.

I jump out of bed and tug off my dress, but as I'm running for the shower, I suddenly remember that Giles said we could all come into the office an hour later today.

Giles. Oh my God. I let the blast of hot water run over my face as I struggle to recall the events of last night. I barely registered what people were saying to me as I ran from the cloakroom and I managed to avoid all contact with Giles after he re-joined our group. On the train home I closed my eyes and put my coat over my head, pretending to be asleep.

What the hell am I going to do when I see him this morning? I'm seized with apprehension. What if he wasn't trying to snog me at all and I've just kneed my boss in the balls for no good reason? I *was* pretty drunk. But no, of course it was his fault. You don't just accidentally slip your tongue down someone's throat. I wonder if he'll call me in to apologise.

I walk through Kemptown village to the office. My brain feels like porridge and I'm not sure what action I should take. Maybe it's best to ignore the situation today, while I'm hungover, then I can chat to Dom at the weekend and decide what to do. Or maybe I could ask Jess; she is in charge of HR, after all.

As I swipe my way into reception, Theresa is bent over the Lego desk talking to Suki. They're both peering at Suki's computer screen.

'Chloe?' Theresa's head snaps up; she looks surprised to see me there.

'Hey, yeah, Giles said we could come in late because of the awards last night,' I say, and they exchange astonished glances.

'You know, the Most Awesome Place to Work awards? We won!' I try again.

'I can't believe the gall of you!' Theresa huffs.

'What?' I frown as she turns and stomps up the stairs. I look at Suki, who ducks her head and starts typing furiously. I can tell she's not even writing real words.

I press the button for the lift, unease threading through me. Surely all the staff should be celebrating our win. As I arrive on the second floor, Rudy and a few of his mates are waiting for the lift. One of the lads lets out a low whistle.

'Wheeee! It's the scarlet harlot herself!'

'Shuddup, you prick,' Rudy mutters, but he doesn't give me his usual grin. His eyes slide away as he walks past me.

With mounting paranoia, I push open the doors to the second floor. The reaction is instant: people stop mid-way through conversations to turn and goggle. There're a few gasps and some of my colleagues poke their heads around their computers to see the cause of the drama.

Verity is on the beanbags with Simone. She stands up with her hands on her hips. 'How could you?' she hisses. 'You've ruined everything!'

I gape at her, feeling slightly nauseous at the palpable hostility in the room.

'Back to work, everyone.' Jess appears in Giles's office doorway. 'Chloe, will you come here a minute, please?' She beckons to me. Her usual dancing dimples have disappeared.

'What the hell is going on?' I ask, shutting Giles's office door behind me. Jess sits down at his desk, rubbing her eyebrows. 'Where's Giles?'

'He's not coming in today, Chloe, not after today's . . . news.' She gestures towards the computer screen. 'I take it you haven't seen it then?'

'No.' I swallow. 'I haven't been online this morning. What is it?'

I round the corner of the desk and gulp at the enlarged image of Giles and me on the screen. His fingers press into my back as he tips me backwards, his mouth firmly covering mine. My hair spools out behind me as my eyes squeeze shut, one hand clutching his shoulder. I realise with a flutter of panic that I don't look like I'm struggling. I look like I'm in ecstasy.

'No!' I whisper, as I read the *Mail Online*'s headline:

HOMEWRECKER: WOMAN MARRYING HERSELF CAUGHT IN ILLICIT KISS WITH FAMILY MAN

'It wasn't like that.' I look at Jess pleadingly. 'You've got to believe me. He grabbed me and tried to snog me!'

Jess's brow furrows and her dark eyes search my face. 'I want to believe you, Chloe, of course, it's just . . . well, it doesn't look good, does it?' She glances again at the screen and I turn to read the rest of the article.

ADULTERY

Today it is revealed that Chloe Usher, who has recently shocked the nation by announcing she will marry herself, is allegedly having an affair with shameless lothario Giles Harper, heir to the Harper's Biscuits fortune and owner of award-winning digital agency, Top Banana. Mr Harper lives with his wife, Angela, and two children in Hove.

EXPOSED

A photo of the oblivious pair in a passionate embrace was snapped at the Most Awesome Place to Work awards in Tottenham Court Road late last night, where Giles's company, Top Banana, had just won the gold award trophy. One guest, Tom Banoff, CEO of White Elephant, commented: 'It's ironic really, that they won for their ethical approach to business – if only they had similar morals in their personal lives!'

MASTURBATION

Miss Usher, who many are branding a narcissist, recently appeared on daytime television, openly discussing masturbation and provoking the wrath of viewers. 'My three-year-old was watching,' one stay-at-home mum complained. 'I had to turn the television off, it was absolutely vile.' See the video of Miss Usher talking about 'pleasuring herself' on *Breakfast with Britain* here.

DEPRAVED

Neither Miss Usher nor Mr Harper were available for comment this morning. Close friends of Mrs Harper admit that she is devastated by the betrayal. One said: 'If Chloe Usher goes through with marrying herself, right after wrecking someone else's happy family, then she must be a complete egomaniac. It's disgusting. No wonder she can't find her own man.'

Chapter 29

'Here, there's double shots of brandy in these.' Yannis puts a tray of three Sidecar cocktails on our table and sits beside Dom. We're sitting in the mahogany booth of a prohibition-themed bar in Kemptown.

'I can't believe they suspended you yesterday.' Dom licks the sugar rim on his glass. The low red lighting casts shadows on his face, which is unusually sombre.

I sigh. 'I guess Jess needs time to follow the proper procedure. At least she listened to my side.'

At first, Jess's expression was tight with caution; she was completely thrown by what she'd seen. But then I told her exactly what happened in the cloakroom; it was upsetting reliving it but at least my tears seemed to convince her I was genuine.

'Chloe, if you tell me it was non-consensual, I believe you,' she said, pulling me into a hug. 'But I'm afraid both you and Giles need to stay away from the office while I deal with it.'

Apparently Giles is insisting that I pounced on him and he was just trying to remove me. He said I've had a crush on him for months and that I should be dismissed for 'inappropriate behaviour'.

'Surely they can't fire you for this,' Yannis says.

'It's his word against mine and sadly he holds more power.'

'Yeah, but creeps don't get away with it these days – look at Harvey Weinstein.'

'Hmm, but I'm hardly the most reliable character, thanks to the tabloids.' I stir my drink desolately.

'Who d'you reckon took that photo?' Dom asks.

'It could have been any one of the guests – a rival of Giles maybe.'

'Well, we *can't* let it ruin your wedding.' Dom slams a hand down. 'Give a shit what some people are saying, your friends know the truth.'

Yannis puts a hand over Dom's. 'But maybe you could delay it until the fuss has died down. It might antagonise the situation further.'

'Why should we pander to them?' Dom throws his hand off. 'We've got to hold our heads high – Pride is in only two weeks.'

I catch Yannis's eye. Part of me agrees with him; my confidence has been crushed and I'm not sure I have the strength to keep fighting my own corner. When I read the *Mail*'s article even I started to hate me.

'So what if Top Banana do fire you?' Dom leans forward. 'You don't like working there and it's not like you need them; your blog is doing so well and you're a really talented writer. You'll get another job, no problem.'

The idea of going through the whole process of job applications fills me with dread; I've done it enough times to know how deflating it can be.

'You think any employer will want me – a masturbating predatory narcissist?'

'Today's news is tomorrow's fish and chip paper,' Dom says stubbornly. 'And Brighton loves its fish and chips.'

After another drink, Yannis gets up to go. 'I'll see you back at the flat?' He ruffles Dom's hair.

Dom just shrugs moodily and picks at his cocktail napkin.

'Please don't fall out with Yannis over this mess,' I say when he's gone.

'But it just proves how spineless he is.' Dom's eyes are steely. 'I don't like bullies. And believe me, I've met a few.'

'And I fucking love your courage,' I say. 'But some people are happier avoiding confrontation. Are you still arguing about his sister's wedding?'

'Yeah. It's become such a big thing now. Yannis thinks if he does invite me I won't be able to resist winding his narrow-minded relatives up.' Dom's mouth twitches. 'As if.'

I snigger. 'You imp. Come on, let's get out of here.'

It's a balmy afternoon as we step onto St James's Street. The sky is bright gold and the restaurants and bars have their doors thrown open; snatches of music and laughter follow us as we turn towards The Lobster.

'Why are we meeting Cube now?' Dom asks.

'Bianca wants some shots of me at the reception venue, discussing the decorations – to build anticipation.' I sigh. 'I couldn't feel less enthusiastic right now.'

'Oh, Chlo.' Dom links his arm through mine. 'This whole wedding is about believing in yourself, right? And of course that's easy to do when everything's going your way – but when it *really* matters is when you're in the middle of a shitstorm, like now.'

Bianca and Seth are filming AJ outside The Lobster as we arrive. Bianca, in a mustard dress, is watching AJ speak. He's wearing his deckchair apron and a white vest top, revealing rippling guns.

'Of course Chloe isn't normal!' he's saying. 'You show me one person in this messed-up world that is truly "normal" and you can have free pancakes for life.' He waves as he spots me. 'Hey, Chloe!'

Bianca turns quickly and Seth, in a Snoopy T-shirt, doesn't meet my eye as he fiddles with his camera. I groan inwardly; I bet they're kicking themselves for choosing me now I've been exposed as a homewrecker.

'Look, about the *Mail* article yesterday.' I walk up to Bianca. 'I'll understand if you don't want to continue filming me – I don't want to lower the tone of your documentary.' I look from her to Seth. 'For what it's worth, none of it is true. Giles forced himself on me.'

Seth presses his lips together, still concentrating on his lens. Bianca blinks, then breaks into a deep chuckle.

'Chloe, don't think the Daily Hate will put us off – we work in media, remember! I could tell Giles was a perv from a mile off! Anyway, there's no such thing as bad publicity.'

'Erm, have you read what they're saying about me?'

'It ain't what they say, it's what you choose to hear!' AJ comes to stand by my side. 'Ignore those vultures, Chloe.'

'It's a bit crowded inside The Lobster at the moment.' Bianca drags two deckchairs onto the pebbles. 'So, why don't you and Dom sit here and tell us a bit about the preparations? We'll get the pier in the background.'

'Well, we've decided on a coastal theme, with a laid-back rustic vibe.' Dom throws himself into the deckchair and beams proudly as Seth trains the camera on him. 'And the bridesmaids' dresses are a particularly nice touch, I think. Chloe, do you want to tell them?'

'No, you go.' I smile.

'OK, well, we thought hard about the colour palette, and then one evening we were sitting on the beach, throwing pebbles for Dora, and Chloe suddenly said, "That's it – pebbles! Let's have the bridesmaids in pebble colours!" To start with I was a bit sceptical; I mean, stones aren't known for their rich hues. But . . . look!' Dom bends over and scoops up a handful of pebbles. 'When you examine them closely, you realise there are so many more shades than you'd expect! See . . . there's dark maroon, light toffee, pale grey, dusty pink. Just in one handful!'

Seth zooms his lens towards Dom's hands but Bianca is looking towards The Lobster, where people are emerging onto the wooden terrace.

'Sounds lovely. What about the food?' she asks distractedly.

'AJ is designing a dream menu, aren't you?' I say, as AJ puts a plastic jug of lemonade down next to me. 'We're going big on fresh seafood platters.'

'Oh, absolutely.' AJ straightens up. 'There'll be chargrilled squid with fennel, braised scallops, tuna carpaccio, shellfish bisque.' He waves his hands about like a conductor.

'Tom, do not leave the children unattended!' A loud, bossy voice floats towards us from the terrace and I look at Dom in dismay.

'Shit, that's Linda!'

Linda spots me and strides over. 'Chloe, what on earth are you doing? You weren't invited!'

'The Lobster is my local.' I stand up and AJ looks between us in concern.

'Well, I hired it for my leaving party.' Linda gestures impatiently at the group of people on the terrace. I see Morag and Duncan talking to Heather, Ray and Jolly and feel a sting of exclusion.

Tom joins us in a salmon shirt and chinos. He hands Linda a glass of Pimm's stuffed with fresh fruit and looks at me askance. 'Good lord, Chloe. This is a surprise.'

'We thought we'd join the party, Tom.' Dom gets up from his deckchair and licks his lips. 'I love public-school totty.'

'We don't want any of that sort of thing here, thank you,' Tom splutters.

Bianca's giggle makes me turn back towards the camera. 'Um, maybe we should go somewhere else.' I pull a face, trying to convey how awkward I feel right now.

'You can come inside now they've all moved to the terrace,' AJ suggests. 'Sorry, I thought you knew about this party,' he says in an undertone to me.

'What is all this set-up anyway?' Linda demands.

'We're making a documentary about Chloe's wedding,' Bianca offers brightly, indicating for Seth to focus on Linda. 'Any thoughts?'

Linda sweeps her ash-blonde hair off her forehead. 'It's utterly preposterous! Chloe clearly isn't in her right mind. Emma and I have been most disturbed by it all, haven't we, Emma?'

She calls to my stepsister, who is wearing a floaty gossamer dress and talking urgently with her husband, James.

'Oh look, it's Polly fucking Anna,' Dom drawls, tapping his foot as Emma reluctantly approaches us.

'Chloe, I didn't realise you were coming.' Her eyes dart away from mine as she frowns at the horizon. Dora leaps forward to greet her, wagging her tail and panting happily, but Emma just puts a restraining hand on her forehead. I feel a pang of sadness; I've never felt this removed from her.

'Chloe has no respect for the sanctity of marriage,' Linda is saying to the camera. 'Especially with recent events.' She turns to me. 'I saw that photo of you and your boss in the papers. You really have gone off the rails; infidelity is the absolute pits.'

'I didn't do anything!' My voice is shrill. 'He forced himself on me!'

'Oh please, there's a photo of you snogging, it's hardly idle rumour!' Linda scoffs. 'I knew you were bitter, but I never thought you were capable of this.'

'And do *you* believe I'm capable of this?' I challenge Emma as she folds her arms, trying to look aloof. 'Is that why you haven't contacted me to offer support?'

'I don't know what to think, Chloe.' Her voice is cold.

'Actually, I play golf with Giles's crowd.' Tom purses his lips. 'And I heard that *you* jumped on *him* – and you've been an emotional wreck for months.'

'Well, that'd make more sense,' Linda sniffs. 'Giles is Eton-bred and an heir to a fortune; he owns three houses, a successful company and has an ex-model wife. Why would he jeopardise all that?'

'Whereas I've got nothing to lose, right? Jesus, you're supposed to be my friends!' I glare at Emma but she stares resolutely at the pebbles. Linda gives a sanctimonious little smile.

'They're not friends, Chlo.' Dom puts an arm round my waist. 'Come on, you don't need this.'

'Yeah, you can all fuck off, I'm out of here.' I shake my head apologetically at Bianca as Dom and I walk back towards The Lobster. 'I hope you choke on your bloody Pimm's.'

'Shit, Chloe, that woman is awful.' AJ trots next to me. 'I'll throw the lot of them out. Her friends are as rude as her.'

'Don't worry; they're probably loaded so you may as well cash in. Anyway, I'm leaving,' I say, hugging him goodbye at The Lobster's entrance.

'Guys, I think we'll have to call it off today.' Dom turns to Bianca and Seth, who are in hot pursuit, Seth still with his camera on his shoulder.

I step aside to allow a pregnant woman with a glossy brown bob to walk past me, eyeing the rose tattoo that curls around her right ankle. It seems familiar somehow.

I take in the dove-grey tunic straining over her swollen bump, the long string of pearls and, with a jolt of recognition, end up staring into a pair of slanted green eyes.

'Saffron!'

'Hello, Chloe.' Saffron glances at Bianca and Seth behind me.

'You're . . . is that . . . ?' Dom is dancing around Saffron like a sparring boxer. I can't even get any words out I'm so shocked.

'Yes, I'm pregnant, and yes, it's Ant's.' Saffron rolls her eyes as if the subject is incredibly dull.

'Speak of the shady devil,' Dom sneers as Ant emerges from The Lobster, followed by Emma's husband, James, who bashes his head on the doorframe as he sees me, grimacing a silent apology.

Ant is wearing a short-sleeved white shirt and his arms are muscly and tanned. I dumbly register how healthy and handsome he looks.

'Oh fuck. Chloe.' He looks around the cluster of people in confusion, pushing away Dora as her attempt at welcome is once again rebuffed. 'I thought you weren't invited.'

'She wasn't.' Linda, Tom and Emma have followed us.

'Can everyone stop saying I wasn't invited – this is a free beach!' I finally find my voice, and it's very loud. '*So*, Linda, you'll judge me but you approve of *this*, do you?' I sweep an arm towards Saffron's pregnant bump. 'You are aware these two were merrily shagging away behind my back and lying through their teeth about it?'

Linda's mouth opens and closes as she tries to rationalise her personal morals and Emma winces.

'Look, Chloe, I can understand why you're angry but we shouldn't do this here.' Ant holds up a palm. 'What's that camera doing? Do you have to make everything so public?'

'Shut up!' I point at him. 'You absolute *prick*! Do you even realise just how fucking *lame* you've been? First, you say you feel trapped.' I hold my fingers up as I count out his pathetic excuses. 'Then you tell me you didn't *mean* to hurt me. Then you make out it's *my* fault, like *I'm* the one who changed. And *now* you're starting a family with my flatmate! And you call me crazy?' I nearly choke at the injustice.

'It wasn't planned, actually,' Ant snarls, like that's supposed to absolve him of everything.

'But we are ready for it.' Saffron rubs her hands over her bump.

'Oh yeah, you look ready, Saffron, with your brand-new swishy hair and your suburban clothes.' I flick her bob and she flinches. 'Chopped off your ratty dreads then, did you?'

'You can take the dreads out of the hippycrite but you can't take the hippycrite out of the dreads!' Dom cautions Ant.

'Oh, I sold your stupid gong, by the way,' I tell her.

'How dare you!' Her snooty expression slips.

'How dare *you*, you sneaky fucking *bitch*!' Fury rages inside me as we lock eyes. If she wasn't pregnant I'd tackle her to the ground right now.

'Look, we all need to calm down – this isn't a nice situation for anyone.' Emma steps towards me, her lips trembling, and James puts a reassuring hand on her shoulder.

'Oh, you're right there, sis, it's definitely not nice,' I whisper.

'Odd motherrrrr!' My heart bounces as Maisie appears in the doorway, her little cherub face aglow. She runs at me, throwing her arms around my waist and laughing wildly. 'I missed you!'

I bend to kiss her, breathing in her sweet scent. 'I've missed you too, darling.' I swallow hard as emotion swells in my chest.

'Look, did you see, there's a baby in there!' We all watch in alarm as Maisie turns and rests her palms on Saffron's stomach with exaggerated care. 'Do you want to talk to it with me?' She cups her hands to her mouth and croons, 'Helllooooo, baby!' into the taut bump. Her blue eyes shine with blissful innocence.

It's more than I can take. Desperately blinking back tears, I grope blindly for Dom and am relieved to feel his arm around me once again. My knees buckle slightly and, as he leads me away from the group, I lean on him and start to weep.

Chapter 30

Dear Chloe,

Ant is going to be a dad? Jesus, no wonder you lost it! I can't imagine how that must feel. If you ask me, Ant's got similar maturity levels to a toddler – I'm not sure he's ready to bring up a child. Can you imagine him changing a sloppy nappy? Not to mention the sleepless nights, you know how grumpy he is in the mornings!

And I can't believe your boss is trying to claim you jumped him! I'm so sorry, Chloe, I know it might feel like your life has collapsed around you, like a house reduced to rubble. But think about it like this: a new door hasn't been opened up for you – there aren't any doors at all. You are free to go – keep on walking, girl!

You've helped me so much these past few months and I want to return the favour and promise you one thing: some days are darker than you ever imagined but you have to keep feeling your way, because just when you think it will never happen, dawn will come and hope will rise again. And that's coming from me – the girl who nearly drowned in her own shadow.

Don't let this ruin your upcoming wedding: it's more important than ever.

Love Katy xxxxx

I lean back against the sofa with my Macbook balanced on cushions on my lap and look towards the French windows, where heavy rain is lashing against the pane. It's Thursday afternoon and it feels strange not being at work; it makes me realise how much I rely on my 9-5 routine. Dora is lying on the carpet watching me; when I look at her she thumps her tail enthusiastically and I smile at her. If only I had the same faith in myself as my pet dog does.

I hit reply.

Dear Katy,

I'm so glad I've helped you. Chatting to you has meant so much to me too – more than you'll ever know. I can safely say it's been the most intense period of my life and, you're right, it does feel a bit like everything around me has crumbled – in January I had a steady boyfriend, a full time job and a flat share.

Now none of those things are reliable. I've interviewed a few potential new flatmates but none of them seemed quite right; one guy asked if I had a problem with nudity in communal areas – haha! – and another was scared of dogs and kept hiding behind the sofa when Dora tried to say hello!

With everything so up in the air, I really don't feel strong enough to stand up in front of everyone and declare my love for myself but I realise I have to follow it through – and my hen do is only in two days so I'd better pull myself together – eeek!

I've been sitting here trying to write personal wedding vows but I keep returning to the traditional ones because they seem to cover everything better than my words ever could. Check this: 'Through marriage, Chloe Usher promises to face her disappointments, embrace her dreams, realise her hopes and accept her failures.'

God, if we could all do this, we'd be laughing, huh?! I guess you and I have both learnt to recognise our failures and not punish ourselves for them.

But I've been debating how to face disappointment . . . I shouldn't push it aside just because it's negative. I should welcome it in: Hello, disappointment!

I'm disappointed that the man I loved doesn't love me back. I'm disappointed because my best friend doesn't understand me

– hell, half the nation doesn't understand me. I'm disappointed in myself. I don't feel like I have a strong enough purpose.

So, what do I do about it?! Maybe I admit that some of this is outside my control. I can't expect all people to love and understand me; they've got their own selves to deal with. So, I should stop seeking approval. If I'm confident enough that what I'm doing is right, that should be enough, shouldn't it?

And the same goes for all of us. I'm struggling with disappointment but you, Katy, you've been facing up to terrors I can't even imagine. It certainly puts things in perspective. You are my inspiration.

And now maybe it's time for us to focus on the stuff that is under our control – realising our hopes and dreams. I love your conviction that hope will always rise, I suppose it is part of what makes us human.

I hope to meet you one day soon.

Love Chloe xxxx

'Listen up, exotic birds.' Dom stands on the scarlet love seat in his flat and blows the silver whistle around his neck. He looks resplendent in an electric-blue feather headdress, with matching wings attached to his arms, silver sequinned hot pants and sparkling platform heels. His naked torso is slick with oil and glitter.

I look around as my friends gather in front of him, their plumage shimmering with vibrant colours.

Jess has come as a bright pink flamingo. Morag and Duncan are both in parrot suits, with great yellow beaks protruding from their foreheads. Kate is in a metallic green bodysuit with wings and Muriel wears a dress with swans and a white fascinator. Jolly have come as two turtledoves, in white feathery onesies with beautiful speckled wings. 'I know they're not that exotic,' Polly said to me apologetically. 'But they mate for life.'

'Please give yourself a round of applause for looking so fabulous!' Dom orders and everyone pats each other between the wings. Yannis and Mum bring champagne from the kitchen and fill up glasses. Yannis looks amazing as a toucan, with a gleaming rainbow bill rising above his head. Mum wears a long gold maxi dress with translucent fabric wings attached to her wrists.

'And Chloe, we'd like to add the final touches to your outfit.'

Dom nods at Yannis, who disappears into the corridor. So far I'm wearing a strapless white velvet dress, with my hair twirled in a bun and a plume of silver feathers on my head.

Everyone cheers as Yannis emerges carrying a stunning white peacock tail; the snowy feathers fan out in an iridescent arc, twinkling at the ends with white glitter eyes.

He kneels behind me and fixes the tail around my waist with a jewelled belt. 'Thank you so much, it's amazing!' I swish in circles, admiring the tail as it floats regally behind me.

'Right, we've got an hour until we get cabs to our carnival float, which gives us plenty of time to create some model penises!'

Dom waves packs of Play-Doh enticingly. 'Split into pairs and make your best cock. The winner gets a bottle of tequila!'

'Blimey, I've forgotten what one looks like,' Mum grumbles and we all laugh.

Jess and I crouch together over our modelling board, massaging the squidgy substance into genital shapes.

'I'm imagining these are John's testicles,' Jess says, squeezing the balls in her hands viciously.

'Still got hubbaphobia then?'

'So bad I've actually started making excuses to stay at work,' she groans.

'And how is the office? It's been so weird not coming in these past two weeks,' I say, pulling a face. 'I'm not looking forward to the disciplinary meeting.'

'I know, babe.' Jess shakes her head. 'I'm afraid I can't find a way to stop Giles throwing shade on you. If he gets rid of you then his wife's more likely to forgive him.'

'More fool her.' I carefully wrap a foreskin around the end of our penis, then dig my fingers into the shaft. 'If only I could perform voodoo, he'd be sorry he ever crossed me.'

We're both giggling and taking it in turns to abuse our model penis when Dom's buzzer goes.

'Is that the stripper?' Muriel shouts, and everyone starts whooping.

'I didn't order one; Yannis and I are the eye candy.' Dom struts over to the door and answers the receiver. He listens in silence, then nods and presses the button.

'She doesn't have to join us if you don't want her to,' he says to me, opening the front door.

Emma stands in the corridor in a yellow shift dress, her curly hair scraped off her pale face. She's clutching something to her chest.

'Bit late now, isn't it?' Mum says archly.

'I wondered if I could have a word?' Emma falters. 'I brought you this.'

She holds out a photo album. On the front is a picture of me holding up Dora when she was a tiny puppy with a handmade sign saying 'Chloe: The One and Only'.

I take it and flick through some of the pages. There's me as a young girl playing with slow-worms, Dad and I fishing, me doing handstands in the park, smoking fags outside the sixth-form common room, doing shots at student house parties, hugging a pregnant Emma, blowing bubbles with Maisie.

I look up and give her a small smile.

'Here, take this.' Dom pushes an open bottle of Prosecco and glasses onto Emma. 'You can chat in our bedroom.'

As we walk down the corridor we hear him yell, 'Right, get your cocks out!'

I sit on Dom's bed feeling strangely shy as Emma pours out the bubbles and hands me a glass. 'Cheers,' she says awkwardly as we clink.

'Look, Chloe, I don't want you to think I'm on Ant's side. I only found out about the baby a few hours before you,' she begins, pacing over to the window. 'And obviously I believe you when you say your boss came onto you – I *know* you're not like that.'

'Right, thanks for the vote of confidence,' I say bitterly and she turns, her eyes flashing.

'I'm *trying* to apologise. I know you've had a crap time and I've let you down but you're not always there for me!'

'I am as much as I can be!' I argue. 'I know it's hard with the kids but I don't see what else I can do to help aside from becoming your nanny.'

Emma's hands curl into fists. 'You can't possibly know what it's like, Chloe! I'm terrified *all* the time. I have no idea what I'm doing. I don't have any time for my relationships or any privacy. It doesn't matter what I want . . . I give a hundred per cent to my two children and I'm just a big fat zero.'

Sympathy washes through me as I see the desperate flare of her nostrils. 'Oh Emma, you're not zero. You're doing an incredibly important job.'

'Yes, I know that,' she snaps. 'And I don't begrudge being a mum; I love my kids so much my skin aches if they're not there. It's just . . . me. I didn't realise I'd lose everything: music, books, eating out, films, clothes, socialising, exercise. I never do anything for myself. Even just popping down the corner shop for a packet of crisps seems like a luxury.'

I bite my lip.

'You're so busy celebrating your independence and self-compassion,' she whispers. 'You haven't even noticed that your best friend doesn't exist any more.'

I feel frustration ripple through me and I shake my head. 'Emma, I'm not a bloody mind-reader. And I still don't think it justifies your resentment towards me. We've made different choices in life; the least we could do is try to support each other. It's not my fault you're not happy – don't blame it on me.'

Emma glares at me, breathing hard, then her shoulders slump and she comes to sit on the chair next to the bed.

'That's what James said,' she says quietly. 'We had a big chat last night, it's the first time we've talked properly in months. I tried to walk out of the room but he grabbed hold of my hand . . . and he didn't let it go. He said he couldn't live with my anger any more.' Her head droops and blonde curls spill forward onto her lap. 'I had no idea he was feeling so cut off, I can't bear the thought of losing him.'

'Oh Em, it'll take more than that to get rid of James. From the moment you met he's been besotted by you.'

'I don't know why.' Emma sniffs. 'I used to be much more attractive and fun. You and I were always breaking the rules together – and you're still doing it! Whereas I'm just boring old Emma – doing the laundry and cooking nutritious meals from scratch. God, even my mother approves of me.' She gives a collapsed little laugh.

'Em, I do laundry too, you know,' I say, poking her.

'I know, it's just . . .' She sighs and looks up at the ceiling. Her eyes are full of tears. 'I see all the parties and stuff you get up to on social media and I get such chronic FOMO. I don't have any interests or hobbies. Sometimes I look at myself through other people's eyes and think how pathetic I must seem. I nearly had a meltdown in the supermarket the other day because I was obsessing over stain removers, thinking, "Is this all my life is now? Clean carpets?"'

I put an arm around her. 'Hun, it's not just you. Most of us question what we're doing most of the time! I've had a "supermarket moment" myself recently. Pretty embarrassing.' I grin. 'But you've got to stop listening to imaginary critical voices. You wouldn't put up with it if I followed you around calling you boring and pathetic, would you?'

She looks at me sideways with a rueful smile. 'No.'

'And I never would, because you're one of the funniest, most interesting people I've ever met.' I give her a squeeze. 'And James will always find you attractive, even with a ripped peri-whatsit.'

'Perineum. Yeah, he said that. He said he's been worrying I'm not attracted to him anymore. But obviously it's not that! I guess I just, dunno, switched off.'

I take a swig of Prosecco. 'Well, maybe that's the biggest passion killer of all – not *feeling* attractive or confident. God, Em, you've got yourself in a right pickle.'

'I know! And I've just ended up pushing away the people closest to me. James said I was being ridiculous arguing with you; he said we've got one of the best friendships he's ever seen.'

I smile at her, chuffed. Knowing my sister has a man who loves her as much as I do fills me with comfort.

'We re-watched your *Breakfast with Britain* interview, Chlo, and I felt so . . . proud.' She chokes. 'I do get why you're doing it. And I'm behind you a hundred per cent. I'd like to join you today and at your wedding – if you'll have me.'

'Of course I bloody will! There's a maid-of-honour place card with your name on it. Literally. I wrote it out just in case.'

She hugs me tightly. 'I promise I'll never bottle everything up and take it out on you again,' she gulps.

'And if all else fails, we can still run off together to become Hare Krishnas,' I say firmly, and her laughter is muffled in my shoulder as I start chanting, 'Hare-hare-hare Krishhnnnaa.'

Chapter 31

I open the maxi-cab door at Hove Lawns and squint in the dazzling sunshine. The pavements are already lined with people waiting for the parade, dressed up in rainbow hats and carrying flags, and the beach is dotted with groups having Pride picnic brunches and swimming in the sea.

My group of exotic birds gather on the edge of Kings Road, admiring the rows of community floats in front of us; Brighton and Hove football club have decorated theirs in blue and white stripes, a local samba company are already dancing on theirs, waving green and yellow pom-poms, and Sussex fire services have a large fire truck where bare-chested firemen writhe around a big free-standing pole.

We hear a whistle behind us and turn as the Cube camera crew approach. 'It's like being in a tropical rainforest with all you sexy birds.' Bianca looks pretty good herself in pink sequinned hot pants and a boob tube. 'Happy Pride hen do!' She fans out my tail in admiration. 'Gather together and make some noise!'

We wrap our arms round each other and whoop as Dom pops a champagne cork and sprays us. Then there's the sound of a truck horn and our float glides towards us. It's magnificent, festooned with huge papier-mâché hearts, balloons and glittering bunches of ruby roses. Up the front near the driver's cab, there's a replica of the famous Mae West sofa shaped like a pair of lips, flanked by two huge speakers and a machine spurting bubbles in a high arc. At the back, on a small raised platform, is a ten-foot gold birdcage complete with a swinging bar, and silver megaphones, rave horns, whistles and confetti bombs dangle from every railing.

On each side of the float, written in huge scarlet letters, are the words: '*Chloe Usher's Self-Love Float: If You Can't Love Yourself, How In The Hell You Gonna Love Somebody Else?*'

'Look!' Mum shouts, and as if on cue, strutting across the road towards us in a purple rubber suit with a winged cape, white platform boots and a massive blonde wig is a very close likeness of RuPaul.

'No way . . .' My mouth drops open as he gives me a massive hug. 'AJ, is that you?!'

He throws his head back and laughs, glossy mauve lips exposing bright white teeth. 'It sure is, honey.'

'You look . . . marvellous.' I stroke his wild mane of hair in awe.

'Thanks!' he preens. 'Are we getting on this self-love wagon or what?'

'Hells yeah!' I jump up onto the float, grabbing a glitter bomb and setting it off over my friends. 'All aboard!'

Inspired by our new drag queen addition, everyone camps it up, shrieking and flamboyantly throwing themselves about as they climb onto the float.

Dom settles Kate and Muriel at the front on the Mae West sofa, then sits down next to them, kicking his long lean legs up over the back so that his platform heels sparkle in the sun.

Emma and Jess climb into the birdcage; Jess clings onto the bars dramatically, pretending to be trapped, while Emma pulls herself up onto the perch, sitting on it like a swing. She's covered herself in coloured glitter and put on wings.

Bianca and Seth confer with Tariq and a few other cameramen, who are going to follow and film us from ground level, then fix a camera to the railings at the front. The driver starts the engine and the truck vibrates. 'We're off!' We sound our rave horns and whistles as we pull away, waving at the crowds on Hove Lawns.

Yannis bends over the sound system and winks at me from under his stripy toucan bill. The next minute Cyndi Lauper's 'True Colours' is blasting out and all my paradise birds burst into song. Everywhere I look there is shining colour and smiling faces as we sing the words, 'Your truuuuuuuueeeee colours are beeeeeeeeyooootiful, like a raaaaainn-bow!'

The streets of Brighton are a seething, sticky mass of glitter, feather boas and flower garlands as we progress slowly through the centre of town and past the Pavilion. Muriel crows with delight, giving everyone the royal wave.

Ahead of us, the Sussex firemen dance on the fire engine, waving their yellow hard hats in the air. Mum and AJ get quite carried away with the hen party vibes, yelling at them through megaphones, 'Oi, show us yer poles!'

I point and laugh as an old man rides alongside us on a mobility scooter draped in tinsel. Seth angles his camera at him as he waves his homemade sign pronouncing him the 'oldest gay in the village'.

'Chloe, I just want to say . . .' Seth turns to me. 'I hope you're OK. You've had a lot on your plate . . . with your boss and ex-boyfriend and everything.'

'Thanks, Seth. I'm just sorry I keep ruining your film shoots with all the drama – it's not exactly what you signed up for!'

'We don't mind, honestly.' Seth frowns.

'What're the other people in the documentary series like? I can't wait to watch it. I bet the cooperative communities are really interesting.'

'Yeah, it's definitely a different lifestyle. In fact—'

'Seth! Come on, dude, no slacking!' Bianca beckons to him. 'There's some guys in gimp masks over this side.'

Seth sighs and moves away, and the next minute I'm flanked by Morag and Duncan and Jolly, all gripping the railing and nodding at each other anxiously.

'What's up, guys?'

Morag clears her throat. 'Chloe, we want to apologise,' she says in her soft Scottish lilt. 'We had no idea Ant's new girl was your bloody flatmate, or that she was pregnant! We only found out at Linda's party.'

'It was awful,' Polly agrees, her pale eyes full of regret. 'And you'd run off before we could talk to you. I'm so sorry.'

'Please don't worry — it's not your fault,' I protest.

'Well, I'm certainly not going to be in touch with him any more,' Duncan says.

'Ant's quite unpredictable,' Jeremy ruminates, stroking his goatee. 'I always thought he could lose his way.'

'Chloe was his anchor,' Morag agrees, and everyone nods. I feel a rush of gratitude and wrap my arms around them. 'Thanks, guys, it means a lot.'

As we approach Preston Circus, I pull a chilled bottle of fizz from the cool box and take it down the back of the float to the birdcage, where Jess and Emma are chatting intensely.

'She's a good girl, this one,' Jess says drunkenly, slinging her arm round Emma's neck.

'Yeah, I know.' I pop the cork and fill their glasses, exchanging grins with Emma.

'I've made a decision, Chlo.' Jess holds up her fists and squeezes her eyes shut. 'It might be cos I've drunk more than a week's worth of booze in one morning and it terrifies the fuck out of me, but I know I've got to do it!'

'Do what?' I look at Emma and she grimaces uncertainly.

'I'm going to break up with John!' Jess opens her eyes and cringes as if she expects someone to hit her.

'Shit, really? I mean, I know you're not getting on . . .' I say.

'Getting on? We're constantly griping at each other and we use the kids to score points. It's gone beyond not getting on, Chlo, it's like we *hate* each other!' Jess's eyes darken. 'The other day we were yelling in the kitchen and I saw my daughter put in her earphones to block out the noise. It was such a natural movement it made me want to cry. We can't carry on like this. We're setting an awful example to the kids of what a relationship is supposed to be.'

'It does sound like you're making each other miserable.' I rub her arm.

'Yeah, and Em was just telling me how her and her husband are going to make more effort to reconnect . . . it made me realise — I want to completely avoid John, not reconnect with

263

him! Omigod, I'm such a bitch!' Jess wails and Emma shakes her head emphatically.

'No you are not! People change, Jess, you can't force a partnership if you're no longer compatible.'

'But all the mothers will think I'm a monster. And the kids will hate me for asking their father to leave!' Jess clings to Emma.

'The most important thing your children need is love,' I say firmly. 'And, in a way, you're doing this to help them. Like you say, they pick up on toxic shit; if you're happier, they will be too. And your family should support your decision.'

'You definitely need some space, Jess,' Emma says, nodding in agreement. 'Do you think John will go quietly?'

'He'll have to.' Jess leans forwards and her gold flamingo beak prods my forehead. 'If he doesn't leave I'll tell him I'm going to section myself because he's driving me insane – then the kids won't have a mother at all.'

'Hmm, maybe don't discuss it with him right after the hen do,' Emma suggests. 'Perhaps wait till tomorrow when you're fully sober.'

'Yeah, I'll talk to him in the morning.' Jess looks between Emma and me. 'Your parents broke up when you were young and you were OK, right?'

Emma and I hesitate. 'It was tough,' I admit. 'Divorce should definitely be the last resort. We're lucky that finding each other was the silver lining.'

'Yeah, I lost a dad but gained a sister and stepdad.' Emma agrees. 'Chloe's right about kids being happy if their parents are – unfortunately neither of my parents have ever seemed happy, even on their second marriages.'

'Same here,' I agree.

'Your mum certainly seems to be letting her hair down today though.' Emma points and we all crack up as we watch AJ teaching everyone how to twerk, while Seth crouches filming them. Mum is taking it very seriously; hitching up her dress, arching her back and shaking her booty like her life depends on it.

★

Our self-love float pulls up at the festival in Preston Park and we reluctantly climb down to the pavement and bid farewell to Kate and Muriel. Muriel, pink with pleasure, hugs us all tightly. 'That was the best ride of my life!'

Tariq pulls up the Cube van on the kerb. 'I got some great footage of you passing through town. Though there was a bit of trouble up London Road earlier; saw some police in riot gear.'

'What kind of trouble?' Mum demands, watching the arriving crowds suspiciously.

'Homophobic thugs, I think.'

'Oh, we don't worry about them,' Dom scoffs as Yannis and Mum exchange anxious glances. 'They're totally outnumbered by us raging queers.'

As soon as we enter the park, the ground under our feet vibrates with a cacophony of sound: whirring fairground rides, thumping house music and the deafening roar of people enjoying themselves. We sit on the grass near a cider stall while Dom and Yannis get a round of drinks in.

I watch as a girl dressed in a tiger suit inhales from a balloon and then lies back on the ground, rolling her head from side to side in a state of suspended hilarity. Another girl, also dressed as a tiger, jumps on her growling and snogs her. As they roll around in a passionate embrace I suddenly recognise the round cheeks and full lips.

'Simone?!'

She starts and tears herself away from the girl's face. 'Oh, Chloe! Hiii! Omigod, you look awesome!' She rolls onto her knees in front of me, reaching out her hands to touch my tail and swaying slightly.

'Having fun, are you?' I raise an eyebrow at the other girl and Simone giggles.

'Yes! I figured it's not breaking the man diet rules if I try women instead, right?' She wiggles a smug finger at me.

'I see what you did there,' I laugh.

'And there's soooo many fucking lesbians in Brighton – it's brilliant!' She dives on the girl again and they tumble off in a blur of stripes.

After a few drinks we check out the drag queen act at the cabaret tent. The compere spots AJ as RuPaul and calls him up on stage. AJ joins in a hilarious lip-syncing competition with two striking queens – Madame X, with flaming red hair, fishnets and a black latex leotard, and Coco Vision, who is in a pink gingham jumpsuit with blonde curls and humongous silver eyelashes.

AJ does remarkably well and I'm starting to wonder if his act today isn't a one-off. Mum gazes up at him with open admiration. 'Why don't more men wear rubber?' she breathes. 'You can see every muscle; look at the buttocks on 'im!'

Dom drags us to the fairground rides but some of our group opt out to look after their tails and wings. As Morag, Duncan, Dom and I get in one of the waltzers, Dom hands around a bottle of poppers.

'Crikey, I haven't done poppers since I was a student!' Duncan exclaims, holding down one nostril and inhaling deeply.

'Ohhhhh shiiiiiiiiiiit!' I grab Dom's arm as we start whirling in crazy circles. The G-force tugs at my cheeks and my eyes feel as if they're bursting out of my head. Morag and Duncan slump against each other groaning, looking like very sick parrots indeed. Dom laughs so hard tears fly across his face.

We have to prop each other up as we step down from the ride, and I fan my hot face with my hand as we walk back to where the others are sitting on the grass.

'Dom! Waltzers and poppers are a definite "no", OK!' I groan, swiping woozily at Seth as he jogs backwards in front of me with his camera. 'Don't get me like this!'

Jess is having a heated row with the guy behind the coconut shy. 'It's fixed!' she yells drunkenly, hopping about and flapping her wings. 'I definitely hit it!'

He finally shrugs and give in, handing over her prize – a toy flamingo – and she holds it up triumphantly as we applaud.

'Brighton Gay Men's Chorus is on in ten!' Polly announces, and we follow her through the crowds to the main stage, pushing our way to the front.

The choir is forty-strong. The men wear black waistcoats over white shirts with purple ties and belt out classic songs in tenor and bass.

As they start singing 'I Will Survive', AJ drops to one knee in front of me. 'Hop on!'

Carefully clutching my peacock tail, I clamber onto his shoulders and the surrounding crowd beam up at me and punch the air, shouting out the lyrics in unison. Seth stands on a beer crate, panning his camera across the scene and zooming in on me as I throw my arms wide and hold my head up high, promising to survive at the top of my lungs, because I have all my life to live and all of the love to give.

'Let's go rave in the Wild Fruit tent,' Dom suggests, looking around our group lying on the picnic blanket. I'm resting my head on Polly's lap, who is resting her head on Jeremy's lap. He keeps bending over to kiss her forehead adoringly, his turtledove wing wrapped around her.

'Yes, good plan!' I sit up. 'Guys, do you want to join us?' I call over to Bianca, Seth and Tariq, who are bent over a camera. 'Surely you've got enough footage by now?'

Seth looks at Bianca hopefully but she shakes her head. 'I want to film more of the main stage acts.'

'I'll try and find you after.' Seth catches my eye and Dom makes an embarrassing show of nudging me suggestively as we head into the dance marquee.

'Dom, stop!' I slap his bum.

'What? Seth's really fit, and he's always looking at you.'

'Duh – that's cos it's his job!' I say, though I feel a little glow of pleasure.

The dance tent pulsates with body heat and lasers. Half-naked sun-burnt bodies gyrate around us, punching out the beat in the rising layers of illuminated steam.

We dive right into the throng, weaving our way to the front where the DJ is bent over her decks, wearing a flowery headdress. When she drops a dirty mix of 'You've Got the Love', Duncan jumps onto Morag's back. Her knees fold under his weight and they're on the floor, yelling under their bright yellow beaks. I immediately jump on top of them and everyone else follows suit until we're all squirming about on the grass, limbs and wings flailing, in a big cuddle puddle. I'm nose to nose with Yannis as he giggles helplessly, wedged underneath AJ's crotch.

After a solid hour of dancing, Dom moves to the tent's exit, sweat dripping down his flushed face. 'Anyone wanna come get some ciggies with me?' He looks at Mum, who is getting quite good at twerking with AJ as a coach.

'No thanks, love, I quit,' Mum pants.

'Have you?' I ask in surprise.

'Yeah, it shortens your life, dunnit?' She winks at me.

I walk to a nearby garage with Dom. The night breeze cools our moist skin as we duck under the police barriers and leave the park, walking past the Cube van parked up on the pavement.

Dom orders Marlboros at the garage checkout and bows graciously as the girl behind the counter compliments his plumage, showing her the full span of his electric-blue wings.

He lights up once we're past the petrol pumps. 'God, that tastes foul.'

Suddenly we hear a high-pitched scream behind us.

'What the hell was that?' I say, spooked. I look up the road to our left but only see shadows where it inclines underneath the railway arch.

'Kids probably.' Dom tips his head back and blows out smoke.

A small figure emerges from behind some bins, bent over double. He limps up the hill under the arch, moaning.

'Are you OK?' I call, but he stumbles away from us.

'Come on, we better check – he might be hurt. Tariq said there was trouble earlier,' I say.

Dom looks across the road to the festival entrance, where a group of people are drinking from tinnies and shouting raucously. 'All right, though I'm sure he's just drunk.'

We catch up with the boy under the arch.

'Hey, are you OK?' I say again, my voice bouncing off the walls.

He turns, his arms cradled around his stomach. 'They tried to bum-rape me,' he chokes, lifting his face. He's older than I thought, probably around sixteen.

'Who did?' Dom asks.

'The bum benders, the shirt lifters, the poofters!' The boy coughs and the words echo around him. I feel a shudder of unease as I realise he's laughing.

'Don't worry, Jez, we'll protect you,' a voice says behind us, and my heart plummets as we spin around to see three older guys blocking our exit back to the park, black silhouettes against the streetlight.

Their lack of decoration makes it clear they're not part of the celebrations. One wears a cap and a red scarf over his face so I can only see his darkly glinting eyes.

'Evening, gentlemen.' Dom greets them smoothly.

'Get out of our way, you filthy fucking faggot,' a short bald bloke in a Reebok shirt hisses.

'With pleasure,' Dom says, taking my arm. His chiselled face is set like stone. 'And may I compliment you on your excellent use of alliteration.'

Sour threads of fear curdle my throat as we take a step towards the park, but the men don't budge. The largest guy, in a black T-shirt with a skull and crossbones, is chewing gum. His mouth opens and shuts gormlessly as he clenches his hands into meaty fists.

'Shall we ruin him, Luke?' he says to the guy in the cap.

'Bob, it would give me great pleasure to take out this little queer,' Luke agrees.

Jez, the kid, starts laughing like a hyena as they advance on us, forcing us backwards, further up the slope under the arch.

'Leave us alone.' My voice is just a squeak and adrenalin slams through my body.

'Nope.' Bob runs at me, head-butting my rib cage and knocking the breath out of me. I fall backwards onto the grass verge; my tail cushions my fall.

'Get off her!' Dom bunches his hands in front of his face and aims a round kick at Bob's head. His glittery heel connects with Bob's temple and it snaps sideways. Bob roars in pain.

As I lurch to my feet, my whistle swings at my neck and I quickly put it in my mouth, blowing loudly. Even as the piercing sound fills my ears I realise how futile it is; today the whole city is full of people blowing whistles.

The kid, Jez, snatches at me from behind and I round on him, slamming the heel of my palm up into his nose, and he squeals and backs away.

'Shit,' Dom mutters, and I follow his gaze to see more shadowy figures coming down the hill. 'We've got to run for it.'

We rush at Luke, Bob and the bald bloke. I try to throw a punch but Luke easily grabs my wrist and twists it up behind my back, holding me in a vice-like grip. Dom elbows the bald guy in the neck and takes a few long strides, then stops in his tracks when he sees I'm caught.

'Run!' I tell him. 'Get help!'

But Bob takes advantage of his hesitation and drives a fist into Dom's face. The crunching sound is sickening. Dom staggers forward as his nose spouts with blood.

'Nooo!' I jerk my head back and it connects with Luke's forehead, then something hits me above the ear and I drop to the floor like a dead weight, my ears ringing.

I roll on my stomach and claw at the grass, not sure which way is forward or back. I can smell the dog shit coming from the bins and waves of nausea nudge at me, but I fight the urge to collapse.

Feet pound the ground around me, echoing under the tunnel so it sounds like an army approaching. I think I hear someone call my name but then a second blow hits my skull and I'm momentarily blind.

When I regain my sight I think for a moment that I'm dreaming. There's a blur of purple in my peripheral vision and I see a white platform boot soaring through the air, striking Bob square in the chest so that his gum comes flying out of his mouth.

The next minute, a six-foot Caribbean RuPaul lookalike, clad in purple rubber, is back to back with Dom, flexing his long legs out in high arcs. Encouraged, Dom follows suit. Blood flows from his nose down his bare chest as he also raises his glitter boots threateningly in the air.

'Come on, lads, they're just fucking queens,' Luke orders the group of thugs, who're hovering uncertainly in front of Dom and AJ.

I yelp in horror as I see Bob picking up a brick. The bald guy jogs to the side of the arch and grabs a short iron pole.

'*Just* fucking queens?!' a deep voice bellows, and I look over my shoulder to see Seth, in his rainbow T-shirt, flanked by a row of drag queens. There's Madame X, her red hair like a halo as she puts her hands on her latex hips, her fishnet legs in a wide stance. And Coco Vision is looking a lot less feminine as she pulls off her blonde wig to reveal a gleaming scalp.

Time slips to a different, somehow leisurely scale as I roll onto my back and watch Coco Vision grab Jez by the throat and hurl him aside like a discarded toffee wrapper, fluttering her silver lashes.

Bob runs at Madame X with the brick clutched in his fist but she neatly sidesteps, holding out a muscular arm and wrapping it around his thick neck, barely breaking into a sweat as she squeezes so hard his face turns purple.

The fight becomes an almost graceful dance, as I'm mesmerised by the whirls of colour and limbs. Wet fleshy noises reverberate around me. Seth pitches towards me, grappling with a gangly guy, and I push myself to my feet, holding onto the arch wall for support as my head swims. Beyond the fight I see people gathering on the verge and hear the distant sound of sirens.

I whack the back of the gangly guy's neck, Seth punches his face and he goes down on his knees. We stare at each other, then I clap a hand to my mouth as, over Seth's shoulder, I see Luke pulling out a brown handle and pressing a button so that a short, fat blade flicks upward, glinting in the orange street light. He advances on Dom.

'Noooo!' I lunge forward too late. There's a flash of blue wing and then Dom crumples sideways and hits the kerb, facing me. Blood oozes out on the road underneath him, dark and thick.

A terrific pain explodes at the back of my ribs and I also fall, stretching out my fingers to try and reach Dom. The bright blue strobes of the police van lights reflect in his eyes as he mouths something at me, then everything goes black.

Chapter 32

When I wake, the first thing I see is my own hands, lying inert on a pale blue blanket. I'm wearing a handwritten hospital wristband on my right arm. I raise it and let it hang, suspended, in the air.

'Chloe.'

I turn my head and the room rocks. My father is sitting on a chair next to my bed, his long limbs bent at awkward angles and his hair sticking out in tufts at his temples.

'Can you hear me?' He leans forward, blinking his blood-shot eyes.

'Uh . . .' I struggle to sit up.

'Don't strain yourself.'

I reach behind my head, feeling two large egg-sized lumps nesting in my knotted hair. I cup my hands over them protectively, nursing their throbbing heat.

'Shit. What . . . when . . .?' I wince as the attack comes flooding back: a high-pitched hyena laugh, scrabbling at grass, sick fleshy thuds echoing around the tunnel.

'It's Sunday afternoon. You've been out of it for about fifteen hours.' Dad's voice trembles. 'You've got cracked ribs and concussion but you're going to be OK.'

He drags his fingers down his face. 'They're maniacs, Chloe. The police caught most of them. I hope they rot in prison.'

'What about Dom?' I jerk forward. 'They had a knife.'

'Shhh, he's OK.' Dad puts a restraining hand on my shoulder and I sink back against the pillows, dizzy with relief. 'His wounds are superficial; the knife missed his main arteries, only caught his elbow. Apparently the costume he was wearing deflected the damage – it was some kind of *bird's wing*?'

Dad's expression is so bewildered I can't help a giggle escaping. It makes my ribs ache, so I quickly stop.

'Thank God, I was so scared when I saw the blood.' I close my eyes as the room spins again.

'Chloe, I'm so sorry. The idea of losing you . . .' Dad chokes. 'I was so awful to you.'

'It doesn't matter—' I begin, but he interrupts me fiercely.

'Yes it *does*. I had a good chat with your mother here last night. The truth is I've been hanging onto such immense guilt for so long. And I'm afraid the only way I've been able to cope with it is with anger.'

I look at him in amazement. I can't believe my parents talked to each other, after all these years. And Dad's actually referring to his emotions; it's like he's speaking a different language.

'I knew you were suffering when Ant cheated,' Dad continues quietly, looking at his lap. 'But I suppose I got defensive, because I put your mother through exactly the same thing when we were younger. Pot calling the kettle black and all that.'

'Oh Dad, you know I always loved you anyway.' I put my hand out and he covers it with his.

'But it was my fault your mother left, my fault you missed out on a full-time father,' he whispers, tired lines etched on his cheeks. 'You have no idea how much I hated myself for doing that to you. I know it's awful to be cheated on, but believe me, hurting the people you love is no walk in the park.'

'Maybe it's time you forgave yourself, Pops.'

He nods slowly, then raises his eyes to mine. 'When you first told me you were marrying yourself, I thought it was another sign I'd damaged you. But you're far more together than I've ever been. And I would love to give you away.'

'That's great, Dad.' I swallow as a dull ache thrums at the base of my skull. 'But I just feel so broken right now.'

I pull the blue blanket up to my chin. I don't know if it's the fact that my dad is finally here for me or the side effects of being smashed in the head, but I suddenly feel as helpless as a newborn baby. The world seems far too big and ugly for me to deal with.

My face wobbles and tears leak from under my lids. 'I c-c-can't do it any more,' I gasp.

'Don't worry, darling.' As Dad stands up and kisses the top of my head, I catch a trace of Imperial Leather. 'You don't have to do anything at all. I'm here now.'

Three days later, I walk down the hospital corridor to visit Dom. I've been allowed to go home and I'm in less pain, but I'm still having vivid flashbacks to the fight which make my heart and breath race. I have to clench my fists and close my eyes until everything calms down.

I watch Dom through the glass door for a moment. He's sitting up in bed, looking at his mobile phone with his good eye. His bad eye is so swollen he can't open it; shiny black ridges of flesh pucker around a tiny glistening slit. His upper lip has tripled in size and billows up towards his nostril, not quite stemming the trickle of sticky fluid.

Every time I see his beautiful face so busted I feel like crying. Yannis obviously has the same reaction because he's lying face down on the bed next to Dom, weeping loudly. Dom moves his screen closer to his face whilst rubbing Yannis's back with the other hand.

'There there, calm down, everything's OK,' he croons distractedly.

'Hey,' I say, leaning against the doorframe. Dom looks up and grins, then winces, putting a hand to his lip.

'Ouch, it hurts,' he says, his voice thick. 'I'm going to be a mannequin until I'm healed.' He adopts a frozen expression and looks around the room with glazed eyes.

'Oh don't, you look more like a zombie!' I giggle.

Yannis rolls over and gazes up at Dom, his usually serene face red and blotchy.

'My love, I don't know what I'd have done if . . .' He closes his eyes, fluttering wet black eyelashes. 'I couldn't live without you.'

Dom looks down at him with his new Stepford wife demeanour and pats his head. 'You would have carried on, but your life would have been significantly less excellent.'

'It's not funny,' Yannis groans. 'Please let's never argue again. And of course, you *must* come as my plus one to my sister's wedding!'

Dom nods graciously. 'I was nearly your "minus one" for a minute there.'

I shake my head grimly. 'We're lucky – it could have been a lot worse.'

Dom's one eye meets mine and I shiver as I remember him lying on the road in a growing puddle of his own blood.

'When I put those wings on that morning, I had no idea they'd save my life,' he agrees. 'Well, them and the drag queens, of course! Have you *seen* the responses the video's getting, Chlo? I can't stop watching it – it's marvellous!' He waves his phone in the air.

'I know, I keep replaying it too.' I go to sit next to him on the bed as we all watch the footage again.

As I was on the ground for most of the fight, AJ and Seth have filled me in on what happened. Apparently, Seth was in the Cube van when Dom and I walked to the garage. He came after us and, alerted by my whistle, realised we were being ambushed so he ran to the entrance of the festival to tell the security guards. AJ was outside the cabaret tent chatting to his new drag queen friends and, refusing to wait for the police, they all charged up to the railway arch to help us. Crowds soon gathered and one of the onlookers decided to film the whole thing on his phone.

The resulting video of such majestic drag queens clobbering the hell out of the vicious thugs is sensational, especially when watched in slow motion. Online viewers have dubbed it *Drag vs Hate*.

The papers have cottoned on to my involvement and are speculating whether or not I was specifically targeted for the attack. The idea makes my skin crawl; online abuse is one thing but witnessing violence in the flesh has made me painfully aware of just how destructive scorn can be.

Several journalists have been in contact, asking if I'll still go ahead with the wedding. I don't know what to tell them; part of me wants to hide in a cave.

Drag vs Hate finishes in a jangle of police sirens and we watch two policemen ram Luke with their shields, slapping handcuffs on him.

Coco Vision sticks both her middle fingers up at the trapped attackers and shouts, 'How's that for fucking queens?' then turns and fixes her blonde wig back on her head, batting her long lashes and strutting away as if she's just encountered a minor diversion.

'God, I love her!' Dom sighs. 'Apparently some web developers in Brighton are creating an online *Drag vs Hate* game, where people can choose their own drag queen avatar and score points destroying enemies with handbag bashing and high kicks. Isn't that awesome?' He beams, then flinches and puts a hand to his mouth.

'Totally awesome,' I agree. It's typical of Dom to focus on the upside of this whole nightmare.

We look up as we hear the squeaking of running feet on lino and Seth appears in the doorway, his chest heaving. He's got a bruised cheekbone and his hair is standing on end.

'Chloe! Your mum said you'd be here. I have something you've *got* to see!' He holds up his laptop triumphantly.

'Yeah? More drag queen GIFS?' I smile. I've really warmed to Seth since Pride, especially as he's the one who raised the alarm; if he hadn't followed us from his van then we might not even be here.

'Oh no, this is way more useful.' He rests his laptop at the end of the bed and we watch in curiosity as he clicks on his desktop. 'This is all you need to sort out your problem at work. I'm pretty sure it means you'll get to keep your job!'

He taps his trackpad and we frown at the screen in confusion for a minute. Then realisation dawns on me and I draw in a loud breath. 'No fucking way.'

Chapter 33

It's a bright Tuesday morning and the beach is empty of people as I walk to the Top Banana office with my laptop in my rucksack. There's a fresh wind and the sea is ruffled with tiny white tips. I'm already feeling that this is going to be a pivotal day.

My ribs are still sore but the bumps on my head are much smaller. I'm amazed that in just nine days my body has healed so well. Dom is also looking a lot better; his swelling has gone down and the bruising is an intriguing kaleidoscope of colours. It makes me realise just how sophisticated the human body is – how hard it works to recover.

Mentally I feel much stronger too. The flashbacks to the attack have started to recede; Dr Fletcher said it might be a touch of post-traumatic stress disorder. I've heard of it before, of course, but I never realised just how visceral and all-consuming it could be.

Mum's been staying with me and making sure I rest. This weekend, we both went for dinner with Dad. It was so surreal, seeing them sitting opposite each other, making polite small talk. After a few glasses of wine, I think they actually started to enjoy themselves – cracking in-jokes and reminiscing about their youth. It reminded me of the banter and shared history Ant and I once had.

I approach Brighton Pier, my eyes running over the familiar contours of its rollercoaster rides and bright white facade. Giles can hit me with whatever he's got; it's not going to make a difference.

'Chloe!' Suki calls from the Lego reception desk as I enter, her eyes bulging eagerly. 'Giles and Jess are in his office waiting for you. What's going on?'

'I'm sure you'll find out soon,' I say.

'Will you go through with your wedding this weekend?'

I start walking up the stairs. 'Don't worry, Suki, all will be revealed.'

It seems I've already developed a considerable aversion to the office. As I push open the second-floor doors and look at everyone bent over their computers I feel a lurch of loathing.

The sound of clacking keyboards grinds to a halt and there's a pause as people eye me warily, unsure how to react. Rudy lopes over, giving me a congratulatory hand slap. '*Drag vs Hate*, mate,' he says. 'Fucking legendary.'

'Oh please, don't encourage her.' Verity's imperious voice comes from the kitchen and I turn to see her and Simone sitting at the table. 'We've all had quite enough of your drama, Chloe,' she says, flicking her hair over one shoulder. 'Let's hope today is the end of it.'

I stare at her with intense dislike. 'It will be.'

Simone looks up at me and opens her mouth but Verity slams a fist down on the table to get her attention.

'Simone, *hello*? Table plans.'

Giles's office light is red but I knock anyway. Jess opens the door and her arms automatically fly up to hug me but she restrains herself, grimacing in solidarity.

I haven't told her what I have up my sleeve so she can remain as impartial as possible.

'Please take a seat,' she says, gesturing to the chair opposite Giles's. 'This is a formal disciplinary hearing and I'll be taking the minutes.'

'Thanks, Jess.' I look at Giles, who is leaning back in the chair opposite in a white linen shirt, playing with his rubber band ball.

'Right, let's sort out this nonsense, shall we.' Giles watches as I sit down, insolent assurance scrolled across his features. 'Chloe, I'm aware you're still recovering from injury so I'll go easy on you.'

'Are you sure you're physically up to this meeting?' Jess checks.

'Absolutely.'

'I'll also take into account the fact that you've had problems in your personal life.' Giles rotates the ball in his hands. 'Which may go some way to explain your erratic behaviour.'

'How have I been erratic?' I ask.

Giles lets out a little snort. 'Erm, you need only refer to the national press to spot the rather large question mark over your sanity – you are just about to marry yourself, after all.'

'You told me you thought it was an ingenious idea, Giles.'

'I try to offer encouragement.' Giles waves a dismissive hand. 'You did well with the award entry but unfortunately it seems you don't deal with success in a healthy way.' He clears his throat. 'Now obviously it's rather a delicate situation, but let's not beat around the bush; I'm afraid I cannot continue to employ staff who are sexually predatory.'

I let out a bark of laughter and glance at Jess, who clenches her jaw in anger.

'You're really going down this road, Giles?' I'm incredulous. 'You won't admit that it was completely the other way around – *you* harassing *me*?'

Giles's pale blue eyes are watchful, like a wolf's. He forces a sigh. 'Oh dear, Chloe, I'm afraid I can't help you.'

'Your denial makes me worry about what else you might have covered up.' I frown, then turn to Jess. 'I'd watch other staff carefully if I were you.'

'Right, that's enough,' Giles snaps impatiently. 'Chloe, you are dismissed for inappropriate behaviour, effective immediately. After this meeting you will leave the premises and Jess will arrange the transfer of your possessions. Your salary will be terminated from today and I'm afraid we won't be offering you a reference. What are you doing?'

I'm unzipping my rucksack and opening my laptop on his desk. 'You might want to see this before your final decision,' I say, clicking on a media file so that the window fills my screen.

Jess lowers her notebook in surprise and Giles looks from her to me. 'What's this about?'

In silence, I press play. We see a slightly out-of-focus shot of an empty red and gold chair that looks a bit like a throne. There's a crackling noise and Tariq appears in the background, dismantling a spotlight.

'Isn't that . . . ?' Giles tails off, frowning.

There's more static and then the audio of Giles's loud voice booms out. 'Ah, there she is, my secret weapon.'

'What? But . . .' Giles starts and leans forward to gawp at the screen. We're still looking at the chair and Tariq, but the audio is recognisably Giles's voice. 'You know, I think we make a great team, Chloe. Everyone's been singing your praises tonight.'

Giles swallows and a red flush creeps up his neck as Jess looks puzzled.

'Giles was still wearing his lapel mic after Cube filmed us at the awards – and the camera and sound was left on record,' I softly fill her in. Her eyes widen as the audio of Giles coming onto me plays out.

As we hear me scream, 'No, Giles! Get your hands off me!' Giles groans and drops his head onto his hands. His Adam's apple bobs up and down.

We listen to a muffled thumping as we struggle, and Giles's strangled 'oooofff', and then he's muttering, 'Fucking bitch!' as my running footsteps retreat.

A stillness falls over the room as the audio ends. Jess stares at Giles, whose head is bowed, his hair falling in strands over his shining forehead. Her expression is a mixture of triumph and disgust. 'Well, Giles, I think you'll agree this changes everything.'

His mouth works as he licks his lips, his eyes darting in circles across the carpet. 'Well, yes. I mean . . . we can obviously put this misunderstanding behind us.' With a huge effort he raises his head and meets my gaze. 'Chloe, you can start work again tomorrow and we'll say no more about it.'

I close my laptop and zip it up in my rucksack. 'No,' I say simply.

'What do you mean "no"?' He lets out a nervous little laugh. 'Look, I'm happy to consider you in an account manager capacity if that's what you want.'

'No,' I say again, standing up. 'I don't want to work here any more, thanks very much. What I *do* want is a tidy redundancy package.'

'I'm sure we can manage that.' Jess gives me a victorious grin.

'Thanks. Sooner rather than later, please. I have a honeymoon to plan!' I open Giles's door and nearly walk straight into Theresa. She jumps away from the fish tank wall; she's clearly been giving everyone a running commentary.

People are hovering halfway out of their chairs as I stride past. 'What's going on?' Rudy hisses.

'Erm, Chloe, hold on one second!' Giles calls in panic from his office doorway. 'There must be a better way to rectify this. Please reconsider. Your departure would be a great loss to the Top Banana family.'

'Pah!' Verity, still in the kitchen, stands up with both hands on her hips.

'Don't pretend there's any team spirit here, Giles,' I scoff. 'You expect us all to be so grateful just because there's unconventional meeting rooms, a cappuccino machine and oversized bloody beanbags. But none of these perks make up for the fact that you're a self-serving, narcissistic wanker.'

There's a collective gasp across the room and Rudy lets out a shout of laughter. Giles shifts from foot to foot, spluttering. His face is bright red.

'That's rich, coming from you!' Verity retorts. 'Always going on about how much you love yourself.'

I turn to her. 'Narcissists don't actually love themselves though, Verity, that's the problem. They're obsessed with their appearance, have a constant need for admiration and are incapable of empathy. Sound familiar?'

Simone's mouth falls open as she looks at Verity, then Giles.

'Look.' Giles clears his throat. 'Don't leave on bad terms. You'll have a long and successful career ahead of you if you stay here, I promise.'

Verity's head whips round; she glares at Giles as if he's lost his mind.

'Giles, I'm not staying a second longer in this place.' I shake my head, feeling giddy with relief. 'I don't want to spend the next thirty years of my precious life clawing my way up a depressing office hierarchy, chasing a dangling salary carrot, sitting in front of a computer all day making corporate brands more money, and attending pointless meetings full of bullshit jargon. How's that for a "helicopter view"?'

'Hear, hear!' Rudy raises a fist in the air and a couple of the lads cheer.

'And what exactly will you do instead? You're not going to a rival agency?' Giles demands.

'I'm going freelance!' I say, opening my arms wide. 'The clue is in the title. I'm free to use my skills for organisations that have a conscience.'

Verity makes a vomit noise. 'Not this crap you were talking about at the awards? No one buys it in the *real* world. You'll be on the dole in no time.'

'Oh yeah? Then why have I already been contacted by three different companies from the awards who are interested in business with purpose?' I raise an eyebrow. 'And Brighton Befrienders have just secured new funding thanks to their recent exposure and will be employing me to do their marketing. So, things aren't looking too shabby, but thanks for your concern.'

'Yes!' Simone jumps to her feet. 'That's fucking brilliant. Well done, Chloe!'

'Simone!' Verity looks apoplectic.

'Oh whatever, Verity, Chloe's only saying what we all think anyway. This job is so fake, I hate it!' Simone's cheeks go pink and she giggles hysterically. 'I hate you too. And I'm totally confused about my sexuality. In fact, my life is a bloody mess right now!'

She bends over and starts laughing uncontrollably and I join in. Other staff start rising from their desks.

'My job is so boring – I'd much rather be a beautician,' Theresa announces, quickly clapping a hand over her mouth at her own audacity.

'Yeah, I'm so over this office and the shit banter,' Rudy agrees. 'I want to teach sports, to help kids with their confidence.'

'Yes, Rudy – do it!' I grin.

'Well, I'm rather inclined to take an early retirement in that case.' We all turn in amazement as Keith sidles out from behind the photocopier. 'Margaret and I ought to do more travelling before her arthritis gets the better of her.'

'Now hang on a minute . . .' Giles is flapping his hands around, trying to contain this unexpected revolt, while Jess leans against his doorframe, cracking up.

'It's wonderful when you realise there are other options, isn't it?' I smile around at my ex-colleagues. 'Goodbye and good luck. And Giles, to your credit, you did once give me some very useful advice.' I smile over my shoulder at him as I turn and leave. 'Your only limit is yourself!'

Chapter 34

Dawn light creeps under my silk curtains and I open one eye to check my alarm clock. 6 a.m. I close my eye again. I should probably get two more hours of beauty sleep but . . . fuck it . . . it's not every day you get married!

I throw my white fluffy duvet off and some stray rose petals fly into the air. Today is the BIG day! My wedding party and I are staying at The Grand hotel for two nights because, well, why the hell not? They do a great wedding package. Last night we had spa treatments and a three-course dinner and they've given me a stunning bridal suite complete with romantic touches.

Feeling a childish glee, like it's Christmas morning, I run on tiptoes to the minibar and get out the punnet of fresh strawberries and mini bottle of Bollinger. Then I pad across the soft carpet, opening the windows and standing in my pants on the balcony.

The panoramic sea view takes my breath away. The sky is washed clean pink like newborn skin and the sea stretches out blue and limitless, beyond the iconic silhouette of the burnt-out West Pier.

To my right is the i360 observation tower, its futuristic glass pod gleaming silver, and the ornate dome of the Bandstand, where I'll be taking my vows later.

I can already feel the enveloping warmth of the rising sun. It's going to be another hot August day. I sit down at the cast-iron table. 'Well, here we are then,' I say out loud.

This year has been a rollercoaster of revelations and life-changing events and I've definitely had the odd pre-wedding jitter, but deep in my heart I know I've made the right choice.

What's most bizarre is how everything suddenly seems to be working out perfectly. I've got three business meetings lined up next week, with people who seem really keen to work with me. They're even willing to wait while I take a casual three-week honeymoon, which is being funded by the generous redundancy package Jess managed to negotiate for me. And Jess has offered to look after Dora while I'm away; she said it'd be nice for the kids to have a dog to distract them while she and their dad take a break.

When I get back I'm going to look to rent that sunny bijou flat I've dreamt of; I know it's out there somewhere. I've never lived on my own before and I can't wait to have a space that's all mine.

It'll double up as a work studio too. I'm going to start writing properly again; I have loads of plans for my blog, and *Stylist* magazine, who've been so lovely and will be coming to the wedding today, are commissioning me to write a solo travel feature for them while I'm away – 'YOLO SOLO!'

I check my social media and smile to see all the good wishes from friends and fans. There's a surprisingly amiable tweet from HotRod:

@HotRod @ChloeWanders Have a good wedding
@ChloeWanders @HotRod What happened to CAPS LOCK?!

I've been ignoring HotRod recently so perhaps he's decided to go easier on me. He replies immediately.

@HotRod @ChloeWanders You're not that bad looking really, I probably would, after about ten pints lol
@ChloeWanders @HotRod I'm touched
@HotRod @ChloeWanders Wanna marry me instead? We can be lonely together
@ChloeWanders @HotRod Promise me one thing? You'll try to love yourself!

I go to his profile page and select 'block' from the menu.

Then I open the itinerary my travel agent sent through: *Gorilla safari trekking, Uganda*. Yep, that's right. It's time to embrace another dream.

Two hours later there's a knocking on my door. I throw it open to find Mum, Dom and Emma outside in the corridor, rolling a breakfast trolley with a champagne ice bucket, fresh fruit and croissants.

We all squeal and have a four-way hug. 'It's strange, isn't it?' Mum says dazedly. 'It feels like the real thing. Even though . . .' She looks up and down the corridor as if half-expecting a groom to emerge from one of the bedroom doors.

'It *is* the real thing,' Dom grins, swinging the garment bag holding my Sofia Dubois dress from his finger. His injured eye is now fully open but there are still deep purple bruises spiralling around it to his cheek.

'Are you nervous?' Emma asks, squeezing my waist. 'I remember I was shitting it on my wedding day.'

'Yeah, a bit, I hope I don't fluff my vows. It'll be scary having everyone I know watching!' I say.

'That's what makes it so special.' Emma rolls the trolley through to my room, leaving a warm buttery aroma in her wake.

After breakfast on the balcony, I have a shower, then everyone snaps into action to get me wedding-ready. Mum curls my hair, Emma does my make-up and Dom fusses with the dress, removing imaginary specks from its long train.

Eventually they're satisfied that I'm polished enough to step into my gown. Dom positions the tiara just above my fringe, pulling the veil back over my shoulders, and slips on my jewelled slippers. We all crowd around my reflection in the long mirror in awe.

The dress is even more beautiful than I remember. Sunlight streams through the windows and catches the sequins, making it shimmer like the sea's surface.

Mum touches my ringlets and sighs mistily. 'You remind me of me on the day I married your father – all wide-eyed and full of hope.' She sighs at her own reflection in the mirror. 'Not that that lasted long, of course. Look at me now, cynical old hag.'

'Joy!' Dom and Emma say in unison, looking appalled, but Mum's cackling at her own wit.

I stand on the balcony feeling like a queen looking over her kingdom while the others get dressed. Then Dom's standing next to me, dressed as the Pope in a gold pointy hat and rich purple robes.

I swoon in delight. 'You look stunning. And the colour exactly matches your bruising!'

'Intentional, darling.' Dom puts his arm around me. 'A last-minute wardrobe change.'

Mum and Emma join us. Mum is wearing a royal-blue two-piece suit which flatters her slender frame perfectly, and Emma has on a beautiful floor-length soft shimmering silver gown – the exact shade of her chosen pebble.

'Oh, Dom!' Emma convulses in giggles as she clocks his outfit. 'I can't cope.' She holds her stomach and howls and Dom looks really chuffed; he's not used to Emma's approval.

My wedding party's waiting for us in the hotel foyer; we're having drinks in the breakfast room before we walk to the Bandstand. Everyone breaks into applause as we descend the grand staircase and we clap back at them.

Duncan, Jeremy, Yannis and James, my ushers, look very handsome in dark blue tuxedos and bow ties, and the brides-maids wear stunning gowns in pebble shades; Morag's in silk maroon, Polly wears a golden toffee shade, and Maisie is wearing a rosy pink puffball dress and wriggling in James's arms.

'You look just like Princess Elsa!' she gasps.

'Can you join Chloe on the staircase?' the photographer asks, and my friends cluster around me. 'Bridesmaids in a row next to Chloe so the bride is the bright white pebble in the middle. Perfect!' He raises a thumb.

I wave as Dad comes through the hotel's revolving front doors with Janice and Dora, who is wearing a yellow bow around her neck to match the sunflowers in my bouquet. As soon as Dora sees me she stands on her hind legs and starts pawing the air in desperation.

'My beautiful girl!' I bend down to pet her and she licks my ears. Dom flaps his hands around us.

'Mind you don't get hairs on the dress!'

I throw my arms around Dad and am surprised when Mum comes up behind me and holds out her hand to Janice.

'Janice.'

'Joy.'

They shake hands and nod, both stiff as ramrods, and Emma and I grin at each other, appreciating their monumental effort.

'Right, excellent.' Dad rubs his hands together. 'I'll get a round of drinks in before we head off.'

As we file into the breakfast room, I bump into Tariq poring over a clipboard.

'Ah, I was wondering where the Cube crew was,' I say. 'Did you stay in the hotel overnight?'

'Yep, we're staying on the ground floor next to the meeting rooms.' He nods across the foyer towards some blue swing doors. 'Bianca and Seth are just running through some of your footage so far, to make sure we're on track.'

'Ooh, OK, it's brilliant having the whole journey captured on film for me. Such a nice keepsake,' I smile.

'Haha yeah,' Tariq smirks. 'It'll make great TV.'

I join my parents on the pale velvet sofas in the breakfast room and Dad passes me an espresso martini, which will hopefully take the edge off this morning's champagne.

'Double shot of Dutch courage in there, my girl,' he winks. 'I was half cut on my wedding days, helps with last-minute nerves.'

I laugh as Mum and Janice roll their eyes in unison. Dad really does seem a lot more chilled out. He doesn't even bat an eyelid when I tell him about my resignation from Top Banana.

'We're living in the age of the entrepreneur, Chloe, there's no reason why you should bust a gut making someone else money.' He purses his lips in approval. 'That Seth did you a favour, I'd like to shake his hand later.'

'Yeah, I'm just going to find him now actually, he doesn't know what happened yet. I'll be back in a bit.'

I cross the foyer towards the meeting rooms, lifting my full skirt up around my ankles. I've been so busy these past few days, I haven't really appreciated just how awesome it was of Seth to give me the audio of Giles. And the way he waded into the fight at Pride and visited me in hospital afterwards was pretty cool. I'm suddenly really keen to see him again.

I break into a jog when I hear a laugh coming from the end of the corridor – sure enough, I see Bianca, Seth and Tariq through the glass of the last door on the left. Bianca and Tariq are sitting at a dark wooden table with their backs to me, their shoulders juddering as they laugh at the footage on the wide-screen monitor mounted on the wall, which Seth is playing from his laptop to the side.

I push the door open slightly, then hesitate as I see what they're watching: a huge bald man with a moustache lies back on his bed looking like a beached walrus. Propped up next to him is a blow-up sex doll wearing a blonde wig, her inflatable red mouth gaping open.

'I wasn't expecting to develop such strong feelings for her,' he says to the camera, shrugging. 'Then one night I just didn't want to put her back in her box.'

'Hahahaaaa!' Tariq takes a grape from the fruit bowl in front of him. 'This is even better than I remember.'

'Yeah, the polyamorous wizard cult is fucking classic too.' Bianca motions to Seth and he flicks through to a scene showing a bunch of people writhing about in a darkened room, wearing galactic cloaks, glow-in-the-dark face jewels and pointy glitter hats. A bare-chested guy wearing a long silver wig sits in the middle, looking into a crystal ball.

'When I have group sex, it's like I travel between dimensions,' he says, giggling. 'I escape my earthly addictions and become all-powerful.'

'Babe, can I have some more teleporting potion?' A girl crawls over to him and rests her chin on his psychedelic leggings.

'Jesus, that lot were so weird,' Seth exclaims.

'Literally all of them are recovering drug addicts.' Bianca snickers as loud distorted circus music blares out and two words bounce onto the screen and crash into each other: 'LOVE FREAKS!'

A jaunty, jeering voiceover says: 'From sexy sorcery to self-pleasuring sologamy – meet Chloe Usher, the woman who married *herself*!'

'You're going to love my edit,' Bianca says to Seth.

I put a fist to my mouth as I see myself looking hideous in the bright pink trouser suit with shoulder pads. There's a fluffy butterfly clip in my hair, holding back my fringe.

'I can do whatever I want, whenever I want,' I tell the camera, and there're quick shots of my erotica coffee table book and a stack of my Disney DVDs. Then it cuts to me slowly bashing my head against the kitchen wall.

'I can't wait to marry you.' There's a shot of me hiccupping, closing one eye and pointing at the camera. 'You're the bessht . . . best thing that ever happened to me. Oops!'

I feel my skin tighten with humiliation as there's a quick montage of Dora licking my nostril in slow motion, Verity and me fighting in the bridal shop, me talking about pleasuring myself, and then me staggering away from the waltzers in my battered white peacock outfit, red-faced from poppers.

Then it's back to me in my pink trouser suit, smiling serenely at the camera and saying, 'I don't think it pays to be bitter,' before it cuts to me yelling, 'you sneaky fucking *bitch*!' at a pregnant Saffron.

'She's totally neurotic,' Saffron says, rubbing her bump protectively and glaring off-camera. Linda and Tom stand next to her, nodding sadly.

'Unfortunately she's always been a terribly envious person,' Linda agrees. 'She can't bear to think of everyone else being content.'

'It's like that film, whass-it-called?' Tom rubs his top lip. 'Ah yes, *Fatal Attraction*.'

I gasp as Liam and Lucy appear on the screen, standing in Palmeira Square with their arms around each other. 'Chloe just doesn't want any competition, that's her problem,' Lucy says snidely. 'She's clearly got a massive ego.'

The final image is of Giles kissing me, overlaid with scrolling newspaper headlines shouting: 'homewrecker', 'narcissist', 'masturbator', 'man-hater', 'desperate feminist', 'spinster', 'schizophrenic'.

'So I was thinking we ply her with booze right after the wedding – shouldn't be that hard.' Bianca gives her throaty chuckle. 'Then Saffron said Ant's going to swing by the reception so we can get an emotional showdown and end with Chloe bawling her eyes out – the tragic solo bride!'

'Perfect!' Tariq laughs and I teeter backwards, whimpering. Blood crashes in my ears and my whole body is shaking. Seth turns in his chair as he starts to say something to Bianca, and his eyes widen when he sees me through the glass.

'Chloe!' He jumps up and comes to pull the door open.

'H-h-how could you?' I stammer.

'Shit.' Bianca briefly closes her eyes and mutters something to Tariq as she stands up. 'Hey, Chloe.'

'What the hell was that – *Love Freaks*? I thought you said your documentary was called *New Love*, about the evolution of love in the twenty-first century.' My voice is high-pitched with shock.

'Well yeah, it is, in some senses.' Bianca fiddles with her two-toned ponytail. 'I mean, Channel 5 wanted it to be light-hearted, you know.'

'Light-hearted?!' I squeal. 'It's a monumental piss-take! This whole time you've been setting me up to make car-crash TV.'

'No! We did get some really inspiring stuff too,' Seth says, scowling at Bianca.

'Bullshit – you haven't included anything remotely positive!' My lips wobble with the effort not to cry. 'And what was that you were saying about Saffron?'

'Chloe.' Bianca sighs. 'As a producer, you get in touch with everyone you think will add to your main subject's story. Verity and Saffron were keen to get involved – it just helps accelerate situations that would probably happen anyway, you know? Think of it as saving time.'

'Verity *and* Saffron?'

'Yes.' Bianca sounds exasperated. 'It was useful having their input – Verity wanted to tie her wedding dress fitting in with yours and Saffron was kind enough to let me know they were having that party at The Lobster. You had to find out about her pregnancy at some point!'

'But not on camera!' I say in disgust, looking at Seth, who's staring at Bianca in silence. 'You don't give a shit about how this might affect me, do you? You made me out to be a complete psycho!'

Bianca chews the inside of her cheek and studies me with opaque eyes. 'Well, Chloe, I mean, you *are* marrying yourself.'

Tariq sniggers and I turn away from them, feeling my confidence collapse in a final sickening wrench. The red carpet seems to wobble under my feet. I woke up in a beautiful dream, which has swiftly turned into a nightmare. I gather up my skirts and pelt down the corridor and across the foyer.

'Chloe!' I ignore the shouts behind me as I push my way through the hotel's revolving doors. Right now, I'd rather be anyone other than myself.

Chapter 35

I stand on Kings Road outside the hotel, blinking in the sunshine. Cars slow down and beep as they pass; children point and wave from the windows. I've never felt more conspicuous in my life. A shout behind me spurs me on and I run across the road when the pelican crossing turns green.

Crowds of tourists gather on the pavement, staring at me as I rush past them, tears streaming down my face. A woman lifts her camera and starts taking snaps and I quickly veer in the opposite direction, jogging down the concrete steps to the seafront.

The lower esplanade is busy with diners eating ice creams outside the cafes, break dancers spinning to tinny beats, and people leaping about on the volleyball and basketball courts, yelling as they score points.

'All right, love?' Several surfers carrying their boards block my way, their wetsuits rolled down to their waists. They flick their wet hair and look at me curiously, and I push past them and streak across the blue basketball court, scattering the bemused players.

Not sure where I'm going, I run towards Brighton Pier. The beach is rammed with friends having barbecues and heat radiates from the pebbles in visible waves. I hear loud exclamations and laughter as I pass and desperately look around for an escape route.

The jangling merry-go-round music of the carousel vibrates in my ears, and a painted wooden horse offers me a rictus grin as it rotates past.

'Chloeee!' I hear a shout behind me and I swerve off to the left. A cloud of sweet-smelling vapour engulfs me and, squinting, I push past some bearded vapers and plunge through a large decorative arch that says 'Doddy's Funfair'.

There's a cacophony of electronic noise and I bump into an arcade machine as my eyes adjust to the darkness. At the back of the building, dodgems whizz around a track in a blur of flashing lights.

Relieved to have found cover, I walk past the bowling alley, through a doorway covered with black curtains. If I can just hide here for a bit, I might be able to get a grip on the sinking horror I'm feeling.

I lean back against a cold glass surface with my eyes squeezed tightly shut, Bianca's embarrassing montage flashing through my head. I can't believe I've been thinking I'm doing something worthwhile when I've actually looked *that* stupid all along!

Hearing echoing footsteps, I open my eyes and yelp as a short, squat bride gapes at me, her face like melting candle wax. I raise my hands to ward her off and her arms also move. I twist away only to see another bride, this time stretched tall, with a long neck like a giraffe. Her eyes are tiny black holes.

'Blllluuerrgh!' She sidesteps just as I do, rebounding into yet another bride, who ripples at the waist, her limbs unnaturally bent and flailing.

'Nooo!' I push her away, and my palm strikes the convex mirror. I turn in panicked circles, surrounded by my own distorted reflections.

'Chloe.' Seth's disembodied head appears through the black curtains. 'There you are.'

He steps into the Hall of Mirrors and immediately his body, dressed in a pale grey suit, elongates, towering over me precariously.

'I trusted you!' I moan. 'Especially after Pride. I'm such a mug; I should've learnt by now.'

'Chloe, believe me, I had no idea Bianca would edit your footage like that.'

'Bollocks! The whole series is about mocking people who're different – don't pretend you didn't know that.' I back away from him.

'OK, yes, I knew Bianca bent the truth a bit when she sold the documentary to you, and that the other contributors were pretty oddball . . .' Seth loosens his collar. 'But yours is such a feel-good story I thought she would do it justice. I guess I overestimated her.'

'She's a callous fucking bitch. And you're no better. What did you say cameramen are – impartial observers? You thought it was OK to stand by and watch while she destroyed me? Pulling strings with my enemies like some evil puppet master!'

'No, it's not OK! She didn't tell me she was doing that.' Seth paces up and down in agitation, followed by his warped counterparts. 'But you're right, I know how she operates and I could've asked more questions. Plotting with your ex's new girlfriend was low – even by Bianca's standards.'

'I can't believe you used to go out with her. I was starting to think you were a nice guy . . .' Seth's head snaps up and he stands in front of me, his brown eyes intense.

'I *am* a nice guy, Chloe, please believe me. I've been trying to break free of Bianca for a while now; it's hard to explain the hold she's had over me – she twists things around and convinces me that I need her, for my career and stuff. It's bullshit; I don't want her in my life.'

'Hhmff, well if your career involves degrading people for cheap laughs then you're bound to meet more people like her.'

'No, that's not what I want to do! I want to shoot interesting video that actually makes people think! Look at *Drag vs Hate* – it's so powerful, it really unites people.'

I let out a dry laugh. 'What's the fucking point, Seth? Everyone judges everything you do anyway so don't even bother trying. Maybe hate will always win.'

'There is a point, Chloe! It's *easy* to sit back and mock others. Showing compassion and kindness is harder, especially to yourself.' Seth reaches out and touches my forearm. 'The more I've watched you, the more I've realised that it is worth the effort. You've inspired *me*, Chloe – you've made me want to be less of a heartless wanker. Think who else you can help.'

'It just feels silly now,' I say in a small voice.

'No! Don't say that.' Seth's tone is ferocious. 'I can't bear to think that we've broken your spirit. Don't let Bianca's lack of humanity put you off.'

I wrap my arms around myself, shivering; my dress feels cold against my skin.

'You have so many people who've come to support you,' Seth continues. 'You haven't even seen the interviews we've done with them yet and theirs are the only opinions that matter – every single one of them has *so* much love for you.'

'And I love them,' I whisper, picturing my family and friends in their smart clothes waiting for me at the Bandstand. 'I don't want to let them down.'

'You don't have to. Come back with me now.' Seth holds out his hand. I stand staring at the short, squat bride morosely; her eyes dribble onto her cheeks.

'Chloe, please. *She* is not the real you.' Seth points an accusatory finger at my weird reflection. 'None of them are.' He turns to face me. 'Your best version of yourself is in here.' He taps my chest, right above my heart.

'Here, hold still while I just . . .' Emma wipes under my eye with a tissue, biting her tongue in concentration as she repairs my streaky makeup in the public toilets on the seafront.

'I'm sorry to call you away from the party, I just didn't want everyone to see me in such a state.' I smooth a hand over my freshly brushed hair.

'No problem, standard maid-of-honour duties.' Emma bends down to reapply my lip gloss. 'This isn't the first time we've had to do an emergency repair job.'

'True.' I stare at her blonde curls as I remember all the times we've done each other's makeup in the ladies', pouring our hearts out over boys we've loved and lost. 'Do you really think I'm making the right decision, Em?'

Emma straightens up and fixes me with an unwavering gaze. 'We are such stuff as dreams are made on . . .' she intones; I grin as I recognise the words from Prospero's final speech in *The Tempest* and we finish it together:

'. . . and our little life is rounded with a sleep.'

Emma laughs. 'Chlo, when you're an old woman sat in your rocking chair, looking back over your life, I don't think you'll ever regret the day you promised to love yourself.'

'I agree.' I link my arm through hers. 'Let's do this.'

We step outside onto the promenade where Seth is waiting and climb the steps up to Kings Road. More cars beep as I walk arm in arm with Emma and Seth towards the Victorian Bandstand, with its curved roof, green pillars and delicate wrought iron, like lace against the summer sky.

People are gathered along the pavements in groups and Emma curses as she sees Bianca and Tariq crouched over a camera.

'Shall I go and tell them to fuck off, Chlo?'

'I'd love you to but I'm pretty sure Bianca's contract is watertight, right, Seth?' I ask.

''Fraid so. The wedding is the main focal point.' Seth sighs. 'But don't worry, I'm going to do everything I can to tell the story properly. I'm pretty handy at post-production myself.'

'Bianca can do what she wants – she can't ruin this moment,' I say, drawing in a breath as I catch sight of the big crowd on the beach below. They let out a huge cheer as I approach, their clapping mingling with the sound of the waves.

Two teenage girls run up to me with their mobile phones, asking for a photo. 'We love your blog,' they tell me. 'Can we watch your wedding?'

'Of course!' I say. 'The more the merrier!'

A girl in her twenties hovers behind them. She has an athletic figure and long chestnut hair in a plait. I meet her speckled grey eyes with a flash of recognition. 'Katy?!'

She smiles shyly. 'I hope you don't mind me pitching up here. I just wanted to see you. You look beautiful.'

'Oh my God, come here!' I step forwards and hold out my arms. 'I feel like I already know you so well and we've never even hugged!'

'I know, it might sound weird but I'm so proud of you,' she murmurs in my ear.

'Proud of you too.' I feel tears push at the back of my throat. Gosh, weddings are so emotional. 'Take a seat at the Bandstand; I'd love you to join us.'

My wedding party is waiting by the Bandstand. They all start chattering at once as I join them, kissing and hugging me in relief. Dad blows his cheeks out. 'We were beginning to think you'd done a runner there.'

'Wouldn't dream of it, Dad.' I wink at Seth and he kisses my cheek and leaves me at the steps. The Bandstand's green and white railings are draped in white ribbons and roses, and my guests are already sitting on the rows of chairs, craning their necks to get a glimpse of us.

Dad lifts my veil over to cover my face and hands me my bouquet. I feel a pulse of nerves when the traditional bridal march starts playing over the speakers. Emma and Maisie start walking slowly in front of us, scattering sunflower petals from their baskets, followed by Morag and Polly.

The veil sheds a pearlescent shimmer over everything as Dad links his arm through mine and we follow them, with the ushers, Jeremy, Yannis, James and Duncan, bringing up the rear.

'Thanks for being here, Dad,' I whisper.

'Hmm, well, I might be giving you away but I'll never let you go,' he whispers back as we climb the black and white chequered steps.

We walk down the aisle between the chairs towards the clearing at the front, where Dom stands waiting in a regal pose, the sea dancing behind him.

Either side of me my guests are dressed in their finery, grinning up at me. There's Mum, Jess with her kids, Keith, Rudy and Simone from work, Kate and Muriel, who is wearing a massive orange hat. Katy has taken a seat next to Dr Fletcher, who gives me a thumbs-up. And there's Jeanne from Bridal Desires, swooning at my dress. There's a loud tongue-popping and I turn to see AJ, in a stunning white satin suit, sitting with Coco Vision and Madame X, who're pumping the air with their fists, their bright wigs towering above everyone else.

Dad and I pause in front of Dom and he waits for the chatter to die down before announcing in sonorous tones: 'Dearly beloved, we are gathered here today to unify this woman in holy matrimony. If any person here can show just cause or impediment as to why she may not marry herself, let them speak now or forever hold their peace.'

I turn to scan the seated audience with mock dread and everyone smiles and presses their lips together tightly. Seth, standing behind a camera, makes a show of raising his hand then slapping his own wrist.

'Good, always a tense moment that one.' Dom wipes his brow. 'Who gives this woman in marriage to herself?'

'Her father,' Dad says, hugging me tightly before stepping away.

I turn to Dom and lift my veil back over my head, casting aside all obscurity and blinking in the clear light of day. There is no disguise, there is no pretence: there is just me.

'Hello, you,' Dom says, his eyes twinkling, and I feel a smile shine across my face.

'Oh, hey there.'

'Chloe' – Dom puffs his chest out – 'this wedding is a mark of your growth as an individual. With fond hope, we assure you our hearts are in tune with yours, for what greater thing is there than one human soul to feel complete – to love thyself, cherish thyself and, indeed, pleasure thyself?' He raises an eyebrow and everyone chuckles.

A wolf-whistle sounds from below on the beach; the crowd has got even bigger, with passers-by stopping to watch the action.

'Mummy, who is she marrying?' A clear child's voice floats towards us, and we all crack up.

Dom waits until there is silence once more and then booms: 'Chloe Usher, will you take Chloe Usher to be your wife? Do you promise to love her, comfort her, honour her and keep her, in sickness and in health, for richer, for poorer, for better, for worse, in sadness and in joy for as long as you shall live?'

There is a collective intake of breath as I step forward with my chin held high. I feel my skin prickle with euphoria as I say the words loud and proud. 'I do!'

My guests and onlookers erupt in applause.

'Would the ringle bearer please step forward?' Dom asks, and Yannis gives Dora a shove towards us. She trots up to Dom and he undoes a gold pouch from around her neck.

'Thank you, Dora. High-five?' She raises her paw and he pats it. Then, encouraged by the crowd, she turns to high-five me too, wiggling and wagging her tail furiously as my guests let out a big 'aaaahhhhhhhh!'

Dom puts the ringle onto his palm. The cherry wood gleams a rich red.

'Chloe, place this ringle on your finger and repeat after me: I give you this ringle as a pledge of my love and as a symbol of my unity. With this ringle, I thee wed.'

I hand my bouquet to Yannis then take the ring and slip it on my finger, clasping my hands over each other as I say, 'With this ringle, I *me* wed!'

People clap and stamp their feet loudly and Dom takes me through the rest of the vows, finishing with a very powerful, 'And so, by the power vested in *me*, Dominic Hart, good friend and confidante, I now pronounce you *wife*!'

I grab my bouquet and raise it in the air in victory and my loved ones give me a standing ovation.

'You may now kiss the bride!' Dom yells gleefully, and I step forward and wrap my arms around myself, running my hands up and down my back so that the audience behind me howls with laughter.

'May your days be good and long upon the earth!' Dom raises his palms and Chesney Hawkes's 'The One and Only' blasts out over the speakers. Suddenly everyone is swarming around me, hugging, kissing and throwing confetti, and I feel so happy I could float right up into the bright blue sky.

Chapter 36

The Lobster looks incredible. Garlands of sunflowers and yellow ribbons hang everywhere and a canopy of netting drapes the ceiling, filled with hundreds of tiny lights which glow like phosphorescence. There are large lobster pot creations dotted around, woven through with fronds of jasmine. Someone's put a waistcoat and top hat on Maude, the stuffed goat, and she looks prouder than ever as she gazes out over the white linen tables, which are decorated with driftwood and starfish, and laden with canapes and drinks.

Most of my guests are looking a bit pink as they stand chatting on the beach terrace in the fierce afternoon sunshine. I see Seth arguing with Bianca on the steps near the pier and walk over. The panic that unravelled me this morning has already shrunk to a hard knot of indifference.

'You've got footage of the ceremony – now clear off, leave Chloe in peace,' Seth is saying. He's taken his jacket off and he's rolling his white shirt up to the elbows threateningly.

'I want some shots of the reception.' Bianca's artificial smile has disappeared and her eyes flick over the crowd on the beach like a leopard watching its prey.

'None of my guests are willing to talk to you, Bianca,' I say.

'And you're officially banned from my premises,' AJ warns as he walks past with Coco Vision and Madame X.

'Are you the queens from *Drag vs Hate*? Could I have a quick word?' Bianca calls.

Coco looks her up and down under long purple lashes. 'Honey, take my lowest priority and put yourself beneath it.'

'But I wanted to discuss a possible TV show.' Bianca is undeterred.

'I'd rather wax my own crack,' Madame X tuts, throwing Bianca a withering look over her muscular shoulder as they sashay off.

Seth laughs. 'You can probably take that as a "no".'

'Christ, what's got into you, Seth? Are you trying to ruin your career?' Bianca snaps. 'I'll make sure everyone in the industry knows how unreliable you are.'

'Do your worst.' Seth shrugs. 'I've got more dirt on you, thanks to your total lack of ethics.'

Bianca glares at him. 'It never used to bother you.'

'Yeah well, I was a coward. I never want to work with you again.'

'Bianca.' I raise my voice so that people start looking over at us. 'I am so over your face. Would you kindly fuck off out of mine?'

There're a few jeers behind me and Dom and Yannis start moving towards us. Bianca locks eyes with me for a moment, then jogs back up the steps to the Cube van, where Tariq gives me a sheepish nod from behind the wheel.

Seth and I go to sit on the terrace just as the Merry Widows start playing sixties tunes on the outdoor stage. AJ and the drag queens are chatting excitedly with Muriel and Kate.

'Chloe, I was just saying, your *One Foot in the Rave* blog post has really made me think,' AJ says. 'I'm going to put on special vintage events for pensioners at The Lobster, with live music and afternoon tea.'

'And Coco and I can provide cabaret entertainment,' Madame X says.

'Yes, you could come as rockabilly gals!' Muriel suggests, and they both clap their hands and start grilling her for style advice.

'This is such an excellent idea.' Kate starts tapping in her phone. 'Our members would love to be involved.'

'I'll contact all the services for older people in the surrounding areas,' Dr Fletcher smiles.

'Can I help organise it?' Jess says. 'I'll bring my kids, they'll love it.'

'Yes, of course, let's make it intergenerational.' AJ throws his arms wide.

'And I can do the marketing if you want,' Simone offers. 'I'm bored of fashion clients.' She winks at me.

The band start playing 'Wild Thing' and I'm pleased to see Mum and Dad get up and start dancing together as Janice looks on with a tight-lipped smile.

'She's such a livewire, your mum.' AJ's voice is deep in my ear as he watches her head-banging. 'I have a lot of respect for her.'

'Ooh, maybe you should tell her that,' I suggest, wiggling my eyebrows.

When the band have finished playing, Seth and I stroll towards the sea. A few kayaks are cruising around the pier. They wave at me as they see my dress and yell congratulations.

'Your wedding moved a lot of people.' Seth shields his eyes with his hand as he looks out at the horizon. 'How did it feel saying those vows?'

'Really powerful, actually.' I smile. 'I'll always remember it.' I kick off my shoes so I can paddle in the shallows.

'Here.' Seth bends on one knee and tightens the ties on my skirt bustle. 'I know this probably isn't the right time . . . but . . . erm . . .' He frowns at his own thigh.

'What?' I look down in amusement at his uncharacteristic shyness, his messy brown hair glinting red in the sunshine.

'Well, I wondered if . . . you'd consider going on a date with me?' He screws up his face as I hesitate. 'I know you probably think I've got a cheek after the whole thing with Cube . . .'

'None of us are perfect.'

'You are though,' he says quickly. 'Your wife's a very lucky woman.'

'I'm not perfect, Seth – and I'm never going to be.' I cock my head. 'Sure, I'll go on a date with you – it'll have to be after my honeymoon though.'

'I'll wait, you're worth it.' He gets to his feet and squeezes me round the waist. His eyes are like melted honey. 'I'm so glad you decided to marry yourself, Chlo. Just think, if you hadn't, I'd never have met you.'

I ponder this for a moment, then grin and kiss his cheek. 'Now that really *is* romantic.'

'Do my eyes deceive me? Chloe canoodling with a man!'

My smile collapses as I hear Linda's strident voice and look over Seth's shoulder to see her approach, stuffing a prawn kebab in her mouth.

'Linda?'

'You did send me an invite,' she says defensively. 'I thought I'd see what all the fuss is about but you're already breaking the rules and pawing another man. Typical.'

'Chloe can do what the hell she wants, Linda,' Seth drawls. 'She made the rules.'

'The whole thing is ridiculous.' Linda's lips are greasy with fish oil. 'You're setting an awful example to your goddaughter.' She looks over at Maisie, who's playing with Emma and Katy on the pebbles behind us. 'I don't know why Emma chose you; it's no wonder she calls you "odd mother".'

'Don't you think it's important for Maisie to value self-love, Linda?' Emma is suddenly next to me, clenching her fists. 'Would you rather she spent her whole youth worrying she isn't pretty or interesting enough to attract the "right man"? Or that she settles for a half-baked relationship because she's too afraid of being single?'

Linda shakes her head. 'Honestly, Emma, I thought you were more sensible.'

'Well, I'm not. I put up with your shit because I was unhappy but I've had enough. You can leave Chloe's wedding if you're not going to say anything nice!' Emma steps forward protectively and I feel a swell of gratitude that I have my sister back.

'Heyyyy!' Maisie comes running at Seth, who swings her up onto his shoulders. 'Can I marry myself and have fifty-nine bridesmaids and build a castle and ride a dragon?'

Linda snaps 'no' just as the rest of us chorus 'yes!' and Maisie puts her imaginary sword in the air. 'Let's go chase the pirates!' We leave Linda gaping disdainfully on the pebbles as we gallop off towards the white froth on the shore.

'Attention, please.' Dom clinks a spoon against his glass. He's changed from his papal robes into a purple suit which is also the exact shade of his eye. 'Before we tuck into AJ's delicious buffet, we're going to have a few words.'

All my guests are seated at tables inside The Lobster, with the wedding party by the open doors. The sun is dipping behind the pier, casting long shadows across the beach and bathing everything in orange.

Along the back wall, trestle tables creak under the weight of elaborate platters of seafood, salads and freshly baked loaves. There are huge joints of honey-glazed ham, roast chicken, stuffed vegetables and pasta dishes.

My dad gets up and makes a very touching speech about my birth and childhood. At the end he gestures to Mum, who is sitting opposite him. 'And Joy, I have you to thank for helping our daughter become the wonderful woman she is today.' His voice breaks a little and Janice puts a supportive arm around him as he sits down.

Mum nods at him and then, unexpectedly, gets to her feet. 'Thank you, Roger, you played a very small part too.' She winks, then clears her throat. 'I didn't plan a speech cos I'm not good at this sort of thing, but I just wanted to thank you, Chloe.' She looks across at me and raises her chin. 'They say you can't teach an old dog new tricks but you've made me realise a few things with this self-love lark.' Her accent grates with emotion. 'When shit things happen, most of us play the victim and point the blame at the person who hurt us. And it may well be their fault.' Her cheeks quiver with the effort of not looking at Dad. 'But at the end of the day, harping on about it is only going to make your life rubbish. So you may as well forgive, right?' She grins around the room, lingering for a moment on AJ. 'I've been the most miserable Joy known to man and I'm sorry for that, Chlo. I'm going to work on living up to my name.' She sits down abruptly to a massive cheer.

Dom leans across to hug her, then stands up to give the best man speech, having the room in stitches with – often exaggerated – stories of my antics, including the time I sat on a discarded sofa in Brighton town centre in my onesie, inviting every passer-by to have tea with me. He neglects to mention the fact that I was high as a kite but I think most people get it.

Maisie, sitting next to Dom, is looking up at him with an enraptured expression. Every time people laugh she throws her head back and cackles loudly, not wanting to miss out on the fun. The more Emma tries to quieten her down, the more she hams it up, until people are laughing more at her than the speech.

'It's a privilege to have shared Chloe's journey,' Dom wraps up. 'Well, aside from the grievous bodily harm, of course.' He gestures to his bruising and everyone groans sympathetically. 'I don't know about you but watching her pledge her vows today has filled me with a desire to make myself a similar promise. You're a shining light to us all, Chloe, thank you!'

Everyone clinks their glasses and roars their approval as I blow a kiss to Dom and stand up.

'Now, the bride doesn't usually do a speech but this isn't exactly a traditional wedding and I don't have a groom, so . . .' I raise an eyebrow and a chuckle rolls across the room. 'I'll keep it brief. I just want to thank every one of you for supporting me today – or should I say humouring me?' I wink at Dad and Emma.

'I know that some might consider this wedding a joke but then I've always believed the moment people start to laugh is when the magic happens.' Maisie demonstrates with a high-pitched guffaw and I smile at her.

'I believe that loving ourselves is as important as loving someone else and that self-love is the foundation on which all love blooms. Love comes in many unexpected shapes; you don't have to be a parent to be a parent, you can have mind-blowing passion for the man you will never sleep with, share your darkest secrets with strangers and be rescued by men in women's clothing.'

I pause as my guests roar with approval and AJ, Coco Vision and Madame X stand up and bow.

'To the haters who refuse to understand, I'd just like to say one thing: I choose love!'

I raise my glass of champagne and chairs scrape across the floor as everyone stands and holds their own glasses aloft. 'To love!'

Chapter 37

After dinner, the staff stack the tables so the floor is free for dancing and The Wallflowers set up on stage. I've worked with them on a brilliant set list that spans all decades.

Everyone is very well oiled and the jackets and shoes are off. Jolly, Morag and Duncan are already in the middle of the dance floor attempting break dancing, and Muriel teaches Mum, Janice and Kate some flapper moves. Dad is standing in the corner, talking to Seth very intently. Seth manages to catch my eye and wink without breaking concentration.

Emma, Jess and Maisie are encouraging Dora up on her hind legs with bits of pitta bread and then grabbing her paws for a waltz. I'm just about to join them when Simone tugs my arm, looking anxious.

'You OK?' I say, turning to her.

'Yeah I am, but' – she looks over her shoulder – 'Verity's outside. I tried to get rid of her but she won't leave till she sees you.'

'Right.' I sigh. 'I'll have a word.'

Verity is slumped against one of the pier's iron pillars in a leather jacket and jeans. She rolls her head towards me as I approach, her swollen eyes streaming.

'I hate myself!' she screams dramatically, smelling strongly of vodka.

'That's a little harsh.' I stand over her with my arms folded.

'That's my dress,' she whispers, looking up at my skirt with glazed eyes.

'Have you come to tear it off me again?'

'There's no point – he doesn't love me any more.' She

310

stares out at the inky black sea, mascara smudged across her high cheekbones.

'Oh come on, Gavin is besotted with you.'

'Not Gavin, stupid!' She thumps her own thigh. 'Giles! Giles, Giles, Giles.'

'What?' I'm having trouble following this conversation.

'I only meant to teach him a lesson for kissing you,' Verity wails. '*I'm* supposed to be his girl.'

I stare at her in silence and she tuts. 'I took the photo of you kissing – duh! But I wasn't going to do anything with it.'

I breathe in through my nose. 'It was *you*!'

'Bianca gave it to the *Mail*! She said she'd get loads of cash for it . . . but she didn't give me any.' Verity sniffs. 'And now Giles hates me.'

'Hang on a minute, rewind . . . don't tell me you've been sleeping with Giles?'

'Yes, Chloe!' Verity yells, her voice echoing under the pier. 'We got together that night at the forest – he chased me in the moonlight. G found my G-spot!'

'But . . . what about marrying Gavin?'

'I just wanted to make Giles jealous.' Verity draws her legs against her chest. 'I don't even want this stupid wedding and I don't love Gav. He's so tedious.'

I press my lips together; there are no words. Verity's red eyes search my face and she juts her chin out defensively.

'Whatever, I'll just cancel it. It's no biggie.' She runs her tongue over her teeth and a flash of her usual cockiness returns. 'I'm still gonna have my hen do in New York though; it can be, like, a "break-up do". I'll need my gals' support. If you can make up random occasions then so can I.'

'Go for it, Verity. Good luck.' I shake my head and turn to leave.

'Wait!' she squawks and I pause. The waves slap against the pillars and her voice is so small I have to lean forward to catch it. 'I don't have any real friends. I don't think I'm a very nice person.'

I open my mouth, then close it. It's difficult to contradict her.

'I know how to make men like me but other girls only hang out with me because they want to look cool. I wish I had friends like you do, ones that always have your back. How do I get them?'

'Christ, that's a tough one.' I think about it for a moment. 'Friendships are reciprocal, I guess, you can't just demand them. Like any relationship, you reap what you sow.'

Verity purses her mouth. 'Sounds like hard work.'

'OK, well, I'm going back to dance.' I turn towards The Lobster again and she erupts into noisy sobs.

I sigh heavily. 'Verity, do you want to come to my party?'

She leaps to her feet as if the pebbles have just scalded her. 'Jeez, I thought you'd never ask.'

'Ah, there you are! C'mon, it's your first dance!' Dom's in the doorway, beckoning me.

'Please make room for the bride.' The band's female singer motions to the dancers on the floor. Duncan is mid-caterpillar and so Morag grabs his ankles and drags him to the edge.

People crowd around, pushing me forward into the middle. The lights dim and dusk melts into the room. Then purple light floods the dance floor and a blanket of dry ice rolls out from the machine on stage. Everyone whoops in excitement.

The singer leans into the microphone and says, 'Well, I think it's time y'all reached out for something new, and that means you too, Chloe.' She points at me and everyone screams again as they hear the first riffs of 'Purple Rain' and a puff of purple glitter fills the air, drifting down over my head.

The band start playing and I swirl around the floor holding my bouquet of sunflowers in the air, mouthing along to the lyrics.

As the tune picks up momentum I beckon to the crowd, inviting them to join me on the floor. We lean into each other, playing air guitar and singing at the top of our voices as the purple glitter rain bathes us. Simone and Verity roll around on the floor and Coco Vision and Madame X fall to their knees, clenching their fists in emotion

'Throw your bouquet!' Emma calls as the song draws to a close, and I get up on stage and turn my back to the crowd, then hurl the sunflowers over my head. There's yelling as a scrum forms behind me and I turn to see Dom and Yannis in the middle, both clutching the bouquet with startled expressions. They turn to look at each other, nodding slowly, and then Yannis bursts into tears just as Dom leans in for a snog.

AJ calls, 'Let's have our cake and eat it!' and wheels out the towering Choccywoccydoodah creation, complete with creamy sunflowers and a solo bride on top. I put both my hands on the knife and close my eyes and wish for nothing more than this; I have everything I ever dreamed of.

The Wallflowers play a two-hour set of floor fillers and by 11 p.m. everyone is sweaty and breathless and some people start to leave, carrying sleepy children and coats.

Jess is taking Dora home with her. I drop to my knees and throw my arms around my dog, breathing in her warm, biscuity smell. 'I'll see you tomorrow, my beautiful.' She rests a paw on my shoulder and snuffles my forehead.

'The kids are excited to meet her,' Jess smiles.

'How're they dealing with John moving out?' I ask.

'They're confused and upset.' Her lip trembles. 'They can't understand why we don't love each other anymore but then, to be honest, neither can I. I've told them that it'll never change our feelings for them.'

'Oh babe, just keep being honest, it's all you can do. And try not to slag each other off to them – it doesn't help.' I give her a tight hug and marvel at how close we've become. Finding such a good friend is at least one upside of my time at Top Banana.

'Time for a bit of drum 'n' bass?' My DJ mate from London walks past, holding up his vinyl case hopefully, and I give him the thumbs-up. 'Always!'

As he sets up the decks I go outside to see Mum off. We stand in front of the pier, where drunk people queue up for late-night fish 'n' chips. One girl points at me and cries, 'Omigod that dress – I want!'

'Something very odd just happened.' Mum's frowning in confusion.

'What's that, Ma?'

'AJ just asked me to dinner. He said he'd close The Lobster for the night and we can have the place to ourselves. I can't make head or tail of it.'

'Brilliant, AJ is a legend – it'd be so cool if you started going out!'

'But surely he can't've meant it like *that*. It's barmy!'

'Why's it barmy?

'I'm six years older than him, Chlo . . . and he, well, he sometimes wears women's clothes.'

'Yeah, but he's straight. And I'm sure he's very capable of "all that".' I wink meaningfully. 'Does it really matter?'

She looks at me for a moment, her grey eyes thoughtful. 'Well, now you mention it, I don't expect it does.' A wicked smile spreads over her face. 'Imagine Barbara's reaction if I took him back to Shillingborne in that rubber suit!'

As we kiss goodbye she gives me a stern mother look. 'Make sure you don't stay out all night partying. You want to make the most of your nice hotel room.'

'Don't worry, Ma, I'll make sure I get to bed at a reasonable hour,' I assure her, and she pulls a sceptical face.

'That'll be the day.'

I watch her walk away and am just turning to re-join the party when a figure emerges from behind the chip queue.

'Chloe.'

Ant stands in front of me in a Stüssy T-shirt, skater shorts and flip flops. His thick curls cast coloured shadows on his face.

'You've always had crap timing, haven't you, Ant?'

'You look amazing,' he says flatly, his eyes dark and brooding.

'What size is the baby now – a grapefruit or a pomegranate?' I ask sarcastically.

Ant sighs. 'A mango, actually. Look, Chloe, I know you lot think I'm a total bastard but I just wanted to say, I didn't mean it to pan out like this. Saffron didn't tell me she was using the rhythm method until it was too late.'

'Ugh, OK, I don't want to know.' I still feel a coiling in my stomach at the idea of them having sex. 'Whatever, I hope you'll be happy together.'

Ant's face twists. 'I miss you, Chlo,' he says quietly. 'You're the only person who knows me inside out.'

'Ah, does Saffron not sit patiently listening to your problems then, Ant? That surprises me.'

'No.' Ant gazes distractedly out at the moonlit ocean, immune to my irony. 'You know, I found out she lied to me – she said she had Romanian gypsy blood and spent her childhood travelling Europe but it turns out she grew up in Milton Keynes.'

I snort. 'Oh dear, not quite the nonconformist you expected then.'

'Hmm, no, she's actually quite controlling. And she's forbidden me from sailing now I'm going to be a dad. I've not been sleeping; I lie awake at night staring at the ceiling. I just don't know how it all suddenly got so . . . *intense*. I never felt like this with you.'

'Tell you what, why don't you ditch Saffron and the baby and run away with me to the Caribbean? We could start again, live on an island and opt out of society altogether?'

Ant's head snaps round and there's a fleeting expression of hope in his eyes, which makes me laugh out loud.

'Jesus Christ, Ant, grow up. Did you really just come here to moan at me?'

He looks affronted. 'God, you could be a bit more sensitive.'

'Sorry, no, I can't spare any sensitivity for you. You had it all once and you threw it back in my face.'

'I know I did – and I'm kicking myself! Don't be so hard, Chloe. You know I loved you.' Ant's voice breaks. 'Love you.'

I swallow, trying to hang onto my righteous anger. He puts a hand out and strokes my bare arm.

'Where are you going on your honeymoon?'

'I'm doing a gorilla trek in Uganda. I'm still that girl.' I give him a small smile.

'I know you are.' His eyes suddenly fill with tears. 'Fuck, I haven't even begun to deal with losing you.'

'Oh, Ant. Look, I'm starting to see it like this: we were just a chapter in the story of each other's lives. OK? It's time we turned the page.'

His lips tremble. 'But I always thought I'd be the hero of your book.'

'Well, it turns out I'm my own hero,' I say softly, squeezing his hand. 'Bye, Ant.'

'Mnnnrrrgggh!' I start awake as Dom elbows me in the gut and blink in the golden light seeping across the room. I'm lying horizontally on my hotel bed, still in my wedding gown and . . . I reach up to my head . . . a top hat, apparently.

Next to me Dom and Emma are curled against each other. Dom's in his shirttails and boxer shorts; Emma's just in a vest top and pants, covered in body paint.

I think it was Katy's idea that we go to The Volks, a small underground club on the seafront; they were quite surprised to see a bride in their midst. And then we ended up at some house party. I remember playing a game where you have to bend over and pick up a cereal box with your mouth. In fact – I flex my leg in the air – ouch! Yep, pretty sure I pulled a hamstring.

I shuffle to the end of the bed, my skirts tangled around me. On the carpet, sprawled out on a pile of cushions and bathroom towels, are Verity, Simone and Katy. Simone is snoring loudly and cuddling Verity's leg.

Well, it does seem I made the most of my hotel room after all. Yawning, I hobble to the minibar and pour out some sparkling water, then go to sit on the balcony. I look out at the ocean, massaging my temples, with a goofy grin on my face.

How could yesterday have just been twenty-four hours long? I didn't ever want it to end. I feel champagne still buzzing through my veins and pull my laptop towards me.

Reader, I Married Me!

19.08.18

Dear Reader,
It was a most excellent wedding and a day I'll remember forever. Promising to always take care of myself in front of my loved ones meant a lot and I'm sure I'll return to the vows in times of trouble. And there will be times of trouble, of course! But what I've learned is, contrary to popular belief, pride comes **after** a fall, not before. When you're knocked down flat, you pick yourself up, dust yourself off and carry on living and that, my friends, is when you fucking celebrate.

I'm sure you're wondering how my wedding night went . . . I'm afraid I didn't even manage to get my dress off, there are so many buttons on this damn thing. But I did stay up dancing till dawn, with friends and strangers, and I woke up in good company.

And next week I leave for my honeymoon – I'm off to see mountain gorillas in Uganda! But you know what? It won't be the biggest adventure I'll have this year, not by a long shot. I've learned loads about freedom these past few months – through my own self-discovery.

I've thought a lot about the difference between solitude and loneliness. Solitude is a bloody marvellous skill that everyone should cultivate. It's a form of meditation; on yourself and the world around you. It's a time for reflection and peace and it gives us the power to adjust our lives.

Loneliness, on the other hand, is an emotional response to feeling unloved and disconnected from the people around you, even if they're in the same room.

And how do we stop feeling isolated? FIND A BOY/GIRLFRIEND RIGHT NOW – QUICK, BEFORE THEY'RE ALL SNAPPED UP!

Jokes.

In my humble opinion, I think it starts with self-compassion. Acknowledge your sense of emptiness; don't run from it. Know that everyone has times when they feel like the odd one out and you are **not** alone – it's part of the human experience.

Maybe your loneliness is a sign that the relationships in your life aren't as supportive as you want them to be (ditch the frenemies!) or that you need to connect with more people. You can fix this!

The good news is that going through this pain gives you empathy for others who feel the same. Have the courage to show your vulnerability. We all have a desire to belong.

I've realised that my life isn't about finding just 'one true love' who'll answer all my prayers. My 'true love' lies in the family I have chosen, the friends I've yet to meet, and in every moment that unfolds, often unremarkably. There's no telling when these moments will end but they're real and they're mine and I'll love every one of them, with all of my magnificent life – Happily Ever NOW!

Yours forever wandering,
Chloe x

Acknowledgments

This book is the joyful outcome of my personal exploration into self-marriage. Ever since I was a little girl, I have wanted to be a published author and the fact that loving myself has helped me achieve my greatest dream is very serendipitous.

I'd like to thank my agent Amanda Preston, at LBA Books, for believing in me right from the start. I remember the fizz of excitement I felt when I first pitched the book idea to her – she looked up from her notebook, her eyes alight with curiosity, and said: 'Tell me more.' Amanda's instinct and passion for great storytelling has inspired me to do her proud.

Next up is my editor, Sam Eades, and the team at Trapeze. Sam's exceptional skill, ballsy attitude and great humour has been the lifeblood of this book and I am so grateful she took a leap of faith with me. It's not often in life that you have someone insisting that you can improve and being extraordinarily *right* every time! Writing can be a fickle and strangely alienating pursuit and Sam's assured confidence in *Reader, I Married Me* has been pivotal in the development of character and plot – she makes me want to be a better writer.

Which brings me on to my support network; I often wonder why these book acknowledgments go on for so long but now I see why. It's your family and friends' unquestioning encouragement that gets you through those 'what the hell am I even writing?' moments.

Thanks to all my family, especially my mum and dad, Sue Usher and Malcolm Tanner, for your constant love and backing – I am so lucky to have you as parents. And thanks to Kay Tanner for looking after Dad so well. And massive big-up to the sisterhood, Holly Edwards and Alex, Jess, Sal and Ames Beveridge; I am so blessed to have you gorgeous girls in my life.

Thanks to those long-standing friends who have always cheered me on: Sarah Nias, Serra and David Kerrigan, Amy Scarth, Henri and Tom Fry-Williams, Nat Sedgwick, Sal and Stef Teska, Kath Ingle, Kat Botterill, Willie Senior, Kel Pegrum, Ed Pugh, Jamiecakes, Morag and Rob McIntosh, Katie Mac and Derek, Shippey, Will and Abs Worthington, Jess Tiffin and Yak, Dee, Wilky, Liam to name a few. The list goes on; you know who you are.

Not only have my friends always boosted my confidence, they've also humoured me by attending my self-wedding, because yes, reader, I did marry me! Vowing to be responsible for my own happiness in front of my loved ones was really empowering and I'll always remember it.

Thank you to James McGeown for being a great gusband and superb pope, George Palmer as the dancing vicar, and the rest of my colourful bridesmaids: Lucy Hodgson, Rosie McNally, Eshe Brown, Anna Bunting, Simone Stevens, Isa Lavahun, Hannah Banham, Jessie Fuller, Jo O'Gorman. Thanks also to Chris Noble, Rhiannon McCluskey, Amy Sanders, Ben Whitehouse, Holly and Morag for capturing my big day on camera.

A huge inspiration for this book's message on overcoming social isolation is Brighton's charity Time to Talk Befriending, run by the amazing warm-hearted Emily Kenward. Working to help raise awareness about befriending alongside Guy Lloyd, Ellie Talebian and Marisha Taylor (Team Jingle) has been so rewarding and long may it continue. Thanks also to Alice Reeves and Sophie Turton at BelongCon for working so hard to champion a culture of belonging; I'm glad we crossed paths.

I can see why people compare writing a novel to giving birth; there's a long gestation process and, when you've finally grown the full body, delivery can be complicated. I'd like to give a massive shout-out to the fabulous Sarah Wadmore for always caring and listening to my moans; you're the greatest doula a girl could wish for – LA vibes forever! And thanks to both couples Jessac and Jonny Paige and Meg Lewis, for being so warm and supportive even whilst going through your own pregnancies – your boys will make fine men. Cheers to Ruari Barratt for helping me with the birthing plan and Rob Smith for the soothing aloe vera. I'd also like to thank my beautiful dog Ella, who is the inspiration for Dora and has unknowingly acted as a living stress ball; a quick cuddle with her has been all the therapy I needed.

Finally, I'd like to express gratitude to you, for choosing to read this story. I hope it's been an inspiring step in your journey to believing in yourself – own it